Seventh Grave
and No
Body

Also by Darynda Jones

Seventh Grave and No Body

Darynda Jones

ST. MARTIN'S PRESS ❧ NEW YORK

SEVENTH GRAVE AND NO BODY. Copyright © 2014 by Darynda Jones. All rights
reserved. Printed in the United States of America. For information, address
St. Martin's Press, 175 Fifth Avenue, New York, N.Y. 10010.

www.stmartins.com

The Library of Congress Cataloging-in-Publication Data
is available upon request.

ISBN 978-1-250-04564-5 (hardcover)
ISBN 978-1-4668-7883-9 (e-book)

St. Martin's Press books may be purchased for educational, business, or
promotional use. For information on bulk purchases, please contact Macmillan
Corporate and Premium Sales Department at 1-800-221-7945, extension 5442,
or write specialmarkets@macmillan.com.

First Edition: October 2014

10 9 8 7 6 5 4 3 2 1

For Dana

You are a font of positive energy.
You are effervescent, exuberant,
brilliant, and dazzling.
Where would I be without you?

Yep, "resting" in an institution, most likely.

Thank you for everything, radiant one.
Your kung fu is strong.

Acknowledgments

The following is a list of people to whom I owe a mountain of gratitude. Some of these individuals are a tad off-kilter, but we'd have it no other way.

My undying gratitude list includes but is not limited to:

Alexandra Machinist: for your amazing energy and unwavering support.

Jennifer Enderlin: for your utter brilliance and enthusiasm.

Eliani Torres: for your tireless efforts and incredible attention to detail.

Stephanie, Jeanne-Marie, Esther, and everyone at St. Martin's Press and Macmillan Audio: for all your wonderful work behind the scenes.

Nick and Mitali: for attempting to keep me in line.

Angie Bee: for the BEST LINE EVER!

Monica Boots and Marjolein Bouwers: for your help with translations.

Cait, Rhianna, Trayce, and Jowanna: for your smarts and dedication.

The Grimlets: for being the best a girl could ask for.

My family: for everything that you do.

Jowanna Kestner: for the diamond thing. JUST AWESOME!

Netters: for letting me hug you in public. You are the light in my heart.

The Mighty, Mighty Jones Boys: for being my gorgeous everythings.

Readers everywhere: for your love of reading.

Thank you, thank you, thank you!

Seventh Grave and No Body

1

If the woman howling from the backseat of Agent Carson's black SUV weren't already dead, I would've strangled her. Gladly. And with much exuberance. But, alas, my ex-BFF Jessica was indeed dead, and ranting on and on about how her death was entirely my fault. Which was so not true. It was only partly my fault. I wasn't the one who'd kicked her off a seven-story grain elevator. Though I was beginning to wish I had. At least then I would've had a reason to listen to her harp ad nauseam. Life was too short for this crap.

After rolling my eyes so far back into my head I almost dislodged them from their sockets, I glanced over at my driver and the owner of said SUV, Agent Carson. Actually, it was FBI Special Agent Carson, but that was way too many syllables, in my book. I'd tried to get her to change her name to SAC—or even FBISAC, since we could've called her Phoebe for short—but she'd have none of it. Her loss. No telling how much time she could save if she didn't have all those syllables to deal with.

Fortunately for SAC, she couldn't hear Jessica, but the other supernatural entity in the car—one Mr. Reyes Alexander Farrow, the hot hunk of corporeal manliness sitting in the middle seat of the long SUV—most definitely could. It was his own fault, however. He was the one who'd insisted on playing bodyguard ever since we found out a group of hell-hounds had escaped from molten gates down under and were on their way to this plane to dismember me.

As a diversionary tactic—since I had the innate ability to visualize my own dismemberment to an alarming degree—I was working on some of the cold cases SAC had asked me to look into, to see if anything caught my eye. And the folder containing an unsolved ten-year-old multiple murder definitely caught my eye.

Well, okay, they all caught my eye, but this one seemed to pull at me. To lure me. It begged to be solved. Five people—two adults and three teens—had been killed one night while preparing to open a summer camp for special-needs kids. They were each stabbed multiple times and found in a sea of blood by another camp supervisor the next morning. Another young girl, the only daughter of the two adults, was never found.

The only real suspect they'd had was a homeless man who scavenged the campsites in the area, stealing food from campers when they went on hikes or slept. But the forensics unit found no evidence linking him to the crime scene. Not a fingerprint. Not a drop of blood. Not a single strand of the suspect's hair.

And so the case went unsolved. Until now. The FBI had finally wised up and put Charley Davidson on the task of bringing a killer to justice. Because that's what Charley did. Brought killers to justice. She also found lost dogs, exposed cheating spouses, and tracked down the occasional skip. And she rarely referred to herself in the third person.

I had a few other specialties as well. Mostly because I'd been born the grim reaper. I could see dead people, for one, a fact that helped me solve many a case. Odd how easy it was to solve cases when one could ask the victim whodunit. Not that I could always rely on that natural advantage. Some people didn't know who'd killed them. That was rare, but it happened. A traumatized brain was a complicated brain. Still, I got good intel most of the time.

In this case, however, the chances of finding the departed just hanging out at the crime scene where they'd died ten years earlier were slim. It was worth a shot either way, which was why I'd agreed to let SAC pick me up at the ungodly hour of 6 A.M. to show me the crime scene first-hand. Along with me, however, came a bit of baggage, and it was sitting in the two backseats. Jessica, my ex-BFF, blamed me for her death. Ad nauseam. Reyes, my affianced, blamed me for his sour mood. I chose to ignore them both.

"The view is gorgeous," I said as we wound up the Jemez Moun-tains. The sun was barely clearing the treetops, casting an orange glow over us. The pine and juniper glistened with the early morning dew, their shadows sliding across the window as we drove deeper into the pass. We didn't see a lot of green in Albuquerque, so the fact that all this lay just an hour away boggled my mind. I loved the Jemez.

"Isn't it?" SAC agreed.

"My dad used to bring us up here on his motorcycle. But isn't all this reservation land?" I asked. "How did the FBI get jurisdiction?"

"Tribal law is complicated," she said, her brown bob swaying as she glanced in her rearview for the hundredth time that morning. But she wasn't checking for traffic. She was checking on the surly man behind her. "In a case like this, we actually would've had jurisdiction, because the campsite isn't on Pueblo land. Either way, it only makes sense to bring in outside authorities. One of the teens was Native American, which is a whole other issue, but the tribal council was more than happy to have us do the investigation."

She tightened her grip on the steering wheel, her gaze darting again to the rearview. I couldn't blame her. Reyes was certainly something to look at. Since I could feel emotions radiate off people like others could feel the weather, I felt every infusion of warmth that rushed through her with his nearness. He affected her like hot tea on a winter's day, but she hid it well. I had to give her kudos for that. She was curious about him but guarded. Since Reyes, dark and dangerous, was an enigma even to me, SAC was smart to be guarded. But there was no denying the raw magnetism, the sensuous allure he unconsciously sent out in sweet, pulsating waves.

Either that or I was ovulating.

No, wait. No chance of that. It was him. A side effect of being created by the most beautiful angel ever to fall from the heavens, forged in the fires of sin and degradation. All the stuff one's mother warns one about.

I struggled to keep from taking a peek every few seconds myself. But just for good measure, I decided to risk a quick look-see. I took out my phone, flipped the camera for a selfie, and focused it on the man riding in the middle seat. He leaned into one corner, sitting spread-eagle across the seat, one arm thrown over the back of it, watching me from underneath his lashes. Studying me.

I raised my chin a notch, refusing to be affected by his shadowy, brooding gaze. I was just as mad at him as he was at me. For two weeks now, he'd insisted on escorting me everywhere, forgoing his responsibilities at that bar and grill he owned to be my babysitter.

Of course, I was now carrying his baby, and she was kind of a big deal. Destined to save the world and all. So I couldn't be too angry. And he was damned nice to look at, even when he scowled. In fact, if I were totally honest, that scowl only added to the allure that was Reyes Farrow. Damn it. When I scowled, I looked constipated. Leave it to the son of Satan to turn a scowl into the stuff of fantasies.

It wasn't like he had a reason to be mad at me, though. Not *that* mad, anyway. I'd tried to sneak out of the apartment without him, to go on this case with Agent Carson alone and get some one-on-one girl time. I soon found out that was the wrong thing to do. He told me so repeatedly before she'd arrived outside my apartment building entrance, reminding me that the Twelve, aka the aforementioned hellhounds, were hot on my heels. But even if they made it through the void of oblivion that resided between hell and this plane, and even if they did manage to escape into this dimension, they would still have to find me. And demons, even hellhounds, had their limitations on this plane.

So, after a ten-minute lecture that involved Reyes reiterating—repeatedly—and me tapping my foot in impatience, Agent Carson pulled up in her SUV. We'd thrown her when we both climbed into her official vehicle, but I quickly explained that Reyes, my affianced, had separation anxiety.

She took it well. She was supercool like that. Most of the time. There was one exception, when she'd threatened to have me arrested and promised I'd spend the rest of my life in prison if I didn't *cooperate fully*. Like I wouldn't have cooperated without her threats. Besides that one tiny incident—and maybe two more where I'd thought she was going to either shoot me in the face or drop-kick me to China—she was full of marshmallowy goodness. And Reyes seemed to be the campfire that melted her creamy center. She was warm. Really warm. And her warmth was making me warm. Like a lot. I couldn't be 100 percent, but I was pretty sure we were in the midst of a ménage.

"As if"—Jessica the departed banshee said from the backseat—"that weren't bad enough, I will never get married. Never! Do you know what that feels like?" Her long red hair shook almost as bad as my hands. Caffeine withdrawal sucked, as evidenced by the quivering of my limbs. But she was vibrating with anger. A vindictive, spiteful kind of rage that turned her hazel irises to a bright shade of green.

Jessica and I had been besties in high school until I made the mistake of telling her not only what I could do—see dead people—but also what I was—the grim reaper. I'd learned that last bit myself only when a robed figure, an incorporeal being I used to call the Big Bad, approached me in the girls' restroom and told me. That robed figure turned out to be Reyes, I found out a decade later. I had yet to confront him on that. What was he doing in the girls' restroom in the first place? The perv.

Jessica didn't handle my admission well. I'd thought her made of kindness and strength before the day she turned on me. Fear transformed her into something I didn't recognize. Her vehemence, her wrath and betrayal, stole my breath. I cried for days—not in front of her, of course; never in front of her—and sank into a deep depression that took me months to recover from.

When she started showing up at Reyes's bar and grill, I hadn't seen her since high school. Lots of women started showing up at the bar and grill when Reyes bought it from my dad. Sadly, Jessica hadn't changed. She still hated me and took every opportunity to be spiteful and manipulative in front of her friends. When a notorious crime lord mistook her for a close friend of mine and abducted her, holding her hostage to force me to do a job for him, events had not ended well. And I thought she'd hated me before!

So, in a vehicle with four people, three of us were angry. I felt like breaking into a chorus of "One of These Things (Is Not Like the Other)," but I doubted anyone but me would get it, especially since Agent Carson didn't know the truth about me. And she had no idea there was a departed crazy woman hitching a ride with us before her inevitable trip to hell. Surely she was going to hell. Jessica had not been a nice person. There must be a special, less volcanic portion of hell that was partitioned off and set aside for people who weren't all bad, just a little vindictive. They could call it the drama queen ward. It would be a huge hit.

Listening to Jessica's rant about how she was going to be a spinster forever—did people still use that word?—I decided to text my sulking affianced:

Can you do something about this?

He dug his phone out of his pocket, an act that was so bizarrely sexy, it mesmerized me for a solid three seconds, then read my missive. His face remained impassive as he typed.

A second later, my phone chimed.

Why would I do that? It's getting you hot.

What? I turned and stabbed him with an appalled expression, then typed back, my fingers flying over the keyboard:

Wrong kind of hot, mister. This kind of hot leaves bodies in its wake. It takes no prisoners. It's very . . . testy.

"The minute you try to get married," Jessica continued, her rant a never-ending drone of threats and complaints, kind of like I imagined the life of an IRS agent might be, "I will rip your dress to shreds the night before your wedding day and, and—"

Reyes was apparently getting hot as well. He offered me a quick wink, his ridiculously long lashes making his mocha eyes sparkle in the early morning sun, then tossed a deadly glare over his shoulder. Jessica's eyes widened at his unprecedented attention, and the yapping stopped immediately. Deciding to pout in silence, she let her fiery red hair fall over her shoulders as she crossed her arms at her chest and stared out the window.

With a satisfied smile, I typed,

I owe you.

I know.

Do you take payments?

I have several installment plans. We can hammer out the details when we get home.

My insides jumped in delight. Gawd, it was hard to stay mad at him.

Deal.

"So, where are you from?" Agent Carson asked Reyes. "Originally?"

I whirled around to face him again, this time pinning him with a warning glare. Carson was an FBI agent, but I was all about stealth. Surely she wouldn't pick up on my silent threat.

He studied my mouth, not the least bit worried about my warning glare, then said at last, "Here and there."

I relaxed against the seatback. He didn't say *hell*. Thank God he didn't say hell. It was always hard to explain to friends how, exactly, one's fiancé was born and raised in the eternal flames of damnation. How his father was, in fact, public enemy number one. And how he'd escaped from hell and was born on earth as a human to be with his true love. As romantic as it all sounded, it was difficult to articulate without garnering a visit from men with butterfly nets.

"You been in Albuquerque long?" she asked him.

Now she was fishing. She knew who he was. Everyone knew who he was. He'd been something of a local celebrity when the state released him from prison for killing the man who'd raised him—*raised* being an insanely generous term. They'd really had no choice when said man showed up alive and well-ish. Reyes did have to sever his spine, but he was still living and breathing. Through a tube! That was the best part. Still, all the news reports about Reyes's wrongful conviction were making him pretty popular. Not quite so popular as Heisenberg and Pinkman, but one could hope.

"As long as I can remember," he said in answer to her question.

"He bought Dad's bar and grill," I told her, changing the subject.

"I heard that," she said. She'd done her homework. She probably knew his shoe size and how he took his coffee.

Coffee.

I started drooling at the thought. It had been several hours since I last had a cup. I'd read a couple of days ago that caffeine was bad for little budding babies and had to psych myself up to quit. I was not going to make it. No way. Nohow. It just would not happen.

"So, you're adjusting?" she asked Reyes, referring to his life on the outside.

"How about AC?" I asked her, changing the subject again. I'd felt Reyes tense with her prying questions, but she was honestly just curious. Surely he felt that as clearly as I did. Then again, we hadn't had the greatest morning. Probably best not to push.

"What?" she asked.

"Your name. Special Agent Carson is rather impersonal, considering all that we've been through, don't you think? And you've repeatedly thwarted my attempts to change your name to SAC."

"You're lucky I caught you. It's a crime to change someone else's name without their consent."

"Details." I waved a dismissive hand. "What I'm getting at—"

"Kit," she said, interrupting me.

"Kit?" I asked, rather stunned.

"That's my first name."

"Your name is Kit Carson?"

She bit down, her jaw working hard, and said through gritted teeth, "Yes. Is there something wrong with that?"

"No. Not at all." I rolled it over on my tongue. "I like it. Kit Carson. Why does that sound so familiar?"

"I can't imagine."

"So, I can call you Kit?"

"Only if you want to be arrested."

"Oh."

Her mouth softened. "Just kidding. Of course you can call me Kit. You can call me George if you want to. Anything as long as you stop calling me SAC."

"I like George, too," I said, "but I've already named Reyes's shower George. I'm afraid it would get confusing if I ever asked Reyes something like, 'Did you clean George's knobs?'" I raised my brows at her. "You see where I'm going with that."

A light blush crept over her face. "How about we stick with Kit."

"Works for me."

"Are you okay?" she asked, and I followed her line-of-sight to my hands.

I knew it. I looked like I was coming off crack. "Oh, yeah, I'm fine. I just quit caffeine."

She blinked in surprise several times before recovering. "Ah, well, that would explain the lack of coffee. It's weird seeing you without a cup in your hand."

"It feels weird."

"So?"

I questioned her with a quirk of my brow.

"Are you going to explain? Why did you, of all people, quit caffeine?"

After a quick glance over my shoulder, I said, "We're pregnant."

Kit had a knee-jerk reaction to that bit of news. Like literally. Her knee jerked and hit the steering wheel, sending us careening into oncoming traffic. Or it would have if there'd been any traffic at that moment.

She corrected the wheel, took a deep breath, then said, "No way. For real? You? A mom?"

I gaped at her. "What the hell? I can be a mom. I'm going to make a great mom."

"Oh," she said, trying not to look so shocked. "No, you're right. You'll make a great mom. You're going to take classes, though, yes? Learn what it takes?"

"Puh-lease. I so have this. I'm going to buy a goldfish. Try that on for a while. You know, start off small and work my way up to a kid."

"You're comparing raising a goldfish to raising a kid?"

"No." I was getting defensive, even though her gut reaction had been spot on. I could think of no one less qualified to be a mother than *moi*. "I'm just saying, if I can keep a goldfish alive, surely I can keep a kid alive."

She stifled a giggle behind a fake cough. That was original. "You do realize there's more to raising a kid than just keeping it alive?"

"I do indeed," I said, sounding way more confident than I felt. "Believe you me, I got this."

"And once you work your way up to a kid, where're you gonna get the kid? You know, to practice on?"

"I hadn't thought that far ahead. I was focusing on the goldfish."

"Ah. Good idea." She said it, but she didn't mean it. I could tell.

I turned to look at the trees as Jessica chimed in from the backseat. "That poor child. Having you as a mother? Talk about cruel and unusual."

Reyes must have shot her another glare, because she shut up. Not sure why he bothered. Jessica was right. And though Agent Carson had been teasing, she still nailed it: I knew nothing about being a mother. The only example I'd ever had was that of a witch in wolf's clothing, a stepmother who thought more of her begonias than she did of me.

Who was I kidding? This kid was in so much trouble.

A heaviness pressed into me. The same heaviness that had been pressing into me since I first learned of our little bun in the oven. The pregnancy was an accident, of course. We hadn't been practicing safe sex by a long shot, but who'd have thought Reyes could get me pregnant? He was the son of Satan, for goodness' sake. I'd just figured it an impossibility.

So, Satan was our daughter's grandfather. Her father was literally created in hell. And her mother worked part-time as the grim reaper. We were the very definition of *dysfunctional,* and that was on a good day. I usually saw the gun clip half full, but this was just not a pristine situation. Nothing about her environment would be safe. I caused more trouble than gonorrhea.

My phone chimed. I glanced down at Reyes's text.

Look at me.

I didn't want to. He had to feel what I was feeling, and he probably felt sorry for me. Possibly even defensive. But both Kit and Jessica were right.

He sat waiting patiently for me to turn around. I swallowed back my self-doubt and turned to look over my shoulder.

To my surprise, his expression had hardened. He studied me with a crackling storm glittering in the depths of his irises. *"Stop,"* he said, his voice soft, dangerously soft—so soft, I had to strain to hear him. He reached out and ran a thumb across my lower lip. *"Je bent de meest krachtige magere hein ooit en je zou je door meningen van anderen aan het wankelen laten brengen?"*

Translation: "You are the most powerful grim reaper ever to exist, and you would let the opinions of others give you pause?"

Response: Apparently.

I raised my chin and tucked a brown lock behind my ear. He'd told me that a dozen times—the most powerful reaper bit—but none of them, not a single reaper who came before me, had ever gotten knocked up. We were breaking new ground here, and he would just have to deal with my insecurities. Normally, no, I would not let the opinions of others give me pause, but I was, after all, still human. At least in part. And being a mother was serious business.

The fact that he was speaking Dutch was not lost on me. It was what he called me: Dutch. What he'd called me from the day I was born. But I'd never heard him speak it, and the beautiful foreign language expressed in his deep, smooth voice felt like warm butterscotch in my mouth.

He lowered his lids and gazed at me, my reaction stirring him. He reached out with his heat, like tendrils of liquid fire, and it washed over me. Pooled in my abdomen. Settled between my legs. They parted involuntarily, as though to give him permission to enter. But now was certainly not the time.

"Stop," I whispered back, echoing his command.

A dimple appeared at one corner of his mouth. *"Maak mij."*

"Make me," he'd said, the challenge glittering from between his lashes almost my undoing.

"This is it," Kit said, either oblivious to our flirtations or choosing to ignore them.

Just as she pulled the car onto a dirt entrance to the campgrounds, my phone rang. It was Cookie.

I drew in a deep ration of cooling air as I answered, pretending my affianced was not trying to seduce me. I couldn't take him anywhere. "Hey, Cook."

Cookie Kowalski was not only my very best friend on planet Earth, but she was also my receptionist slash research assistant who was darned near becoming a fantastic skiptracer. And she was my neighbor to boot, who cooked a mean enchilada. Like, really mean. Like so hot under its corn tortilla collar that my taste buds tingled for days after eating them—aka, perfect.

"Hey, boss. How's it going?" she asked.

Normally we had coffee every morning and discussed the day's business, but I'd left so early, I didn't get to explain that I couldn't have coffee with her anymore. And I'd never get to have coffee with her again. The thought sent me into a deep, dark depression, the one where I curled into a ball and sang show tunes to myself. Then I remembered it was only for another eight months or so. Maybe I'd get lucky and the little bun in the oven would pop out a couple weeks early. I'd have to do jumping jacks and run a couple of triathlons when I reached the beached-whale stage. Hurry her along.

"I'm investigating a cold case with Agent Carson. What's up?"

"Oh, sorry to bother, but your uncle called. He has a case for you."

Kit pulled up to the main gate, turned off the SUV, and started riffling through her briefcase.

"No bother, but Uncle Bob can bite me. I'm not talking to him." I was a tad irked at the moment with my uncle, a detective on the Albuquerque police force.

"Okay, but he has a case for you," she said again, her voice singsong.

"Don't care."

"It's right up your alley. There's been a rash of suicide notes."

"That's not right up my alley. That's, like, two blocks over from my alley."

"It is when the people who supposedly wrote those notes are missing."

I straightened. "Missing? Where'd they go?"

"Exactly," she said, a satisfied smirk in her voice. "Right up your alley."

Damn. She had me. I felt rather than saw Reyes smile from the backseat. "We'll be back in a couple. Fill me in then."

"You got it."

We hung up as I took in the area. The sign that used to announce a visitor's arrival to the Four Winds Summer Camp was now covered with boards that simply said CLOSED with a few NO TRESPASSING signs posted here and there for good measure.

I glanced at Kit. "I'm surprised they've kept the camp closed all this time."

She shrugged. "Would you send your kid to a camp where a mass murder took place?"

"Good point."

"And I guess it's partly out of respect as well," Kit continued. She gestured toward the metal gate. "We'll have to hike it from here. The gate is padlocked and I don't have a key."

From our vantage, I still couldn't see the outbuildings or lake, but I felt a gentle tug from just over the hill. There was certainly something there.

This was going to be tricky. Kit didn't know anything about my *abilities,* for lack of a better term. And after my high school fiasco with Jessica, only several of my closests knew. Even with them, I'd kept it to myself as long as I possibly could. So, investigating a crime scene with her so near and nothing else to really distract her could prove sticky, as I tended to talk to dead people.

Hopefully, however, my plan would work. If Reyes was going to tag along, the least he could do was be a distraction. We got out of the SUV and I nodded toward him. He nodded back, albeit reluctantly, and we were officially on a *Mission: Impossible* episode. I so wanted to dart around humming the theme song, but I didn't want to add to Kit's already low opinion of me.

I closed my door and started the hike up the trail to the grounds. Reyes seemed to magically appear beside me, but he didn't press the issue of my—gasp!—walking away without him. He was just going to have to deal. I needed him to direct Kit's attention elsewhere if we came upon any departed. I could always use my cell phone, pretend to talk into it when I was actually speaking to a departed, but that got me only so far. Sometimes the situation demanded a more assertive approach. For example, I'd once had to put this guy who died in a convenience store robbery in a headlock. It was really awkward, since there had been several cops standing nearby. I barely escaped a padded cell with that one, but the guy told me what I needed to know, so it was totally worth it.

But for some reason, I didn't want Kit to see anything like that. She was good people. I didn't want her to think of me as a raving lunatic. It tended to put a damper on relationships.

We hiked through thick foliage and across overgrown brush to get to a clearing sprinkled with outbuildings and a small lake. The grounds before us, once a thriving summer camp for kids, were now a series of crumbling cabins and neglected vegetation.

"This didn't happen on Friday the thirteenth, did it?" I asked, noticing a small wooden rowboat in the middle of the lake, completely empty. It rocked gently to and fro. This was way creepier than I'd thought it would be.

"No," Kit said, walking up behind me.

I strolled to the sunlit clearing, stepping carefully around a patch of prickly pear, and watched as children, all girls, skipped rope, played hopscotch in the dirt, created Jacob's ladders out of threadbare pieces of string, and fell back in the grass, giggling until their bellies hurt.

The scene reminded me of my childhood. Long before Jessica came around, I'd had a best friend like that. Her name was Ramona. She had skin the color of dark coffee and wore her frizzy hair in two braids that started behind her ears and ended before they touched her shoulders. They stuck straight out to the sides more often than not, and that is one of my most cherished memories. I thought the sun shone just for her. Her laughter warmed me to the deepest depths of my soul.

She was hit by a car while riding her bike to my house when we were seven, but we played together for years afterwards, until she figured I'd be okay if she left. When she crossed through me, I saw the true meaning of love, and I've never forgotten it. It wasn't until I met my current BFF, Cookie Kowalski, that I realized that that kind of love could exist more than once in a lifetime. *Philia.* A deep, selfless friendship. A loyalty of epic proportions, in which one is willing to sacrifice anything for the other.

And looking at these girls, who'd surely died under tragic circumstances, I saw that kind of love, that kind of closeness, no matter the horrid circumstances that brought them together. They played and skipped and laughed as though their lives were filled with cupcakes and cotton candy.

"It's sad," Agent Carson said, taking in the view before us. "Seeing it abandoned like this. Run-down. So utterly lifeless."

"Explain to me again how many people were killed that night," I said.

Reyes leaned against a tree and was watching the serene tableau with a gentle smile on his face. I'd forgotten how much he liked kids. Thought they were cool. He would make a fantastic dad. Maybe his longcomings could make up for my short ones once we entered into the sacred realm of parenthood.

"Five," Kit said. "And one girl disappeared that night. We've never found her."

I nodded. "Any suspects named Jason?"

She scoffed softly. "No, but there was a Mrs. Voorhees on our persons-of-interest list. She had seemed troubled." Kit gazed at me a long moment as I watched a little girl, quite a bit younger than the rest, take a cautious step closer to us. She had startlingly white hair with a pixie cut that matched her doll-like face, and she wore a dress that fairly exploded in a cascade of powder blue ruffles. Not exactly the attire one wore to summer camp. But one of her most adorable qualities was her ears: They stuck out and curved up a little, and if I believed in elves, I'd swear she was one. Or perhaps she was a tree sprite.

"What?" Agent Carson asked at last, doubt and curiosity in her tone. "Why did you want to know how many were killed when you've been over that file with a fine-toothed comb?"

I knelt down, pretending to take a closer look at the ground, as though I were some kind of tracker. I coaxed the elfling closer with a smile. "Just double-checking," I said, opening a hand out of Kit's line of sight. Many more had died here than just those five victims. I scanned the grounds again as the elfling made up her mind. At least eight girls played in the field around us. Possibly nine.

The elfling gazed at me, her attention rapt as she took in the bright light that forever surrounded me. Only the departed and a few other supernatural beings could see it. I could not, however, but it was apparently nothing short of amazing.

Reyes knelt beside me, and the elfling took a wary step back. When I looked over at him, he nodded toward the tree line, where another little girl stood in the shadows, hidden almost completely behind a pine. If not for her pale striped shirt and turquoise shorts, I would not have spotted her.

I gestured toward Kit, and he agreed with another nod.

"Can I see the file again?" I asked her.

She handed it to me as Reyes stood. With space between them, the elfling relaxed visibly. She raised a hand in the air and laughed softly at something I couldn't make out. Her grin was infectious. Reyes and I each wore one quite similar.

"Would you like to see the crime scene?" Kit asked me, beginning to wonder what I was doing.

It was the perfect segue. "Sure. Can you show it to Reyes first? I'll be there in a sec."

Kit looked from me to Reyes and then back, not sure what to think. Then, with a shrug, she led him off to the cabins.

The main one, probably the meeting lodge, was the only one with slight remnants of police tape on it. The tattered strips swayed loosely in the soft breeze, stirring the dirt and debris below them. Most of the windows had been broken, and the roof sat slightly askew. Neglect had a way of aging a place.

Free to talk privately, I sobered and winked at the little girl in front of me, who was so utterly fascinated with my light. Before I could get down to business, Jessica materialized beside me. She looked out over the girls. They had stopped what they were doing and were now watching us. Most were merely curious. A couple seemed to withdraw. Those would probably disappear before I could ask them anything.

"What happened?" Jessica asked, astonished.

"We aren't sure," I said. "But we're working on it."

Another girl, perhaps nine or ten and wearing a seersucker jumpsuit, joined the elfling as she danced and played. Looking as though they were running through sprinklers on a summer afternoon, they laughed and tried to catch particles of my light in their hands, clasping them together midair, then bringing them close to their eyes and peeking inside. Then they would burst into a fit of giggles. While I couldn't help but laugh with them, Jessica stood confused. Mortified.

"I don't understand," she said, her brows drawn in concern. "What happened to them?"

"I don't know, Jessica." I thumbed through the file until I came to a news article that included a picture of the homeless man who had frequented the area. The police were taking him in for questioning and someone had snapped a shot. "We're trying to find that out." I held the file open to the girls. "Can you answer a few questions for me?" I asked them.

The older one crept forward first. The elfling followed suit.

After pointing out the suspect, I asked, "Is this the man who brought you here? Did he kill you?" It was a horrible thing to say, to *have* to say, but there was simply no delicate way of putting it. One thing I'd found to be a truth 99 percent of the time was that the departed handled their deaths better than the living did.

The older one leaned in, squinted, then shook her head. But the elfling nodded vigorously.

"That's not him," the older one said.

"Is so. Look." The elfling pointed, but when she did, her finger traced over the news column until it came to a figure in the background. It was a cop or a deputy of some sort, and he was standing off to the side and talking to a woman, possibly a reporter. The photographer had snapped the shot just as the man looked over his shoulder toward the camera.

"Oh," the older one said. "That *is* him. He came to my house after school before my mom got home. He said she was in an accident and I had to go with him to the hospital, but we didn't go to the hospital."

The elfling bowed her head. "I was at a party and tried to walk home by myself because Cindy Crane threw up. Then I didn't feel good, so I left. But I got lost. He said he would help me find my mom." When she glanced up at me with those huge green eyes, my heart constricted. "He was so nice at first."

I slammed my lids shut. I just didn't get it. Why was there so much evil in the world? What had any of these precious girls done to deserve such a horrifying fate? I couldn't help but think of my own daughter, of what she would have to deal with. To face. It was not a pleasant thought.

Forcing myself to keep calm, I took in a deep breath, then continued. "Do you know about the people who were killed here? They were setting up for a summer camp when they were attacked."

The elfling pointed toward the cabin. "There. They were killed there."

"Do you know by whom?" I asked.

She pointed to the picture again. To the deputy.

"He brought Vanessa out here," the older one said. "They saw him."

Ah, they'd caught him burying one of his victims, so he killed them all. "Do you know where you are buried?"

"Of course," the elfling said. She pointed to the tree line surrounding the retreat. "We're over there by that big rock."

At least I could tell Kit where to look. She would, of course, question everything I told her, but she knew enough about me to follow through anyway. Each one of these girls deserved a proper burial, and their families deserved closure.

"Except for Lydia," the older one said.

I thumbed through the file again. "Lydia Weeks?" I asked, scanning the notes. "The girl from the camp? They never found her." I looked up at them.

"Yeah, he took her off somewhere else. She's not with us. She sticks to the trees mostly."

That time, they pointed in the opposite direction, at the girl in the turquoise shorts.

"That's her?" I asked, standing.

"That's her."

I bent to the girls. "I'll be right back, okay?"

They nodded before trying to catch particles of light again, like dust motes in the sun.

Though Jessica seemed totally distraught, I asked her for a favor. "Would you mind watching them until I get back?"

"What? Me?" She acted as though I'd asked her to shave her head. "I— I can't— I mean, I don't know anything about children."

I winked at her. "Join the club."

Before heading toward Lydia, I glanced at the cabins. Kit was explaining something to Reyes in front of the main lodge, her back to me. Accepting that as my cue, I took off in a dead sprint, barely catching the glare on Reyes's face as I put even more distance between us.

Lydia sank farther into the shadows as I neared. At eleven, she was actually a bit older than the other girls in the area. Her brows formed a hard line. She looked part Asian with dark, almond-shaped eyes and straight black hair that hung past her shoulders.

I slowed and eased up to her, afraid she would disappear before I could ask her anything. "Hi, Lydia," I said. Fighting my already burning lungs and racing heart, I pasted on my best smile and tiptoed closer. "I'm Charley."

Without uttering a word, she took off in the opposite direction.

"Wonderful," I said, ducking past a branch and hurrying after her. "I suck at tag. I was always It." My breaths came in quick, shallow bursts as I tripped on a leaf or something. "I contemplated changing my name to It when I was a kid to make playing tag more ironic."

She zigzagged past a log for my benefit, then cleared a fallen tree in one graceful leap. I, however, did not. After scraping my shins on the thick bark, I scaled the obstacle instead, huffing and puffing as I jumped over the other side. Before I could rant much more, I caught up to Lydia. She'd stopped running and was staring at the ground. I struggled to get oxygen to my red blood cells as I stumbled forward. When I got closer, I realized there was a distinct impression in the dirt. Leaves and debris had accrued, but on the edge of what looked like a shallow grave were the remains of a small, skeletal hand.

"I'm so sorry, Lydia," I said between gasps.

"I wanted you to see."

I knelt down and wrapped my fingers around the bones of hers before looking back at her. "I'll make sure they find you."

She nodded, tears threatening to spill over her lashes.

I wanted to tell her she could cross through me, she could be with her parents who'd died that night—but a growl, low and guttural, caught my attention. Alarm raced up my spine and over my skin as my gaze darted from one shadow to the next. "Is that a bear?" I asked. "I hope that's not a bear."

Lydia's expression had changed. She looked at me worriedly. "I shouldn't have brought you here. I'm sorry. I just wanted you to see."

I stood. "I know, honey. It's okay."

"No, it's not. It was selfish of me." She lowered her head.

"Not at all," I said, my voice stern.

Her mouth forming a lovely pout, she whispered, "You should know, they were summoned."

I put a hand on her arm and leaned closer. "Who, sweetheart? Who was summoned?"

She cast a worried glance over her shoulder. "The monsters." The growl grew louder as she spoke. "They were summoned. All twelve of them."

I stilled, my thoughts snagging on the word *twelve*. I straightened and whirled around, looking for the hellhounds, the beasts who'd escaped eternal damnation to frolic on earth. And to rip me limb from limb.

Before I could ask any more questions, she whispered to me once again. Her words curled around me like dark, ethereal smoke as she said, "You should run."

2

We are all searching for someone whose demons play well with ours.
—BUMPER STICKER

I raced back to the campgrounds so fast, tree limbs and pine needles whipped across my face with cruel intent. I didn't care. I flew over the fallen log and zigzagged past the trees, the landscape blurring in my periphery as I focused on sound. Not just any sound. A specific sound. A growl. But I had yet to hear it again.

I felt Reyes near me, incorporeal. His heat encircled me, but I didn't have time to explain. I burst from the forest and sprinted back to the cabins, shouting, "Time to go! Chop, chop!"

Snapping at a very confused Kit, I scooped up the file I'd laid on the ground and raced toward her SUV. She didn't argue. She followed behind me, grabbing her keys as she ran.

"Is there a bear?" she asked as we hustled into her SUV.

"Something like that," I said, eyeing Reyes.

He bit down and examined the area as Kit maneuvered the SUV through a perfect three-point turn, stirring up dirt and clouds of dust.

I felt bad about leaving the girls behind without so much as a by-your-leave. I'd have to go back for them when this Twelve business was all said and done.

"Okay," I said once we were on the road, "there are at least eight girls buried near that big boulder to the east of the cabins, just past the tree line."

"What?" she asked.

"And Lydia Weeks is buried at the opposite end of the camp, in a shallow grave. There is a fallen tree nearby."

Kit pulled to the side of the road. Our pause in forward momentum had me nervous again. Had the Twelve seen me? Would they hunt me down? Drag me out of the car for my dismemberment?

"We should keep going," I said to her, my hands slick with perspiration. From physical exertion or from nerves, I had no idea.

"What are you talking about? What girls?"

"Oh." I pulled out the file and opened it to the news article. "And this is your killer. He was using the area as a dumpsite. The campers got there on the wrong night. But we really should keep going."

She took the file without looking at it. "How do you know all of this?"

I sighed in helplessness, unable to answer to her satisfaction. "It's what I do, Kit. You just have to trust me. Say that we were investigating the area and we found a body. I can draw you a map of where to find her."

"You can show me." She started to make a U-turn.

I stopped her with a hand on her arm. "No, I can't."

We were idling in the middle of the road when a car approached. The driver slowed upon seeing us, unsure of what we were up to.

After a moment, Kit depressed the gas pedal and continued down the mountain. "I want a map," she said.

"You'll have it." I pointed to the deputy in the photo again. "Do you recognize this man?"

She finally took a look. "No. Why?"

"Was he ever a suspect?"

"No, but one of the agents on-scene described a confrontation he'd had with a sheriff's deputy from Los Alamos. Said he was asking all kinds of questions, which is natural, but he just remembered the guy as being dodgy. He'd wanted to know everything that was going on, even though it was well out of his jurisdiction."

"He's your killer."

She blinked at me in surprise, then refocused on the road. After navigating a few tight turns, she said, "One of these days, you're going to have to tell me how you do that."

"One of these days," I said, relieved beyond measure to be alive. And fully limbed.

Giving up all pretense of normalcy, I turned to Reyes in the backseat. "Are we safe?"

"For the moment. But we need a plan."

"Like what kind of plan? I mean, they're—" I gave one last fleeting glance toward Kit. She would never look at me the same again. Come to think of it, she might never look at me again, period. "They're hell-hounds," I said, resigned to the fact that I might lose SAC. "What can we possibly do to them?"

"First off, I don't think they're as sensitive to light as the first ones that escaped onto this plane, but they still can't go into direct sunlight. Nothing from hell can without insulation."

"You mean, without having the advantage of a human host?"

"Exactly. And I don't think they can actually possess people."

"You aren't sure?"

"Not really. I never dealt much with the hounds. But I know who has."

It only took me a moment to guess: "The Dealer."

The Dealer was our newest acquaintance, a slave who, like Reyes, had escaped from hell and now lived on earth as a human. He was centuries old yet barely looked nineteen.

"Yes. He was Daeva. He was a slave, and part of their job was to take care of other slaves, like the hounds."

"You know, someday you're going to have to explain to me in great detail exactly what hell is."

Kit's grip was so tight on the steering wheel, her knuckles shone white. I couldn't help that now.

"I understand what you meant earlier," Reyes said.

I still wanted to know more about hell and the hounds raised there. "Changing the subject will not help your— Wait, what do you mean?"

"This world," he said, his jaw working as he gazed out the window at the last of the pine and juniper as we emerged from the mountains and onto flatter land. "Bringing a child into it. What happened to those girls."

I wrapped my arms over my chest. "I guess it doesn't matter now, but still, it kind of breaks my heart. Especially knowing what our daughter is going to face."

Without looking at me, he said, "It breaks mine, too."

Hoping Kit couldn't give me a ticket for not wearing my seat belt, I unbuckled it and crawled into the backseat with my affianced. He took my hand in his, lacing our fingers together, his heat soft and stirring.

As we got closer to town, I called Cook to fill her in, as promised.

"How'd it go?" she asked in lieu of a salutation.

"Well," I told her, "we not only figured out who committed the murders ten years ago but also IDed a serial killer."

"Another one? We seem to have a lot of those around here."

"We do, don't we?" I'd never thought of it that way, but we really did seem to attract our share of crazies. I explained about the little girls. I shouldn't have. Cookie sank into that same deep, dark depression I'd been experiencing, but her depression was much more noble. Mine was just kind of whiny.

After a moment where Reyes studied the hand he was still holding, running his fingertips along my lifeline, Cookie asked, "What would you attempt to do if you knew you couldn't fail?"

"Calculus, prolly. Why?"

"Just curious. What if you could create the perfect murder? Like literally? Who would you kill?"

"Well, if I could create the perfect murder—of which there are none—I could probably time travel, too. I'd go back in time and kill Hitler."

"Interesting," she said.

"Why?" I asked. "Whom would you kill?" This was so not a conversation to be having in the back of an FBI agent's SUV.

"My ex," she said.

"Probably best not to mention that to your lawyer."

Her ex, whom I had yet to meet in the three years I'd known Cookie, was giving her a hard time about putting their daughter in danger. Apparently, he'd found out about an attack in my apartment, one Amber had witnessed, only she'd been too sleepy to realize what was happening at the time. Amber must have put two and two together and mentioned the incident to her dad. She would never have said anything if she knew what kind of strife it would cause her mother. Amber didn't know her dad as well as Cookie did.

"But if you're shopping, I know a guy who knows a guy."

"Nah," she said, dropping the idea, which was probably for the best. "But thanks. Still, if I could get away with murder, I'd hunt down serial killers and take them out one by one. I'd be a serial killer serial killer. Like *Dexter,* only with curves."

"I get that. Hey, I could be your assistant! I'd be an Assistant Serial Killer Serial Killer. I'd be an ASS. Or do I need the *K*s in there? Because that wouldn't sound nearly as cool."

She chuckled. "So, what's with this note you left on my desk?"

"It's a list of words."

"Yes, which is why I'm confused. Are these words significant in some way?"

"Are they ever? It struck me recently that if you put an *A* in front of a word, it negates that word. Like *amoral* or *asymmetrical.*"

"Yes—"

"I mean, I knew that, naturally. I just don't think we're taking full advantage of the precedent."

"Right. I got the list. But I don't think *a-smart* is a real word."

"That's what I'm talking about. It *should* be a real word. And it's nicer than saying dumb."

"Did you call your uncle Bob?"

"Not yet. But I could use a paycheck since, you know, I have to pay you. Eventually."

"That'd be awesome. I could eat this month."

"Well, now, I didn't say I was going to pay you enough to eat the whole month long. You might want to ration your food. And get rid of that kid. She eats entirely too much, now that she's turned thirteen." The part I was leaving out, of course: Amber was roughly the size of a twig in winter.

"Right? I don't know what to do with her."

"Don't get me started," I said, pulling my hand out of Reyes's grasp to wave it around dramatically before he took hold of it again. "She's so demanding. Food. Water. Next thing you know, she's going to ask to be unchained every time she has to go to the bathroom."

Cookie scoffed. "Like that will happen. So, Robert is at the court-house this afternoon, but he asked that you call him later."

"This whole suicide-note thing sounds suspicious. I think this is a ploy to get me to call him."

She laughed softly. "Honey, you need to talk to him."

"You're just saying that because you're dating the guy. You have to be on his side now."

"I'm not on anyone's side."

"Oh yeah? Two weeks ago, you would've had me kicking him to the curb."

"No, I wouldn't have. And you know it."

I let out a deep, annoyed sigh. "Whatever. I'll just go by the courthouse and talk to him face-to-face. Make him squirm like the rabid dog he is."

"Oh," she said, hesitating. "I don't think that's a good idea."

Interest level: 10. "Intriguing response. And why is that?"

"He's observing the trial of one of his cases."

"And?"

"And the presiding judge is, well, not your biggest fan."

"The Iron Fist?" I screeched. "Holy cow, I am so there."

"Charley," she said, her tone warning, "you know what happened last time you saw her."

"Pfft. Water under the bridge, Cook. It's a-relevant."

"Isn't there already a word for that?"

"A-relevant again. You're on a roll."

Kit dropped us off in front of Calamity's, the bar and grill Reyes bought from my dad. Her pallor had turned a chalky shade of white, but she said she'd have a team at the campgrounds immediately. She'd make something up. Tell them we found the remains somehow.

I wanted to set her mind at ease, but we both had work to do. Explanations would have to wait. It was still pretty early and Calamity's wouldn't open for another hour, but Reyes had a lot of work to do as well. I decided to remind him.

"You have a lot of work to do," I said as we walked behind the bar to our apartment building, where my cherry red Jeep Wrangler, aka Misery, sat waiting for me.

"I told you. I hired a manager." He was trying to sound all nonchalant, but I could feel the tension in his body. Better yet, I could see it. His arms corded with sinew and thick muscles, flexing in reaction to every sound—and on Central, that meant a lot of flexing. But he had a killer poker face, his gait relaxed, his smile charming.

"Right. I keep forgetting. Wait," I said, coming to a stop, "who did you hire?"

"Teri," he said with a shrug.

"No way." I started walking again, digging for my keys through the used Louis Vuitton I'd gotten off eBay—because a used Louis Vuitton was better than no Louis Vuitton—and mulling over the fact that Teri was the new manager of Calamity's. She had been a bartender for my dad forever, and even though she was a little rough around the edges, I couldn't think of anyone more suited for the job. "She's awesome."

"Mm-hm."

"And she's honest."

"I know."

"And she's been sober for over five years. It's crazy, though. Why would an alcoholic become a bartender? Isn't that setting the bar a little high? Pun intended, of course."

"I suspect for the same reason a person like your sister with extreme OCD might become a therapist. To help others."

"Oh, yeah. That makes sense. Teri's really good at spotting people who have had one too many. They call her the key thief. So, are you going to relax anytime soon?" I stuck my key into the lock and opened the door.

Reyes stepped behind me and shut it. Keeping his arm braced against the door, he pressed against my backside. "Is that an offer? I am feeling a little tense across my shoulders."

I turned to face him. "I thought you were mad at me."

"I am."

"Well, I make it a rule never to have sex with anyone who's mad at me."

He arched a brow. "It's a wonder you've ever had sex at all."

"Right? Okay, I'm going to the courthouse. I have a case. And I have to give Uncle Bob hell."

"What did he do now?"

"He— He—" I shook my head, unable to say the words out loud. "I can't talk about it. It's too painful."

A dimple appeared at one corner of his mouth. I so very much wanted to kiss it. "That bad, huh?"

"Worse. I don't know how we're ever going to get past this."

"So, all the times he's saved your ass, come to your rescue, helped you with cases—?"

"Null and void." I turned to open the door again. He shut it again. "Reyes, I'm never going to get there at this rate."

"Were you planning on going somewhere without me?"

I twisted around again. "It's daylight. You said that even if the Twelve really are here, they can't go into direct sunlight."

"And the fact that you were just almost attacked by one?"

"I told you. I never saw anything. I just heard a growl. It could have been my stomach, for all I know."

His expression hardened. "They aren't like regular demons, Dutch. I don't know exactly what they can and cannot do. Thus," he added, swiping my keys, "I'm driving."

"Oh, no, you don't," I said, jumping for the keys as Reyes raised them above my head. I felt like I was in second grade and Davey Cresap was holding my juice box just out of my reach. Until I kneed him in the groin. He damned sure never did that shit again.

I tried the same move with Reyes, but he was way too fast. He easily caught my knee and raised it until my leg was practically encircling his hips. It was such a nice fit.

He backed me against Misery again, pushed into me, whispered into my ear. "Next time you try to sneak out without me," he said, curling a hand around my buttocks and pulling me against his crotch, "we are going to have a serious discussion about the well-being of your ass." He squeezed, causing an infusion of warmth to flood my nether-neaths.

I wrapped my hands around his steely buttocks, pulled him into me, and said, "Next time you threaten my ass, you'd better have your own covered. I can swing with the best of them."

He leaned back. "Did you just threaten to spank me?"

A bark of laughter bubbled up out of me. "As a matter of fact—" I left my sentence hanging as I playfully swatted a steely derriere. I could only hope he felt it. Freaking son-of-Satan crap. He was like a boulder with zero pain receptors. But I was super good at the whole denial thing. Pretending my swat registered, I said, "Maybe you should remember that the next time you threaten me." I pulled my lower lip between my teeth, then added, "Or my exquisite ass."

He sobered, his gaze dropping to my mouth. It lingered there, a delicious glint in the gold flecks of his irises. "I can assure you, Dutch," he said, his voice husky and deep, "I will never forget it. Shotgun!" he added. He dropped my leg, tossed me back my keys, and strolled to the passenger side.

I stood stunned a moment before his statement registered. Gawd, that man was beautiful. After climbing in, I looked over at my intended, all sexy and . . . waiting for me to unlock the door. Wearing the mother of all smirks, I started the engine and put Misery in reverse.

"You do realize," he said through the closed window, "I could rip this door off its hinges."

I gasped. "You wouldn't."

His lids narrowed in challenge, and my mother of all smirks fizzled. Withered like a begonia in the Sahara. I unlocked his door and glared.

He didn't care. He laughed. It was a very uncaring laugh.

Freaking son of Satan.

3

I'm diagonally parked in a parallel universe.

—BUMPER STICKER

I tried to convince Reyes to sit outside the courtroom, that I'd only be a minute, but he insisted on going in. We emptied our pockets for the guard, went through the metal detector as my purse was inspected, then went inside. Ubie—that's the nickname I used to call him before I changed it—sat in the third row, his shoulders straight as he listened in rapt attention. I tiptoed to sit beside him. The captain was on his other side. And like any delinquent forced to enter a courtroom, Reyes chose a seat in the back of the room. He spread out, threw an arm over the back of his pew, and made himself comfortable. Ubie, on the other hand, looked anything but comfortable. He glanced over at me, slid his brows together in consternation, then returned his attention to the witness on the stand.

"Yes," the Caucasian man in the prison uniform said. "I met Vikki about a year ago at a bar and we started sleeping together soon after. She told me she'd been slowly poisoning her husband, Steve, for several weeks for the insurance money."

Vikki must have been the defendant, the one staring at him like he had two heads. The man's testimony shocked her. And I felt that shock to my core. It rippled through me, knotted my stomach, made me feel woozy with nausea and utter disbelief. Either that or the morning sickness was kicking in.

"And we're just supposed to believe you?" the female defense attorney asked. "A convicted felon who has perjured himself to get a reduced sentence before."

"I'm telling the truth."

I doubted that. The man in his late thirties seemed about as trustworthy as that guy who was selling pre-owned underwear out of his trunk the other day. I was with the defense attorney on this one.

Without looking at my scumbag uncle, I whispered, "He's lying through his teeth. What do you want, Traitor Joe?" That was his new name: Traitor Joe. Because he was a traitor, and he was mean. A joke was one thing, but—

He cleared his throat, obviously uncomfortable talking at a trial. "I have a case for you," he said back, his voice low. "And what do you mean, he's lying through his teeth?"

I was busy concentrating on the defendant as she sat at a large table to the left of us. She was a heavyset woman, young with soft brown hair pulled back from her face. She wore an ill-fitting dress, the sleeves too tight around her arms. Wringing her hands in front of her on the table, she looked the type to feel more at home in jeans and cowboy boots than a dress. And her hands were rough. She was a worker. A hard worker. On top of that, she was completely innocent.

"Is this your case?" I asked Joe.

"Yes. We've spent months building it."

"Well, then maybe you shouldn't be hiring Wynona Jakes to help you solve cases. Because the woman sitting at the defendant's table is as innocent as my left pinkie toe."

My uncle shifted in his seat. I felt dread saturate his entire body.

The captain frowned at us. I could feel his knee-jerk reaction to my statement, that reaction 100 percent negative. But he'd learned a lot about me during our last powwow. He knew I could sense things others couldn't.

"What are you talking about, pumpkin?" Joe asked, so patient with me even when I was doing my darnedest to be mean. But he'd been mean first. "I told you, I never hired Wynona Jakes. It was a setup. Payback, remember? For when you set me up?"

Fine. I set him up.

For happiness!

He wasn't asking Cookie out when he'd so clearly wanted to, so I constructed a scenario that would change his mind. The plan was to send Cookie on a few dates to make him so jealous, he'd feel compelled to ask her to dinner. Only he figured out what we were doing. For payback, he'd brought in a fake psychic to consult on a case. Or he pretended to, anyway. Thought he'd ruffle my feathers a bit. I got that. I understood. I was setting him up. He set me up. But what he did next—unforgivable.

"You know what you did," I said to him, crossing my arms over my chest.

"I really don't."

I closed my eyes, counted to ten, then said as calmly as I could, "The book."

After taking a moment to absorb my meaning, he doubled over into a fit of coughs to suppress his laughter. Everyone looked, but he recovered quickly, coughing into his handkerchief, his face red with humor. "She did it?" he asked from behind the white material. "Wynona Jakes sent you the book?"

"I didn't even know she had a book out," I said, my words a hiss through my teeth. "She is as fake as a porn star's orgasm. How did she get a book deal?"

He bent toward me and said in an understanding whisper, "Is that what all this is about?"

"Maybe." I stared straight ahead, unable to meet his gaze.

"She asked if I thought you'd like a copy of her book."

"She knew damned well I didn't want one. I made my opinion of who she was and what she did perfectly clear the day we met."

People like Jakes were dangerous. Period. And those who followed her, who believed the cockamamie lies she dished out . . . well, I felt sorry for them. There was the real deal, and then there were the charlatans. She'd ruined people's lives and refused to take responsibility, to come clean to the public. Maybe someone would have to expose her. Or, I thought, conjuring a plan, I could just have Reyes sever her spine.

No. Severing spines rarely solved anything. And I couldn't turn to his spine-severing service every time I needed to incapacitate someone. The consequences were so permanent.

"I didn't know she actually sent you a book, pumpkin. Is that why you've been ignoring my calls?"

"I haven't ignored all of them," I said, defensive.

"Okay, well, when you do pick up, you pretend like we have a bad connection."

My shoulders concaved.

"Sweetheart?"

"I thought you were making fun of me. Of my reaction to her."

"Like you have anything to worry about from someone like Wynona Jakes."

"But she's making money, Uncle Bob. Off innocent people."

"And she's the first?"

"Detective," the captain whispered, his impatience palpable. "The defendant."

Ubie nodded. "Right. Back to this. Are you telling me this woman is innocent?" He gestured toward the defendant.

I nodded. "Completely."

The captain cursed under his breath and leaned toward me. "This isn't a game, Davidson."

Before I could say, *Really? 'Cause it looks so much like tennis,* the judge cleared her throat. Loudly. My gaze snapped to the front of the court-room to see the witness being led away in cuffs on his way back to prison.

The judge, a large African American woman who could kick my ass so fast, I'd need CPR—she'd done it before—leveled a hard glare on me. Refusing to take all the blame, I pointed to Uncle Bob.

"Mizzz Davidson," she said. Her voice, loud and razor sharp, echoed against the wood walls. Everyone turned to look at us. At me.

Judge Quimby always called me Miz Davidson, buzzing out the Z sound like a bee to let me know just how unimpressed she was with my existence. And, like the sound of running water, it had a way of making me want to pee myself.

I clenched Virginia just in case. "Your Honor," I said, my cheeks burning in mortification.

"Would you care to enlighten me as to why you are in my courtroom when you have been banned from ever stepping inside my humble hall of justice until the day one of us dies?"

I refrained from mentioning the fact that if I died first, the point would be moot. "Oh, that," I said, adding soft laughter. "I just—"

I glanced over at the defendant. She was the only one in the entire room not looking at me. She sat with her head bowed as absolute misery washed over her. The man had lied and she was filled with anger, hurt, and hopelessness. Two women who bore a striking resemblance to the defendant sat directly behind her. One looked like her mother. Same soft brown hair pulled back. Same work-hardened hands as she wiped at a tear and leaned forward to rub the defendant's shoulder. But the one next to the older woman caught my interest the most. The emotions rolling out of her were filled with deception. I strained to single out her feelings, which were stronger than most of those around her.

Gloating.

She was gloating on the inside, quite enjoying the defendant's agony. It took a special kind of evil to enjoy the agony of others. She put a hand on her chest and wrapped her fingers around something just beneath the sweater she wore. A necklace of some sort, it had special meaning. It made her happy knowing she had it near, as though she wore it on purpose.

"I just—," I started again, unable to tear my gaze away from her. "May I call for a recess?"

Part of the room gasped in horror. The rest simply looked on in horror, probably afraid to gasp aloud in the presence of the Iron Fist, a nickname Judge Quimby had earned her first year on the bench. I hoped it had more to do with her judging principles than, say, her ability to beat scrawny white chicks to a bloody pulp. I always saw the cup half full like that. Tried to see the good in any situation.

The prosecutor, ADA Parker, scrubbed his face with his fingers. He did that a lot around me.

"Fifteen-minute recess," Judge Quimby said before pounding her gavel.

"Oh, my god," I said to no one in particular. "It worked."

"You," she continued, pointing her gavel at me. "In my chambers."

Holy crap on a cracker. This could not be good.

I looked at Ubie in helplessness and grew even more mortified when I saw the humor playing about his mouth. Annnnd we were back to Traitor Joe.

"You, too," the judge said, scowling at Joe with a stern look of disapproval.

It took every ounce of strength I possessed not to say in a singsong voice, *Ubie got in trouble.*

At least I wouldn't go down alone. I'd drag everyone with me that I could.

"What about the captain?" I called to her as people stood all around us, waiting for the bailiff to excuse them.

"Him, too," she said.

Sweet! Surely I could deflect some of the blame for my disrespectful behavior in her courtroom over to them. They should have known better, inviting me into a courtroom. It was their own fault. This was assuming, of course, that my trespass into her courtroom was the reason for Judge Quimby's orders. If it was about that other thing, we were all screwed.

I tossed a shrug to Reyes as we were led into the judge's chambers. He had stiffened, not wanting to let me out of his sight, but he'd just have to hold that thought. Nothing to be done for it now.

The Iron Fist walked out of a side room, a toilet flushing in the background. "I had to go something awful."

I knew how she felt.

"Sit down, gentlemen," she said to Ubie and Captain Eckert as she sat behind a massive desk. It was all very stately.

Since there were only two chairs, I took that as my cue that I was meant to stand. I stepped to the side so that Ubie and the captain didn't have to stare at my ass.

The door opened again and both the prosecutor and counsel for the defendant stepped inside. Now it was getting awkward. And cramped. The ADA scrubbed his face again when he saw me. Maybe he had allergies that made his face itchy.

"Now, Miz Davidson," Quimby began, riffling through papers as she spoke, "what on God's green earth made you think stepping into my courtroom was a good idea?" She stopped riffling and leveled one of her infamous glowers on me. It rivaled my own infamous death stare and was a thing to behold, especially when her top lip twitched, as it did now. I'd have to add that to my death stare. I could twitch. No, wait, I could twerk. Different body part entirely.

"I needed to talk to my uncle," I said, hanging my head in shame. "I didn't realize you were presiding today."

"Really?" she asked, tapping a stack of papers into place. "The name on the door outside didn't give it away?"

"I— I'm having problems comprehending what I'm reading today. I have a condition."

"Interesting." She looked over at my partners in crime. "Detective, Captain, would you care to elaborate?"

"I'll try, Your Honor," Ubie said. "I called her in on a case, and she needed some information. I apologize. I should have met her outside."

"Yes, you should have. Captain?" she asked him.

He shook his head. "I got nothing."

"I didn't expect that you would."

"You know," I said, trying to put an end to the torture, "about that last incident. If I'd known that guy had schizophrenia, I never would have made that face. But daaaang, girl," I added, going the homegirl route, "you were the bomb. I mean, those moves were tight." I did an exaggerated head nod and threw in some gang signs for good measure.

Uncle Bob closed his eyes, unable to watch.

"Seriously, girl, the way you threw me over your shoulder like that? Sheeeee-uht. I had lower back pain for days."

"I will hold you in contempt," she said, her voice a dangerously low octave. "Don't you ever pull that gangsta garbage in my presence again. Do you understand me?"

"Yes, Your Honor." That didn't go as well as I'd hoped. "But what if we're at a bar and a rival gang comes up threatening to shank our asses and all we have is our wit and acting skills?"

"Are you mentally challenged?" she asked me. She was serious.

"Not that I know of."

"Then shut up."

"Okay." Gah. Testy. Unlike hers, mine was a legitimate question.

"So, what were you saying about the defendant?"

I blinked in surprise. Uncle Bob blinked in surprise. The captain blinked in surprise. The ADA and the defendant's lawyer—a pretty blonde with big bones and a tired face—just kind of stood there.

"I'm sorry?" I asked.

"Oh, now you don't have no sass for me, huh?"

I wasn't sure a judge should use a double negative like that.

"What were you saying about the defendant? And don't look at me like I just stole your lollipop. I know all about you and your antics, little girl."

"Your Honor," the ADA said. He was young, hungry for the top spot, and working his ass off to get there. He certainly didn't have time for underlings like me. He'd actually said that to me once when I tried to tell him the man he was investigating was on to him. He would have saved a lot of time and a lot of face if he'd just listened to me.

God, if I had a nickel for every time I'd said that.

"I don't know what this woman has told you, but she is always causing trouble. I have no idea why APD puts up with her, besides the obvious." He cast a sideways glance at Uncle Bob, implying nepotism, and that's where I took offense. Not about the nepotism but about the glance. Nobody cast sideways glances at Ubie but me.

I straightened. "Look here, Nick," I said, leaving off the last part of his name: the Prick.

"Did you just speak in my presence after I told you to shut up?" Quimby asked.

I bit my bottom lip. "No."

"That's what I thought. I will not ask the same question three times. I have my limits."

When everyone turned to me, I said, "May I speak?"

"If, and only if, you have something to say about this case that might be of benefit to anyone in this room with a law degree."

There were three things wrong with this picture that I could decipher right off the bat. First, a judge never asked people if they had information pertinent to a case. Wasn't that the lawyers' job? Judges presided. Lawyers deposed. Second, she'd actually called a recess to get said information. Things like that just didn't happen in real life. And third, what would make her want to listen to anything I had to say, whether it was about a case or not?

I cleared my throat and said, "In that case, the defendant's completely innocent."

Nick the Prick threw his hands in the air. "Gosh, if only we'd had you during the months-long investigation into this crime to tell us these things. However did you break the case?"

"Mr. Parker," the judge said, "would you please let me do the questioning here?"

"Yes, Your Honor." His face darkened to a purplish hue. Disturbing? Yes. Entertaining? Even more so. "But, begging Your Honor's pardon, why would you even listen to her?"

I was right there with him.

The judge gave him her full attention. "Because her instincts have a way of . . . How shall I put this?"

I shrugged, at a complete loss.

"Her instincts have a way of bearing fruit."

Aw. She thought I was fruity. I got that a lot.

She placed a much gentler glare on me than normal. It made me very uncomfortable. "Any thoughts on who actually killed Mrs. Johnson's husband?"

After a hesitant nod, I said, "Her sister did it."

"Of course she did," Nick said, tossing his hands in the air again. He was such a drama queen.

"I can prove it," I said, growing desperate.

Every gaze landed on me.

I swallowed hard and said, "She's wearing a necklace underneath her sweater. I think it's significant. I think it's the poison she used to kill her brother-in-law." When everyone just sat there, gaping at me, I added, "She was fondling it, secretly rubbing her sister's nose in it."

"Detective?" Judge Quimby said, raising her brows at Uncle Bob. "Did you question the defendant's sister?"

Ubie shifted in his chair. "We did, Your Honor, but she was never a suspect. In fact—" He shook his head in disbelief. "—she was the one who convinced us of her sister's guilt."

The defendant's lawyer spoke with a confidence she hadn't had moments earlier when she said, "Your Honor, may I ask for a continuance until we can look into this further?"

"You have twenty-four hours."

The fatigue slid from the woman's features. "Thank you," she said, beaming at me. "I know my client is innocent. Thank you for this opportunity to prove it."

I nodded. "You might want to get that necklace. Like, now."

"Your Honor?"

"Go," she said. Standing from behind her desk, the judge waved a dismissive hand. "All of you, out."

I was the first to obey, practically sprinting toward the exit. Of all the strange events in my life, that was by far the weirdest I'd had in hours. But the day was early.

The defendant's sister had been detained by security before I even got out of the building. I stopped and watched as they escorted her to a waiting patrol car. They could question her, but if she didn't give up the necklace, they'd need a warrant. Hopefully, the Iron Fist would help with that as well.

Uncle Bob stood down the hall, gripping his phone. He was both angry and relieved. I couldn't blame him. He worked hard on these cases. It couldn't be easy to have me waltz in and tell him he was wrong, with no real proof to back it up. He had to take a lot of what I said on faith, just like Kit. It made me appreciate them all the more. And if everything went as planned, we'd just stopped an innocent woman from going to prison. Nothing felt better than that.

Well, perhaps one thing. Reyes walked up behind me, his heat reaching me long before he did, and its warmth saturated my clothes. My hair. My girlie bits.

"Did you save the day again?" he asked while wrapping his arms around me, his mouth at my ear, his warm breath fanning across my cheek.

"Hopefully. For one person, anyway."

"And that's enough?" he asked. "Saving one person?"

I turned in his arms. "I wish I could have been there during your trial. I would've told Uncle Bob you were innocent, too."

"I don't think even the great Charlotte Davidson could have kept my ass out of prison. Earl made sure there was more than enough evidence for a conviction."

It still crushed my heart every time I thought about him spending so many years behind bars for a crime he didn't commit. At that moment, I could think of nothing worse.

His eyes, a deep, shimmering chocolate with gold and green flecks, narrowed in warning. "You aren't feeling sorry for me, are you?"

He knew not to dismiss my empathy where he was concerned. There was little I could do about it, and he knew that. At least, he'd better if he didn't want a spanking.

My mouth tilted into a playful smile at the thought, and he grew intrigued, but before he could ask me about it, Ubie walked up to us.

"Parker's having a fit," he said, the humor in his voice unmistakable.

I tore my gaze off my affianced. "ADA Parker does that."

"I think you do that to him."

"It's his own fault," I said, slipping out of Reyes's hold so we could walk out the exit. He laced his fingers into mine, and I paused for just a moment. He'd never done that before. Just held my hand as we walked. His warmth spread up my arm and over my chest to settle around my heart. I continued walking beside Uncle Bob. "So, what's this case?"

"Ah, yes, I have a copy of the file for you in the SUV. We've had two suicide notes over the last couple of weeks."

"Cookie told me," I said as he led us across a parking lot to his department-issue dark gray SUV.

He grabbed a file out of the front seat, handed it over to me. Reyes took the occasional peek over my shoulder while I perused, but for the most part, he kept a weather eye on our surroundings.

"Just notes," Uncle Bob said as I looked through the case file. "Both people who wrote them have disappeared."

"They killed themselves?"

"We have no idea. But we just got another one a couple of hours ago. Woman says her husband left a note in the middle of the night and just disappeared."

"Was there any sign of a struggle?"

"Don't know. Haven't been to the scene yet. We have a team over there now."

I read one of the notes, typical yet sad, then the next. All kinds of stuff about how the author didn't deserve to live the glorious life they'd been given. In fact, both authors used the word *glorious.* That could not be a coincidence. The third note was very different, but it had the same word in it: *glorious.* "They're remarkably similar," I said, marking other strange phrases in all three letters, but the handwriting was unique. As were the signatures.

"Yes, they are. We have three almost identical suicide notes and no bodies."

I looked up at him. "So, really? They just disappeared?"

"Far as we can tell. No signs of any kind of struggle at the first two scenes, and none of them had ever attempted suicide before. We figure they were forced to write these notes by the same person, then taken somewhere else and were either killed or are being held hostage."

I leaned against his door. "So, the notes were just to throw you guys off? To stall you? What?"

"You tell me," he said with a shrug. "I thought maybe you could, you know, poke around and see if they were still alive."

"I can ask Rocket," I said. "What's the connection among the three?"

"We haven't found any, besides the notes themselves."

"Okay, you keep looking and I'll go talk to Rocket after lunch."

"Lunch?" he asked, his interest piqued. "You buying?"

I snorted. "Not even. But I do know an incredible cook at this local pub." I tossed a wistful smile to Reyes.

He winked, offered Ubie a head nod, then took my hand into his again and led me to Misery.

"So," I asked, enjoying the warm, sunny day and the feel of Reyes's hand in mine, "are you holding my hand because you want to get in my pants or because you're afraid I'll escape?"

"You couldn't escape if you wanted to."

He did not just throw down that gauntlet.

"And, in case you missed the memo, we have twelve angry hell-hounds on our asses."

I leaned behind him to check out the aforementioned backside. "Can't say that I blame them. If I were a hellhound, I'd be after your ass, too."

A reluctant dimple appeared at the side of his mouth.

"Actually," I said, rethinking that statement, "even if I were an angel, I'd be after your ass. Or a saint. Or a gerbil. I like this." I indicated his hand in mine. Or, well, mine in his since his was fairly swallowing mine. I stepped in front of him as we strolled to Misery and walked backwards for a minute until I could resist no longer. I jumped into his arms.

He laughed softly and cradled my ass, pulling me closer. "What's 'this'?"

"Romantic. Like in the movies." I leaned in and kissed a dimple. "No, wait!" I hopped out of his arms, leaned into him again, placed the back of one hand over my brow, then bent backwards, hoping he'd catch me.

He did. First one arm went around my waist to keep me from falling; then the other went under my knees. "And this?" he asked, lifting me into his arms.

I arched farther back. "It's even more romantic," I said, keeping my eyes closed. "Like in a paperback novel, when the Duke of Hastings catches the girl who has just fainted into his arms."

He stopped then, and the world was ours. There were no onlookers.

No cars whizzing by or people talking a short distance away. It was just the two of us.

He pulled me against his chest and I nestled my head into the crook of his neck, but I kept my arms limp at my side. I had a role to maintain, and being an English debutante in the middle of an Albuquerque parking lot was not as easy as it might seem.

"And what does the duke do with her?" he asked, his voice suddenly hoarse.

Completely lifeless, I let my head fall back again, effectively giving him access to my neck. "Whatever he desires."

He took advantage, causing a slew of microscopic earthquakes to quiver through me.

I had to run a couple of errands with Reyes in tow, but when I was done, I dropped him off at his office, aka the kitchen of Calamity's, then headed up to my office, which sat above said bar and grill. I had a special package and a couple of bags hampering my normally pantherlike movements. Thus, with arms filled to the brim, I missed a stair and had to drop to one knee to keep from falling back, ramming the edge of said stair into my shin and causing a sharp pain to rocket through me. I cursed just loud enough for the whole of Albuquerque to hear.

"You okay?" Teri called up to me from the bar. I'd taken the inside stairs, but the only barrier between Teri and me was an intricate wrought-iron balustrade. My misstep was visible for all to see. Thankfully, they were still minutes away from opening for the day.

"I'm good," I said, but Reyes's head was out the door of the kitchen instantly. "No, I'm good." I had to assure him I wasn't being attacked by a hellhound. "Go back to work. Nothing that an ice pack and a mild surgical procedure can't fix." My shin was throbbing and each movement after caused a jolt of agony.

I struggled to my feet as he looked on and continued up the stairs to the back entrance of my offices. I was carrying precious cargo. I was on a mission, and no stair on earth was going to stop me. Of course, if I'd tumbled down them, knocking my head a few times and landing in a heap at the bottom of the staircase, that might have stopped me.

The coolest thing about this bar was the old-fashioned ironwork laced in with the dark woods of the pub. The metalwork led to an ancient iron elevator no one actually used, because it was as slow as molasses in the Artic, but it looked awesome. I'd secretly wanted to live in this building for a long time. It was built by the same people who'd made our apartment complex. But that building had no elevator, iron or otherwise.

I had to shift a bag or two so I could open the door, but I managed to get myself inside.

"Honey, I'm home!" I called out to Cookie.

She leaned forward to look at me from her desk in the next room. "What in God's name are you carrying?"

I put all the bags down but one and walked to stand in front of her desk. "This," I said, pride swelling in my chest as I held up a clear bag filled mostly with water, "is Belvedere."

"You bought a goldfish?"

"Yep." I was putting the bag on a stack of papers, which Cookie whisked away before I set my goldfish down completely; then I went back for the other bags, one of which contained a round fishbowl. "I'm practicing."

She watched with mild curiosity as I walked into the restroom and filled the bowl with water.

"I know I'll regret this, but practicing for what?"

"Motherhood." I rubbed my belly to demonstrate. "I'm pregtastic."

"I know you're pregtastic."

"I should hope so. Either that or your rubbing my belly is completely inappropriate."

"I just like saying hi to her," she said defensively. "But what does a goldfish have to do with your condition?"

"The way I see it, if I can keep Belvedere here alive, I can keep a kid alive. And that's half the battle, right?" I untied the knot at the top of the clear bag and started to pour Belvedere into his new home. "Moving day!" I said happily.

Cookie lunged across the desk—and caught the bag just in the nick of time, if her relieved expression was anything to go by. She cradled Belvedere and glanced at me accusingly. It was weird. I never thought she'd be so protective of a fish.

"You're still my number one," I said, teasing.

"First of all," she volleyed, retying the knot, "you can't just toss a goldfish into water that has not been treated and is not the same temperature as what the fish is already living in."

I blinked. "Why the hell not?"

"Because. Our water has all kinds of crap in it that's bad for him, and it's a different temperature than what he's in right now, so if you dump him into it, he'll go into shock and die. Didn't the clerk at the store tell you that?"

"I'm not sure." I thought back. "Reyes kissed my neck while she was talking. I was so enamored, I kind of tuned her out."

"Oh, okay. It's so hard to concentrate with that man on the planet."

"Word."

"So, you think if you can keep a goldfish alive, you can keep a child alive?"

I took out the fish food to examine it. "Sure. You have to feed both of them, right?"

"Yes, but—"

"And you have to take care of them both, right?"

"You do, yes, but I think—"

"Then surely if I can do one, I can do the other."

"I think you're missing the point."

"And you've kept Amber alive for thirteen years, as of last week," I added. "How hard can it be?"

"I can't believe I have a thirteen-year-old."

"I can't believe you've kept her alive that long," I said. "I mean, it's so . . . daily. And kids are so needy. Like, you have to feed them every week. I couldn't even remember to water my plants every week."

"Well," she said, giving me her schoolteacher face, "there is one huge difference between a kid and a plant: Kids make noise when they're hungry. Trust me when I say you will not forget."

"Sweet."

She snorted. "Tell me that in a year."

4

I don't think I get enough credit for the fact that I do all of this unmedicated.

—T-SHIRT

I was busy perusing the suicide notes and waiting for Belvedere's water to finish its treatment when I heard a thud from Cookie's office. Then a mousy squeak. Then a throaty moan.

"Cookie," I said, wiggling my fingers at Belvedere to get him acquainted with our strange ways, "are you masturbating?"

"No. I got a paper cut."

Oh. I didn't see that coming.

"A bad one," she added, her voice more whiny than usual.

"Sucks to be you." It was the best I could offer. I cared on the inside. Which was exactly where it would stay.

She made a sucking sound and another squeak.

"Are you sure you're not mastur—?"

"I had a thought," she called out to me.

"Okay."

"You know how you heal really fast?"

I stood and walked to the doorway that separated our offices. "Yes," I answered, wondering where she was going with this.

She was sucking the side of her index finger. "Maybe if you lick my cut, your spit will heal me fast, too."

"Dude," I said, tamping down a giggle, "I'm not licking your cut."

"Just lick me." She held out her finger. "This is going to be tender for days."

"I'm not licking you." A line I rarely said aloud.

"Come on, Charley. Every time I file a document or type at the computer, it will hurt. Just lick me."

Reyes walked in behind me, but for once Cookie was too wrapped up in her own agony to give his majestic presence her full attention. She was much more concerned about her nigh-fatal injury.

"Or at least spit on me."

"Cook," I said, walking to her desk, "it's not that the thought isn't appealing, but my spit is not going to heal your cut."

She deflated. "How do you know until you try?"

"Mr. Farrow heals faster than I do," I continued, teasing him with a wink. "Let him lick you."

Her gaze landed on my affianced, hope and a spark of lust brightening the smoky depths of her blue irises.

I glanced over my shoulder at the curious smirk he was wearing. "Paper cut," I explained.

"Ah," he said. "Let me see."

I could tell by the way he said it—*Let me see,* his voice soft, his head lowered with one brow quirked—this was going to be interesting.

He walked over to her, but she hesitated. "It's okay. I'll live."

She tried to laugh it off, but he caught her hand in his, turned it this way and that, tsked when he came upon the life-threatening cut. Paper cuts hurt like the dickens. I understood her agony all too well. I also understood the spike of adrenaline that shot through her when Reyes brought her finger to his mouth. Locking his gaze with hers, he kissed the injured extremity, and Cookie visibly melted in her chair, every muscle in her body turning to mush, but Reyes didn't stop there. He parted his lips, pressing them into her skin as he suckled her injury. Cookie's heartbeat skyrocketed. Her nerves leapt, probably with joy, and I could feel a hot rush of desire flood her body.

I was right there with her. He had yet to release her gaze as his tongue slid along the cut, wetting it with what she believed was super-healing mojo. He placed one last kiss, a tiny peck, on the finger before releasing her hand with a soft wink.

She pulled her hand back, cradled it to her chest, and while normally I'd chuckle at her reaction, I could only stare in fascination.

I pointed to my shoulder. "I have a bruise."

He walked over to me, peeled my shirt back, and kissed my shoulder, the heat of his mouth scalding as that simple act sent the butterflies in my stomach into a frenzy.

Just as I was about to drag him into my office by his shirt collar, Uncle Bob walked in. It was probably for the best. I had yet to get it on with my affianced in my office, especially with Cookie in the next room, and now was hardly the time since, you know, Cookie was in the next room.

She snapped to attention. Her face bloomed a bright pink as she busied herself, straightening papers.

"Where you been?" I asked him, taking a second to draw in cool air as Reyes stared at me from underneath his thick lashes. His eyes glistened with intent. He knew exactly what I'd been thinking. The rake.

Ubie nodded an acknowledgment. "Had to tie up a couple of things. But I'm starving. What's for lunch?" he asked Reyes.

The Cheshire smile Reyes gave him almost made me laugh. "It's a surprise," he said.

Ubie frowned in suspicion before taking a good look at Cookie, his new flame. Cookie may have lusted after Reyes, but her feelings for Ubie were just as strong. Just as undeniable. The desire she felt toward Reyes wasn't her fault. Pretty much everybody lusted after Reyes—a side effect of his supernatural heritage was my guess. But what she felt for my uncle was real. I felt a deep admiration for him every time she looked at him. An absolute trust. And, yes, an unmistakable attraction.

I felt pretty much the same thing coming from Ubie, but with one addition: astonishment. He was still astonished that Cookie liked him. That she was dating him. That she wanted to be with him. Their mutual respect and admiration were what would see this relationship through. Unlike the last dozen or so women Ubie had dated, none of whom had gotten my approval.

Cookie stood when he stepped to her desk, and he leaned over to kiss her cheek, unsure if she'd want him to display his affection in front of us. He was like the shy kid at school picking up his prom date, his nerves jumbled and his palms sweaty. I could hardly miss an opportunity like this.

"So, are you two hitting it yet?"

Ubie did his deadpan thing, the one that made me laugh inside.

Cookie pressed her mouth closed, but the emotions that leapt inside her when I mentioned premarital sex told me everything I needed to know. Probably more than I needed to know.

I gaped at her. "Cookie!" I shrieked just loud enough to make them both super-duper uncomfortable. Then I asked, "Are you being safe?"

That time, Ubie clamped his teeth together.

"Fine," I said before he could reprimand me. "Whatever. Let's eat."

My phone rang as Ubie waited for Cookie to round her desk so he could escort her downstairs. He treated her like a queen. He treated her exactly as she deserved to be treated. I loved it.

There was already a crowd, the dull roar of conversation wafting up to us as I answered a call from Kit.

"Hey, homey," I said to her, hoping she felt the same way about me. I was busy watching Reyes's ass as he took the lead, intrigued with the way his glutes flexed with each step.

"So, that deputy you told me about—" She stopped talking a few seconds and I heard mumbling in the background.

To bring her back to me, I said, "I'm not sure that was a complete sentence."

"Sorry. That deputy transferred to Alaska about nine years ago."

I stopped, bringing the whole procession to a halt. Cookie and Ubie stepped past me after I gestured for them to grab a table. Reyes had stopped, too, waiting for me to go in with them.

I cupped my hand over the phone. "Reyes, they are not going to attack me between here and our table."

He crossed his arms over his chest and leaned against the banister, refusing to proceed without me. But I wouldn't be able to hear Kit in the pub. The Calamity's crew was a rowdy bunch, so I continued to stand on the stairs.

"Do you think he's still killing? Do you think it's him?"

"Hard to say. It seems they've had a lot of disappearances up there, but from all over the state."

"And Alaska is a big state."

"Damn right, it is. But we did find out something very interesting."

I leaned against the iron banister, too. "Yeah?"

"He has a pilot's license."

I stood up again. "Really? Do you think he's been abducting girls from around the state and flying them out to a central location?"

"That's the working theory."

"Was he doing that here?"

"That's what we're trying to find out. The authorities in Juneau are very excited to work with us on this. They're pulling up all his flight plans. We're doing the same here and cross-checking them with missing persons cases. So far, we have two hits."

"What can I do?"

"That's my question. What can you do? How did you know all this?"

"It's just my thing," I said, trying to play it off.

"Can you do your thing with the missing girls in Alaska if it comes to that?"

"I could try. I'd have to fly there. I'm totally in, though. You're paying for that, right?"

"Absolutely. How about we work on this end first—then if we need you in Alaska, I'll get it approved. Somehow."

"Sounds like a plan."

Reyes was glaring. I glared back. He was so not tagging along on our girls' week out. It just wouldn't be the same.

"We have a team at the campgrounds now, searching for bodies. They found one set of remains already."

"There's more."

"I understand. We're on it."

We hung up and I offered Reyes another glare before stepping past him. The noise had subsided and I realized that the restaurant, filled mostly with women—as usual—could see us. Dozens of pairs of shadowed and mascaraed gazes flitted shyly toward him while others stared openly. Unapologetically. Brazen hussies. I needed to get a wedding band on this man, and fast, lest they try to seduce him behind my back. Then again, I thought, glancing around the crowd, some of these chicks would have few qualms about doing so right in front of my face.

I decided to blame him.

"You're a ho," I accused over my shoulder, a sly smile spreading across my face.

"What does that mean? I haven't slept with anyone besides—"

"Look at this room." I stepped off the staircase and started for the table Reyes had clearly reserved for us, because every other table in the joint was taken, and several other people waited up front. "They're only here for you."

We wound past chairs full of women hungry for an item that was most definitely not on the menu, and men craving either the same or Reyes's demise, many toxic to the core with jealousy. Reyes did bring out the emotions in people.

He wrapped a hand around my arm from behind, and I turned, my brows drawn in curiosity. He pulled me close to talk soft, even though we were still in the middle of a crowded room. "It's not me," he said, and the sting I felt radiate off him sliced into me.

I placed a hand possessively at his hips and stepped closer. "Reyes, what?" I asked.

"I'm not— I don't mean for this to happen." He scanned the crowd, feeling the exact same emotions I was feeling, only they were all zeroed in on him. All focused directly at him like laser-guided missiles. "I never asked for this."

"I was just kidding," I said, flexing my fingers against his hip. "I didn't mean to imply that you do this on purpose." I looked around helplessly. "I was just kidding."

I didn't know what else to say. My remark had actually hurt him.

He leaned in and confessed in my ear, his voice soft, hesitant. "It's suffocating."

The possibility of his being hurt by the emotions of others had never occurred to me. Being able to feel others' emotions was both a blessing and curse. At times like this, it leaned toward curse. For me, anyway. I'd never imagined it would bother him. Why should he care what others think?

But he was right. Sometimes the emotions wafting off others were so powerful, so . . . well, suffocating, I had to block them, a trick I'd learned in high school. Up until that point, school could be utter agony. Sure, I knew things others didn't, but I also knew things I didn't want to know. No one could "talk behind my back." I always knew the truth about how they felt about me. It kept my friendships to a minimum. The bare essentials. And once I lost my BFF, Jessica, I really didn't have another person I could call a best friend until I met Cookie a couple years ago.

One thing I'd learned growing up: People were never, ever, ever 100 percent honest about their feelings.

Never.

But that was something I'd learned to live with a long time ago.

This time, I wrapped my hand into his and led him to a small hall that accessed the restrooms and a storage closet. I held up an index finger to Cookie to let her know we'd be right back, then pulled him around a corner and into me. "I'm sorry, Reyes. I didn't mean that. It was just a joke."

He kept his features schooled. "I was just kidding, too."

"No, you weren't." I lifted my hand and ran my fingertips along his lower lip.

But just like every other time I'd tried to get him to open up, he grew resentful. He edged me against the wall, his hand placed lightly around my throat, his body pressed into mine, effectively changing the subject. He knew better than to order me to stop: To stop caring. To stop empathizing. To stop feeling. We'd been over it a hundred times. He couldn't just order me not to care. But he could switch the focus off himself and onto me. And he was very, very good at that.

He held me loosely against the wall, considered my mouth a long moment before I felt the tension ease out of him. This was his life. He could hardly run from it. People just . . . *wanted* him. He had a singular animalistic allure, a steely magnetism that anyone who looked at him had a hard time ignoring. He'd once told me that his attraction was so powerful, a girl he met in one of the plethora of apartment complexes Earl Walker had dragged him to throughout his childhood tried to kill herself when they'd moved out a month after unpacking. They moved out because their rent check had bounced, but Reyes was relieved. The girl's desire had been so thick. So palpable.

Then he began to tell me another story, one that involved a boy in the apartment building where I'd first seen Reyes, over a decade ago—the one where I watched Earl, the monster who'd raised him, beat him bloody. He'd dropped the anecdote abruptly and refused to elaborate on what happened, so I took it upon myself to look into the history of the building around the time he'd lived there. A thirteen-year-old boy hanged himself in his closet a couple of days after Earl had absconded into the night with Reyes and his nonbiological sister, Kim. According to the boy's parents, he'd become very distraught after his best friend moved away, but the kid's friends had said he was in love with a boy from the building who didn't reciprocate. After the boy moved, the kid killed himself.

That neighbor had to have been Reyes. And he knew what the boy had done. What would that guilt do to a person? How would it affect one's psyche?

And the ogling didn't stop there. I'd noticed departed hanging around more and more. But Reyes looked different to them than he did to humans. He was forever enshrouded in a dark mist, and underneath that mist was the soft glow of a fire. The angrier Reyes became, the brighter that fire. I'd seen it only once, after almost dying at the hands of a raving lunatic. And, as incredible as Reyes was in human form, he was startlingly beautiful when seen from another plane. I'd been told I could perceive things from that plane, and in that form, whenever I wanted to, but I had yet to master said talent. Because of this handicap, I wasn't sure if the departed who followed Reyes around were like the humans— insanely attracted to him—or like some form of spiritual gawkers, unable to believe what they were seeing, curious about him, testing their own courage by how close they could get to him.

Right now, my guess would be the latter, as there was a departed woman totally in our space bubble. The blonde stood against my shoulder, staring up at Reyes in wonder. In her defense, the departed were unused to being watched back. Maybe she didn't know we could see her. Reyes was still studying my mouth, completely ignoring her, so I turned and pinned her with an annoyed frown.

Stepping back as though coming to her senses, she cleared her throat. "Sorry," she said a microsecond before disappearing. But not before one last longing glance at the prince of the underworld.

That answered that. At least in her case.

"Tell me what it's like," I said, gesturing toward the patrons with a nod. "What does it feel like to have them want you so badly? Is it, you know, because of your father?"

He dipped his head and didn't answer for a long moment. When he did, it was a mere whisper on the air: "It feels . . . It feels like I'm drowning."

I wrapped a hand behind his neck. Brought him even closer. "Reyes, I'm so sorry."

The loose grip he'd had on my throat tightened minutely. "Your pity is hardly a step up."

"Empathy," I corrected, running my fingertips along the back of his neck soothingly. "And there's little I can do about it."

After another long moment of his probing gaze, he blinked to attention and released me. The coolness that rushed over me with his absence gave me goose bumps as he escorted me to the table. I sat down with Cookie, Uncle Bob, and my sister, Gemma, while Reyes strolled back to the kitchen to grab our lunches. Every head turned to watch him, conversations dying down as he passed, and I felt the weight of their emotions from where I sat. I felt the suffocating pressure. I felt him drowning, but he walked without betraying a hint of that distress.

The door swung back and he was already putting on the white apron he always wore. I sat there, marveling at how utterly stunning he was. Was there anything sexier than a hot guy in an apron, cooking? I could only hope he wouldn't grow tired of me. Would we ever get tired of one another? Would our desire to be touched by the other, to be embraced, ever wane? I couldn't imagine it, but I prayed not.

"So?" Gemma asked. Her brows arched in question as a lock of her blond hair pulled loose from a tidy chignon. She wore chignons and that particular navy blouse and skirt only when she was meeting someone important. Someone not me.

"Who's the VIP?" I asked back as I dipped a blue corn tortilla chip into Reyes's salsa, otherwise known as the devil's dipping sauce. I absorbed the spice and heat with something akin to ecstasy. His salsa was becoming famous and he'd been asked to bottle it several times, but it was usually by women gazing at him with fire in their loins, and I was never sure if they were talking about bottling the salsa or Reyes himself.

I glanced over at him as he brought out our plates. Either way, I'd be the first in line to purchase at least a case.

"What VIP?" Gemma asked.

"Your duds. You never wear navy unless you're meeting someone super important."

"Oh." She looked down and shrugged. "It was all I had clean."

"Ah," I said, clearing a place for my plate. She was lying, but I'd let her. For now.

Reyes set down a plate for Cookie, Gemma, and Ubie, his long, sinuous arms flexing in a way that had me mesmerized. I tore my gaze away to see what was on the menu. Red chile enchiladas. Sweet. I glanced up at him askance, wondering where my plate was.

He waited as one of the new cooks brought up the last entrée. "I hope you like them," he said, gesturing toward the plate.

"I love your enchiladas." I gazed down at the flat enchiladas as he waited for us to sample them. A symphony of moans echoed around me as everyone took a bite, and while Reyes's enchiladas were always to die for, their reactions were a mixture of ecstasy and surprise. I was a little worried Cookie was going to climax, her expression was so sensual.

More curious than ever, I buried my fork, cutting through the soft blue corn tortillas and scooping a bite into my mouth. He sank beside me, balancing on the balls of his feet as I ate—and just like Cookie, I almost climaxed. My taste buds were gifted with an explosion of unexpected flavors and textures, the spices warming my mouth.

I glanced at him. "You used chili. Oh, my god, this is amazing."

A shy smile reshaped his features, and he bowed his head like a kid unable to take a compliment. The act was so charming, I reached out and put my hand on his cheek.

He kissed my palm quickly, then stood. "I'll let you guys eat," he said.

"Why don't you join us?" Ubie asked, and I could tell the question surprised Reyes. It surprised me.

After a moment, he said, "I can't, but thanks. I have to put out a few fires before this one—" He nodded toward me. "—runs headlong into a hot mess of trouble again."

The appreciation in Uncle Bob's expression was undeniable. "She's a full-time job."

I tried to be appalled, but when Reyes said, "She is indeed," and bent to kiss me, my misgivings melted.

I watched him leave—his steely buttocks amazingly sexy, framed the way they were with the edges of the apron. I scooped up another bite before checking out the rest of the fare. He'd covered the *papas* with chili as well, topping them off with a ladle of warm red chile and cheese. It was like crack on a plate. And the scent helped mask the aroma of coffee lingering in the air. How would I ever get through the next eight months without the elixir of life?

"So, what exactly happened between you and Judge Quimby?" Ubie asked me.

I snapped out of my pity party to answer him, but changed my mind. There were some things he was better off not knowing. "I'd rather not talk about that," I said, diving in for another bite.

"She seems to like you," he said.

I lifted a shoulder in a halfhearted shrug. "She did seem way more understanding of the fact that I'm alive and kicking than she normally is. I wonder what changed her mind about me."

A knowing smile flashed across his face, but he hid it quickly.

Not quickly enough, however. I gaped at him. "What?" I asked.

"What?" he asked back.

"You know something."

He cut into an enchilada, stuffed a bite into his mouth, then said, "No, I don't."

I leaned close to him. "Yes, you do, so let me put it this way: You can tell me and spare yourself the embarrassment of me reminiscing about the time I caught you stumbling around in our backyard in the middle of the night screaming, 'Stella!' or you can sit there and squirm while I recount the entire story in great detail, including a description of your attire that fateful evening."

He straightened. "You wouldn't."

"Do you know me at all? I suffered. Seeing you in that particular style of underwear? I was traumatized for hours. Maybe days."

"That's blackmail."

"Duh. Do you really know something about the judge I don't?"

He caved. "I only know that you somehow helped her sister come to terms with her husband's death."

"Her sister?" I asked, thinking back.

"She'd been devastated and developed some kind of eating disorder."

I gasped. "No way! That was her sister?"

"It was."

That poor woman was so distraught over her husband's death, she hadn't eaten for weeks. I'd never seen anything like it. The husband had come to me and asked me to intervene. He knew she would take his passing hard, so he hadn't crossed when he died. Together, we came up with a plan to help her cope. It basically involved me relaying his messages to her. The whole ordeal was heartbreaking, but with some professional therapy thrown in, she'd slowly come out of it. I had the most rewarding job ever.

"Who's that?" Cookie asked, her voice sharp with concern.

I turned to see a woman speaking to Reyes near the entrance. She had thick black hair that fell like silk over her shoulders and startlingly blue eyes.

"Is that the newswoman from Channel 7?" Gemma asked.

"I don't know," Cookie said, and I felt her ire rise. "But she is getting just a little too friendly, don't you think?"

Cook was right: The woman was leaning in to Reyes as she spoke to him. She placed a hand on his shoulder when he apparently said something funny. It was an intimate gesture that had me seeing a vivid, crystal scarlet. I was used to women fawning all over themselves to get closer to him, to touch him, but this was ridiculous.

"You have got to get a ring on that boy," Gemma said. "Speaking of which, did you look at those links I sent you? Those are some prime venues, and you two need to decide on a date soon if you want to book any of them."

"Oh," Cookie said, combing through her bag, "and we need to decide on where to have the shower."

"I showered this morning," I said absently.

Gemma ignored me. "The shower, yes, but are we doing one shower for both the wedding and the baby, or one for each?"

"Heavens, that's a good point. Charley, what do you think?"

"I like Reyes's shower," I said, not bothering to look at them. Instead, I watched as the newswoman, whom I now recognized from the six o'clock news, spoke softly to Reyes. She laughed at something he said, taking the opportunity to toss her hair over her shoulder flirtatiously.

Reyes glanced back, then realizing I was watching, angled himself between the newswoman and me. Completely affronted, I stiffened.

"Oh, I like that place, too," Cookie said, responding to something Gemma had said. "It's gorgeous in the summer."

"True, but I think it will be too late to get it for this summer. It books fast."

"Okay, well, what else do you have?"

As Cookie and Gemma planned my wedding, a job I did not envy in the least, I watched Reyes. I tried to single out his emotions, but there was so much blisteringly raw lust in the room, I couldn't get past it all. Damn him and his sexual tractor beam.

A giggle floated toward me, and I saw the woman's head tilt back again. Clearly, Reyes was slapping on the charm, but why? Was this about an interview? He'd been asked a dozen times for one and never gave any of the other reporters the time of day. Even *60 Minutes* had wanted to do a story on him and got the door slammed in their face. But this woman came in, pinned him with a glittering smile, and he caved?

That was not like Reyes.

"I need a pretzel," I said, ignoring my food.

Before any of them could say anything, I rose and walked to the bar, which put me a few precious feet closer to the happy couple. If he were ever to break up with me, I would so be that stalker ex-girlfriend who stole his underwear and hid in the hedges outside his bedroom window. But finally I had a clear path and could read Reyes's emotions. Only I still couldn't feel him.

He was blocking me!

He'd done that trick before, but it took a concentrated effort on his part. The sting stemming from the fact that he was doing so while a gorgeous woman flirted with him hit me hard and quick, and he visibly sucked in a lungful of air when it did. He'd felt my reaction to his reaction to my reaction at having a hussy put her hands on my man. But still he stood with his back to me, barring me from the conversation.

Fine. I grabbed a pretzel out of a bowl on the bar and turned my back to him as well. If he wanted to block his emotions from me, I would do the same to him.

Except I didn't know how. Damn it, I needed *The Idiot's Guide to Grim Reaperism.*

I took another quick peek from over my shoulder as I headed back to our table. The woman's hand was resting on his arm again, her fingers curling over his biceps clearly visible in the outlines of his tee, and I nearly tripped.

Well, okay, I did trip, but I caught myself quickly, grabbed my plate and fork, and said, "I'm eating in my office. I have some work to do."

"Charley," Gemma said, her tone scolding, "we need to make some decisions."

"I have complete faith in you," I said before taking off for my hidey-hole.

As far as I was concerned, if he was going to flirt so openly with a skank who wore enough hair spray to thin the ozone a good two inches, then he could have at it. I had better things to do with my time than watch him. For example, I needed to put the song "Jolene" on repeat and listen to it about a thousand times. It was the song where Dolly Parton begs Jolene not to take her man. But I wouldn't beg. I would never beg. It would be really bizarre if her name were Jolene, though.

I took the interior stairs back to my office, refusing to spare another glance his way. Just as I put my plate on my desk, I noticed a priest waiting in Cookie's office. He was wearing a jacket and jeans, but the collar gave it away every time. We'd apparently forgotten to lock the door, but in all my years as a PI, a priest was new. I felt like I should do the sign of the cross as I walked forward, but I could never remember if it was up-down-left-right or up-down-right-left. I was so bad with directions.

"I'm sorry," I said, going over and holding out my hand. It was shaking even more now than it had been that morning. Shaking from too much coffee was one thing, but shaking from none at all? Utter agony. Torturous. Inhumane. Of course, Reyes and his new gal pal could have had something to do with my trembling. "I didn't mean to leave anyone waiting here," I continued. "I'm Charley."

He stood and took my hand into his. He looked like one of those jolly priests who preached about hellfire and damnation but then qualified his sermon with an assurance that if his parishioners strayed, they need only repent to be washed of their sin. I'd tried to be washed of my sin once, but I ran out of Dial. Tricky business, that.

"I'm Father Glenn," he said, his voice and manner full of exuberance. He had sandy hair, thinning up top, and wire-framed glasses fitted over chubby cheeks. "I didn't mean to interrupt your lunch." He gestured toward the lunch he could see through the adjoining door. It sat on my desk, calling my name. Metaphorically.

My stomach growled on cue. I offered a sheepish grin, then said, "Oh, no, I'm saving it for later. I'm not the least bit hungry."

"Gutsy," he said as I sat in the chair next to the one he'd been sitting in.

"Gutsy?"

He followed suit, crossing his legs to get comfortable. "Fibbing to a priest," he explained.

"Oh, that." I laughed and waved it off. "I do that kind of crap all the time. Except to my clients," I assured him. "I don't lie to my clients."

"Then I hope to become one."

I liked him. "What can I help you with?"

"Well, I'd like to think we could help each other."

"Works for me."

He settled back into his seat and then looked at me pointedly. "What do you know about possession?"

Ah, a supernatural gig. Interesting. "More than I'd like, sadly."

"Do you know what the three kinds of possession are?"

"There are three? I just thought possession was, you know, possession. An entity takes over a body, and that body is then possessed."

The scent of New Mexico–grown red chile infiltrated every air molecule around me. I had no choice but to inhale as my mouth flooded in response and my stomach growled again.

"You're not entirely wrong," he said, taking an envelope out from a pocket inside his jacket, "but that's only one kind, and despite the fact that it's the least common, thanks to Hollywood, it's the most well known. I just thought with your . . . background, you'd know more."

"My background?"

He took the envelope into both hands and held it while we spoke. "Yes. Your experience."

I shifted in my chair. "And what do you know about my experience?" It wasn't a defensive question at all. Just a curious one.

"Well, let's just say when I discovered what I discovered—" He tapped the envelope. "I did some research on you."

Wonderful. I suddenly felt the need to explain that night with the chess club. It was all a blur, but I was certain of one thing: Chad Ackerman's tattoo of a female impersonator was not my fault. Not entirely. "So you went down to the local library?" I teased him.

"Actually, the Vatican has a rather extensive file on you."

"Shut up," I said, flattered and appalled at the same time.

"No, it's true. You're of great interest to them. I thought you should know."

"Wow, thank you, but aren't you betraying your vows or something?"

"My vows are to our Heavenly Father and to the Church. They're not to a file in the Vatican's archives labeled 'Charlotte Jean Davidson.'"

"They know my middle name? They're really good."

"They know quite a bit. I actually found much of it to be a little hard to swallow." I nodded, but he pinned me with a knowing stare. "At first."

"Oh, so you swallow the whole thing now?"

"I do, yes. And can I just say, it's an honor to meet you."

"You make me sound like a saint."

"Not a saint. More like a warrior."

My spine lengthened. "A warrior. I like it. But what exactly did you discover that set you on this path?"

"A different kind of possession." His face softened. "I'm kind of a specialist."

"Okay, I'll bite, but first, would you like some coffee?" I pointed through the adjoining door to the Bunn. The one that was residing on a counter in my office. Not the one residing a tad southeast of my belly button. Because that would have been awkward.

He brightened. "Sure."

Cool. I could live vicariously through a Catholic priest. A thought that rarely occurred to me, for obvious reasons. I stood, crossed over to my office and poured him a cup, then asked if he liked his coffee like I liked my Death Stars: gigantic, on the Dark Side, and powerful enough to destroy a planet.

He laughed softly. "A little cream is fine."

"One coffee high coming up," I said through the doorway. I loved diner lingo.

My body reacted to the scent, to the act of pouring the dark elixir, like a Chihuahua when face-to-face with a pit bull—by shaking uncontrollably. It was a Pavlovian response to java anytime I went longer than an hour or two without a sip, and it had now been almost seventeen hours since my last slug of joe. I couldn't help but note that, for one reason or another, I'd been shaking for quite a while. Hopefully, it wouldn't become a habit.

"Can you explain the different kinds of possessions, so we're on the same page?" I asked, coming back and handing him the cup. Reluctantly.

"Absolutely." He took a long, sensuous draw. Either that or I was projecting again. "The first is infiltration, which is a possession of a space."

"Like the house in *Poltergeist,*" I offered, swallowing back my inner Chihuahua.

"Exactly. But with a little less drama."

"Of course," I said, pretending to be more knowledgeable than I actually was.

"Then you have oppression, which is where a demon is focused on one person."

"Like a stalker, only less creepy."

He chuckled. "Why not? The third kind is the most known, and that is possession itself, where a demon occupies a person."

I nodded. "My very favorite flavor. So, which kind brought you here?"

"That would be infiltration."

"Really? So there's a possessed house somewhere in Albuquerque?"

"It would seem so. I have a young family who just bought their first home and is terrified to go inside it. They end up sleeping at relatives' houses quite often."

"That's awful, and I'd love to help, but what does any of this have to do with me?"

He put the envelope on the coffee table stacked with magazines in front of us and fumbled through another inside pocket for his phone. After thumbing through a couple of menus, he passed the phone over to me. "Scroll through these, then ask me that again." He wore a mischievous grin as I took the phone.

The first picture was hard to make out. "Is this a wall?" I asked.

"Probably. But there's more."

"Okay." No idea what that was about. There were scratches on the wall, but the camera didn't pick them up clearly. So I scrolled. The next one was of a doll. One of those lifeless dolls with dead eyes so often used in horror movies. It, too, had scratches in its plastic skin, but I couldn't decipher what they were supposed to mean. I continued to do that for a few more images. Paper. A broken toy. A Lego construction worker. Another wall. Then a pattern started emerging. I finally saw a *C*. Sometimes an *R* or a *Y*. I went back to the beginning and started over, zooming in when I needed to, until I realized the scratches all said the same thing: Charley Davidson. Over and over. That couldn't be good.

"So, you think this demon is trying to send you a message?" I asked, making light of an eerie situation. 'Cause that's how I rolled.

Father Glenn raised a thick brow. "Can't be certain. It sure seems to like you, though. An old flame, maybe?"

"Could be. I dated some doozies." I handed his phone back. "Never took any of them for demons, though. Can you send those to me?"

"Sure." He put his coffee cup on the coffee table and took one of my business cards to get my e-mail address off it.

I cringed. I'd recently run out of my current business cards and had to set out an older stash of them: my very first attempt at professionalism. Thankfully, when I'd hired Cookie, she talked me into getting new cards. But the one Father Glenn had just picked up said, CHARLEY DAVID-

SON, PRIVATE INVESTIGATOR, BECAUSE NO ONE IS BETTER AT INVESTIGATING YOUR PRIVATES.

Yeah.

He arched that brow again but didn't look up as he typed my address into his phone. In the meantime, my attention wandered to the Bunn of steel. So inviting. So seductive. The aroma wafting off it lured me like a caffeinated Casanova. Like Romeo below the balcony. Coffee by any other name—

"Ms. Davidson?"

I snapped back to the father.

"Are you okay?"

"I'm fine!" I yelled. No idea why.

He eased away from me.

I cleared my throat and tried again. "I'm fine. I just— I'm trying to quit caffeine." When he raised that same brow, only this time questioningly, I explained. "Bun in the oven."

"Ah." He nodded. "Last time I had a bun in the oven, I had to give up whiskey. Worst twelve minutes of my life. Thank goodness those brown-and-serve rolls bake fast."

I chuckled and stood as he pocketed his phone and rose to leave.

"When would be a good time for you to meet our guest?"

"I'm pretty open and very intrigued."

"How about Friday morning. Around nine?"

"Perfect." I wrote the appointment in my calendar, but only so I could rip the page out and tell Cookie not to let me forget.

He shook my hand, then started to leave.

"Oh, you left your envelope," I said, picking it up to hand to him.

"No, that's for you. Consider it a down payment."

"Works for me."

I opened it after he left. The thick envelope held about ten photo-copied pages of what amounted to the file the Vatican had on me. They had pictures, dates of strange occurrences with which I'd been involved, a short description of what part the investigator believed I'd played in those strange occurrences, and his final thoughts, which always read, " 'Further investigation recommended.' "

Now, wasn't that interesting.

5

Of course I'm an organ donor.
Who wouldn't want a piece of this?

—T-SHIRT

I set Cookie to finding out everything she could on the missing suicide-note victims. There had to be a connection between them somewhere in their pasts. In the meantime, I would go talk to their closests, but first I needed to know if the victims were still alive. If they'd been abducted, this would quickly become a much different case. We would probably have to get the FBI involved, if they weren't on to it already.

Reyes was still working, so I decided to cut out alone. I knew he'd freak. He wasn't about to leave me alone for long, and neither would he put up with my running off without him, so I decided to pick up a passenger. Well, *another* passenger. The one I had at the moment would be of no help in a fight against hounds from hell, should they spot me in a crowd.

Jessica was harping again, this time about how her friends were at the restaurant, fawning over Reyes as though she had never died. She'd called dibs the moment she saw him, and they seemed almost relieved she was out of the way. I refrained from reminding her that (1) I'd had dibs long before that, and (2) she was as dead as the Twizzler I was gnawing on

in an attempt to forget about my extreme caffeine depletion. Poor little
Twizzler.

"She said that!" Jessica shouted. "Like, she said it. Right to Reyes's face."

"Wait, what?" I almost slammed on the brakes, then realized my foot
was already on the brake, as we were idling at a stoplight. "Who said
what to Reyes's face?"

"Oh . . . my god. Have you heard a word I've said?"

"Not especially. Who said what?"

"She said she'd do anything, *any . . . thing,* for an interview."

I turned to her. "Are you telling me you heard what Reyes and
Jolene—I mean, that hooch—were talking about?"

"Duh. I was so upset with Joanie and the girls that I started to walk
out when that—that ho practically assaulted our man."

I'd just taken a sip of water, because Cookie had told me water would
be good for the bun. Who would've guessed? I sucked in a quick gulp of
air, sending water down the wrong pipe, at which point I sputtered and
coughed until the car behind me honked. I honked back, then put the
pedal to the custom Bugs Bunny floor mat and booked it to my on-ramp.

"First of all," I said, my voice sounding like Dobby's from Harry Pot-
ter, "you actually have a friend named Joanie?"

Ignoring me, she crossed her arms over her chest to pout.

"And second—'our' man? Really?"

She shrugged one noncommittal shoulder. "I think he likes me."

"It's amazing you're still single."

"Right? I just have so much love to give. If I were still alive, Reyes
would see that."

"Yeah," I said with a snort and another light bout of coughs, "and then
he'd run in the opposite direction."

"That's so uncalled for."

"Do you even remember how you treated me in high school? How
you've treated me since? Why are you here? Why don't you just . . . go . . .
away?"

"You are the worst greeter in the history of greeters ever. In the history. Of time. And greeters."

"Okay, what?"

"You heard me." She turned to pout out the window this time.

"Greeter? You think I'm a greeter?" Talk about a demotion.

"Yes. To the other side?" She pointed up.

I whizzed around a little red Corvette to make my exit sometime this century, wondering why nobody paid me to drive professionally, because I kind of rocked at it.

"Dude, calling me a greeter is like calling Saint Peter a ticket taker."

"Whatever. Where are we going?" she asked.

"Well, if you must know, I need to talk to a guy I know who may or may not be a demon." I could ask my intended for the information I needed, but he was currently on my list of persons resembling and/or wallowing in fecal matter.

"I knew it!" she said, glaring at me. "You're in league with the devil."

"Duh. I'm affianced to him. Or, well, his son. I guess that makes me 'in league' with him, but you can't judge people by their in-laws. In-laws are all crazy. Everyone knows that."

She shrugged. "That's true. My sister's in-laws wrote the book on crazy."

"Willa? Really? Who did she marry?"

"Oh, no you don't."

"What?" I said, taking an extremely sharp right just off the exit.

"You don't get to change the subject like that. And you never even liked Willa."

"Sure I did." Where Jessica got the idea that I didn't like her sister, I'd never know.

"You *spit* on her."

Oh. Yeah. I did. Kind of. "I didn't actually spit on her," I said, taking another extremely sharp right followed by a left, just as sharp. It was odd how sharp those suckers got the faster I drove.

"You're going to flip us over," Jessica said in protest.

"Please, I so have this. And I spit on the ground in front of her. It was a gesture."

"Of what? Hatred?"

"More like contempt, but yeah, at the time it was a little of both."

"Why?"

I did the deadpan thing. "You have a very selective memory." The last thing I was going to do was remind my ex-BFF that I'd spit at her sister's feet only after I dragged said sister off her when Willa had attacked like a berserker craving the taste of blood. And all over a pair of socks Jessica borrowed without asking.

Lesson learned: Never borrow socks. From anyone. Ever.

We were almost at our destination when I began to get worried about Reyes. If he didn't detect me out and about, he'd never know I left the place without him. As far as he was concerned, I was up in my office, eating.

In an act of desperation, I summoned Angel—a thirteen-year-old gang kid who'd died in the '90s—my best investigator. But he'd been AWOL for a couple of weeks. Ever since I found out he wasn't exactly who he said he was. From the first time we'd met, he told me all about his family, how his mother was a hairdresser and had a shop with his aunt. He told me about his nieces and nephews, his uncles and cousins. And it had all been a lie. He'd been posing as his best friend, the one who'd died the same fateful night he did, and pretending his friend's mother, along with her entire family, was his.

Who could blame him? He'd come from nothing. Grew up with nothing. Unfortunately, he thought that just being Angel—the precious boy I'd grown to love the way someone who's grown numb to the pain of tattoos learns to love them—wasn't enough. As though he could ever fall short in my eyes. He could be a royal pain in my donk, but he was family.

So, I understood why he did what he did. Deep down, he knew that—but he was embarrassed nonetheless and hadn't come around for a while. I was trying not to force the issue, but I needed advice. And grim reaper info.

He popped into the backseat, one foot on the hump thing in the middle of the floorboard, an elbow propped onto his knee as he, too, stared out the window to pout. I had a lot of pouters today. I really wanted to say, *A pouter's a doubter,* but couldn't think of how it applied to this situation.

"Hey, mister," I said, hoping to brighten the somber mood.

"Who's the babe?" he asked without looking at me or Jessica.

She turned around, fuming with a spark of indignity until she spotted him. He had his usual bandanna headband worn low over his brow with a smattering of peach fuzz along his young jaw. He'd been on the verge of becoming a man. No, he'd become a man the night he stopped his best friend from firing into the house of a rival gang member by crashing the car they were in and killing them both.

Jessica chilled instantly. "That's rude," she said, facing front again.

"Sorry."

"You haven't been around much," I said, looking at him in the rearview. "No complaints about how you were in the middle of one of your nieces' birthday parties or at a *quinceañera* when I summoned you?"

"You know they aren't my family."

I pulled Misery over, even though we were only a couple of blocks from our destination. Turning in my seat, I nailed him with my best nurturing glower. "Angel, you heard what Mrs. Garza said. You were like a son to her, and she welcomed you into her life with open arms."

And she had. Mrs. Garza, who'd been hoping the presence she was feeling was her son, was not terribly disappointed when it turned out to be her son's best friend. She'd loved Angel. I could tell. But getting him to face that fact now could be difficult. Stubborn little shit.

He scoffed softly, pulled in his lower lip, and studied the pattern on Misery's seat cushion.

I reached back and took his chin into my hand. "Angel."

"That's not my real name."

"Yes, sweetheart, it is. It's your middle name and the name you went by before you passed away." I was stroking the fuzz around his mouth with my thumb. "Look at me," I said softly.

He did, but quite reluctantly, his deep brown gaze settling on mine.

"This changes nothing. I still adore you. You're still the best investigator I have."

"I'm the only investigator you have."

"That doesn't lessen your importance."

"Can I see you naked, then?" he asked, his gaze traveling south of the border, aka my neckline.

"Up here, buddy," I said, pointing two fingers at my face. "And no."

"It would make me feel better."

"Is he always this frisky?" Jessica asked.

His gaze found hers again. He gestured a greeting with a nod and a saucy wink. I tried not to giggle.

"I summoned you for a reason, you know," I said, drawing him back to me.

"Okay, who am I following now?"

"I just need information. Can I block Reyes from feeling my emotions?"

"I keep telling you, *pendeja,* you can do anything you want to." He glanced back at Jessica. "She's loca, yeah?"

I fought my eyes' natural urge to roll back into my head. "Yes, but how? How do I do something like that?"

"You just speak it. Remember when you bound Rey'aziel to his body so he couldn't leave it and, like, float around and shit?"

"Yeah, but that was, I don't know, in the heat of the moment. I was desperate."

"Then get desperate. Just do it."

"Just do it." I nodded and shut my lids to concentrate. "Okay. Just do it."

"Just say the word."

That was easy for him to say. Which word? I had several thousand to choose from. But what exactly did I want to accomplish? I wanted to hide my feelings. My emotions. At the moment, I didn't want Reyes to know I'd left without him. But it was more than that. I didn't want him to feel it every time my insides turned to mush around him. Or every time I felt a streak of jealousy slice through the chambers and antechambers of my heart—a very new sensation for me. I'd never been the jealous type, but today with that newswoman, I bordered on stalker with a heaping side of lunatic. And that made me weak. I didn't want Reyes to see me as weak. I could be strong. I could take anything he threw at me.

Of course, if I really did block my emotions, he wouldn't be able to feel them if I got in trouble. Thankfully, that didn't happen often. If I needed Reyes, I would just summon him. Easy as pie.

With that settled, I bowed my head, drew in a lungful of air, and said the first word that came to me. *"Occultate,"* I whispered, focusing my energy behind the word inside myself.

Hide.

Hide my feelings. Hide my fears. My doubts about being a mother. About raising a child in our world. If demons weren't attacking, maniacs were. There was always another murderer around the corner, or a messed-up departed person who mistook me for his overbearing mother and came at me with a butcher's knife. What kind of world was I bringing the bun into? How could I ever keep her safe?

"You know," Angel said, his voice full of humor, "you could say it in any language. You're the reaper. What you say goes."

I blinked to attention. "I know. But it just feels right giving commands in Latin. Or Aramaic. Or even Mandarin. It sounds more important. I don't really feel any different, though. Did it work?"

"No idea. It works only if you want and believe it will work. You are the center of your power. Only you can determine what works and what doesn't. Are you finished?"

"I guess, but I wanted to talk to you about something else. We're supposed to have a few unwelcome guests on this plane soon."

"Yeah, I heard. The Twelve."

"What do you know?"

He shrugged one shoulder. "Not much. Just that they're, like, hellhounds or something, and they were summoned."

My ears perked up. "I heard that today, too. They were summoned. They didn't just escape and make their way here willy-nilly. Do you know who summoned them?"

"Nah. I only know the general gossip. Some of these dead people are worse than old women."

I was neither disappointed nor surprised he didn't know more. But I really wanted to find out who on earth—literally—would summon hounds from hell.

"Just be careful, hon. I don't know what these things are capable of. What they'll do."

He smirked. "You worried about me?"

I took hold of his chin again, drew him forward until our lips met, giving him a gentle kiss before breaking away. "I'm always worried about you."

His head dipped shyly. "Let me know if you need anything else."

"Where are you going?"

"Mrs. Garza's niece has a recital. She's going."

"You mean *your* niece. They're your family, too, remember? She wants you to call her Mom. That's a pretty good validation of how she feels about you."

He lifted a shoulder again before disappearing. He was on his way back to me. We'd been together for over ten years. Surely my learning that he'd been lying about his identity this whole time wouldn't stop us from remaining friends. He constantly reminded me that, technically, he was older than I was, but times like this, I always felt like the older one. Probably because he still looked thirteen.

I shifted into drive again and pulled onto the side street.

"You lead a complicated life," Jessica said.

"Tell me about it." I screeched to a stop in front of an abandoned mental asylum, the kind you see in horror movies and music videos.

Jessica shriveled at the sight of it. "Is this the demon's lair?"

"Nope. This is a friend of mine's lair. I just have to make a quick pit stop to see if a few people are still kicking or not. Next stop is the demon's lair. It's a nice adobe off Wyoming. Very discreet. But I've heard that those pristine plaster walls were painted with the blood of virgins. Or a terra cotta latex from Sears. Not sure which."

"You're evil," she said.

"Tell me something my stepmother didn't yell in my face every day since I was two."

I grabbed my flashlight out of the backseat, got out of Misery, and found myself facing a digital lock on the chain link surrounding the asylum. The tall gate as well as the rest of the fence was topped with razor wire, a nice but superfluous touch. In this neighborhood, the residents would see the razor wire as more of a challenge than a deterrent, but Reyes had felt the security measure necessary. I found his concern endearing. He knew what Rocket and his sister meant to me, and he'd bought the building and the land around it to preserve it so Rocket would always have his home.

Rocket was a large man-child who'd died in the '50s in this very mental asylum. He was a savant—an incredible being who knew every name on earth—and he could tell me if a person was still alive or had already passed. I took advantage of that more often than I probably should. While his sister—who'd died of dust pneumonia around the age of five—also lived at the asylum with him, I rarely saw her. She was cute as a bug's ear and painfully shy.

So here I was again, trying to break into an asylum that I now owned, but because of the razor wire, scaling the fence was out of the question. I didn't know the security code. Reyes had yet to give it to me, and I wasn't about to call him and alert him to the fact that I'd ditched him. I should have stopped at the Daeva's house first and convinced him to come along with me. He would be a measure of protection, one that would tamp Reyes's wrath once he found out what I'd done. Wouldn't tamp it a lot, but it's the thought that counts.

I wasn't a moron. I wasn't really putting myself at risk. I knew if one of the Twelve showed up, I could summon Reyes instantly. He could still be my protector incorporeally, since the hellhounds would be in the same state—incorporeal—but he'd be mad nonetheless, seeing my actions as reckless and impulsive.

Maybe they were. I placed a palm against my abdomen. I really did have more to worry about than just my own ass now. According to prophecy, the bun was a lot more important than I would ever be, any day of the week. But I still had a job to do and bills to pay. I could hardly expect Reyes to follow me around for the rest of my life, no matter how delicious the thought.

I walked up to the gate and decided to try my luck. I punched in Reyes's birthday, to no avail. Then my birthday, also to no avail. Then, just for shits and giggles, I punched in another date and stood stunned when a dot on the display flashed green and the gate unlocked. I paused, surprised he'd remembered the very first time we met in the flesh—the night I saw Earl Walker beating him. The night I'd tried to stop said beating and almost got into even more hot water than I could handle.

But the ordeal had been worth it. Every moment with Reyes was worth it, and that first sighting, as heartbreaking as it was, had changed my life.

I strolled up to the metal doors, punched in the same code, and gained entrance again. At least his security measures would keep out the riffraff. Mostly partiers who wanted to destroy the place once their alcohol levels reached the size of their IQs. This place was historic, fascinating, and to many, creepy as hell. It was awesome.

But even for Reyes, these were a lot of security precautions for a run-down building that had been abandoned in the '50s. Thankfully, there was no alarm system, but even without one, I had to question all the other electronics. Unless he was storing weapons of mass destruction down here, I had no idea why we'd need this much protection.

I stepped inside the lobby and continued down a darkened corridor.

"Rocket?" I said, my voice soft as I trampled through dirt and debris left by partiers. Much of the surface had been tagged, but Rocket's etchings made them look rather beautiful, like crumbling pieces of ancient abstract art.

The last time I saw the Rocket Man, he'd been scratching my name into one of the walls. He wrote only the names of those who had died or were about to die, so seeing my name up in scratches was sobering. But that was before I knew about the bun. This was a whole new game, and I was not about to die anytime soon. My daughter had to be born. Her birth was prophesied according to some guy way back when, before the invention of sliced bread. Rocket was wrong, however—and this wouldn't be the first time. Well, okay, technically he hadn't been wrong yet. He'd prophesied Reyes's death, and Reyes did die for a few seconds before I brought him back to life with a kiss—according to my affianced, anyway. So I had to believe that Rocket's record was yet untainted, but was about to be. If there's one thing I'd learned as a supernatural being thus far, it's that there's always a loophole. No way was I going to die now. I would lie, cheat, and steal to make sure nothing happened to the bun. And I needed info to assure my survival.

Sadly, Rocket wasn't the easiest being to get information out of, but he was going to give me a few more details if I had to strangle them out of him. First, however, I needed to know about the suicide victims. I could keep his attention for only so long. If I had to choose between me and the suicide victims, I'd have to choose the latter. They could've been abducted. They could still be alive and suffering. Their safety had to come first in this situation. Then maybe I could convince Rocket to tell me something about my own demise. Demises in general sucked. My own would probably suck even worse from my point of view. It was hard to tell at this juncture.

I took the stairs to the basement. He'd been favoring the basement lately, as it had a few unused walls. I turned on my flashlight and slowed the lower I got.

"Could this place be any creepier?" Jessica asked, appearing behind me, her hands cradled at her chest as though afraid to touch anything.

"It is now," I said, refraining from doing a fist pump and shouting, *Score!*

A singsong voice fluttered through the air toward me. "Somebody's in trouble."

I recognized the voice as Strawberry Shortcake's—not her real name— a girl who'd drowned when she was nine. She'd taken up residence with Rocket and his little sister, Blue Bell. My gratitude with respect to that fact knew no bounds, because before SS had taken to squatting at the asylum, she was better known as a crazy stalker chick who warned me repeatedly to stay away from her brother, David Taft, a police officer in my uncle's precinct. And she often tried to scratch my eyes out. Not an endearing quality.

Since Taft and I could barely stand each other, her concerns had never truly been an issue, but she'd seen me as a threat until her brother started dating skanks. Her words. After that, she decided I needed to date him after all. Thankfully, she was too busy being Chrissy from *Three's Company* to push the issue.

Jessica and I turned toward her. SS wore her usual pink Strawberry Shortcake pajamas that were all the rage back in the day. Her long blond hair hung in tangles down her back as always, and her baby blues shimmered a silvery color, even incorporeal as she was. Though her luster had a general grayness to it, she was as solid to me as the walls around us.

The grayness often gave the departed away. And the cold. But more than that, their lack of emotion was a real tip-off—I couldn't feel any radiating off the dead, as I could the living. Even without those signs, there was something intangible about the departed that made me instinctively know they were no longer among the living. It just registered in the back of my mind when I met someone who'd departed. I could always sense it. From the day I was born, I knew there were two kinds of people: the living and the dead.

What took me much, much longer to comprehend was the fact that not everyone was able to see the departed. My confusion had caused me problems growing up. Especially with my stepmother. But that was a story—or, well, a dozen or so stories—for another time.

Strawberry stood there, petting a ragged Barbie doll with its hair chopped off in large chunks. Which wasn't creepy at all. Poor Malibu Barbie. All her Malibu friends would be horrified. Taft told me his sister had always cut off her dolls' hair. A fact that kind of scared me. I did have to sleep occasionally, and the thought of a departed child in dire need of therapy cutting my hair in my sleep did nothing to ease my mind as I fell into oblivion.

"Why am I in trouble this time?" I asked her, kneeling down and wiping a smudge off her cheek. She really was quite beautiful. It pained me to imagine who she would have become, given the chance. For the life to be ripped away from someone so young just seemed so terribly, terribly unfair.

"Because you're going to die soon."

On second thought, maybe she was better off. Away from other people and most sharp objects. I had a sneaking suspicion she would have become a serial killer. Or a telemarketer. Either way.

"Well, I'm hoping I don't."

"I hope you do. You can live with us."

"She is adorable," Jessica said, kneeling beside me. "What's your name?"

Strawberry frowned. "I can't talk to strangers. And I especially can't tell them my name is Becky. Or that I'm nine. Or that—"

"Have you seen Rocket?" I asked, interrupting. We'd be there all day.

"I see him all the time."

"Do you know where he is now?"

She lifted a shoulder. "Maybe. But you need to run the mean man out first."

My brows slid together. "What mean man?"

"The one sleeping in the cold room. He eats cat food out of a can with his fingers."

I tried not to gag on that thought. "Hon, are you telling me there's someone here? Someone living here?"

She nodded, petting her bald Barbie harder and harder.

What the hell? How could anyone get in with all the security measures? I knew the razor wire wouldn't deter anyone, but the code on the doors should have helped.

"He cut a hole in the fence out back with this big whacker thing and he crawls in through a basement window. He brings little brown bags."

Oh. Well, that explained that. "He must be homeless."

"No, he has a home."

"What makes you think that?"

"Because he goes there." She pointed. No idea why. I got so turned around in the place, I barely knew which way was up. "He goes to that ugly house and then comes back here."

Was he breaking into a home while here? I'd have to find out.

"Okay, pumpkin," I said, lifting her into my arms with a groan. The departed were also heavy. How a person who walked through walls could be that heavy was beyond me. "Why don't you take me to him?"

She pointed again, and Jessica and I followed her lead. We came to a swinging door to the kitchen.

I flattened against the wall. "Is he in there now?" I whispered to Strawberry.

She stopped chewing the Barbie's little plastic head and shrugged, her lashes round with concern. This guy really scared her.

I turned to Jessica. "Go in there and see if the coast is clear."

"What?" she screeched. "Me? Why me? You go in there and see if the coast is clear."

I let out a loud sigh. "Jessica, you're departed now. He won't see you. You can stick your head through this wall, and no one will be the wiser."

"Screw that." She set her jaw and turned away from me.

Wonderful.

"Fine," I whispered. "You can keep watch out here. Just warn me if anyone comes, *capisce*?"

Honestly, what was the good of having departed ex-friends if they refused to spy when I needed it most? I leaned forward and tried to peek in through the round window on the door, but years of grime and a huge face with a sheepish smile kept me from looking very far.

"Rocket," I whispered, and then in a soft hiss, "is there a man in there?"

He continued to smile and I thought for a moment he didn't understand, but he turned and looked over his shoulder at last. He faced me again and shook his head, the smile still shaping his pudgy features framed by a bald head. A little like Malibu Barbie's.

I hefted Strawberry closer and pushed into the kitchen. "Hey, Rocket Man," I said, using my free arm to give him a hug.

"Miss Charlotte, you're not dead yet."

"I'm aware of that, thank you. Have you seen the man who has been coming here?"

He nodded and pointed to the "cold room," literally an old walk-in freezer. Strawberry's description of it being a cold room must have come from Rocket, who'd lived—and died—here in the '50s, because now it was just as warm as the rest of the place.

I plopped Strawberry onto an aluminum counter and eased up to the darkened room, keeping my flashlight front and center. Jessica, completely ignoring my orders to stand guard, was right behind me, clinging to my sweater as we inched our way to the half-open unit. One quick sweep told me it wasn't occupied, but it had been recently. More than one McDonald's bag littered the area where someone had been sleeping. The stench of old cigarettes clung to the air as a makeshift ashtray over-flowed with butts. Blankets and a dingy pillow lay on one side of the unit, while other homey items like a lantern and a couple of porn maga-zines sat beside them. I could only hope Blue Bell and Strawberry hadn't seen the skin mags. Or him while he read them. No telling what a UV flashlight would pick up.

"I have a couple of names for you," I said while studying the area. It didn't really look like your everyday, garden-variety homeless lair. There were no clothes. No supplies like normal homeless people had. No blan-kets or cans of food like my friend Mary had in her shopping cart.

I did a quick check on Strawberry. She sat chewing on Barbie's head, scanning the area with a worried expression. Why she would be afraid of a human was beyond me. If that's what she was afraid of.

"You feel different, Miss Charlotte."

I looked at Rocket from over my shoulder. "How so?"

"There's more of you in there now." He was staring at my stomach.

After a soft laugh, I said, "Yes, there is." I was amazed he'd picked up on that. The bun was so brand-new. I'd conceived only a couple of weeks earlier. Hadn't even had a pregnancy test yet, but I felt her warmth from the moment her journey began. Still, how Rocket felt her, I'd never know. She wasn't even the size of a black-eyed pea yet. Maybe that's what I'd call her: Black-Eyed Pea. B-E-P. I could call her Beep for short.

"How did that happen?" he asked, regarding me as though I'd grown another head.

I was so not going there. He'd lived without the facts of life thus far—so to speak—he could live without knowing about the birds and the bees a little longer. I sorted through a pile of trash in one corner, lifting items between my thumb and index finger as though they'd bite me, hoping to find a name or other identifying information, but all I found were old

McDonald's receipts, tissues, and cigarette butts. "Are you ready for the names?"

He leaned over me to study my every move. "Ready, set, go."

"Okay. Fabiana Marie Luna. Born in Belen."

He straightened and lowered his lids, his lashes fluttering as he searched his files, and I wondered what it would be like to have all those names, billions and billions of names, floating around in my head. I could barely remember my sister's name at times.

He bounced back to me and refocused. "Dead."

"Damn," I said, stepping to a piece of paper I'd seen wedged between the wood slats in the floor.

"No breaking rules, Miss Charlotte."

"Sorry, Rocket Man," I said, lifting the paper out of the crack. Cursing was breaking the rules, and Rocket was all about rules. "How about Anna Michelle Gallegos."

"Forty-eight dead. Twelve alive."

"She would have passed recently. She was born in Houston but raised here in New Mexico."

He responded faster this time. "Dead. I can show you."

He started to pull me out of the freezer, but I held my ground with a pat on his hand. He was going to show me where he'd written the name in one of his walls. "I believe you, hon. It just makes me sad. I was hoping they were still alive. One more: Theodore James Chandler from Albuquerque."

I had high hopes for this guy. His wife had just found the suicide note that morning. Maybe, just maybe, he was still alive.

"Not dead," he said, and as my hopes soared, he counted on his fingers.

"So, he's still alive? Do you know where he is?" I asked him.

"Not where. Not how," he said, still counting down slowly on his fingers, each pudgy digit folding down one at a time. "Only if."

I started to fish my phone out of my front pocket when he'd counted down to zero and said, "Dead."

"Wait, what? Ted Chandler is dead? He was alive two seconds ago."

"No, no, no. Not anymore."

I blinked at him, waiting for an explanation.

"He probably didn't pay his electric bill," Rocket said, arching his brows and nodding as though issuing a caveat.

The impact of Ted's death hit me hard. While I was busy playing detective—not that I wasn't one, but still—poking around old receipts and porn magazines with the pages stuck together, a man had been dying.

I texted Uncle Bob, my message somber and pensive at once:

> They're dead. All three.
>
> Son of a bitch. Are they with you?
>
> No. Probably crossed over already.

Uncle Bob didn't know exactly how it all worked, but he knew enough to believe anything I said, no matter how . . . unusual it sounded. One day I'd tell him who—no, what—I really was. For now, he took anything I had to say as gospel.

> Going to talk to some of the relatives of these victims.
>
> Let me know what you find out.
>
> Will do.

With a heavy sigh and a heavier heart, I turned back to the task at hand: homeless perv living in the freezer. I didn't really know if the pages of the porn magazines were stuck together, and I was not about to find out. I totally needed to start carrying plastic gloves, but that was all I needed, to launder gloves along with my license and car keys. I went through more fobs that way.

"Has he been here today?" I asked Rocket, trying to gauge whether there was anything in the area to identify the man. When I received no answer, I turned around.

Everyone was gone. Jessica. Strawberry. Rocket.

I walked slowly back into the kitchen, shining my light into the darkest corners, but saw nothing. I did, however, feel something. The cold hand of an attacker as it slammed roughly over my mouth.

6

My life is just like a soap opera
filmed in a psychiatric ward.

—T-SHIRT

I was pulled back against a skeletal body as a sharp piece of metal jabbed the skin at my neck. Not a knife, but something long and sharp. A screwdriver perhaps, which could do a lot of damage in the right hands. The man held it there as a warning while he got a better hold, tightening the opposite arm around my ribs just under Danger and Will Robinson, my breasts. He pulled me close.

I wasn't fighting terribly hard just yet. No need to cause a ruckus when I had no idea what he wanted. Maybe he just wanted me to leave, which I'd oblige willingly. Homeless people, for the most part, were harmless unless you invaded what they considered their turf. I wasn't using that freezer space anyway. It was all his.

"You sure talk a lot when ain't nobody else in the room," he said, his voice full of sand and gravel.

I glanced down to assess what I could: a grimy hand, Caucasian, midthirties. He was much stronger than he felt because all I could feel were bones. I caught a glimpse of the end of a tool in his other hand. Definitely a screwdriver. Long bony fingers curled around it until their knuckles shone white.

I'd dropped my flashlight, but I would have been able to see the others, no matter how dark it was. I couldn't fathom why they'd left. A mere mortal wouldn't have sent them packing. I had to wonder what had made them turn tail. At the same moment, I realized my order to hide my emotions from Reyes must have worked. Otherwise, the second my adrenaline spiked, he would have been there. Materialized right in front of me, and after severing the spine of my attacker as he was wont to do, he would have glared at me, given me a scolding for leaving without him.

Instead, nothing. I stood there parked against a homeless guy with a rusty screwdriver at my throat, and I had to wonder how I got into these situations so often. It wasn't like I went in search of crazy people. They just seemed to find me.

"Look," I said, holding my hands up in surrender, "it's yours, okay? I never liked that freezer much anyway."

He waited a long moment, his breath raspy as his lungs filled with air. Then he leaned forward and did the strangest thing. He bit the tip of my ear. Rather hard. As though he enjoyed inflicting pain on others.

I jerked in his grip, but he only tightened it more.

"You think I'm living in this shithole because I want to?" he asked, the smell of stale cigarettes on his breath suffocating me. "This is the only place you go without that pretty boyfriend of yours."

Dread began to fill me, and I was on the verge of summoning Reyes when the man continued, his words convincing me to suspend the summons.

"I'll kill him quick. He won't know what hit him, I swear. And you get to walk away. If you can." He brushed a thumb over Will Robinson to demonstrate his meaning. "You're going to call him and get him over here, but if you tip him off, I'll make it slow for him and even slower for you." He buried his face in my hair and inhaled.

"Why?" I asked, searching the area frantically for a weapon. I could still have summoned Reyes. It wasn't as though the man could hurt him in his incorporeal form, but I really wanted to know why he was after my affianced. Why he wanted to kill him quick. Why he wanted to kill him at all. Reyes charging in here and maiming the man before we got answers would do neither of us any good. "What did he ever to do you?"

The man barked a humorless laugh. "Ain't never done anything to me. Just the price of being who he is, I guess."

What the hell? Was this guy possessed? Was he sent to kill Reyes? And why lie in wait for me? From the look of things, he'd been waiting for at least a week.

"Who sent you?" I asked, relaxing against him in the hopes he'd respond by loosening his grip. I'd spotted a grungy wooden spoon half hidden under the brushed aluminum prep table. It wasn't much, but if I dropped to the floor, letting my weight jerk me out of his grip, I might could get to it, break the handle, and use it to defend myself before he had a chance to sink the screwdriver into my back. Which would suck on several levels.

Did I dare risk summoning Reyes? He would be so angry with me. The dread of that scenario was almost more than the dread I felt toward screwdriver man.

"Call him. Get him over here. And make it good or you get a shiv in your throat before you can cry uncle."

That seemed horridly unpleasant. When I reached into my front pocket, his grip tightened.

"I'm just getting my phone. But you must not know Reyes very well if you think you're going to take him on with a screwdriver."

"I've taken on bigger with less," he assured me.

"Right. Like I said, you must not know him."

I took out my phone, but he stopped me with a thoughtful, "What do you mean?"

"I mean that on Reyes's first day in gen pop, three of the biggest, baddest members of the South Side gang were sent to take him out. Less than thirty seconds later, they all lay dead on the cafeteria floor while Reyes remained completely unscathed. Winded, but unscathed. They'd had weapons, too."

"Son of a bitch," he whispered to himself. "I fucking knew it. Dollar, that fucking piece of shit."

"I don't understand," I said, trying to reason with an addict. An impossible feat on my best day. And clearly today was not my best day.

He twisted a hand into my hair and jerked my head back. His emotions gushed out as though a dam had broken. The drugs he was on, most likely meth, were making him unpredictable and even more dangerous. His emotions went from a sadistic joy to an absolute rage within the span of a heartbeat. He'd been duped by someone, but I couldn't quite figure out what was going on. Did someone named Dollar send him? Was that even a real name?

"Only thing you got to understand is now I got myself a predicament," he said, pulling the tip of my ear between his teeth again, his teeth sinking lightly into the cartilage before moving to the lobe.

I tried to jerk away, but his fingers entangled in my hair would have none of it.

"Do I shove this flathead into your skull or—?"

I locked my focus on to the spoon and waited for him to give me option B, hoping it would prove to be far more appealing than option A. If I didn't survive this day, Beep wouldn't survive this day, and that was not an option at all. So I gave him a moment to evaluate his choices, to make me an offer I couldn't refuse, but after a pause that seemed to stretch for several minutes, I heard a sound like a tear or a rip, then a gurgling sound. His grip didn't ease, even when I felt a warmth saturate the back of my neck to trickle down my shirt.

Startled, I pushed out of his grip, but he tried to hold on to me when I turned to face him. His lids were saucerlike, shock and fear radiating out of him in hot waves as blood gushed out of his throat, his esophagus and surrounding tendons laid open as though a lion had taken a swipe at him. I shoved to break his hold, but he kept a grip on my shirt. Warm, sticky blood sprayed out of him and onto me in pulsating bursts, his mouth open in horror as his life drained from his body. As his expression faded.

I fell back and he lurched forward, still clinging to me. We fell to the ground, his blood soaking my shirt and my hair in seconds.

My mind instantly jumped to Reyes, but he had never done anything like this before. He worked much cleaner, causing internal destruction with no external trauma whatsoever. Without an MRI, there was no way of knowing exactly how much damage he'd done to someone on the inside.

The man's head lolled onto my shoulder, the deluge slowing as his weight pinned me to the filthy, now blood-soaked floor. Before I could come up with another theory, a sound raked over me, low and vicious, the deep, raw undertones reverberating through to my bones. I paused a solid five seconds as absolute terror took hold of me.

Before I lost control of my faculties altogether, I squirmed beneath the deadweight of my attacker. I felt a sharp tug on my left arm followed by a raging sting as I scrambled out from under him and ran for my life. Literally. I didn't look back. I didn't dare. I scaled the stairs, the adrenaline pumping through me like rocket fuel, and ran down the hall to the front doors, heedless of the trash and debris in my path. Hitting the door like a nuclear missile, I stumbled into the blinding daylight and sprinted to the gate, where my mind couldn't quite latch on to the code. My gaze darted around wildly, trying to spot the beast before it ripped my throat out as well. Somewhere in the frantic recesses of my mind, I registered a blistering pain in my left arm and the thundering beats of my heart. I backed against the gate, laced my fingers through the chain link, and stared at the front door like a sentry. Waiting. Dreading.

They can't come into the daylight.
They can't come into the daylight.

They can't come into the daylight.

I repeated that mantra, my chest heaving, my lungs burning, having no idea if it was true or not. No one, not even Reyes, really knew about the hellhounds. What their vulnerabilities were here on earth. Their strengths. They were not demons, but a product of hell. Created there by Lucifer himself. So while demons could not come into the light without some kind of protection, like a human once possessed, hellhounds were a different breed entirely. They might be just as comfortable in daylight as I was.

With that thought, I turned back to the lock on the gate, forced myself to calm down, and punched the date into the number pad. The second it unlocked, I pushed through it and jumped into Misery. I took out my phone while turning over the engine. I had to get to someone who had answers, who might know what to do.

There were only two people on this plane that I knew of who might have some answers. Reyes, naturally, and the Dealer, a Daeva, a slave who had escaped from hell centuries ago and now lived in Albuquerque, New Mexico, running illicit card games and tricking humans out of their souls. We'd come to an agreement on the soul thing. He could sup only on very bad people. But he seemed to know a lot more about all of this than anyone else. In fact, he was the one who'd told us about the Twelve and the fact that they'd escaped from their prison in hell and made it onto this plane. He'd wanted to help protect me from them, but Reyes refused his assistance. I was beginning to think he'd made a grave mistake.

So, I could run either to Reyes or to the Dealer, and only one of the two would become enraged with the fact that I'd left without him.

The Dealer it was.

Only after I brought up his name in my contacts did it occur to me that I'd torn out of a building, soaked in someone else's blood, and raced away as though I'd committed murder. I could only hope no one had seen me. No one called the police. I'd do that myself.

My lashes clung together, the blood coagulating and creating a thick, sticky residue, and I dared a quick glance at my reflection in the rearview as the phone rang. I regretted it instantly. I looked like the second-to-last victim of an axe murderer in a B-grade horror movie. If I was going to look like the second-to-last victim of an axe murderer in a horror movie, it'd damned well better be grade A.

The Dealer picked up the line. "This must be important for you to call me, the dreg of society."

"You home?"

"Maybe."

"Be there in two. Have your door open."

"Pregnant women are so demanding. Anything I can do in the interim?"

"Unless you can dematerialize and rematerialize in my Jeep while I'm going ninety-three in a twenty-five, then probably not." I hung up to concentrate on the road before he could say anything else.

That had to have been one of the twelve beasts of hell. Who else—no *what* else—could have done that? And if Reyes had materialized, could they have killed him? Was his incorporeal spirit at risk? He would have fought it, tried to kill it, just to get it out of the way. Picking them off one by one was a tactic he'd taught me: Weaken the pack slowly. Methodically. He'd never been one to sit around and wait to be attacked. He preferred the hunt. Craved it. I'd felt his hunger, his voracious appetite the last time we took on a horde of demons.

Still, I couldn't believe my binding spell, for lack of a better phrase, had worked. I couldn't believe Reyes hadn't materialized.

I sped around anything that got in my way. Getting pulled over for speeding while covered in blood wasn't suspicious at all, but I just couldn't seem to slow down. I whizzed around a delivery truck and screeched to a stop in the Dealer's driveway. He had a nice adobe in a decent neighborhood. Hopefully none of his neighbors were out.

I charged out of Misery and ran for his front door, which stood wide open with a kid leaning against the frame, arms crossed, top hat sitting at a flirtatious slant. Though he looked nineteen, he was centuries old. From what I could piece together, he'd actually been on earth for over a millennium. Tall and wide-shouldered, he had black hair—the tips of which brushed his collarbone—the most incredible bronze-colored eyes I'd ever seen, and a persistent smirk that could be charming one minute and deadly the next. I still didn't know the Daeva's name, but Reyes did. The first time we met the kid, Reyes had recognized him from their days back in hell, said he was a champion of some kind. His description of the Dealer had made me think of a gladiator, a slave fighting for the entertainment of his owners.

If the kid was surprised by my ravaged appearance, he didn't show it.

I hurried past him and went straight for his bathroom. But because I didn't know which room it was in, I had to try a few doors first.

"Next right," he said, following me down the hall.

I went inside, turned on the light, and checked my appearance.

"You didn't kill him, did you? We might need him if we're going to keep you safe." When I blinked at him, he continued, with one of those smirks playing upon his mouth, this one teasing. "Rey'aziel," he clarified. "He can be an ass, but—"

"They're here," I said, taking a towel off the rack and wiping my face.

He straightened slowly. The alarm rocketing through him hit me in one sharp wave.

"They killed a man right in front of me. Or, well, behind me. I didn't see anything." I looked down at the towel. "There was so much blood."

He stepped to me. Lifted my shirt. "Is any of this yours? Did they get you?"

"I don't think so."

He peeled off the shirt despite my squirming for him stop. But I was drained of all energy, as though gravity had leached it out of me. After a detailed examination, he wrenched my left arm. A scalding heat seared through to my bones, and I felt anger rise within him.

"Where is Rey'aziel?" When I glared at him, the Dealer stepped closer. Lowered his voice. "Where is your fiancé?"

"At the bar," I said, exasperated.

After ripping the towel out of my hands, he stalked out. "I'll get a clean one and find something for you to wear. Get in the shower. I have bandages in the kitchen."

"I need to call my uncle first. If anyone saw me, they'll think I was trying to cover up a crime. I need to report— Bandages?"

I looked down at my arm as the Dealer—who refused to tell me his name—returned with another towel and some disinfectant. Blood gushed freely from a wound on my arm, and I suddenly remembered the pain I'd felt while underneath the dead man's body.

"It bit me," I said, my shock complete.

Before today, the Twelve had just been a mild threat. A vague possibility. Escaping hell was one thing. Making it onto this plane was quite another. The fact that they had done both, that they were here to finish what they'd started, was slowly sinking in.

He took a closer look at the wound, dabbed it with a bandage to check the flow of blood, then turned me around to face the shower.

"This wasn't an accident," I said to him as he undid my bra and pushed the straps over my shoulders.

I covered Danger and Will as he turned me around and started to unbutton my pants.

"They were summoned," I said.

His fingers stopped and his gaze, as dark as his black hair, turned incredulous. "How do you know?" he asked after a long moment.

"A little girl told me this morning."

"And you believed her?"

"Yes."

He took a step back and braced an arm on the wall as though trying not to fall down.

"Who could do such a thing?" I asked him.

For several long beats, he stood in silence. "I have no idea," he said at last. "There's no one with that kind of power on this plane." He raised his lids. "Besides you, that is."

Was he accusing me of something? "Why would I summon the Twelve beasts of hell? I didn't even know there was such a thing."

"There's no one else," he repeated. Shaking off the moment, he went back to the task at hand: struggling with the blood-soaked button on my jeans.

"This is your world," I said. "Your area of expertise. You have to know who did this. Maybe if someone out there controls them, we can stop them by stopping him."

He shook his head to indicate he had no clue.

My clothes fell on a fuzzy beige rug underneath my feet, effectively ruining it as the Dealer stepped past me and turned on the shower.

"It'll take a minute. You need to get warm."

Only then did I realize every part of me quivered visibly. "It's probably the fact that I haven't had any caffeine in twenty hours."

It was the oddest thing. I stood there in front of him, completely naked, and felt no shame or guilt—though he did look just over half my age. There was something between us. Something pure that had tugged at me the first moment I saw him, but it wasn't attraction. He was stunning—no doubt about it. But what I felt was more like . . . trust. Deep down inside, I'd trusted him despite his heritage. I felt I could trust him with more than my life. I felt I could trust him with my most prized possession. With something that meant more to me than my life.

Was that why I'd gone to him instead of to Reyes? Or was it simply because of the fact that Reyes was going to kill me?

Dread caused nausea to spike within me. That combined with all the blood, with the memory of seeing a man's throat literally ripped out, made the world topple beneath my feet. The Dealer caught me to him with one arm, pushed the shower curtain back with the other, and then lifted me over the edge of the tub, soaking and bloodying himself simultaneously.

"That's never going to come out," I said, gesturing toward the crimson stains on his meticulous white shirt.

He offered me a tilt of his mouth before I slid the curtain closed.

I scrubbed every inch of me. The soap he had smelled good. Clean. It almost concealed the coppery scent of blood. The dark red substance turned pink as it mixed with the water around my feet and swirled down the drain. I couldn't wait much longer. I had to call Uncle Bob. But I was taking a shower—washing away crucial evidence. What would he think? Even he couldn't cover up the fact that my fingerprints were surely all over that kitchen. Smeared in the blood on the floor. Trailed along the walls and over the door I'd burst out of.

Even Uncle Bob could cover up only so much. How was I going to explain the fact that the man's throat had just magically ripped open? That I'd had nothing to do with it? That a beast, essentially an escaped prisoner from hell, had tried to kill me and got the man instead?

It sounded crazy even to me.

The injury to my arm, clean slices along my biceps, stung under the warm water. They were deep but not deep enough to need stitches. They still bled, though. I'd need to bandage them tightly and lay off the strawberries, a natural blood thinner.

After I'd calmed down enough to stop shaking uncontrollably—now my shakes were much more controlled, more of an orchestrated effort—I turned off the shower. The heat from it had permeated every inch of me. Saturated and soothed. Or so I thought. Then I realized it wasn't the shower heating me but something much hotter. Much more dangerous.

Without another thought, I threw open the shower curtain, practically stumbled over the edge of the tub, and rushed into Reyes's arms. He was angry. Outrage reverberated around him, but he held me as though I were the last morsel of food he would ever see.

I was getting him soaked. He wore a light blue button-down with the sleeves rolled up, and when I leaned back to see if I was bleeding onto him, the shirt clung wetly to his wide chest.

"I'm bleeding," I said, trying to back away.

He didn't let me. He pulled me close again, and we both shook against each other. Me with a combination of terror and relief. Him with a combination of anger and, well, anger.

"How did you know I was here?" I asked into his shoulder.

"The Daeva called me."

"Oh." It was all I could say. But I'd wanted to say, *the traitor.* I should have known the Dealer would call Reyes. It was pretty brave, actually, since he'd just seen me naked. Not many men would risk calling the son of Satan after that. "You got here really fast."

"He said you were in the shower. It was incentive."

"Oh, again. He was closer," I explained. "And I was covered in blood. Since we live in a high-traffic area, I was afraid people would see."

I could feel him fight with that judgment call despite my reasoning. I hadn't gone to him. I'd gone to what he considered to be a lesser life-form. A being who could not protect me when push came to shove. But I would argue with him on that point. On all of them.

After a moment, his hold eased. He put me at arm's length. Frowned. Studied me and frowned again.

Then, as though a revelation had hit him, his anger flared to life again, as strong as I'd ever felt it, and I knew that he knew. I'd meant to change it back before going home or to the office, but I forgot.

He bit down, worked his jaw until he said, "You blocked me."

I lowered my head, confirming both my guilt and my hesitation in admitting it to him.

His grip tightened. He'd never known his own strength, and he was proving that once again. One hand had a firm hold right where the hell-hound had swiped at me like a hungry tiger. I winced, but he didn't notice. He wouldn't. Not with the all-consuming anger riveting through him as it was now. "First you leave without me, knowing what we are facing, and then you block me from feeling you. From finding you." When I didn't answer, he scoffed. "No wonder I didn't pick up your distress when the Daeva called. I just thought it was because I was so worried, but—"

"I just didn't want you to know I'd left. You were . . . busy."

"What the fuck does that mean?"

My own anger roared to life at his condescending tone. Had he forgotten his little encounter with the celebrity temptress? "Let's just put it this way," I said, pushing out of his grip, "you blocked me first."

"I've never blocked you. Not like this. I've kept you from emotions at times, but—"

"Physically," I said, turning to search for my clothes. They were gone.

The minute I turned around to yell at the Dealer, he threw a pair of jeans, a pair of boxers, and a T-shirt over Reyes's shoulder. I caught them in midair, waiting for Reyes to turn on him. He didn't. He was too busy glowering at me.

"What are you talking about?"

"The chick in the bar. You purposely blocked me from seeing you while you talked to her."

"There was a reason."

I jerked the shirt over my head. "And?"

"I don't think she's right in the head."

"Really? That's your excuse? If I give you more time," I said, jumping into the boxers that fit alarmingly well, "do you think you can come up with a better one? That one is as lame as my uncle's dead horse."

He watched as I tried to step into the pants and lost my balance. He started to help me but I held up a hand to stop him.

"I don't need your help."

"I didn't want her to see you, Dutch. Not the other way around. There's something wrong with her."

"She looked fine from my vantage point."

"Mentally, I mean."

Unlike the boxers, the pants were about two sizes too big. I stormed past my man in search of the Dealer. "Do you have a belt I can borrow?" I called out.

"Right here," he said, coming out of a bedroom. He nodded with a grin. "Not bad. And the bleeding stopped. I'll find those bandages."

"It's okay. I don't need any. Can you just put my clothes in a bag?"

"I'm burning them," he said, matter-of-fact, handing me a thick black belt.

"Burning them?" I was starting to panic again. "I have to call my uncle." I threaded the belt through the loops. "He has to know what happened. There's a dead body on what is now *our*"—I turned to glare at the only person in the hall glaring back—"property. I can't just leave him there. I have to tell them what happened. I took a shower. I burned my clothes. It's all going to look a tad suspicious, don't you think?"

The doorbell rang and the Dealer strode past me without comment.

I followed him. "So when you say you're burning them, you mean you were *planning* to burn them, right? They aren't actually on fire yet, are they?"

"Sorry, sugar," he said as he opened the door.

Garrett Swopes stood on the other side of it.

"What are you doing here?" I asked him, taken aback.

"I'm the backup plan," he said, a sly grin lighting his face. Garrett was a skiptracer who happened to have died recently—an incident that may or may not have been my fault. The doctors revived him, but he'd seen some pretty dark stuff while surfing the afterlife, including Reyes's father, the big man down under.

"Backup plan?" I turned to Reyes. "Why do we need a backup plan?"

The Dealer tossed a pair of socks and my boots to me. "I cleaned them the best I could," he said. "They're still wet, but I don't have anything that will fit you."

I took a black athletic sock and hopped on one foot to get it on while following the Dealer into the kitchen. "I need my phone. I have to call my uncle."

"No can do, sugar," he said, grabbing a beer out of the fridge. He winked before downing the entire contents in three huge gulps. "Liquid courage." He pitched the bottle into a wastebasket and went for another.

"I need you sober," Reyes said, his voice razorlike.

"As luck would have it, your particular needs don't interest me. My only concern is the reaper. She needs to stay here."

"You can't keep me prisoner," I protested.

"I told you," Reyes said, stepping close as I hopped into the other sock, "she doesn't leave my sight. What if they show up here while we're there?"

"They can't come in here, demon spawn, or don't you feel that?"

Reyes stepped back and lowered his head before pasting on a smirk. "You think one minuscule blessing and a little holy water are going to keep them out?"

"You got a better plan?"

Reyes pulled a leather cloth from the back of his pants. He unfolded it in his palm to reveal Zeus, the only knife in existence that could kill a demon, any demon, with one thrust.

"What good will that do you?" I asked him. "You can't even touch it."

"I can if it's encased in leather." He held it out for my inspection. Who knew a Sham Wow had so many uses? "But it's not for me. It's for you." He took my hand and placed the knife in it sans the chamois. "If they attack, don't hesitate to use it, Dutch. Not even a microsecond."

I began to get more and more worried. "What do you mean? Where are we going?"

He gave me a quick once-over and I felt something dangerously close to pride swell inside him.

I took a quick peek myself. Loose Blue Öyster Cult T-shirt, baggy jeans held up by a belt, and my usual dark brown ankle boots.

"We have to go back," Reyes said, and I froze.

"We have to call my uncle, Reyes. It's a crime scene now. We have to get the police involved."

He nodded, then said, "What if you do call your uncle? What if he goes in there, Dutch? What if the same thing happens to him?"

I leaned back against the wall, astounded with my idiocy. "I didn't even consider that. I'm so stupid."

"You're not stupid," Garrett said. "But why are *we* going in there again? I mean if these things are so bad."

"*We* aren't," Reyes said, heading toward the door. "The Daeva and I are. You are staying out front in the sunlight, guarding my fiancée with your life."

"Oh," Garrett said. "Okay, then."

"We don't even know if that sunlight thing is true, Reyes." I rushed to keep up with his long strides. "You said yourself, neither of you have any idea what they are capable of. They could frolic in the sun on a daily basis, for all we know." When he kept going, I added, "They attacked with no warning, Reyes."

He paused midstride and I almost ran into him. Instead he turned and wrapped one arm around my waist and waited for me to continue.

"You don't understand. I never even saw them. I just heard a growl. Saw that man's throat ripped to shreds. Felt their teeth. I never even got a glimpse. We have no idea what they are capable of."

"There's only one way to find out," he said, giving me a light squeeze. "Just keep that thing close."

"You think Zeus can kill them?" I asked, my voice quivering.

"No," he said, running a thumb along the cleft in my chin. "I think *you* can kill them."

7

We pulled up to the asylum again in two vehicles. Since Misery's driver's seat was still drenched in blood, Reyes and I took his black Plymouth 'Cuda while Garrett and the Dealer took Garrett's black pickup. Black in New Mexico was just not a sane choice, no matter how good it looked, but boys will be boys.

I thought about summoning Angel or even Artemis, but I had no idea if the Twelve could kill them. I couldn't take the risk. Artemis, a gorgeous Rottweiler, had been sent to guard me, but I would die if anything happened to her. Possibly quite literally.

When we pulled up, Strawberry was sitting on the curb out front, chewing absently on Barbie's head.

I jumped out before Reyes could stop me, and ran to her. "Strawberry," I said, kneeling beside her, "are you okay?"

"No," she said past the plastic in her mouth. "I'm okay. There's an awful lot of blood, though."

I took her into my arms, hoping none of the surrounding neighbors were watching. It would just look odd. Apparently, no one had seen me tearing out of the building earlier, covered in someone else's blood. There were no cop cars about or crime scene teams scouring the place for evidence, like my bloody fingerprints all over the place. Thank heavens for small favors.

"Where are Rocket and Blue?"

She answered with a soft shrug.

I set her back so I could look into her eyes. "Did you see them, sweetheart? The big dogs?" I asked.

She lowered her head. "No. I just heard them."

I embraced her again. "I'm so sorry. You can't go back in there for a while, okay?"

"Okay."

"Thank you."

As I sat rocking her in my arms, I felt a sliver of cold metal encircle one of my wrists with a click.

I looked up at Garrett, who had the other cuff around his wrist. "What the hell?" I said, standing awkwardly, one hand imprisoned.

"Boss's orders." He gestured to Reyes with a nod.

I gaped at my husband-to-be. "What is this for?"

Reyes didn't dignify my question with a response. "If she tries to go in there for any reason," he said instead, addressing Garrett with a hard stare, "you have my permission to restrain her by any means necessary."

"Sweet," Garrett said.

Reyes cast one last glare before turning to the number pad on the front gate and entering the date. "How did you know?" he asked over his shoulder.

I knew what he was talking about: How had I guessed the key code? If he wasn't going to answer my questions, I wouldn't answer his. I crossed my arms over my chest, but just as quickly dropped them, as the action brought Garrett's cuffed hand dangerously close to Will Robinson.

Not waiting for an answer, Reyes propped the gate open in case they'd have to make a quick exit before he and the Dealer—I would have to get that kid's name someday—walked up the sidewalk to the building entrance, punched in the same code there, then entered what I now considered the mouth of hell.

"I'm going to go look for Blue," Strawberry said. Before I could warn her not to go back into the building again, she was gone.

"This is so wrong," I said to Garrett.

"Nah," he said, checking messages on his phone, which was really inconvenient for me. "It'll give us some quality time."

Quality time, my ass. Garrett was that tall, sexy friend one almost wants to bang. A friend-with-benefits kind of thing, only we'd never taken our initial flirtations that far. Thank goodness, because every conversation from there on out would have been filled with those awkward silences as we tried to decipher what the other was thinking. But he was more than handsome enough to give me pause when we'd first met, during my pre-Reyes hookup days. He had deep mocha skin and silvery gray eyes that turned heads everywhere he went. Not to mention killer abs. I could've done laundry on those abs.

"Okay." I leaned against his truck, a move that could be considered an act of war in some cultures, but he didn't seem to mind.

He quickly did the same, his gaze glued to his phone. "What happened in there?" he asked without looking up.

I scratched my affronted wrist. "Let's just say 'they're here.'"

He expelled a long sigh. "I was hoping the prophecies were wrong."

"Have you gotten any more of the translations from the cow doctor?"

"Dr. von Holstein is not a cow doctor."

I knew that, of course, but his name was Dr. von Holstein, for goodness' sake. It screamed cow doctor.

"And he's flying in tomorrow."

I straightened in surprise. "He's flying here?"

He nodded. "Yes. Apparently, he's translated a large section that he feels we need to see. He says it's not what we think."

"What? What's not what we think?"

He lowered his phone. "He wouldn't say. Did you ever get that DNA for me?"

"Swopes," I said, leaning against the truck again, "how on planet Earth am I going to get your ex-squeeze and her infant child's DNA?" I'd made a deal with him to secretly get the DNA of an ex-girlfriend of his. She'd had a baby, and he believed the child might be his. But how did one go about getting someone's DNA without her knowledge?

"I told you," he said. "Not my problem."

"Well, you better make it your problem if you want to know who that kid's father is."

"But he looked like me?" he asked. "You saw him, right? Didn't you think—?"

"Yes, he looks like you, but so does your ex's new boyfriend."

"How much like me?"

I stood again to assess him. "Well, he's not quite so squiggly around the edges. And his nose has never been broken."

He leveled an expressionless expression on me, then went back to his messages. In reality, the guy wasn't anywhere near as good-looking as Garrett, and yet he did resemble him. I was right there with my surly skiptracer friend: I felt like Marika was up to something. Like she'd planned on getting pregnant with Garrett.

"Heart," I said.

"You mean that thing you don't have?"

I gasped. "I have a heart. Her name is Betty White." I slammed a fist against my chest passionately, wincing slightly. "She's right here with me, hand in hand—or ventricle in ventricle—through thick and thin, day in and day out. Otherwise, I'd be dead."

"Your point being?"

"Heart. The music group. They sing a song about this chick who picks up this guy and has sex with him. He sees her later with a kid and the kid has his eyes. The chick explains that she just needed his sperm. Those weren't the exact words, but apparently, her husband couldn't get her pregtastic, so she went out and seduced a guy just to get knocked up. Maybe it's the same thing with Marika?"

He stuffed his phone into his pocket. "Maybe."

"I mean, you said she'd just come over for sex in the middle of the night and then leave. There was no real relationship, right?"

One shoulder went up in a halfhearted shrug.

"Maybe she just wanted a baby daddy." I looked toward the building, growing more impatient by the second. They'd been in there awhile. "You need to call Reyes," I said, but the moment I said it, I heard a shrill scream coming from the asylum. I straightened once more and pulled against my restraint.

"What?" Garrett said in alarm. He couldn't hear her.

"Strawberry," I gasped, then ran for the gate.

Reyes had propped the front door open, too, and I rocketed through it and flew down the stairs and to the kitchen. I came to a screeching halt in front of Reyes, the Dealer, and Strawberry. She glanced around the room wildly, her face in shock as she tried to make sense of her surroundings. The other two looked from her to each other, then back again until they noticed my presence.

"Dutch, son of a bitch," Reyes said, storming toward me, his expression not pleasant in the least. "What the fuck are you doing in here?"

I blinked, taking in the scene with a mixture of shock and awe. It was clean. Sterile, in fact. Not a drop of blood anywhere. Not a body. Not a speck of dirt out of place. "What the hell?" I asked, turning in a full circle.

"There's nothing here," the Dealer said. "But the guy's shit is still in there." He nodded toward the freezer.

Reyes took my arm to drag me back out, but I stood my ground.

"Where did he go? Where did all the blood go?"

"There isn't any, but the scent is still strong." The Dealer inhaled through his nose. "I can smell it. Blood. A lot of it."

Reyes jerked me to attention. "What are you doing in here?"

"I heard Strawberry scream."

Garrett finally found me, having burst through the door and come face-to-face with a very angry demon.

In a microsecond, Reyes had let go of me and clutched on to Garrett's throat. If he'd wanted to, he could've crushed the larynx with very little effort.

I clutched on to Reyes's arm to stop him, but the anger flaring inside him scorched me. I held my ground, placed a hand on his cheek, spoke with a soft yet firm voice. "Reyes, let go." But the surreality of the situation hit me just as it had Garrett, who didn't look scared or angry as Reyes sank his fingers into his throat. He looked . . . surprised. And he was looking at me despite the fact that the son of Satan was choking the life out of him.

"Evade," I said to Reyes.

Caught off guard, he released Swopes, then turned his anger my way.

But, picking up on Garrett's astonishment, I looked down at my wrist, completely handcuff free.

"Did it break?" I asked Garrett as he coughed and wheezed to get air. People did that a lot around me.

"No," he said through his abused esophagus. "You just—" He blinked at me a moment, then continued. "You just . . . went through it."

He held it up, the empty side still adjusted to the size of my wrist, still locked in place.

"My hand doesn't even hurt," I said, rubbing it. "I don't know how it slipped off."

Garrett focused on Reyes, who was still tamping down his anger. Freaking demons. "She went through it," he repeated. "Her wrist . . . just slipped through."

"I don't understand," I said.

"You don't have to." Reyes wrapped an arm around me again. "I told you not to come in here."

My anger reignited. "I told you, I heard Strawberry scream." I suddenly remembered her and knelt beside her. "Are you okay, honey?"

"Where did it all go?" she asked. "Where did that man go?"

I scanned the room. "I wish I knew." Glancing at the Dealer, I asked, "How is this possible?"

He shook his head as though he couldn't form the words to explain his bewilderment.

"Get her out," Reyes said to Garrett.

Garrett took hold of my arm to escort me out, but I needed to talk to Strawberry. "Honey, I need you to leave and don't come back for a while, okay? Remember?"

"I was looking for Blue and Rocket."

"Okay, but not in here, okay. Go outside and call them."

She nodded and stuck the Barbie head back into her mouth before disappearing again. From my kneeling position, I could see something under the slats of the pallet floor as I looked into the freezer. It looked like a driver's license.

I stood and fished it out. I was just about to take a good look when Reyes grabbed my arm again.

"I said get her out or spend the rest of your days drinking your meals through a straw," he said to Garrett.

Wrenching out of Reyes's grip, I stuffed the license in my back pocket, then jammed my hands on my hips as I turned to him. He could be such a bully. "That is just about enough," I said. I lifted an index finger and poked his chest. That'd show him.

But just as I was about to continue my tirade, I caught a glimpse of something behind him. Something dark and sleek like a panther, only five times bigger. I couldn't see the whole thing at once. Its coat appeared and disappeared as the muscles underneath it rolled with movement like very well-controlled smoke. Then I saw a set of amber eyes. They disappeared the second I focused on them, to be replaced with a glimpse of an ear, tall and pointed. Or was it a horn?

It all happened so fast, I'd barely had time to draw a breath when a massive paw materialized and swiped through the air. In the same instant, another being on the other side of Reyes surfaced out of the void of emptiness, smoke winding around it as its monstrous jaws opened wide and sank into Reyes's shoulder.

Before either of us could react, a third beast clamped down on my calf and jerked my feet out from under me. I hit the concrete hard and it dragged me across the floor. But all I saw was Reyes pushed to his knees as he tried to fight off the beast.

A searing pain shot through me when the Dealer caught my arms and pulled. I thought my leg would come off, but the beast let go and, in a collage of appearing and disappearing sleek black muscles, attacked the Dealer himself. He tried to scramble out of the way, but five slash marks scored his chest, streaming blood in an eerie pattern across his shirt. The last thing I saw before grabbing Zeus from the back of my pants was a glimpse of long white teeth as they opened behind the Dealer's head.

I heard bones crunch and a final sharp crack that echoed along the walls. The monster had broken the Dealer's neck. He went limp, crumpling to the floor as I lunged forward and sank the blade blindly into the now invisible hellhound. But the blade did its job. The beast yelped, materialized in its entirety for a split second, then disappeared. I sat stunned for a solid five seconds. It was massive, the size of an elephant, darker than a starless sky, its coat sleek like wet ink.

"Get her out!" Reyes shouted, catapulting me to attention.

Garrett obeyed without hesitation. He wrapped his arms around me protectively and dragged me across the floor kicking and screaming.

"No!" I shouted, grabbing for Reyes. Blood gushed out of the wound at his shoulder faster than I imagined possible, making me dizzy and nauseated with fear.

He fell forward onto his hands, and only then did I see the wounds on his back. The beast's paw had hit home, slicing Reyes open, shredding him.

I slashed through the air, trying to hit a target that might be lurking there, invisible to us. When we reached the door, I fought harder, but

Garrett was not budging. He wanted out of there and he was not about to leave me. Just then I realized Artemis had appeared after all. She barked and growled at what I could only assume was a beast. I couldn't see it, but apparently she could. I had a target.

"Garrett, wait!" I shouted, but he kept his hold strong, not giving me an inch this time.

Until he did.

His hold broke and I fell forward, my limbs splaying across the floor gracelessly, Zeus wrenched from my hand to slide under the prep table. I looked over my shoulder just in time to see Garrett crash against a far wall and tumble to the ground, unconscious.

Fear engulfed me utterly. I forced myself to go calm and concentrate on one thing.

"*Quiesce,*" I said, slowing time, grinding it to a begrudging halt. And in the brief second between the momentum of time and its opposite, its constant, they materialized. In all that melee, all that carnage, there were only three of them.

They disappeared again, but in that split second I got a good look. I'd never seen anything even remotely similar to these creatures. A cross between a panther and a Doberman, but the size of a small elephant on some serious steroids, they were hulking beasts. Their growls were a mixture of a lion and a gorilla's, deep and guttural. Volatile and angry. I could still see the sleekness of their muscles as they moved, just barely at first, as though gaining their bearings, as though adjusting to the shift in time. After a couple more seconds, they were able to move fully, their features like silver dust outlining their invisible bodies as they turned on me, all three of them, in perfect unison.

I froze in place, my heart stopping as I tried to see them. As I tried to assess from which direction the deathblow would come. One swipe of their massive paws, one graze of their shimmering teeth, and I would cease to exist.

It killed me that Satan would win. That he'd get his wish. That I would die before having the chance to face him, because I had every intention of doing that very thing once Beep was born safely on earth. But he was essentially killing both of us and guaranteeing his chance of survival for many millennia to come, because according to the prophecy, it wasn't me who would take him on, but the precious cargo I was now carrying.

As one hellhound drifted toward me, silvery black dust shifting and rolling with each step it took, I dived for the prep table. I barely fit underneath it as I scrambled for cover, pushing and scraping against the filthy floor, but I couldn't let Satan win. Sadly, I couldn't reach Zeus from my vantage either, so I went for the wooden spoon I'd seen earlier.

The beast paced the floor beside me, its growls ricocheting against my bones, and I periodically caught a glimpse of its paw. One claw was the size of my hand. And it had five of those on each paw. Its feet alone must have weighed more than I did. It pawed at me periodically with one of them, the claws scraping against the metal table, the screeching sound disturbing on so many levels.

The fact that Artemis was still barking and growling registered in the back of my mind. My time suppression never affected her either, but I could hold it back only so long. I could stop Reyes from bleeding out for only a few moments more.

I glanced across the floor. He lay in a colossal pool of his own blood as I sat quivering under a table like an addled schoolgirl. Fear laced up my spine and watered my eyes. I closed them, pushing the wetness past my lashes. The shelf I lay under was so low, I couldn't turn my head, I couldn't see the Dealer or Garrett, but I could feel Zeus. He lay next to my right foot. If only I could nudge him toward me . . . but I could barely move my leg without exposing it.

I had no choice. I had to kick the knife out from under the table, then try to get to it before the beast's claws met their mark. I felt time slipping away from me. When it bounced back, it would feel like a runaway train crashing through a railway station. It would knock the air from my lungs and disorient me.

It was exactly what I needed.

I readied myself by inhaling a long draft of air and releasing it slowly. Counting down from five, I tucked Zeus under my foot, focused on my goal, and released time.

It slammed into me, as I kicked Zeus from underneath the table and scrambled after it. My head grazed the leg of the pacing hellhound, but it had yet to orient to the time shift, giving me precious seconds to get to the knife. But I was also fighting gravity, as though time had its own gravitational force field. The barrier slowed me down and I had to push against it with all my strength.

Once free of the table, I lunged for Zeus, scooped him up in one hand, and buried the razor-sharp blade into the hell beast's paw. The creatures adjusted even faster than before, coming to life with deafening growls, the loudest snarls coming from the one I'd stabbed.

I pulled the knife out and slashed blindly, trying to get to Reyes's side. One swipe actually met its mark, and another howl reverberated over the sound of time ricocheting into place.

My measly cuts would barely faze the animals, much less kill them. But the lacerations would sting like the dickens, enough to get their attention. Enough, I prayed, to convince them to back off. When the third beast stepped forward with a growl, I finally sank my blade. From what I could tell, it landed in the thing's shoulder. My hold on Zeus slipped, but I doubled my efforts to withdraw him, screaming for the beast to leave now or die trying later.

And then they were gone.

My gaze darted around me as I whirled this direction and that, but even the silvery black dust was gone. Still, for how long? I looked up. The windows sat high, as this was a lower level, and they were covered in a brown paper or cardboard or something.

We still didn't know if daylight affected them, but the idea was worth a shot. Before they could return, I scurried onto the countertops at the far end of the room and started ripping at the paper. Some of it was stuck to the glass, so I did the next best thing. Using Zeus's handle, I broke the panes out of the frames until sunlight streamed into the room.

I heard a moan and looked toward Garrett. He was struggling to stand. I hustled down and hurried over to help him.

"I'm fine," he said, scanning the area warily.

"We have to get them out," I said to him, indicating the Dealer and Reyes, but the Dealer was already up, his head bowed, his hands clenched into fists as he glared from underneath his dark lashes.

Reyes had told me the kid was a champion fighter, and in hell, one could only assume that meant fighting to the death. He said the Daeva, or slave demon, was the fastest and strongest fighter in the games, not only among slaves but any of the demons there, too. He'd been a champion, afforded luxuries other slaves didn't have, which led to his ability to escape centuries before Reyes had.

He was clearly in his element. Even with his back raw and dripping with blood and remnants of flesh, he stood deathly still. Watching. Learning. That had been his gift. His stillness. His patience. His ability to wait out his opponent, to let the fighter get the upper hand just long enough for him assess the beast's strengths and weaknesses before attacking, because once the champion attacked, it didn't take long for his opponent to die.

I literally felt the force of his anger as he pushed it aside, turning it off so he could appraise the situation.

"Holy fuck," Garrett said, rushing toward Reyes.

I was right behind him. I dropped Zeus and slid onto my knees as Reyes braced a hand against a counter. He tried to lift himself off the ground but couldn't quite manage it. Garrett was there instantly, helping him to his feet as I took his other side.

"We need to leave," the Dealer said, his eyes unblinking as he continued to scan the area. "Now."

He didn't have to tell me twice. Garrett and I eased Reyes toward the door. I slipped on his blood but was able to right myself before making a bigger disaster of an already disastrous situation.

"The knife," the Dealer said, and I knew he couldn't just pick it up without some kind of protection. No demon could.

"There." I nodded toward a dirty dishrag on the floor.

But we didn't wait for him. We hurried out the door and up the stairs, Reyes's feet tripping as we almost carried him up. Or, well, Garrett almost carried him up. I felt more like a hindrance than a help.

Reyes had definitely taken the worst of the attack. Not only was his back in shreds, but his shoulder had almost been ripped off as well. The jaws on those beasts could manage it effortlessly. I shuddered at the thought as we burst through the front doors and into the glorious sunlight.

Feeling safe for the first time, I lifted my head toward the sun. If we made it to our vehicles with no one noticing us, that would be the third miracle for the day. I'd already used up two, the first being my last trip to my vehicle, covered in blood with no one the wiser. The next being the fact that I had nary a mark on me. But Reyes sure did.

After we exited out the gate, I started for Reyes's 'Cuda, but Garrett steered him in the opposite direction. Artemis followed us out, bouncing around and whining helplessly. I understood completely.

"My truck," Garrett said, indicating the bed with a nod. "He needs to lie down."

"We have to get him to a hospital this time. He's lost too much blood."

"No." The Dealer brought up the rear, then sprinted past us to let the tailgate down. I saw him wince when he pulled the handle and lowered the gate.

"Look, Dealer or Daeva or whatever your name is," I said as we eased Reyes onto the tailgate. Garrett jumped in, hooked his arms under my man's shoulders, and dragged him into the bed. Reyes's head lolled back and Garrett carefully lowered him onto the metal bed.

That time I winced. His right shoulder was mangled, and I honestly worried his arm would come clean off. Blackness blurred the edges of my vision. I almost fainted, but the Dealer wrapped an arm around my waist.

I pushed off him. "We have to get him to a hospital. Look at his shoulder."

He regarded Reyes's unconscious form, then turned to me. "Got any duct tape?"

8

Most of what I call "cooking" is just melting cheese on stuff.
—T-SHIRT

We snuck Reyes—who'd woken up mid-trip and insisted on going home instead of to the Daeva's house—up the stairs and into my apartment. The Dealer drove Garrett's pickup, since he was better equipped to fight the hellhounds should they show up, and Garrett drove Reyes's 'Cuda to our place. We avoided the interstate in favor of a residential, and thus less traveled, route. We couldn't risk someone in a truck seeing Reyes and me covered in blood in the bed of a pickup and have them call the police.

"It's okay, Mrs. Allen," I said to my elderly neighbor as she cracked open her door for a peek. "We're rehearsing for a play."

"That was so lame," Garrett said, huffing with the burden he carried. The Dealer seemed to be handling it okay, but I felt pain radiate out of the kid with every movement. The slashes on his back were deep.

"I know," I said, acknowledging my lame reason we were all covered in blood. "It was all I had." I was still quaking from our most recent efforts and in fear for Reyes's life.

"We aren't safe here," the Dealer said as he helped Garrett carry a grimacing Reyes up the second flight of stairs. We totally needed an elevator. "We're making a big mistake coming here. My place is much safer."

"They can't come in here, demon slave," Reyes said from between clenched teeth, echoing the Dealer's earlier words, "or don't you feel that?"

The Dealer paused, absorbed whatever it was he could feel that I clearly couldn't, then nodded. "That'll work."

"What?" I asked, rushing ahead of them to open my door. "What will work?"

"The whole area has been blessed. It's not exactly sacred ground, but it'll do for now."

"Blessed?" I asked Reyes, wanting to help but not knowing where I could touch him without it causing him even more pain.

"After the basement."

"Oh. Right." We'd had an infestation of demons in the basement once. I'd never thought about having the place blessed to keep them away. Then it hit me. "I knew that new bug guy looked familiar. He was a priest or something, wasn't he?"

Reyes tried to nod but cringed in agony instead.

He must have had holy water in that canister instead of bug spray. "No wonder I've been seeing so many spiders lately." Holy water may fend off demons, but spiders were completely unfazed by it.

I made a mental note to call a real bug guy ay-sap. Not that I had anything against spiders. I liked them as much as the next girl. Not.

After much effort, bickering, and fussing on my part, we got both the Dealer and Reyes cleaned up, duct-taped, and on the road to recovery. I could hardly look at Reyes's wounds. Or the Dealer's, for that matter. There was only so much flayed flesh I could take, and I'd been feeling quite nauseated as it was.

We put Reyes in my bed, which still butted against the head of Reyes's bed, where there used to be a wall before Reyes went all *This Old House* on me. I had yet to discard mine. Artemis curled up on the end of it, resting her head against Reyes's leg. Then we put the Dealer on the couch and Garrett in a rather comfortable recliner we'd moved into my apartment from Reyes's.

They all fell fast asleep. Garrett didn't want to let on how hurt he was, but I'd have bet my bottom dollar he had a cracked rib or two. His arm and ribs were also scratched up, but because his injuries were nothing compared to Reyes's and the Dealer's, he didn't feel he could complain.

After I said my belated hellos to Mr. Wong, the departed Asian man hovering in the corner of my living room, I sat at my kitchen table and listened to the men's shallow panting as they all tried to heal. But I couldn't get the image of the beasts out of my head. I had never been so scared of something I could barely see. In an effort to take my mind off them, I picked up my phone, called Cookie at the office, and broke down, sobbing, until she finally hung up on me, locked the doors, and rushed over with Belvedere slopping in his fishbowl to get the story firsthand.

As the guys slept, I also called Uncle Bob over. The three of us sat at my tiny kitchen table, watching Belvedere do the dance of his people as I quickly and quietly explained everything that had happened. Through tears of shock and grief, I fought past my stupor and told them about the man who had attacked me, his horrific death, and the fact that I'd gone to the Dealer's house. How the Dealer had burned my clothes trying to protect me. How we went back and were attacked again. And I told them about the Twelve. They had a right to know. If I was going to bring them into this, into my life, they had a right to know everything. I'd considered looping in the captain since he now knew more about me than most, but decided to leave that up to Ubie. The bottom line was, we had a dead body on our hands. A missing dead body, but a dead body nonetheless.

"Would they—? Would the Twelve hound beast things have taken the body?" Cookie asked, her expression grave as she held my hand.

"I have no idea." I sobbed into a paper towel, as I was out of tissues. Shopping for the mundane was never my strong suit. "I'm sorry," I said, blowing my nose for the fifteenth time. "I think I'm hormonal."

"You're suicidal," Ubie said, his ire rising. "Why the hell did that bastard take you back to the asylum after what happened the first time?"

"Trust me, Uncle Bob, the last place Reyes wanted me to go was back inside. He was a tad angry. But you can't go there," I said, handing him the license I'd found in the freezer. "This is the guy who attacked me, but he was really after Reyes. Either way, you can't go there. Promise me."

"Pumpkin, that's a crime scene."

"Not if you don't tell anyone."

He bit back a curse.

"Ubie," I said, leaning forward, pleading, "you can't go in there and you can't send anyone in there. You could be sending them to their deaths. The only reason Reyes and the Dealer are alive is because of their heritage."

"Is that what you call it? Their heritage?"

"Uncle Bob, I'm not kidding. These beasts are like nothing I've ever seen, and I've seen a lot."

After a long, thoughtful moment, he drew in a deep breath of resignation. "I'll run a background on this guy, see what I can dig up, and let you know."

"Thank you. Are you going to tell the captain?"

"I don't know yet. I'll have to think about it."

"I'm so sorry to put you in this position."

"Pumpkin," he said, taking my hand, "this is not on you. You're not like us, and we all know it. I'm just glad I can be here when you need me."

I was taken aback by his admission, and the waterworks flowed again. I lunged forward and hugged him. "Thank you."

"I like him," Cookie said, nodding toward the kid sleeping on Sophie, my couch.

I kissed Ubie's cheek, then released him. "You like all kids."

"Not my own," she said, teasing.

"I heard that." Amber, Cookie's offspring, had come in and was standing behind me.

"Oh, I had no earthly idea you were there." Cookie winked at me as Amber started scouring my cabinets. "How was school?"

"You know those days where you wish the earth would open up and swallow your teachers whole?" she began. Then her gaze landed on the sleeping beauty sprawled across Sophie. His shoulder-length black hair splayed across a throw pillow, and an arm was covering half his face, but those didn't detract from the fact that he was gorgeous. Her gaze slowly meandered toward the other sleeping beauty set up in the recliner. Then she rose onto her toes and could just see into my bedroom, where the third sleeping beauty lay resting.

"Is Reyes okay?" she whispered, worried and wondering what had happened. I could feel curiosity rise like a tide within her.

"He'll be fine," I replied.

"Sweetheart, why don't you go raid our own cabinets? Aunt Charley's food is dangerous. It has green fuzzy stuff on it."

"Not on my Twizzlers," I protested.

"Um, okay," she said, her gaze latching back on to the Dealer and staying there. "Can I bring you anything? Crackers? Coconut water? Bubble gum?"

I almost laughed, but couldn't quite get past my stupor enough to do it. And I'd even showered for the third time that day, but my mottled senses refused to bounce back to their state of stasis: extreme ADHD.

"We're good, hon," Cookie said. "You run along."

"Okay, but don't forget about my carnival. You guys have to come."

"I wouldn't miss it for the world," I told her as she hugged me good-bye. After she left, I asked Cook, "She's joined the circus? I had no idea."

"No. Don't worry about it. You don't have to go."

I straightened. "Of course I have to go. I live for carnivals. Carnivals and Oreos, but not necessarily in that order."

I really didn't live for either, but I needed a drink so bad, I'd started babbling. A mocha latte would hit the spot, but noooooo. I had to be carrying a Beep around. I was never going to survive this whole pregtastic thing.

"I'm going to run a search on this guy," Ubie said. He stood to leave and Cookie followed suit.

"Okay." Guilt leached into me once again. He did have a job to do, and this was a lot to lay on an officer of the law. *Oh, so yeah, there's this dead guy on my property, but you can't tell anyone or investigate or anything. Also I burned my bloody clothes. Does that seem suspicious at all?* I was the worst niece ever.

"You realize your sister is coming over in an hour," Cookie said.

I dropped my forehead into my palm. "I totally forgot. She's going to kill me."

"She's just excited about the wedding and the baby. I'll call her."

"Thanks, Cook."

"And I'll bring dinner over in a few. You just keep watch over the guys."

"Will do."

After they left, I went to check on my affianced. He lay sleeping with his good arm thrown over his forehead. I leaned in to check on his wounds. What little the duct tape didn't cover was already fusing, his cells merging at an incredible rate to make him whole again. I could only pray the internal damage to his shoulder was doing the same.

I wanted to lie down beside him, to curl him into my arms, but I didn't want to risk waking him, so I strolled back to my living room and sat on the coffee table near the Dealer so I could check on him. He lay on his back, as did Reyes, a feat that floored me. Their backs had been ripped to shreds. How they were able to get sleep while lying on them was beyond me. His arm, lean and sinewy like Reyes's, covered most of his face, but I could tell he was awake.

"What's your name?" I asked him, sipping a cup of water.

"I can't tell you my real name," he said without removing his arm.

"Why?"

"Knowing a demon's real name gives you power over him. I'm surprised you know Rey'aziel's."

That was the second time that day I'd heard something along those lines. The priest had said the same thing.

"Well, we are affianced."

He removed his hand at last, letting it hang over Sophie's arm. His bronze irises shimmered in the low light as he studied me. There was simply something about him, something alarmingly attractive but not in the usual way. There was nothing sexual about my interest. I just trusted him. I had no idea why, really, but I'd trusted him from the moment I saw him.

"And yet," he said, gazing at me with the same regard, "Rey'aziel has never told you *your* real name, has he? So who has more power?"

"I do," I said, matter-of-fact, completely full of shit.

One corner of his mouth lifted. "Good. You'll need that confidence in the days to come." He glanced down at my abdomen. "May I?"

I leaned away warily. "May you what?"

"Feel her?"

Looking down at Beep, I hesitated, then nodded, unsure of what he meant.

He brought his arm around, wincing at the pain it caused, and placed his hand gently on my abdomen. I couldn't imagine he would feel anything. She was little more than cells. Her heart hadn't even started to beat yet. But I felt her warmth like a tiny light pulsing inside me.

His lids drifted shut as though the act soothed him, eased his pain. "What's her name?" he asked, keeping his lids closed.

I glanced over to see if Garrett was awake. He was. He looked on silently as the Dealer, the slave demon from hell who had no reason to help us and yet risked his life to do that very thing, somehow connected with my daughter.

"You show me yours and I'll show you mine," I told him.

He grinned, his fingers sliding dangerously close to Virginia, my girlie part. Clearly Beep was lower than I thought. "I'll tell you what you can call me. How's that?"

"That'll work. I looked up your utilities and stuff. They're all under the name of the guy you rent from. I can't believe that, despite everything I have to go on, I can't find a thing about you."

"I've been around a lot longer than you, sugar. I'm careful."

"I'll buy that. So what can I call you?"

He finally lifted his lids, his bronze irises feverishly bright when he said, "Osh. You can call me Osh."

"Osh," I said, absorbing the name, associating it with the demon who looked like a kid lounging on my sofa. Such an unassuming name for such a dangerous, dangerous boy. "I like it. You got a last name?"

"It's not my demon name, if that's what you're asking."

"Not at all." I took out my phone. "I just need to know what to put your number under. If anyone found my phone and read 'The Dealer,' I could be in trouble."

He flashed me a brilliant smile. "It's Villione. It was given to me many centuries ago, after I first arrived on earth."

I stilled a moment before punching the name into my phone. "Does it stem from what I think it does?"

"A life of debauchery and mayhem?"

"Something like that."

"Yes, Charlotte," he said, his voice smooth like fine whiskey. "I was a very bad boy once upon a time."

I nodded. "Okay, well, that'll work for now. But Reyes knows your real name, right?"

"He does." He said it almost regretfully. "Not that he ever used it in hell."

"Then I'll just ask him. Until then, Osh it is."

"And her name?" he asked.

"I don't know yet. I've been calling her Beep."

He laughed softly, giving my belly a light rub, then pulling back his arm. "I don't know why, but that seems very appropriate."

"Thank you. I like to think so."

He winced as he rolled fully onto his back again.

"Why are you and Reyes sleeping on your backs? Your wounds are horrible. Wouldn't you be more comfortable on your stomachs?"

He rubbed his eyes, his lids drifting closed every so often, no matter how hard he fought against it. "You learn things where we come from, and one of them is that you are much more vulnerable on your stomach. No demon worth his salt sleeps on his stomach."

"Oh." That was certainly not the answer I'd expected. A survival instinct. Interesting.

"What you should be asking yourself," he said, indicating Mr. Wong with a nod as the departed man hovered in my corner, "is why a being that ungodly powerful is hanging out in your apartment."

We spent a quiet evening at home, and I used much of that time studying Mr. Wong. I'd heard that before, of course—that Mr. Wong was powerful—but he'd been here when I first looked at the apartment, not the other way around. It wasn't like he showed up later to stalk me or anything. Then again, why was a being that powerful hovering in the corner of an apartment in Albuquerque, New Mexico? Wouldn't he have better things to do?

Before I could ask Osh any more about it, his lids had drifted shut once more, as though he could no longer hold them open. So I dropped it. For now. But studying Mr. Wong wasn't getting me anywhere either. I couldn't help but wonder if it was all connected. Mr. Wong. The Twelve. Even the house that was possessed. Did a recent demon possession have anything to do with the Twelve showing up? I'd find out soon enough. I was meeting Father Glenn there in a couple of days. Hopefully,

I would find some answers, along with the demon that liked to carve my name.

Cookie and Amber brought dinner. Uncle Bob joined us, too. He had so many questions, but I just didn't have the energy or the desire to answer them. I'd been drained and I was barely injured. I couldn't imagine what the boys were going through.

Reyes hardly stirred enough to eat, but Osh explained that the deeper he slept, the faster he'd heal. He could actually go almost comatose and be healed from a near-fatal injury in a matter of hours.

"We all can," he said, staring at me pointedly. "Since he got it the worst, however, one of us needs to stand guard."

"So, you won't heal as fast as he does?"

"No. But I will once he wakes. I'll go into stasis and be as good as new in a day." He looked up in thought. "Maybe two days. This is fantastic," he said to Cookie and Amber, twirling spaghetti around his fork.

Amber blushed, the little hussy. She had the biggest crush on Quentin, a Deaf acquaintance, but I could understand her fascination with Osh, though I was still having a difficult time connecting the name with the kid. He didn't look like an Osh at first. Maybe the more I used it, the more he would become Osh. Osh Villione. I wondered if he'd let me call him OshKosh B'gosh. Prolly not.

"That guy who attacked you today," Ubie said, keeping a wary eye on Osh, "was in prison with Reyes."

I nodded. "He seemed a little rough around the edges. When did he get out?"

"That's just it. He didn't."

I put down my fork. "What do you mean?"

"According to prison records, he died two weeks ago."

"What?" I asked, completely taken aback. "There's no way, Uncle Bob. I can tell a living person from a dead one."

"You haven't asked me the best part yet."

"Okay, what's the best part?"

"He died of a heart attack. He was in his sixties."

"This guy had some issues, but I doubt heart disease was one of them."

"We're looking into it, pumpkin. It has to be some kind of clerical error."

"Please, keep looking. And while we're on the subject," I said, biting my lower lip in hesitation, "did you tell the captain?"

"I did. I'm sorry, hon. I was kind of at a loss on what to do."

"No, it's okay. And?"

"He agrees with me. We need to let this one slide for the time being. The guy you identified as the perp is already dead on paper. We can't send in a crime scene, knowing they could be attacked. And how would we explain it, anyway?"

I relaxed visibly. Another day without being arrested for murder and/or covering up a murder was a good day in my book.

"But he does have some questions for you," he said.

"Of course he does. Oh, and I asked Rocket. All the people in the suicide notes have passed. But the one from this morning," I added curiously, "lived until this afternoon. You got the letter at what time?"

"The wife said she woke up and it was in the kitchen. Nothing was gone or missing except him."

"Had he changed clothes? Taken his phone? Made coffee?"

"None of the above. From what she could tell, he just disappeared in the middle of the night."

"I'll go talk to her tomorrow and to the families of the other two."

"There's a fourth," Cookie said, surprising us.

"What do you mean, hon?" Ubie asked her. Hon. So cute. And kind of disturbing.

"Right here." She retrieved some papers she'd brought over earlier. I hadn't paid attention, but she'd certainly piqued my interest now. "Okay, according to a news article from *The Los Angeles Times,* a woman named Phoebe Durant went missing about two months ago. She left a suicide note saying she was going to jump off the Golden Gate Bridge, but she left everything behind: her purse, phone, car keys, the car itself. And there was a sign of what the LAPD said looked like a struggle, but they couldn't be certain. A cup was broken in her bathroom, and a few scuff marks marred the walls. They said it could have been shoe prints of someone being taken against their will, but it could also have been just general wear and tear."

She handed us the article.

"Look at the note," she said, pointing to a scanned copy of the suicide note. "The handwriting matches the woman's, but—"

"The words," I said, reading the note. "How many people use the word *glorious* in their suicide notes?"

"Exactly."

"Nice catch," Uncle Bob said to Cook.

She smiled shyly.

"How did you get this?" I asked her, holding up the copy of the note.

"A very nice young man in Records sent it to me. I had to promise to look him up if I was ever in the City of Angels." She winked to Uncle Bob. "He liked my voice."

"Mom," Amber said, utterly appalled. "You used your feminine wiles on a man you don't even know."

Cookie smiled. "That's what they're for, honey. Eat your salad."

Amber crinkled her nose as Garrett, a skiptracer who'd been to hell and back, and Osh, a slave who'd escaped from said hell, both laughed behind a façade of soft coughs.

Gawd, my life was strange.

After Cookie, Amber, and Ubie left, I asked Osh if we should change his duct tape. Which sounded odd even to me.

"The duct tape doesn't get changed until I'm healed," he said. "Do you know what it feels like to peel duct tape off an open wound?"

I winced. I couldn't imagine, and, oddly enough, I didn't want to try. "So, you'll just know when it's time?"

He took the recliner that time, and Garrett took Sophie.

"I will," he said, settling into the plush chair.

"Do you need anything?" I asked Garrett.

"A foot rub would be nice."

I threw a pillow at him instead. It was a throw pillow, after all. He stuffed it behind his head and closed his lids, a smile playing about his mouth. I couldn't fathom what he had to smile about. Since meeting me, his life had been turned upside down. I was like a small but devastating plague upon humanity. It was weird.

9

See owner for mounting instructions.

—NOVELTY UNDERWEAR

After giving Mr. Wong a kiss on the cheek—or, well, his jaw just under his earlobe because that was all I could reach, with his nose being in the corner and all—I slipped into bed beside Reyes. I didn't want to wake him while he was in stasis, a state that resembled a well-deserved coma. And I certainly didn't want to jostle him. His back and shoulder had been through enough. As he showered with Osh and Garrett's help, I could hardly look on. The Twelve beasts of hell were there for me, and I was the only one to leave that building relatively unscathed.

I lay there a long time, unable to sleep, letting Reyes's heat wash over and warm me. Having him around sure saved on the heating bill at night. But the more I lay there, the more terrified I became. It was no longer about me. I rubbed my abdomen thoughtfully. Perhaps it was never about me. According to the prophecies, I was simply the vessel that brought in the true heroine of our story: Beep.

Clearly she needed a better name. Heroines, those who saved the world from evil, deserved great names. I'd have to think on it, but she would forever be Beep to me.

And the world needed her. I hadn't died today. I had bought another few hours of life, postponed Rocket's prediction of my demise. Technically, he'd never been wrong, so if I could just stay alive long enough to bring her into this world, I could die happy.

I looked at Reyes's profile. He'd thrown an arm—the good one—over his forehead, just as Osh had. I wondered if it was a demon thing.

"You're so serious," Reyes said, his voice hoarse and scratchy.

I leaned onto an elbow in alarm. "Reyes." I wanted to hug his neck but didn't dare risk hurting him. I leaned toward my nightstand and got the bottle of water I'd brought in earlier. "It's warm now. I can get a cold one out of the fridge."

"This is fine," he said, taking a sip before handing it back to me.

"How are you?"

"Peachy."

"I need to tell Osh you're awake."

He looked toward the living room. "He went into stasis the moment I came out," he said. "He'll be fine by morning."

"So that's how you do it?" I asked him. "That's how you heal so much faster than I do? You go into some kind of deep healing state like a monk? Or a ninja?"

"Something like that. You do it, too. I saw you the night after Earl Walker tortured you."

I cringed at the thought of that night. It was not my favorite.

"You went into a deep sleep and healed your wounds almost overnight."

I scoffed. "It didn't feel very instant."

"Dutch, how many people can go through that, then get up and around the very next day?"

"Oh, well, maybe you're right. But it still hurt like the John Dickens."

"John?"

"I went to school with him. He used to twist my arm and give me carpet burns."

He laid his arm over his forehead again. "I could sever his spine."

"It's all right," I said with a soft laugh. "Last I heard, he was selling insurance out of his Buick. He's paying for his impertinence tenfold. But, so, are you still mad at me?"

"Yes."

"Okay." After a long moment, I asked, "Do you know how long you'll be mad at me?"

"No."

"Okay."

"Why did you block me from accessing your emotions? Why did you leave without me after everything we discussed?"

"I don't know. I was just going to Rocket's and— I just— I don't want you to think I'm this fragile thing you have to protect 24/7. I want to be able to take care of myself. I want you to know that I can take care of myself."

"You can. I know that you can better than anyone. And you'll get better at it as you come into your powers, but until then, what is so wrong with my company?"

"What?" I asked him. "What are you talking about?"

"It's like you can't get away from me fast enough."

"That's not it, Reyes. That has nothing to do with it."

"Right."

"I was mad, okay? You were talking to that woman and you blocked me first."

After a long moment, he said, "I can't feel you. I have no idea if you're lying."

But I could feel him. I could feel the hurt I'd caused, and a wave guilt washed over me. I'd never meant any of this in the vein he was taking it.

I brushed a lock of his hair over his brow and said simply, *"Aperite."* And with that word, I laid bare my emotions again.

He inhaled sharply with the reemergence of my feelings.

"I didn't want you to feel my jealousy," I said, embarrassed. "That newswoman seemed very into you."

"Dutch," he said, wrapping a hand around my neck, "all the women who come into the bar are into me."

I almost laughed. Self-deprecating, he wasn't.

"Or they think they are." His voice hardened with resentment. "They don't even know me, Dutch. Their need is exhausting."

I truly could understand that. Well, not from personal experience or anything. I tended to repel instead of attract. But I felt it from the women and men who came into the bar. He was like a flame, drawing moths from all walks of life, only to have their wings suffocate the fire within him.

"I know where they're coming from. I'm the same way. I've lusted after you since the first time I met you. And I still am, Reyes. I'm your biggest fan."

He ran his thumb along my jaw and over my mouth. "No. It's different with you. You were never a sure thing."

I snorted. "Clearly you have misinterpreted my interest."

"No, I haven't. You were never like them. I wish you could feel what I feel. You're amazingly different. You may not believe this, but you could take me or leave me any day of the week. You could drop me in your wake and be fine."

I shook my head. "No, Rey'aziel, I couldn't."

"I love that you believe that."

"There's no winning with a man who just defended me against a hound from hell."

He dropped his hand, and I felt a wave of shame radiate out of him. "A man who *tried* to defend you. A man who failed."

"What?" I shrieked a little too loudly. I slammed my lids shut and waited to make sure I hadn't woken the two in the living room. When they didn't so much as stir in their sleep, I whispered, "What the—? You fought a hellhound for me. Three of them, to be exact. What more could I ask from my affianced? I'm so sorry I went in there."

"If you hadn't, we might not be here." He nodded toward Osh. "They incapacitated us before I could do anything. It was so fast." He smiled at me, his dark eyes shimmering in the glow from my bathroom night-light. That thing was really bright. "But you were faster."

"I was slow. A bumbling mess. I stopped time just long enough to send myself into a complete panic."

"You're wrong," he said. "I saw you. You moved with the speed and stealth of a cheetah. They didn't stand a chance."

"Only because of Zeus. He worked."

"The god?" he asked, teasing me.

"The knife."

"Zeus, huh?"

"Well, I thought about calling him Reyes, but I didn't want to confuse anyone. Including me."

"And what about that one?" he asked, glancing toward the bun. "She got a name?"

"Beep. For now."

"Beep?" he asked, his expression humorous.

"Short for Black-Eyed Pea. She isn't quite as big as one yet, but she will be soon."

"It's perfect."

"It'll do for now, but we need to come up with a great name," I said, lying back in thought. "Something that shouts, 'I will lay waste to the evil in this world!'"

"I agree." Still covered in duct tape, he turned on his side to face me, his flesh straining against the binds. "You would tell me if something were wrong, right?"

"What do you mean? Of course, I would."

"So, if you knew something could happen to you, you'd let me know."

Where was he going with this? "Yes. Nothing is going to happen to me. Well, unless the Twelve get ahold of me. Other than that, I should be fine."

He nodded in thought.

"Reyes, what is it?"

"I think you keep secrets from me."

"You keep secrets from me," I said, teasing. "Seems only fair."

He leaned forward and nibbled on my ear. "We can decide who gets to keep secrets and who doesn't later. Until then, want to do it?"

"Reyes!" I said, appalled. "You just had your arm nearly ripped off at the shoulder." That and the fact that a grown man asking me if I wanted to "do it" was hilarious.

"We can still do it."

I giggled. "No, we can't."

"I'm very creative with my mouth."

"I am well aware of that."

"You should sit on my face."

A bubble of laughter escaped again. "I am not sitting on your face. Oh, my god."

"Just sit on my face. I'll make all your dreams come true."

"You really need to practice humility," I said.

"Humility is overrated."

"Besides," I said, pushing him back when he leaned into me, "we have company."

He looked down at Artemis, her stubby tail wagging a hundred miles a minute. She was almost as happy as I was to see our man back to his normal self. "How are you, girl?" he asked, reaching down to scrub her ears.

I was floored he could even move that arm.

"Go get the ball," he said, pretending to throw one.

Artemis bound off the bed and dived through the wall in search of an invisible ball as I sat gaping at him.

"That was so mean," I scolded.

"What?" he asked, leaning into me again. "She likes balls. You do, too, if I recall."

"You are incorrigible. What about your shoulder?"

"I don't plan on using my shoulder for this," he said, sending his hand down the front of my pajama bottoms, the ones that read MELTS IN YOUR MOUTH. A delicious jolt of pleasure rushed through me as his fingers found the core of my being and buried themselves inside. I drew in a lungful of air.

"What about your back?" I asked.

"I'll put my back into it. I promise."

"No, Reyes," I said, pushing him away again. "I mean it. You were almost ripped apart, and suddenly you're okay to have sex?"

"Dutch," he said, squeezing the inside of my thigh, "if I weren't okay to have sex, do you think I could do this?"

He parted the folds between my legs, his fingers deftly caressing the most sensitive, most tender part of my flesh. He wrapped his other hand around my neck and drew my mouth up to his.

After an initial rush of pleasure that left me trembling with need, I broke off the heated kiss and whispered, "Okay, you win."

He leaned over me and said into my ear, "Dutch, I won the moment you crawled into bed."

He really did need to work on his self-esteem.

I reached down and wrapped my fingers around his erection. He sucked in a sharp breath of air through his teeth. Then, pinning me to the bed with his weight, he grabbed both wrists and locked them over my head, keeping them at a safe distance while he did as he pleased. It was hardly fair, since I wanted to explore the hills and valleys of his body as much as he wanted to explore mine. I wanted to point out the fact that his were much more fascinating than anything I had to offer. They were hard and smooth at once, rigid yet pliant when they rolled under my touch, flexed in response to a kiss.

He lifted my top over my head to gain access to Danger and Will. As he suckled the hardened peaks, giving each one the same amount of attention, swirling his tongue in a maddeningly erotic move, he lowered my bottoms with his other hand. And people say men can't multitask.

Impatiently, I kicked off the leggings as he rose from the bed. The chill from his absence gave me goose bumps. He closed the door, then turned to me in all his naked glory, his skin shimmering in the low light. I stilled and allowed myself to absorb every inch of him. He reached on top of my dresser and brought back something I couldn't quite make out. Then I heard a ripping sound as he walked forward, his gait like that of a predator readying to attack.

The bed dipped when he climbed on. He straddled me, his heat settling over me like a warm blanket. Reaching up, he wrapped a wrist with something cold. Something sticky.

A bubble of laughter escaped me. "Duct tape?" I asked.

"Hush," he said, his brows drawn in an adorable look of concentration. "This is a delicate procedure." He ripped off another strip and bound my wrists together.

A shiver of anticipation ran down my spine as he worked. My pulse accelerated. My skin tightened.

His erection lay between Danger and Will, and my mouth watered, wanting to taste him in the worst way, to feel the rush of his blood beneath my tongue, but he wouldn't allow me to rise or to use my hands. He left me again and grasped an ankle, ran his fingertips along my instep, sending a startlingly sharp wave of pleasure up my leg before ripping off another strip of tape and wrapping it. He seemed to be growing more impatient as he worked. He pulled, spreading my legs wide, and secured it to the frame with another strip. After showering my calf and the inside of my knee with soft, hot kisses, he did the same to the other ankle, spreading me even farther.

Then he stood over me like a king observing his conquest. I lay open and exposed. I'd never been particularly self-conscious, but I couldn't help a moment of doubt as he gazed at me. His expression was so intense, so magnetic, however, that all doubt melted. But I could never have imagined what would happen next.

He started at my ankles, first rubbing them with his thumbs, then leaning in, placing the tiniest of kisses along my skin, grazing his teeth a microsecond before he bit down. Just barely. Just enough to cause a slight spike in pain.

I gasped at almost the precise moment he did. Then I understood. I felt his reaction to my pain. Felt it bounce off him and into me like a ricochet of pleasure that stabbed into my center. He did the same to the other ankle. Each bite crackled like lightning beneath my skin, and I squirmed with need and uncontrollable delight. He licked, then drank, then bit as though taking tequila shots up my legs, and the insane exhilaration washing through me, filtered through his own tactile response, caused me to cry out softly. But it was enough to get his attention.

He straddled me again and tore off another strip of tape, only to secure it over my mouth before descending on Danger and Will. His teeth grazed an erect nipple, just hard enough to cause another spike, another stab, another ricochet.

I threw back my head and wiggled helplessly as he did this over and over, giving every inch of my body the same amount of attention. Even the insides of my wrists, covered by tape, were not safe. He just bit harder to get the reaction he wanted, tensing each time and pausing to let the pain wash over him and back into me.

Without warning, he dipped lower, forced my legs even farther apart, and suckled the folds between my legs, feathering soft strokes with his tongue, whipping me to the brink of orgasm. I gasped behind the tape as an intense pleasure pooled in my abdomen. I became molten lava, scorching hot beneath his touch, and the swell of climax flared to life deep in my core. I moaned as it flourished and grew in size and strength like a summer tide. He pushed his fingers inside me, milking it even closer until I almost begged for release.

Then he sank his teeth into the delicate folds, the pain pushing me higher, up and up until the bittersweet sting of orgasm burst inside me and spilled through me like a boiling sea.

Before I came down entirely, Reyes crawled on top of me, grabbed a handful of hair to secure me to the spot, and slid inside me, burying every inch of his erection in one quick thrust. I bit down, whipped my head back as my climax rebound. He began to move inside me, exquisitely slow at first, then harder, faster, as though desperate with need. With hunger. Another wave of pleasure rippled through me as I felt his own orgasm growing. Pulsating. Rocketing through him.

He thrust into me with a fierce fervor, seeking that high until it cracked and shattered inside him, the ethereal sensation crashing against his bones. I followed suit, coming for a second time, pleasure so sharp and raw, I forgot how to breathe. His climax felt like white-hot sparks falling over my skin as reality settled around us once again.

10

You're the reason I get up in the morning.
That, and I need to pee.

——E-CARD

I woke early the next morning to sticky wrists and a raging headache. I felt like Barbara, my brain, had exploded into a liquid goo but Fred, my skull, was keeping everything intact. I slipped out of bed quietly, trying not to wake my affianced, and stumbled to the bathroom. My head and everything attached to it hurt. My hair hurt. My lashes hurt. My brows hurt possibly most of all. Even my earlobes hurt. Perhaps that last orgasm caused a mini-stroke. I checked my mouth to see if it was lopsided.

Seeing nothing out of the ordinary, I took my morning tinkle and brushed my teeth—not at the same time or anything, though I could multitask like that when in a hurry.

Having left my brush in Reyes's bathroom, I went through the now open bedrooms and into his apartment. Before I made it to the bathroom, however, I heard a painfully soft knock on his door. As I made my way toward it, the doorknob jiggled as though someone was testing it.

I furrowed my brows and stepped closer. Since I was wearing only a nightshirt, I cracked open the door to peer into the barely lit hall. A woman with long black hair stood on the other side. She was clearly just as surprised to see me as I her. She jumped back, startled; then a slow dawning spread over her, and the stark jealousy I not only felt but also saw in her expression raked over my frayed nerve endings.

"I'm looking for Reyes Farrow," she said, her voice low, as though not wanting to disturb the neighbors. "I'm Sylvia Starr."

I knew who she was, but why in the hell was she showing up at Reyes's apartment so early in the morning? I decided to call her on it.

"This is his apartment, and it's way too early to receive visitors."

She blinked, appalled, but I wasn't sure if it was my tone or the fact that another female was in her love interest's apartment.

She tried to hand me her card. "Can you ask him to call me? We need to set up a time for an interview I'm doing for *News at Seven*."

Refusing to take the card, I let her hand hang in the air. "I think, Ms. Starr, he's made it clear he doesn't want an interview."

Anger surged out of her in a hot wave. "And you are?"

I couldn't help it. Reyes might not want me in her crosshairs, but I could handle the likes of a Barbara Walters wannabe any day of the week. I didn't say it gloatingly, but I did make sure to pronounce every syllable with infinite care when I said, "His fiancée."

A soft gasp escaped her and she stepped back. After a moment, she shook back the long locks that had fallen over her shoulders and said, "Funny, he didn't mention you the other day when I suggested we have dinner."

"That's because he had no intention of having dinner with you, Ms. Starr. There was no need. And aren't you a little early for dinner?"

"Just tell him I dropped by," she said, turning to leave.

The emotions radiating out of her were downright volatile. Reyes was right about her. She was nuts.

I retrieved my brush, but combing it through my hair proved too painful, so I tiptoed into the living room to check on the boys. While Osh lay sleeping in the exact same position I'd left him, Garrett was just waking up. Looking to my left, I figured out why. Cookie was in my kitchen cooking breakfast. She was a saint.

"Hey, Cook," I said, nodding an acknowledgment toward Garrett as he stretched in the chair, then grimaced as a jolt of pain seized him. I knew how he felt. A jolt of pain seized me with the nod. No more nodding for me. "You will not believe who showed up at Reyes's door a few minutes ago."

She stopped what she was doing and checked the delicate watch on her wrist. "This early?" she asked.

"Yep, and it was none other than Sylvia Starr."

"No," she said.

"I kid you not. She wanted an interview. She's tenacious, I'll give her that."

"I'll give her a shiner if she doesn't stay away from our boy."

I gave her a thumbs-up before I had to do something about the wetness on the side of my mouth. She'd made a pot of coffee and I drooled. Like literally. I had to get a napkin.

"Have a cup," she said, handing me a mug out of the cabinet and filling it to the brim.

"Cook, you know what I'm going through right now. And my head hurts."

"Does it feel like a raging inferno engulfed your brain?"

"Yes."

"Like a volcano went off and your everything exploded inside your skull?"

My god, she was good. "Exactly like that."

"It's caffeine withdrawal. I told you what would happen if you cold-turkeyed it."

I grabbed my head as another spasm of pain jerked me sideways, slamming my head into an open cabinet door. Which did not help at all. "What the fuck? I thought you were exaggerating."

"Nope. You'll just have to suffer through it. But I've decided to join you."

About that time, I noticed a coffee can sitting on my counter next to the eggs. A green coffee can. The color of the devil!

"What is that?" I asked, screeching as Garrett walked into the kitchen looking like a sleepy, sexy zombie.

He yawned and reached over our heads for a coffee cup.

"If you're going to suffer," Cookie said, "I'm going to suffer with you. I'm giving up caffeine, too."

I scrutinized the mug in her hand. "What are you drinking now?"

"What we're both going to be drinking for the next eight months. We're switching to decaf."

The horror that riveted through me, the absolute terror with a taint of nausea, stunned me speechless for three, maybe four seconds. I put the mug down and made a cross with my fingers, screaming, "Death before decaf!" as Garrett poured himself a cup. The fool.

"Oh, stop it." She put down her cup and tried to give me mine back. "Just give it a shot."

"I can't. That's like asking me to cheat on Reyes with Garrett."

He scowled at me as he doctored his cup of devil's blood with cream and sugar.

"Suit yourself," Cook said, picking hers up and taking a long, lingering draw.

After a few agonizing moments, the aroma started to get to me. I almost caved because of that, not because of Cookie's coffee porn. Really, who sucked on a mug like that? I leaned closer as she licked a drop sliding down the side and moaned in ecstasy. It was so wrong and yet so very, very right.

"It doesn't smell like decaf," I said, watching Garrett take a sip and waiting for his reaction. It was much the same as Cookie's, without the licking and moans, but he did seem amused by her dedication. I was surprised she wasn't gyrating against Mr. Coffee. Maybe if I stuffed a ten-spot down her bra.

"You've never even tried decaf?" she asked, sliding my mug closer.

I let the suspicion I felt show in my wary expression.

Her brows inched up, waiting. Clearly, she wasn't going to give up until I did the deed.

"Fine, I'll try it. But don't be disappointed when I spit it out in disgust. Or when I vomit. Or when my head does a three-hundred-sixty-degree spin on its axis."

"I'm not overly worried."

"Okeydokey. You've been warned." I lifted the cup as though it carried a lethal pathogen, carefully brought it to my lips, and sipped. Warm, rich, fake liquid gold slid over my tongue and down my throat, bathing my taste buds in utter ecstasy. My eyes rolled back into my head and I almost collapsed. "Oh, my god," I said, taking another sip. "This is awesome."

"Told you." She turned her attention to scrambling eggs, because eggs rarely scrambled themselves.

"Wait!" I said, causing another spasm to seize my fine motor skills for a split second before I could finish my thought. "Even though this is decaf, will it help my headache?"

"No," she said over her shoulder.

"Darn. You know, you really don't have to quit caffeine just for me."

"Are you kidding? I'd do anything for you. Although quitting caffeine is going to be hard. I'd be more inclined to sell my firstborn."

"Word."

"Want to help me with this tape?" Reyes asked as he strolled into the kitchen in nothing but pajama bottoms. Was there anything sexier than a shirtless man in pajama bottoms, even one covered in duct tape? I doubted it.

"Are you sure you're ready?" I asked in alarm as Cookie dropped several items in concert with his entrance. I was pretty sure a couple of them were eggs. And something splatty, like bacon. "Three-second rule!" I shouted without looking back at her. I didn't want to draw attention or anything. Or embarrass her.

Reyes tossed her a playful wink before saying, "Sure as I'll ever be."

I imagined the tape ripping off the skin, and another seizure hit. After a long, eventful recovery, we went into the living room and he sat on the coffee table as I went to work. I peeled ever-so-slowly, worried I'd rip the flesh from his bones. But it was incredible. The skin was pink where it had been injured, but completely closed. There wasn't a single open wound.

"What about the inside? The muscle and tendons?" I asked him. It had literally been shredded the day before.

He tested it, lifting his elbow slightly and flexing his muscles from different positions. They swayed and rolled beneath his perfect skin like a swimmer's. "They all seem to be back in working order. Just really sore."

"I can't imagine why. I've never seen anything like this." I rubbed my fingers along the newly formed skin. Even more bizarre was the fact that his tattoos, for lack of a better word, the marks he'd been born with that formed a map to the gates of hell, had re-formed in perfect symmetry with his uninjured side. Not a single line was marred or misshapen, and his flesh had been laid bare. It was a sight I would never forget. "That's how you healed so fast after getting shot that time."

"It is." He stood, tested his back before turning toward the recliner and its occupant.

"Breakfast will be ready in ten," Cookie said, "with a few added nutrients from the floor."

"Attagirl. Can't let that stuff go to waste."

Reyes was studying Osh, whose name I was still having difficulty applying to the Daeva sleeping so soundly in the plush chair. But when I thought of him as a kid instead of a thousand-year-old demon, it worked better. I tried to focus on that, because he really did look like a kid. His shoulder-length black hair needed brushing and his lashes fanned across youthful cheeks. He had a perfectly straight nose and a full mouth, as though caught between the stages of teen and adult. I had to remind myself at times what he was. And, possibly more important, what he was capable of.

"We should let him sleep," I said to Reyes.

"He's coming out of stasis now."

"You can feel it?"

"Yes," he said. "And once he's out, I have some questions for him."

"What kind of questions?" I asked, worried at the turn of events.

"He has ulterior motives. I can feel it."

"Doesn't matter. He fought with us side by side yesterday. We owe him our trust." Then I thought about Reyes's words. He could have fought for an ulterior motive just as easily as anything noble. I had no idea what that motive would be, however. "Okay, but just in case," I added before he came out of stasis completely, "what's his real name?"

"What did he tell you?"

"Osh. Osh Villione."

He nodded. "The Villione is new, but his name really is Osh. It's short for Osh'ekiel."

"Osh'ekiel. And because I know this, I have power over him?"

"You do. Just like you do me."

I grinned, never believing for a minute I had power over a man named Reyes Alexander Farrow. Or an offspring of Lucifer named Rey'aziel. Either way. "What's on your plate today?" I asked him.

He gave me a once-over, his dark eyes shimmering in the early morning light. "You."

"Do I need to leave?" Garrett asked from the sofa.

Reyes and I answered simultaneously, one with a yes and one with a no. Three guesses as to who said what.

Garrett shrugged and went back to reading the news on his phone.

"No," I said to Reyes. "I mean workwise. I have several stops to make today, and if you're going to insist on tagging along, we need to get our schedules straight."

"I don't think now is a good time to be leaving your apartment," he said.

"It's daytime. The perfect time. I still have a job to do, Reyes."

"I figured as much. I cleared my schedule. I'm all yours."

"Sweet," I said, offering him a flirtatious wink.

He bent to offer me a kiss on my earlobe and whispered, "He's out," a microsecond before he pushed me out of harm's way and lifted Osh out of the recliner by his throat.

Garrett had caught me to him and held me as Reyes threw Osh across my living room and against the wall to our bedroom.

I screamed something unintelligible as Osh fell to the floor, landing on his hands and the balls of his feet like an animal. He had just enough time to look up from underneath his lashes, his gaze furious, when Reyes body-slammed him again, this time bracing him high against the wall.

"Who summoned them?" he asked, his voice sharp with vehemence.

Osh smiled down at him, as though he'd longed for the entertainment. Then he easily broke Reyes's hold and attacked.

What happened next defied the laws of physics. They moved so fast, too fast for my mind to register as they each fought for dominance. I made out a flip here that shook the building's foundation, and a toss there that almost took out my west wall. I tried to yell for them to stop, but it did no good.

Garrett scrambled out of the way as Cookie screamed in the background, but I couldn't tear my gaze from the domestic dispute happening in front of me and all around me at once.

Their movements were animalistic, agile and graceful and yet fierce, utterly deadly like those of a seasoned predator. And they moved so fast, they disappeared for split seconds at a time.

Having no other choice, I filled my lungs with air and focused. "Stop," I said, forgoing the Latin and getting down to business.

When time slowed, the fighting began to look like an MMA fight I'd seen on TV. The MMA fighters were fast, but I could still see what they were doing. Now, everything froze except the two brawlers who were literally tearing my living room apart. They were moving at almost a normal speed. But they were still moving. So I took it to another level. I centered my energy, let it build, then sent it out in one solid wave. *"Quiesce,"* I commanded, and finally even the two prizefighters slowed until they didn't move.

It would take them a minute to realize what I'd done, to join me in my current time zone. Before that happened, I walked toward the frozen scene. Reyes had Osh on the ground, his fist barely an inch from plummeting into Osh's face. But Osh was still grinning and it didn't take long to figure out why. His elbow was headed straight for Reyes's left eye.

I should have just let them continue. If not for my apartment, a space I considered sacred, I would have let them rip each other apart.

Either time began to slip, or they were adjusting to my shift and the fight would recommence any second. I couldn't let that happen. I quickly knelt beside them, placed a hand first on Reyes's chest, and said, "Rey'aziel, *suffoca."* Then I placed my other hand on Osh's head and said, "Osh'ekiel, *dormi."*

This would either work or I would die. I was rooting for the former. I was very pro-life.

I bit down and said softly, *"Redi,"* commanding time to come back.

And boy, did it. As always, time crashed into me hard. Stunned me. But I'd taken it further this time, and the bounce-back felt like a brick wall slamming into me. I held my ground. If I was as all-powerful as everyone kept telling me, I would soon have two very cooperative boys on my hands. If not, I was about to get the ever-loving crap knocked out of me. There was no way they could stop the punches they'd thrown that fast.

As the brick wall shattered and I moved between increments of time, I felt like the world had splintered into a million pieces and gravity pulled at me from every direction until I would be ripped limb from limb. I braced myself and fought through it, tumbling back to the present where two men were in the midst of beating each other to death.

I lowered my lids and waited for the blow that would surely end my life. At the very least, it would mess up my hair. The two demons in the room may have been strong enough to absorb such powerful blows, to shake them off and go back for more, but I had a feeling my delicate ass would crumble into dust after the first one.

I clenched my teeth and waited. Nothing happened.

Well, a lot happened, but I didn't get hit. Instead, Cookie's scream shot through me like a battle cry. The man under my left hand collapsed mid-punch, going completely limp under my palm, and the other one, the only one in the room with a fallen angel as a father, doubled over, gasping for air.

I let him suffer awhile, just long enough to get his attention and for his face to turn red from either lack of oxygen or extreme anger, I couldn't be sure.

"*Anhela,*" I said, letting him breathe again.

He collapsed onto his hands and knees, drinking in huge gulps of air, and in that moment, a flashback hit me so hard and so fast, I almost buckled as well.

I lunged toward him, cradled his head, fought the images swarming my mind.

The first time I'd seen Reyes in the alley that horrible night, when he'd managed to escape Earl Walker and collapsed onto the frozen ground by a Dumpster, he'd been on his hands and knees, gasping in pain, struggling to get air into his abused body.

How could I do to him what Earl had done? How could I ever cause him pain? Refuse him air?

"I'm so sorry," I said, my eyes stinging with emotion. "I didn't mean to do that."

He pulled away to look at me and flashed me a pained grin. "Good girl," he said, and I felt pride well within him, a fact that astonished me. "You're getting more and more powerful every day. Just like I said you would."

"I didn't mean to do that, Reyes. I'm so sorry."

"No," he said, coughing into a shoulder, "no, that is exactly what you need to learn to survive. You did the right thing."

Cookie's scream slowly died down and ended with a little squeak as Reyes and I looked at the sleeping beauty on my floor.

"He didn't summon the Twelve, Reyes."

"Dutch," he began, but I held up a hand to stop him.

"I know what you're going to say. He was the only one who could have. But there are others on this plane we don't know about. For all we know, your father could be on this plane. He could have allowed them to escape, then followed them through the gate."

He stiffened. "It would be just like him to send the Twelve after us. He used them for his dirty work. They were created for his dirty work. And his entertainment."

"See? Osh didn't do it. I can feel his desire to help us just as easily as you can. His desire for us to win. He's not exactly a fan of your father's. Why would you attack him like that?"

Still shirtless, Reyes lowered himself to a sitting position, his wide shoulders resting against Sophie, and braced an arm on one knee. I knelt beside Osh, touched his face. He looked like an angel. He looked like a child.

"I don't know," Reyes said. "I'm getting desperate. If we don't find out who summoned them, who controls them, we may never win this."

"We have to," I said, matter-of-fact. "For Beep, Reyes, we have to."

"I know." He nodded toward Osh. "What is it about him that you trust so much?"

"I'm not really sure. I feel like he's . . . important. That's all."

"If you'd seen him in hell—"

"The same can be said about you, Rey'aziel," I reminded him.

"Point taken. By the way," he said, looking at the mass destruction he'd caused, "how the fuck *did* you completely incapacitate two of the strongest demons ever to walk through the fires of hell?"

I shrugged. "Latin. Works every time. Though so does English and Ancient Aramaic and Farsi and pretty much any of the thousands of languages we know. Not sure why Latin. It just feels right. You know, when I wake him up, he's going to be pissed."

The wickedest Cheshire grin I'd ever seen spread across Reyes's lovely face. "I'm counting on it."

Cookie squeaked. I had to agree with her.

Turns out, angry demons actually do wake up swinging. I was sure I'd heard that somewhere. Maybe growing up in church or at a séance in middle school where a girl named Rachel Dunn said she'd been in league with the devil since she was seven. Because she'd been so young, I always assumed she'd been talking about little league. Probably coach pitch, but one never knows. It could have been juniors. She could have been an aficionado.

After I soothed an extremely angry OshKosh—at the same time learning that calling him OshKosh did not help his mood—he stormed out of the apartment, his temperament blisteringly hot. And a small part of him had been hurt by Reyes's accusation. Not the attack itself, though. He seemed to thrive on violence, but I'd felt the same reaction from Reyes. They were like boys wrestling in a backyard called Charley's apartment.

"It's all fun and games until someone loses an eye," I reminded them when they literally growled at each other. "Or a testicle." I stepped between them when they came within reach of each other. "Do not make me angry again."

Instead of challenging me, or possibly out of respect, Osh left.

"Eggs?" a very nervous Cookie asked from the kitchen.

Amber had come running with the sound of World War III echoing out of my apartment. I was surprised, once again, that no one had sicced 5-0 on us. Gawd, I loved calling the cops 5-0. It's the little things.

Fortunately, Amber had missed the best, most violent parts of the morning, but she saw Osh storm out and took it upon herself to glare at me all through breakfast. Me! Her favorite albeit only and not particularly blood-related aunt! To say the tension could have been cut with a knife would have been an understatement. A regular knife wouldn't have scored it. Maybe a machete. A really sharp one. Like *Kill Bill*–katana sharp.

As worried as he was, Garrett left soon after. He had a date with a skip and a cool five grand if he brought him in. Reyes took his leave to visit George, his deliciously sexy shower, as I opted for another cup of devil's blood and a quick check to see what was on the agenda for the day. According to my online scheduler, which I never actually used, I was scot-free. I could whittle away the day if I wanted to. Sadly, that was not the case. Despite the raging state of my headache, I had things to see and people to do. I was just about to head to my own shower, the less spectacular but just as useful Roman, when Cookie barged in.

"Turn to Channel 7," she said, taking up my remote and turning to channel 7, leaving me to wonder why she told me to do it at all.

The TV blared to life, causing my ears to bleed before she turned down the volume.

"Though Reyes Farrow had no comment," the newswoman said into the camera, the same one who'd assaulted Reyes in the bar, "he did assure me that his lawyers are looking into the matter. Back to you, Tom."

"What is she talking about?" I asked Cookie.

"Robert. She said that Reyes and his lawyers are looking into suing not only the city, but Robert as well, since he was the lead detective on Reyes's case ten years ago."

"Reyes is going to sue Uncle Bob?" I asked, confounded.

"No, Reyes is not suing anyone."

I turned as Reyes entered the room in a towel.

"But she said other things," Cookie said, sending a worried expression toward Reyes. And I had to hand it to her. Her gaze dropped to the towel only once. Maybe twice. "She seemed to know an awful lot about you. About what you were like in prison. And how you reacted during the trial."

"Really?" I asked, pinning him with an accusing glare. "You must have had a lot to say yesterday."

He shrugged. "All she got out of me was 'no comment' and 'stop touching my ass.'"

Ugh. He just had to say that. He knew how I felt about other women fondling his ass. Normally it was kind of funny, since I got to touch it anytime I wanted, but for some reason, the thought of news chick touching those steely buttocks did not sit well with Betty White. Her right ventricle contracted in a jealous rage.

Reyes sucked air in through his teeth when Betty's reaction hit him. That kind of jealousy felt like microscopic razor blades slicing across the skin. It was painful and oddly seductive. That combined with the towel, and I'd never leave my apartment.

"She showed up here this morning, hoping for that interview," I told him.

He frowned and a spark of anger flared to life inside him. At least I knew he hadn't invited her.

"What did you tell her?"

"No," I said, tearing my gaze away to address Cookie. "What kinds of stories? What exactly did she talk about?"

Cookie turned off the morning news and put the remote back on the side table. "She said that he saved a man's life during a lockdown and that he took out three assassins sent to kill him on his first day in the general area thing. Whatever that's called."

"Neil Gossett," I said through clenched teeth, hunting for my phone. "And it's called gen pop."

"Deputy Warden Gossett?" Reyes asked me. "He would know better."

"No, he *should* know better." I punched his name into my contacts and pressed the number to his cell. Phone. Not prison. They didn't have phones in prison cells as far as I knew, not that Neil was actually *inside*.

"Well, if it ain't Charley Davidson," he said, answering in a most chipper mood. If he'd seen the newscast, he had to know why I was calling.

"Hey, Neil," I said, being chipper right back.

Cookie leaned in and whispered, "I'm heading to the office. Stop by before causing any trouble."

I gave her an incredulous look and pointed to myself in question.

"What's up, sweet cheeks?" Oh, yeah, Neil knew. He was being way too nice. We'd gone to high school together, and the only time he was nice to me was when he wanted to date my sister, Gemma.

"Well, for starters, Reyes and I are affianced. And we have a bun in the oven. Her name is Beep."

"That's not a name you hear every day."

I didn't see Neil for ten years after high school, and when I did, it was only because of Reyes. Neil was a deputy warden at the state pen in Santa Fe, where Reyes was residing. But today would mark a new era in our friend-ish-ship. I was about to bust his hussy ass.

"While we're on the subject, did you just happen to spill your guts to a very pretty yet skankish newswoman lately who may or may not have been asking questions about the father of Beep?"

"You make it sound so dirty."

"Neil," I said, appalled. "Isn't that, like, against regulations or something?"

"Technically, yeah. But she wined and dined me."

"Meaning she got you drunk enough to spill your slutty guts."

"Something like that."

"You are such a slut."

"I am. I really am. But she was a charmer."

"Yes, I'm sure she was."

"No follow-through, though. After all the flirting and innuendo, she said she was saving herself for Superman. So, yeah, she was a nut. It's become a pattern."

"Women looking for Superman?"

"No, nutcases hitting on me."

"Can't say I didn't warn you. You're one of those men who wants a lady in public but a whore in the bedroom."

"Um, that's pretty much every man alive."

"Oh, right. My bad. Well, don't get any STDs in your quest for happiness."

"Is that the only reason you called? To bust my balls?"

"Duh." I hung up. At least we knew who news lady's source was. Not that it did anyone any good, but it killed the curiosity burning inside Betty White.

11

"A wine, please."
"Ma'am, this is McDonald's."
"Okay, a McWine, please."
—MCDONALD'S DRIVE-THROUGH, 2 A.M.

I let the scalding water wash over my aching head while dodging a stray departed animal that was part Rottweiler and part waterfowl. Sharing a shower with a hundred-pound Rottie was not my idea of sterile, even if she was incorporeal. And there were safety concerns. I could slip and break something vital.

Alas, Artemis didn't care. She jumped on a stream of water as it splashed against the tub floor, her ears cocked and ready. She growled at it, focusing all her attention on stopping the rogue water stream when another popped up and demanded her immediate attention. The water surged right through her, of course, but she didn't seem to notice as she pounced, growling to give it a stern warning. To give them *all* a stern warning. No splashing allowed! So it is written. So shall it be done.

Just when the throbbing in my head had dulled to an excruciating but nonstabbing ache, a shrill voice sliced through the air straight to the center of each and every pain synapse Barbara had.

"Someone stole my body!"

Oh, my god. I slammed my lids shut and gritted my teeth in agony. She'd scared Artemis off, too. The big baby.

The offending woman stuck her head through the shower curtain. "It's gone! You have to find it!"

I scrubbed my face and turned off the shower. Clearly the day was going to proceed as usual: hectic and slightly bizarre.

"Do you remember where you last saw it?" I asked her, reaching for a towel.

A young girl—perhaps sixteen, with shoulder-length hair dyed the dull color of charcoal—stood back and let me dry off before answering.

However, the second I slid the curtain aside, she started in. "You have to find it. I think my ex-boyfriend stole it. He was cray-cray." Her clothes were modern and a touch dark, so she couldn't have been dead very long. And the slang would suggest a recent death as well.

"Okay, but really, where was it when it was stolen?"

She blinked at me. "In my grave at the cemetery. Where else would it be?"

"Oh, so you're not an unsolved homicide or anything?"

She held out her wrists, her shoulders rounding as she tucked her chin. Several cuts marred her perfect skin. A few were deep enough to sever the arteries, and blood streaked down from them and over her palms.

"I'm sorry I did it, if that helps. I had no idea what it would do to my family."

I wrapped the towel around me.

"I'm going to hell, aren't I?"

"No, hon. If you were going to hell, you'd already be there. Don't even get me started on that all-suicides-go-to-hell crap. There are always loopholes. Extenuating circumstances, so to speak."

"That makes sense. I was adopted. I don't know anything about my birth parents, but I think they were crazy, too."

"You think you're crazy?"

"Yeah, but not like drama queen crazy. I mean like literally. I could never keep my head right, you know? I could never keep facts straight or remember things like others could. They put me in special education when I was a kid, and some girls called me stupid."

She was still a kid, though I kept that to myself.

"Even my best friends growing up turned against me and laughed at me."

I knew the feeling.

"I think maybe my mom was on drugs or something when she was pregnant with me, you know? Anyways, that's why I did it, I think. My head just didn't work right. But my mom—" She hid behind her hair and wiped the back of a palm across her eyes. "My adopted mom. I just didn't know how much I meant to her."

"I'm so sorry, hon."

"I wish I could tell her I'm sorry."

Caving completely, I wrapped an arm around her. "We'll figure out a way, okay? She'll know how much you loved her. But for now, what's this about your body?"

"It's gone!" she screeched again, and a searing knife pierced my delicate skull and plummeted into my head to scramble my already exploded brains. Poor Barbara. I didn't know how much more she could take. She wasn't the most reliable of brains to begin with.

"Yes," I said, holding my head to keep it from falling off, "I got that the first time."

I hurried and dressed so Reyes and I could make a quick pit stop at the bar before heading off to interview the suicide-note victims' families and to check out Lacey Banks's missing body. But stepping out of the apartment building, the one that had been blessed by a priest and thus offered some protection against the Twelve, proved more difficult than I had expected.

"We can go back inside," Reyes said, a sexy smile playing about his mouth as he stood behind me.

"And do what, exactly?" I was getting frustrated. I had a job to do. I couldn't be cowering around every corner, worried about one of the beasts of hell filleting the flesh from my bones.

"You have to ask?" he said, teasing.

"Please. I know exactly what you'd do."

"What?"

I did the deadpan thing before explaining. "You would call Osh over to stand guard while you went in search of the Twelve. I know you would."

He looked across the parking lot, totally busted. "I would, but I can't trust you. Or him."

"Then work, it is."

I forced my leg past the threshold of the building and waited a second for it to be ripped off. When nothing happened, I eased out into the open, praying we were right about the sunlight. After a few steps, I grew more confident. Reyes checked on things downstairs as I ran up to the office to check on Cook before we set out for the day. She'd seen a lot that morning. Not everyone could handle that kind of violence without some kind of side effect. Like horrendous nightmares or a twitchy eyelid. I hated when that happened.

But she seemed fine. A little traumatized by the demon showdown that morning and the newswoman implying Reyes was going to sue her honey bunny. Other than that, she was ay-okay. We went over my schedule for the day before I set her on the task of finding a connection between the suicide-note victims. "And I want to know more about that newswoman. Do a background on her."

"Blackmail?" Cookie asked just as Reyes walked in.

I smiled and laughed, dismissing her statement with a wave. "I've never blackmailed anyone in my life," I explained to my affianced.

"What about—?"

"That wasn't blackmail, Cook," I said, shutting her up. "That was a mutually beneficial arrangement. And can you keep trying my dad? He's not picking up."

"Maybe your stepmother's psycho and he really is sailing the ocean blue," she offered.

"My stepmother *is* psycho. That's never been in question. But not about this. Dad always makes sure we can get ahold of him. This just isn't like him."

A woman's voice drifted to us from inside my office. "They told me you were up here."

We turned as she walked through my office door. The one that led to the stairs that led to the bar that Reyes usually ran. She wore four-inch heels and sauntered up to us like she owned the place.

"You," she said, pointing toward Reyes, "are a difficult man to catch." When Reyes didn't answer her, she turned toward me. The woman whose back he'd been caressing. She held out her hand. "So nice to see you again."

"And in real clothes this time," I said, still flinching over the fact that our first meeting involved pajamas and bed head.

She hooked her fingers around mine as though she expected me to kiss her hand. "Aren't you darling?" she asked.

That wasn't patronizing at all. "Well, thank you. My fiancé seems to think so." I leaned back into his shoulder, at which point he placed an appreciative kiss on my head. Right on cue. It kind of hurt, since Barbara had exploded from lack of caffeine, but I sucked it up.

While Cookie looked on longingly and a soft sigh escaped her, Sylvia Starr's emotions were more along the lines of sociopathic. They leapt inside her, and a boiling hatred spilled out in hot, razor-sharp waves. Yet she managed to keep her cool. That superstar smile plastered on her face didn't waver an inch. It was creepy.

Feeling the same thing I did, Reyes wrapped his arm all the way around my waist and pulled me close. How did she even get in? It was eight o'clock in the morning and the restaurant wasn't open yet. She was a sweet-talker.

Neil had been right. She probably knew how to talk her way into any situation. Or out of one.

"I'm Cookie," my faithful assistant said, standing behind her desk and holding out her hand. "I see you on TV all the time."

"Well, thank you."

I wasn't sure how that was a compliment, but okay.

The sugary texture of her voice was making my teeth ache, but she turned back to Reyes and spoke again nonetheless. "I was wondering if now would be a good time for that interview."

Anger welled within him, so I intervened. "Actually, we have some people to interview ourselves. We're on a case at the moment, but thanks."

"A case?" she asked. Not me. She had yet to speak directly to me. It was weird how everything she said, even to other people, was directed toward Reyes. As though he had to answer for us simple girl-folk.

"A case," I said, pointing to the *front* door, the one she didn't come through, that had my name on it.

"Oh, right. You must be the Davidson in Davidson Investigations."

Oh, my god. She didn't even look at me when she said it. It was as though she would almost look at me, but her gaze would stay locked on Reyes.

"If you'll excuse us," I said, gesturing toward the door. The front door.

"Another time," she said, turning and going back the way she'd come in.

I stood stunned. Not for very long, but still. "She's nuttier than a pecan tree."

Reyes didn't say anything. He just glared.

"Okay, well, that was fun," I said to Cook.

"I liked her, except her homicidal attachment to your affianced," she said.

"You noticed that, did you? I wasn't sure you would with all the work you're doing."

"Mm-hmm." Cookie sat concentrating on her computer screen, really into that game of spider solitaire.

I patted her cheek, and said, "Okay, then. I'm off to affect somebody's life in an irreversible devastating way."

"Good luck," she said without looking up.

I think it was her lack of caffeine that morning that made her zone out. "And get some work done. I'm not paying you minimum wage to play solitaire."

"I'm on it, boss."

Gawd, she was good.

.

"I was hoping to avoid that," Reyes said as we made our way to Misery. Sometime during the evening, Uncle Bob had had Noni detail her innards, removing the blood I'd smeared across her seats and floorboard. I must've resembled Carrie when I left the asylum that first time yesterday. And the second time. And red was not my best color. Thank the gods Ubie'd had her detailed, because blood simmering under the New Mexico sun was never a good scent choice for cars. I preferred pine. Or plants of the tropics. But I was most fond of the one I had now, mocha cappuccino. Odd how that flavor came in a scent for one's car. It turned the inside of Misery into a little coffeehouse on wheels. A decaf coffeehouse, sadly.

Our first stop was the widow of yesterday's suicide-note victim. Of course, she didn't know she was a widow yet. I'd have to be very, very careful with my words.

"Since you're going to follow me around all day, I've decided to pretend you're my bodyguard," I said to Reyes as he followed me up the walk to the woman's house. "And I am very, very wealthy. So wealthy, I need a bodyguard."

"I am your bodyguard," he said, scanning the area for any sign of the Twelve. "And you are very, very wealthy."

"No, I'm not. You are. And you can't be my bodyguard for reals. You're my affianced." I rang the doorbell. The Chandlers had a modest house in the Northeast Heights with a well-manicured lawn and lots of nonindigenous flowers. "Affianceds can't be bodyguards to their better halves. Bodyguards have to keep their distance," I explained as we waited. "They can't get too attached to their subject matter."

"Their subject matter?"

"The body they're guarding. They have to keep a cool, level head and stay detached, lest they let their emotions overrule their better judgment. Thus, I am pretending—emphasis on the *pre* and the *tend*—that you are my bodyguard. I need a Chihuahua with a diamond collar."

I glanced at my button-down, soft leather vest hanging to my knees, and my boots. I had to wear the knee-highs so I could bring Zeus along. When I carried him out in the open, people hurt themselves trying to get away.

"I so don't look like a woman with a bodyguard. I look like a bohemian."

"I like bohemians."

I glanced up at him. "Are you sure you're okay? You were almost ripped apart yesterday, and today you seem . . . off."

He glanced around again. "I just think we should be looking at the bigger picture."

"Which is?" I asked as the door opened.

"Twelve angry hellhounds that want nothing more than to rip out your throat and sup on your blood."

Thankfully, there was a glass door between Mrs. Chandler and us, and Reyes had said those last words softly.

I pasted on my best sympathetic smile as she opened the glass door. She was a pleasant-looking lady in her mid-fifties with short brown hair she probably had done every week at the beauty shop. After digging out my PI license, I explained who we were, introducing Reyes as my associate, Mr. Farrow, and why we were there. I doubt she heard a word we said.

She let us in, her eagerness to find her husband making her desperate. I was surprised at the lack of uniforms. I'd expected a cop to be there or an FBI agent. She sniffed into a tissue as we sat in her pristine living room.

"I'm so sorry, Mrs. Chandler," I said, as she sniffed again. "Was that your husband's handwriting on the suicide note?"

"No," she said, raising her chin. "Like I told the police, that's his handwriting when he's drunk."

"He'd been drinking?"

She stood and rummaged through a drawer before coming back and showing us a coin. No, a chip. A sobriety chip from Alcoholics Anonymous.

"This is his nine-year chip. He carries his ten-year chip with him everywhere. He hasn't taken a sip of alcohol since . . ." She turned away from me to gather herself. When she turned back, her expression was filled with vehemence. Determination. "He hasn't taken a single sip in all that time. Then suddenly he's drinking *and* suicidal? Just out of the blue like that?"

"Mrs. Chandler, do you know any of these people?" I asked, slipping three pictures out of the file I carried and showing them to her. They were the other three suicide-note victims. Perhaps if we could find a link, we could figure out who was doing this. And why.

But my bigger motivation for being there was her husband. Every once in a great while, I would get lucky and the departed victim would still be hanging out at his old stomping grounds. I glanced around but saw no one. Though I did catch a glimpse of a stuffed shi-tzu on a bookshelf. Stuffed animals freaked me out.

"I don't recognize any of them, though this one looks faintly familiar," she said, handing back the pictures and pointing to Anna Gallegos. "Are they involved in my husband's disappearance?"

"No, not exactly. Did the police tell you your husband's suicide note wasn't the first they've seen lately?"

"Yes, they mentioned that. They said there was another man and a woman missing as well. Why aren't they doing anything?" She was starting to panic. "Why aren't they looking?"

"Mrs. Chandler, they are. That's why we're here, too. We're looking in on the case."

"A private investigator?" she asked, surprised.

"I'm also a consultant for APD. Has your husband had any problems with anyone lately? Any fights with coworkers or—?"

"He's an accountant for a law firm. He has issues every once in a while with a lawyer or an investigator billing beyond what they actually worked, but nothing that would explain this."

I nodded, asked her a few more questions along the same lines, but I got the feeling Reyes was making her nervous. He stood and looked down the halls occasionally. Peeked into her kitchen. Moved aside a curtain to look through the window.

"If you think of anything," I said, handing her my card as she led us out, "please give me a call."

"I will. Please find him," she said, breaking down again. A Buick pulled into the drive with Oregon license plates. Mrs. Chandler ran to the car and hugged the woman getting out of it. They looked like sisters, so I left them to it and walked Reyes to Misery.

"This would work much better if you'd relax."

"This would work much better if there weren't hellhounds after my fiancée."

He had a point.

Next stop was an elementary school where the sister of the local female victim was working. The sister taught third grade. As much as I hated to interrupt her class, I needed to get on this. I made Reyes wait for me outside, because nothing about a man loitering outside an elementary school seemed creepy. But I couldn't risk him making her nervous.

After a thorough cavity check, a retinal scan, and the drawing of a sample of my DNA, I was allowed to walk two doors down the hall of the school to Marie Gallegos's classroom.

Ms. Gallegos was a petite Hispanic woman with a short bob and pretty face. And she was just as distraught as Mrs. Chandler. I asked her the same questions and showed her the same pictures as we stood at her desk, to no avail. The children were working quietly at their desks. The brave ones glanced up on occasion, curious as to what we were talking about. The really brave ones stared openly. But the longer we talked, the more restless they became. I was worried we'd have a mutiny on our hands if I stayed much longer. Either that or Reyes would be arrested for hanging out at a schoolyard.

"If you think of anything," I said as I let her get back to her third-grade math class before they drew blood, "please give me a call."

"Thank you, I will."

I put the pictures away, then headed back to the office to check out, hoping another cavity search wouldn't be necessary. My ass could take only so much probing. Reyes would get jealous.

"Ms. Davidson," Marie whispered just as I reached the office. She'd opened the door and was peering around it.

I walked back to her with fingers crossed.

"Anna did mention something rather odd the day before she disappeared. I only just remembered it."

"Anything will help," I assured her, trying not to get my hopes up, and failing.

"She said that a woman got in touch with her, claiming to be an old friend and wanting to have coffee. But then she said the strangest thing."

"And what was that?"

"She said she knew the woman, but they had never been friends. In fact, she said she'd felt threatened by her at one time. She seemed genuinely worried about the call, but still laughed it off."

That could have been a very costly mistake. "Did she meet with her?"

"I don't know. I know she didn't want to, but my sister was a people pleaser."

I knew the type. I'd been accused of being one myself once or twice. I took out my memo pad and made a note to check Anna's phone records. "Did she give you a name?"

"She did, but I can't remember what it was. I'm so sorry." Guilt engulfed her.

"No, please don't be. Did she ever mention a Phoebe Durant?"

"Not that I recall." She glanced down, and the pain that leached out of her hit me like a wall of sorrow.

I strained against the crushing weight of it, the direction of her thoughts so tragic, so heartbreaking. And there was nothing I could do to reassure her.

"She's not coming back, is she?"

I lowered my head, too, and answered her as vaguely as I could. "I wish I could say."

She nodded and closed the door between us.

All in all, the morning had been a complete bust. And my headache was becoming a pain in the ass. No other family members remembered anything about a phone call from an old friend. They didn't recognize any of the other victims or their names. And they couldn't say for certain if their missing family members were having any trouble at work or in their personal lives.

Uncle Bob had Anna Gallegos's phone records, but all the calls she received had been accounted for. The only people who'd called her were family or close friends.

"Maybe this woman called her at work," I said into the phone as I ordered my usual mocha latte at the Java Loft, only in decaf. The woman behind the counter gazed at me like I'd crossed my eyes and stuck my tongue out at her. "Can you get those records?" I asked, ignoring her.

"Sure can," Ubie said. "She worked at the Plant Source, a nursery over on Candelaria."

"Thanks. Let me know."

"Oh, before I forget," Ubie said, "Zeke Schneider, the guy who attacked you yesterday, was in prison, all right, but he was down in Cruces. Got out a couple of months ago. The guy who died in Santa Fe was his father, Zeke Schneider Sr."

"Sounds like he had a healthy home life."

"Doesn't it? There was apparently a clerical error when recording the man's death, and they accidentally entered the wrong Schneider. And guess who Zeke Schneider Jr. worked for when he got out."

"God?" He said *guess*.

"Bruno Navarra."

"The crime boss?"

"The crime boss who was in prison with Reyes."

I turned and looked out the plate-glass window at my intended. He leaned against a post outside, keeping a watch on the horizon. The guy took his bodyguard responsibilities very seriously. He just needed a suit and some dark aviator shades. As it stood, he looked more like a supermodel relaxing in the sun. Poor guy.

"Thanks, Ubie. I'll get back to you."

"We still on for dinner tonight?" he asked.

"Does it involve food?"

"I sure the hell hope so."

"I'm in." I had no idea there was a dinner in my very near future, or what the special occasion was, but who could say no to free food? "Later, gator."

I hung up and did a 360, checking out the patrons in the room. Everyone seemed legit. Or, well, alive at least. But I felt a departed close by. I could feel the coolness radiating off one, the gentle vibrations that hummed through me whenever one was near, and I caught the subtle hint of a cologne I hadn't smelled in years. White Shoulders. It had been one of my favorites growing up.

Seeing nothing out of the ordinary, I dialed Neil Gossett's number for the second time that day.

"If you're going to call me a slut again, you can save your energy. I already know."

"Wait, did she call you back?" I asked. "You're not actually going out with her?"

"No. And no." Disappointment saddened his voice.

"Oh, okay. I'm calling about another matter." I was half whispering into the phone even though Reyes was outside. But just in case . . . "Was there anything between Reyes and a crime boss by the name of—"

"Bruno Navarra, aka Bumpy."

"Um, yes. That was a really good guess."

"You know the three guys I told you about who attacked Farrow his first day in gen pop and he took them out in less that thirty seconds?"

I knew the story well. Neil had been a rookie guard, and what Reyes did that day had affected him greatly. He'd never forgotten it. "Of course."

"They were Bumpy's men."

"No way."

"Sorry to say. Bumpy's not a nice guy."

"And did a man named Zeke Schneider Sr. know him?"

"He did. Why?"

I couldn't tell him any more than that. I was taking a huge risk as it was. If anyone figured out my connection to Zeke Schneider Jr., I could be accused of murdering him.

"Let's just say that the man makes an impression."

"So, you're not mad at me anymore?"

"Gossett, I'm not mad at you. I met the woman this morning. She has a silver tongue, I'll give you that."

"Told you. So, did she mention me?" he asked, his voice filled with hope.

"You're such a slut."

12

I don't want you to forget this moment.
In about a week, I'll come up with a scathing retort.

—T-SHIRT

I'd called Dad and left another message while we headed toward the nursery where Anna Gallegos worked, but we were met with the same answers the families had given us. No one knew anything. Even Anna's closest coworker—a man everyone called Gallagher because of his resemblance to the comedian—had no clue about the phone call. Anna had never told him.

So we were at a dead end once again.

"I feel like a salad," I said as we climbed back into Misery.

"You don't look like a salad," Reyes answered.

"Maybe it's the fact that we are at a nursery with plants and crap. You should totally make me one of your famous taco salads with grilled chicken in green chile and top it off with guacamole and sour cream."

A delectable dimple appeared at one corner of his mouth. "I have a famous taco salad?"

"You do now. You should call it the Charley Davidson."

He laughed softly as he buckled his seat belt. "Last week you wanted me to name a burrito after you."

"And?"

"The week before that, it was a burger with both red and green chile."

"Yes, Christmas style, like me. I'm multicolored and sparkly like Christmas. I'm not sure what your point is."

I steered Misery back to the bar, turning south on Wyoming as Reyes lounged in my passenger's seat, his powerful legs slightly parted. He rested one arm across the console, his long fingers absently touching the gearshift between us. I decided to find out a little more about this crime boss before I told Reyes that the man who'd attacked me worked for Bumpy. Angering most people wouldn't get you killed. A crime boss was not most people.

He sat staring out the window and seemed a thousand miles away when he said, "If you keep looking at me like that, we aren't going to make it to the grill."

"I'm just so amazed at how fast you healed."

He turned toward me. "You can, too, once you figure it out."

"I hope I never have to."

"I hope so, too. What else did you find out from your uncle?"

"What?" I asked in alarm. "Nothing."

He paused a long moment before he said, "About the suicide-note victims."

"Oh," I said, relaxing, "not much. They still haven't found a connection. We just don't have much to go on at this point. They're sending the notes off to the crime lab. Hopefully there will be some residual evidence that we missed."

He nodded.

He'd been so quiet all day, it really had me wondering. "Are you okay?"

"Don't I seem okay?"

"I don't know." I slowed to a stop at a light and regarded him suspiciously. "You seem a little distant today."

He turned to look out the window again. "I'd be better if you didn't lie to me."

Damn it. I should have known he'd feel that. "It's nothing."

"Then why lie?"

"Because," I said, having no plausible excuse. And I usually rocked at coming up with excuses on the fly. I thought about saying, *Because you're a sissy and I'm not,* but that made no sense even to me. "I need to do some research before I can explain."

We entered a packed bar with nary a seat to be found. Reyes went straight for the kitchen as I hunted down the little *señoritas'* room to relieve myself for the ten thousandth time that morning. Either decaf produced more urine than regular coffee, or Beep was already pressing on my bladder.

"It's hormones," Cookie said as she came out of the end stall.

"Oh, fancy meeting you here."

"I came down for lunch, but there are no tables."

"I noticed. Wait, hormones are making me pee every five minutes?"

"Yep. At first it's hormones. The third trimester is a different story entirely. There's nothing like a baby kicking your bladder for the sheer enjoyment of it."

"Well, that sounds fun."

"Did you get anything good today?" she asked me.

As we washed our hands, I told her what we didn't learn and the miniscule bit that we did. "Uncle Bob is getting the phone records from Anna's work. Hopefully whoever called her is the key to all this."

"Perfect. I'll cross-reference them. If there are any names they don't recognize, I'll see if Anna's sister remembers her mentioning them."

"That'd be great." We stepped out into the restaurant and were met with the dull roar of conversation.

"I'm getting mine to go, if you want to come up," Cookie began, then stopped short.

Uncle Bob was sitting at the bar, looking at a menu.

"I might," I said, watching her drink in my surly uncle. "I lied to Reyes and he busted me. Now might not be the best time."

"What did you lie about this time?" she asked, keeping her gaze zeroed in on Ubie.

I frowned. "You act like I lie every day."

"You do. I know because you suck at it."

"Why does everybody say that? I rock at lying. I could totally be a criminal lawyer."

She patted my head. It hurt. "What did you lie about?"

We stood waiting by the to-go counter for Cookie's order. I glanced around to make sure Reyes wasn't hovering nearby. "I believe the guy who attacked me at the asylum was sent by Bruno Navarra."

That was enough to get her attention. "The crime boss?"

"The one and only. Remember the three assassins sent for Reyes while he was in the big house?"

"Yes."

"Bumpy sent them."

She gaped at me. "No."

"Yes."

"No, for reals."

"Yes, for reals. Zeke Schneider Sr. worked for him there, and Zeke Schneider Jr. was working for him on the outside."

"So, is Bumpy still in prison?"

"I actually don't know. I didn't think to find out. I have to do some research before I tell Reyes."

"Fine, I'll find out and let you know."

"Thanks, Cook! God, I love research. Especially when you do it."

She turned her attention back to Ubie.

I laughed softly. "I'll wait here for your food. Go talk to the man. You haven't seen him in—" I looked at my invisible watch. "—hours."

She ran her hands over her hair—not sure why, since it stuck out every which way regardless—and did a quick shimmy before heading toward her main squeeze. Uncle Bob's expression when he saw her was priceless. Those two were so in love, it hurt. Like literally. My head was killing me, and contemplating their love only made it worse. And it was kind of nauseating.

"Can I help you?" Reyes asked, sidling up to the to-go counter like he owned the joint.

"I would like a Reyes Farrow's famous taco salad."

"I don't think Reyes Farrow has a famous salad, taco or otherwise."

The noise had died down, as it always did when he entered the restaurant. "I bet he can whip something up."

"He does have a taco salad. I'm just not sure how famous it is."

"That'll do."

He pretended to take out a pad and hold it with his left hand while his right retrieved an invisible pen from behind his ear and wrote down my order. I smiled and propped my elbows on the counter, plopping my chin into my palms to watch him. I felt the longing glances and hoped Reyes could shake them off. He wasn't really himself today, and I didn't want anything to rock his boat off center. I figured getting almost ripped apart and then healing overnight took its toll. He was still recovering. He had to be.

He put the pen back, tore a page out of the order book, then passed it to Sammy, who was cooking today.

Sammy's brows slid together. "You spelled *anchovies* wrong," he said.

"No," I called to him. "Taco salad."

"Oh, then he's a worse speller than I thought." He winked at me, playing along.

Reyes copied me, propping his elbows on the counter and leaning close until his mouth was at my ear. "What are you hiding from me?" he asked, his breath warm against my cheek.

I turned my face into him, inhaled his earthy scent. He always smelled like a lightning storm at dusk, but he also smelled like sandalwood, one of his favorite soaps.

"You show me yours and I'll show you mine."

"Despite what you may think, I am not keeping secrets from you. I have nothing more to hide."

"I beg to differ. What's my name?"

He leaned back for a better look at me. "If I tell you, I'll lose you."

I placed both my hands on his face. "That's not possible."

After slipping on a sad smile, he said, "I'll lose you forever," then turned and went back to the kitchen to work on our lunch.

I couldn't ever remember seeing him that sad. What did he know, and what secret did he think I was keeping from him?

Since there were no tables in the bar, Reyes and I ended up eating in the kitchen in silence. He knew I'd been lying earlier, but he'd also been talking about some secret I was keeping since yesterday. What happened yesterday that made him think I had some huge secret I was keeping from him?

I shook my aching head, befuddled.

"Where to now?" he asked, taking my salad bowl.

"I have to make a quick stop at the Sunset Cemetery and check on a grave there."

"I'll be ready in five."

I hurried to my office to get cleaned up after lunch and to check in with Cook. She'd already found Bumpy Navarra's whereabouts. Lo and behold, they were right smack in the heart of Albuquerque. He owned a series of strip malls and had a management office on Menaul, though I couldn't imagine he kept many hours there. She also had a home address and an address where he had most of his mail sent. It was another business address with no business name attached. Interesting.

"Great," I said to Cook. "Now I just have to figure out how to ditch my affianced and go talk to him."

Cookie whirled around from her computer monitor. The movement was very silver screen dramatic. "You're kidding, right? After what happened last time?"

"I know. Effing hellhounds. They're really effing up my plans for a long and prosperous life."

"Why are you using the fake F-word?"

"I don't want to use the real F-word in front of Beep." I decided to be just as melodramatic and turned in a huff to leave, but the door to my office was slightly ajar and I ran into it face-first. "Fuck," I said, holding Barbara as she absorbed the brunt of the injury. "And now I said *fuck*. Son of a fucking bitch. I'm going to be the worst mom ever."

I met Reyes at Misery, still holding on to Barbara for dear life. When he raised his brows in question, I scowled at him. He didn't ask. Smart boy.

On the way over to Sunset Cemetery, I took out my phone and dialed Ubie. He'd been called away before I got a chance to talk to him at the bar.

"Hey, pumpkin, what's up?" he asked, but he seemed distracted. Possibly even a little distressed.

"I don't understand, Uncle Bob. If someone did this to them, why take the body? I mean, why not kill the person and pretend they committed suicide?"

"Suicide is a lot harder to fake than people think. Could be that whoever is doing this is worried the medical examiner will figure it out."

"Then why even have a suicide note at all? It makes the whole thing even more suspicious and bizarre."

"Maybe they were hoping we would just give up once we couldn't find a body. Maybe they thought the note would be enough."

"I don't think so," I said, thinking—not the safest thing for me to do. "I have a theory."

That seemed to intrigue him. "Shoot."

"I think that this is very personal for the assailant. I think that whoever is doing this is making a statement. He wants people to know that the person who supposedly wrote the suicide note did not deserve the life they'd been given."

"You're getting pretty good at this stuff."

I deflated. "You already knew that."

"It's one of several working theories. But you're definitely on the right track. This is very personal, and whatever these people have in common will lead us to a suspect. I'm certain of it."

"Okay, well, let me know what you find out."

"Will do. You do the same. See you tonight."

I disconnected the call and turned into the cemetery. The Sunset Cemetery may be marinating in death, but it was not the local hangout for the departed. On the contrary. Most dead people had little reason to hang out in such a lifeless, depressing place. A simple fact that explained beautifully why I liked cemeteries so much. Not many live people. Not many dead people. Even as a child, I preferred the morbid atmosphere of an ancient burial ground over the lovely grasses of parks. People rarely died at cemeteries. Parks, on the other hand, seemed a magnet for mayhem. And the murders that happened in parks were almost always particularly brutal, as if evil fed on the innocent intentions found there. Thus, cemeteries were one of my favorite places on earth.

The girl from the shower, Lacey Banks, was standing by her grave, and she waved me over when she saw me. "You came!" she said as I stepped out of Misery.

"Of course I did. This is you?" I asked her, but she'd spotted Reyes, and her jaw fell open.

He walked a few feet from the Jeep to survey the landscape.

"Lacey?" I said, waving a hand in front of her face.

She snapped back to me. "Sorry, it's just, he's very— He's so—"

"I know. This is you?" I repeated.

"Oh, yeah. Home sweet home."

I poked around a bit before stating the obvious. "The site is completely intact. There's no sign of disturbance. What makes you think your body is no longer here?"

"Because my coffin is empty."

"What?" Her statement caught me off guard. Not sure why. "You can see into your coffin?"

"Well, yeah. Duh. If I go down there."

I had never thought of that. "But why would you want to?"

She jammed a fist onto her hip. "I am slowly decomposing. It's awesome! I want to see it in stages. You know, check out what I look like every so often. Sadly, the embalming fluid is slowing down the process drastically."

"Yes," I said, kicking at the ground with my toe, "that is a sad dilemma." The grass covering her grave was a little softer than it should have been. It did feel disturbed. It just didn't look like it.

"Oh, and I searched my ex's house. No Lacey anywhere to be found. Maybe he didn't do it after all."

"If he did, I'll find out." I called Ubie back. "Sorry!" I said before he could say anything.

"No problem. What's up?"

"Can I get a warrant to have a grave dug up?"

He laughed. "You ask the strangest things. And no. Not without some very compelling evidence as to why it should be. Exhuming a body is a serious matter."

"Darn. Well, that's the problem. There's no body in there."

"Three others are missing as well," she said to me.

"Ew, what?" I asked.

"What?" Ubie said.

"Hold on," I said to him, then turned back to Lacey. "There are three more empty graves?"

She nodded. "Yes, I checked. I can show you. They're all girls, and they were all buried within the last five years."

"Yuck," I said, wishing I hadn't asked. "Just yuck. It looks like we have a grave robber, Uncle Bob. But the site looks completely undisturbed."

"I can check with the captain, but again, exhuming a body is kind of a big deal. I'm going to need something. Some kind of evidence the grave has been seriously disturbed. Not just vandalized."

I sighed aloud. "Okay. I'll figure something out."

"Should I bring wine tonight?"

"Um, sure." I still had no idea what the hell he was talking about. "And sparkling grape juice for me."

"Got it."

We hung up again and I looked around for Reyes. When I didn't see him, alarm shot through me. The Twelve.

"No," I said, running to where I last saw him. "This is consecrated ground. They can't come on here."

"Are you looking for the guy who came with you?" Lacey asked. "He's over there."

She pointed toward the mausoleum. I hurried toward it, worried the Twelve had shown up, and spotted Reyes talking to someone. I stopped short and ducked behind a tree. He was talking to a woman. A beautiful, tall woman with hair the exact color of honey. She wore a flowing white evening gown and a million-dollar smile. And she was dead.

I caught the soft scent of White Shoulders on the breeze, and I knew she'd been at the Java Loft earlier. I'd felt a departed. It had to have been her.

She turned and saw me, said something to Reyes while gesturing toward me with a delicate hand, and flashed that brilliant smile. He didn't turn around. Instead, he turned away, and I felt the heat of his anger from where I stood.

"Time to go," I said to Lacey, hurrying back to Misery.

Being left high and dry would infuriate him, but my number one goal in life at that moment was keeping Reyes out of jail. I had a feeling the woman had been spying on me at the coffee shop. She probably overheard my entire conversation with Ubie about Bumpy Navarra. But I knew something he didn't. I knew where Bumpy lived and did business.

I'd go to the businesses first and try to get an explanation out of him. There was no telling what Reyes would do to him, and that temper could land my fiancé right back in prison. He'd spent too much time incarcerated for a crime he didn't commit. I couldn't imagine what he'd do to Bumpy if Reyes thought the man had sent Zeke after me, but I was fairly certain it would land him right back in a six-by-eight.

"But what about my body?" Lacey said.

"No worries, hon." I tapped Barbara on the temple. "I have a plan."

"Oh. Okay. So, I'll just wait here?"

"Yes. Perfect. You do that."

I jumped in Misery and turned the key just as my driver's door opened. And boy was the opener peeved.

"Oh, hey," I said, offering him my best guileless smile. "Just warming her up."

He lowered his head and glared at me. Glared! "You knew," he said, his voice deep. Accusing.

Clearly the charade was up, but I had a few things of my own to be peeved about. "You sent that woman to spy on me."

He eased forward, his anger exploding around me like aftershocks. "After that little stunt you pulled yesterday, I sent her to keep an eye on you. To make sure you were safe."

"And to spy," I said.

"You knew who Schneider worked for and you kept it from me."

I turned off the engine. "Because I also knew what you would do."

"You had no right to keep that from me."

"I was going to tell you. I just needed to talk to him first."

He stabbed me with an incredulous look, a harsh one that needed no interpretation. He thought me a fool. The laugh that followed proved that.

"Do you have any idea what he would have done to you if you'd just waltzed into his place and asked him why he sent a man to kill you?"

I fought past the sting of his opinion of me. "He didn't send him to kill me. He sent him to kill you. Remember?"

"For fuck's sake, Dutch," he said, pushing off Misery and away from me. "Will there ever come a time when you take this shit seriously?"

"I do, asswipe," I said, restarting my car. "And you can walk."

I slammed my door shut before he got back to me and floored it, leaving a trial of dust as I hurried out of the cemetery. I risked one look in the rearview. Reyes stood, furious, fists at his side as I pulled onto the road. I could still make it to Bumpy's place of business before he even figured out where the man was.

Thinking ahead, I texted Cook and told her not to let on she knew about Bumpy or his addresses. Then I told her to text them to me.

"What are you doing?" a female voice said from my passenger's side.

Jessica had decided to pop in. Wonderful.

"Go away," I said to her. "I am so not in the mood."

"He's only trying to keep you safe," she said, her voice sad. "No one has ever gone to those lengths for me, and you get mad at him every time he tries to help."

"No, I don't. He's being an ass. And he sent a spy. A spy!" A tumultuous rage roiled inside me. His true feelings about me, about what he considered incompetence, stung more than anything he could ever say to me outright. It wasn't even about the woman. It was about his belief that I could barely walk and chew gum at the same time. His reaction had proved it.

I wanted to cry. I actually wanted to cry. I never knew he thought me so incapable. So inept. Then again, I wasn't completely stupid. I picked up my phone and dialed my go-to guy.

"Hey, Charles, a little busy," Garrett said.

"Reyes thinks I'm inept."

I heard a thud and some glass breaking in the background. "No, he doesn't. Where are you?"

"Where are you? I need backup."

"I'm in the middle of a bust. Give me an hour."

"I don't have an hour. It's okay, I'll call Osh."

"See you tonight for dinner?"

"Sure." What the hell was tonight? Whatever it was, everyone was going to be there.

I called Osh, but he didn't pick up. Probably still angry about being attacked by the asswipe known as my affianced. He could just stand in the cemetery and stew all he wanted. I was going to reason with Bumpy. Though I probably wouldn't call him that to his face.

I tried his residence first because it was closer and kind of on the way in an out-of-the-way sort of way. A maid answered and said he wasn't home, so I went to the business address that lacked a business name. I pulled into the parking lot, which was in an alley, and walked around to the side entrance, the one with a door slightly ajar and music leaching out.

After gathering my nerve, I stepped inside. Once my vision adjusted to the low light, I realized it was more like a pool hall with music and a bunch of guys standing around drinking beer. The few women in the place were serving drinks and dressed in short shorts and tanks. Their heels were higher than Denise's IQ. The interesting part of my entrance was that everyone, every single gaze in the place, turned toward me.

I waved shyly. "Hi. I was just looking for a Mr. Bruno Navarra."

"What do you want with him?" someone asked. I think it was the man tending bar.

"I have a business proposition."

The woman closest to me laughed. "You're too dressed for that, honey."

The rest of the room burst into laughter at my expense as she examined me from head to toe.

"He likes a little more skin and a little less attitude, if you know what I mean."

I rocked on my heels and waited for the comedy club to die down.

A male voice wafted toward me then. "What kind of business proposition?"

Cookie had texted me a picture of Bumpy, and I recognized him at a table, playing cards.

I stepped forward and said softly, "I'd like to save your life today."

Again with the laughter, but Bumpy held up a hand and it stopped instantly.

"And who is it you're saving my life from?"

"I think you know the name Reyes Farrow."

Bumpy stilled. After a moment, he looked around as though expecting Reyes to show up. "How is Farrow?" he asked, but his tune had changed completely. Everyone sensed it and kept their snickering down.

"Angry," I replied.

He nodded. "Let's go to my office."

I had Zeus in my boot. I could only hope he would be enough if I needed to defend myself.

"Can I offer you a drink?" he asked as he led me to a cluttered office in the back.

"No, thank you."

"So, as far as I know, Farrow and I are cool. Why the sudden interest?"

In his office, away from the others, I got a good read on Bruno Navarra. The only word I could use to describe him at that moment was *afraid*. I felt genuine fear emanating out of him. If he was afraid of Reyes, why would he send a guy to take him out?

"Zeke Schneider," I said, and Navarra bowed his head.

"One of my best men. He'll be missed."

"Not that one, the other one."

Before Navarra could reply, Reyes had burst through the door, his anger bathing me in a blistering heat. He gave Navarra a once-over, then focused the full force of his anger on me.

I'd stood the minute he barged through the door and found myself backing up a little. Not because I was afraid of Reyes Farrow. On the contrary. I was still hurt. Angry.

"Farrow," Navarra said, growing more nervous by the moment. "I have no idea what this woman is talking about."

Reyes turned his anger on Navarra now, granting me a short reprieve. "You sent a man after me." He stepped closer to the crime lord's desk. "He found my fiancée first."

Navarra shook his head, bewildered.

"And even now, I'm surprised, considering our history." He pointed past Navarra, toward the wall behind him.

"Weapons down, boys," he said, raising his hands. Two men came out from behind a false wall and placed their guns on Navarra's desk. "Better?" he asked Reyes. "But I remember our past quite well. You know I wouldn't send anyone after you or your fiancée."

He wasn't lying.

"What is this about?"

"Zeke Schneider," I repeated. Before he could tell me again he was dead, I added, "Junior."

"Son of a bitch." Navarra sat back down at his desk and wiped a hand over his mouth in frustration. "That little piece of shit. The only reason he's alive is out of respect for his old man."

"Why would he come after me?" Reyes asked.

Navarra sighed. "He wanted in. I said no. His dad must've told him about you. He must've thought that if he took you out, I'd let him in." He shook his head again. "That kid is a troublemaker and a snitch. I wouldn't have let him back in if he'd given me his firstborn."

"He was a snitch?" I asked, growing a little worried. "Was he a CI for anyone?"

"Not that I know of. Mostly in prison. Used to suck any dick he could for information. Had something going on with one of the guards. His father, God rest his soul, was ashamed they shared the same name."

I did notice Navarra's use of the present tense when speaking about Zeke. He didn't know anything about what the guy was up to.

"See?" I asked Reyes while pointing to Navarra. "Handled. And without any deaths or severed spines."

"Thanks to me."

"Navarra was a complete gentleman, unlike someone else in the room. I was never in any danger, despite your low opinion of me."

"My low opinion? What the fuck—?"

"You think I'm inept, and that's fine," I said, not meaning a word of it. "But—"

"Inept?" he asked, taken aback. "I've never thought that."

"Please, Reyes, I can feel emotions just as well as you can. I felt your reaction, your *gut* reaction, in the cemetery."

He ground his teeth together. "If you're going to read my emotions, at least read them correctly. I do not think you inept. On the contrary. I was just amazed that you would insist on handling the suicide investigation, that you would prance to a cemetery to look for a body—"

"Prance?"

"—that you would try to talk to a crime boss alone, all the while knowing what you know."

"Did you say *prance*? Wait, what do I know? No, better yet, what do you think you know?"

"The wall. I know about the wall."

"What?" I asked him, baffled.

He stepped closer. Dangerously close. I could drop him. I knew that now, and I'd do it if he threatened me. "The wall. I saw it." When I still didn't understand, he lowered his voice and said, "Rocket's wall. Your name on Rocket's wall."

Realization rushed through me, causing a tingle of understanding as it laced down my spine. "That's what this is about?" I asked.

"You know it is. Rocket is never wrong. There's a reason for that, and you know your name is on that wall. You know he saw your death, and yet you rush headlong into any fucking situation that strikes your fancy." He turned away from me as though in disgust.

"Your name was on there, too," I said, raising my chin a notch.

He whirled around in surprise.

"There are always loopholes, Reyes. I found one with you. You didn't die like you were supposed to that day."

To say he was astonished would've been an understatement. He gazed at me, completely stunned, his eyes watering from the turbulence rocketing through him. "Then I should have died, and you risked your life needlessly."

"What did you just say?" I marched up to him, appalled he could even think such a thing.

"You risked your life for me." He took my shoulders into his hands. "When are you going to learn, Dutch: No one matters but you and the baby. You keep risking your life—" He threw one hand out to indicate our surroundings. "—on things that are not the least bit important." He stepped even closer. "On people who committed suicide and crazy chicks in cemeteries and—" He stopped and dropped a heated gaze on me. His voice cracked when he said in a hushed tone, "I can't lose you."

"And I can lose you?" I asked, almost screaming at him.

He lowered his head and pinched the bridge of his nose with his thumb and index finger. Then he admitted what was probably his greatest fear. "I don't know how to win. I don't have the faintest idea of how to kill the Twelve. And when I saw your name on that wall." His breath hitched in his chest. Then he focused his coffee-colored gaze on me. "If you die," he said with a savage vehemence in his voice, "I will go straight to hell and kill every demon there. Or I'll perish in the attempt."

I put my hands on his face to force him to look at me. "I'm not going to die, Reyes. Think about it. The prophecies say that our daughter—" I put a hand on my abdomen. "—is destined to destroy him. I can't die. There's another loophole; I just haven't found it yet."

"Prophecies can be misread. Misinterpreted. And they're based on fate, on events from the time of their writing. A trillion things could happen to change them."

I shook my head. "Not this time." I took his hand and put it on my abdomen. "I'll figure this out. I'm not going anywhere."

Reyes gazed at his hand. "I can feel her," he said. "She spoke to me."

"Seriously?" I pushed his hand aside and replaced it with my own. "She's never said anything to me. What the heck, Beep? Talk to me, baby."

He laughed softly, then said, "Inept?"

Embarrassed, I said, "That's what I felt."

"Then you suck at interpreting other people's emotions."

"No, only yours." I lifted my gaze to his. "You confound me."

A set of charming dimples appeared at the corners of his mouth. "Then you know exactly how I feel. But he's still a crime boss." He turned back to Navarra.

"Hey," the man said, raising his hands in surrender, "I don't have any issues with you, Farrow. You know that."

"Then we have an understanding, but just in case you're thinking of somehow repeating history and trying to control me through her," he said, arching a brow in warning, "do you remember how fast I am? How deadly?"

Navarra nodded without hesitation.

Reyes leaned toward him and raised his own hand to cover part of his mouth as though telling a secret. "She's faster."

13

Help someone when they're in trouble,
and they'll remember you when they're in trouble again.

—FORTUNE COOKIE

We left the clubhouse with a bottle of fine scotch and a bottle of sparkling grape juice. It made me happy. "Navarra is so nice," I said, and Reyes laughed.

"You see people very differently than I do."

"Word. So, can I risk my life one more time today?"

He raised a brow. "Where to now?"

He walked me to my driver's side door and I turned to him. "I thought we could enjoy the afternoon, maybe go play laser tag or something."

"Laser tag?"

"Wait." I looked around. "How did you get here?"

"I ran."

I reached into his pocket and pulled out his phone. Scrolling through his menu, I said, "You called a cab."

"But I ran to the cab when it got to the cemetery."

I giggled at the thought. "How did you know where Navarra would be?"

"I keep tabs on everyone who's tried to kill me in the past."

"Ah. That's a good habit to get into."

"I think so. But laser tag?"

My phone rang before I could give him my sales pitch. The allure wasn't the laser tag itself, but the cool uniforms and dark corners involved in playing the game.

"It's Swopes," I said, then answered with a "'Sup?"

"She's here."

"Oh, man, that sucks. Well, tell her hey for me."

I'd almost hung up to go macking on my affianced when Garrett said, "Marika. She's outside my house. Just sitting there."

"Go talk to her."

"I can't go talk to her. She has a boyfriend."

"Oh, my gawd, you're such a girl. Want me to pass her a note before gym class?"

"Get over here and do your thing."

"Are you kidding me? Reyes and I were going to take the afternoon off and play laser tag."

"Do people still play that?"

"'Parently."

"Dark corners, huh?"

"What is it about them?"

"I don't know, but it's creepy. There are kids everywhere. Get over here instead and figure out what she wants. This is your chance to get close to her. To go undercover, pretend to be her friend, and figure out what's going on."

"While she's sitting outside your house? Don't you think that's a little obvious?"

"Come on, Charles. I've done a lot of shit for you. It's your turn to repay the favor."

He did go to hell when I got him shot. I did owe him.

"Fine," I said, "but you can deal with Reyes later. He had his heart set on laser tag."

Reyes didn't really seem to mind missing laser tag. Or that I was risking my life to play go-between for Garrett and his ex sex kitten. It's all about communication. Laundering the dirty air or airing the dirty minds. Something like that. If the look he was giving me was any indication, however, we might have to find one of those dark corners ay-sap. God, the man had bedroom eyes to die for.

I called Cookie. "Did you ever find anything out about that woman Swopes was banging who may or may not have had his kid?"

She sighed. "Did you look at the memo?"

"What memo? We're getting memos now?"

"I sent a memo a week ago. I've been sending you a memo every week with a list of all the updates and my notes on all our cases for weeks now."

Holy cow. Missed the boat on that one. "Oh, *those* memos. I totally knew that."

"You're not even reading them, are you?"

"I thought they were optional." Note to self: *Stop making paper airplanes out of Cookie's memos.*

"You're using them as paper airplanes, aren't you?"

"What? No way, José. But I kind of just skimmed the last one." Skimmed the top of my ceiling fan. Stealth fighter: best design yet. I was hoping to master the F-14, but . . . "What did it say about Marika?"

While Cookie told me what she'd found out, I grew more and more in awe. "And, Garrett? For real?"

"For real. There are parts of the world where he'd be considered royalty. And now this? If this baby is who I think it is, we could write a book."

"Dude, this is the coolest thing ever," I said, pulling up to Garrett's.

"Tell me about it. No, really, take notes or something. I want to know everything."

"You got it." I hung up and pasted on a smile. "Sometimes the world is a really cool place."

"It's even cooler without hellhounds," said Reyes.

"True. Killjoy."

He grinned. "I call 'em like I see 'em. This is his house?"

"This is it."

He raised his brows either in approval or distaste. His brows were mumbling. The message wasn't quite clear. Garrett's house wasn't anything to write home about, but it was cozy and comfortable, with lots of plants and greenery outside and beer on the inside.

"Rife," I said as we walked up to the door.

"Rife?"

"I need to use more complex words. Beep will be able to hear soon. No time like the present to incorporate a more colorful vocabulary. And I definitely need to use the word *rife* more."

He laughed softly as Garrett opened the door.

"Is she still there?" he asked, craning his neck.

Since his shirt was unbuttoned, I first took in the lovely sight of his manly chest and abs. He must unbutton his shirt the moment he comes home every day. Every single time I'd come over, it hung open, exposing his six-pack. Not that I was complaining.

I finally turned to see where he was looking. A maroon sedan sat down the street about half a block away. "Are you sure that's her?"

"I'm sure. She hasn't been back in months. Why now?"

"Maybe she wants to introduce you to your son?"

He ushered us in and went for a beer, grabbing one for Reyes, too. They had become quite chummy over the past few weeks. I loved it. Of course, it could be Osh's influence and Swopes was the lesser of two evils. Whatever worked.

"So, what are you going to do?" I asked as he handed me a diet orange soda, a drink he stocked just for me.

"I'm not going to do anything. You're going to go talk to her."

"Why me? She doesn't even know me, Swopes. And did you ever figure out if she's actually married to that guy I saw her with before?"

"No. I thought they were, but they aren't."

"He looked a lot like you," I said. "I'm telling you, it's weird." I used to think that had everything to do with her getting pregtastic until Cookie's report, but I wasn't going to tell Garrett that. Marika needed to spill the beans on that one herself.

I sat on his sofa. Just like the last time I'd visited, he had old books and documents scattered about the place. "Are you still trying to figure out that prophecy?"

"Sure am. That's why Dr. von Holstein is coming in. He was supposed to be here already." He checked his watch. "He's going to text me when his plane lands so I can pick him up."

"Cool. It's all very rife with mystery."

Reyes grinned as he sat down and started picking through the stacks of papers.

"Okay," I said, "what are we doing again?"

Garrett took a swig and went to look out his window. "Just go talk to her."

"You do realize how odd it's going to be when I just walk over there and knock on her car window."

"Yeah, but I don't want her boyfriend seeing us talk, just in case."

"Fine. I'll be back." I swung my legs to give me enough momentum to get out of the chair. It was a really comfortable chair.

After achieving enough escape velocity for success, I walked out and marched directly up to Marika's car. Reyes followed me to Garrett's front door, but let me go to her vehicle alone. It took a while. She was half a block away. The walk was awkward, especially after she spotted me. Should I make it clear that I was walking right up to her or pretend I was just out for a stroll instead and surprise-attack her at the last minute? So many decisions. I was just beginning to feel the pressure when her gaze locked onto mine like a laser-guided missile. Marika had dark blond hair and beautiful hazel eyes that rounded the closer I got.

I waved and knocked on her window. When she rolled it down warily, I said, "Come inside. We need to talk."

"I can't," she said. "I have the baby." She had a soft French accent that seemed very appropriate, given her background.

Her son was asleep in the backseat, and Betty White leapt in her chest cavity. "He's so adorable. Just pull up to the house and bring him in. It'll be fine."

"I shouldn't."

"Marika," I said, and she was surprised I knew her name. "He's driving me crazy, and I think I know why you did what you did." When she raised her brows in question, I said, "I know your heritage. I know Swopes's, too."

She nodded, acquiescing, and started the car. I followed behind her, wishing I'd hitched a ride. Half a block was half a block, and I'd had a tiring week thus far.

After she grabbed the baby and his diaper bag, I took the bag from her and we walked up to the door. Garrett, thankfully, had buttoned and tucked in his shirt.

"Marika," he said, offering a congenial nod.

"This is Reyes," I said, introducing them. "And I'm Charley."

"This is Zaire."

I smiled, knowing exactly where she'd gotten the name from; Cookie was that good. And Marika had a blog, so that helped. Zaire was waking up in his carrier, so I knelt beside him when she placed him on the floor next to the chair Garrett led her to. I could hardly wait to have one of my own. There was something about babies few women could resist, but I had never in a million years seen myself as a mother. Until I had no choice. Odd, that.

Garrett took a seat across from her, and with all the hubbub about not being able to talk to her, he went for the jugular the minute he settled in. "Is he mine?" he asked.

She lowered her head. It took her a moment to answer, and when she did, she did so quietly. "He is. But not for the reason you may think."

Garrett took another swig, then said, "Because you lied to me when you said you were on the pill?"

"Holy crap, Swopes," I said. "You fell for that? When will men learn?" I turned back to Zaire and was busy cooing about the gullibility of men since the dawn of man when Marika answered him.

"I did lie to you. Yes."

Garrett began a rant that could have scalded the ears of a nun, but he didn't get very far.

"He'll be powerful," she said, interrupting him. "Our son. He will be very powerful."

"What do you mean?"

I nodded encouragingly, knowing where she was going.

"You are the descendant of a very powerful voodoo queen. Probably the most famous in history: Marie Laveau."

"Yeah, I know," he said before gulping the last of his beer.

"I am the descendant of Sefu Zaire, a very powerful Haitian *houngan,* a vodou priest. Voodoo and vodou are not the same thing, but they're related. They were both born out of slavery and poor conditions. They both originated from the traditional ways of African diaspora. And they both weave Christian elements and symbolism into their beliefs and ceremonies. There are many differences as well, but I believe they are much more alike than vice versa."

"Okay," Garrett said, opening his arms in question. "What does that have to do with me?"

"Both of our ancestors were very powerful. And I believe that by combining our bloodlines, our son will be just as powerful as they, if not more so."

"That's it?" he asked. "That's what all of this is about?"

"It is."

"You do realize that's all a crock of shit."

I jumped to cover Zaire's ears. "Language, Swopes. I can reach your shins from here."

He was hurt. He'd been played like a violin at a symphony, and I understood his bitterness, but he was the one having unprotected sex. I decided to have *the talk* with Zaire while I had the chance. "Can you say STD?"

"I come from a long line of con artists," Garrett said, "most of whom spent half their lives in prison."

"Garrett," I said in my best scolding tone, "we are talking about religions here, not con artists."

"Right." He stood to get another beer. "How brash of me. So, bottom line, what's this going to cost me?" he asked.

"I'm not here for money. I just— I felt I could not be right with Bondye until I told you the truth."

"Bondye?" he asked, strolling back in with a fresh brew.

"God," Reyes said, listening in while he perused an old manuscript. "Of course."

"And I don't think this says what you think it says."

We all turned toward Reyes as he studied a copy of an ancient document, probably part of the prophecies that were supposedly about yours truly.

"What do you mean?" I asked. "You can read that?"

"Not really, but I do recognize a few words, and according to this, it's not the Twelve that is going to be the undoing of the Daughter of Light, but the Thirteenth Warrior."

"Antonio Banderas is going to be my undoing? I'm rife with anticipation."

Since Reyes didn't really know what he was reading and was picking up only bits and pieces, I took that as a sign Antonio Banderas was probably not going to be my undoing, though he was certainly welcome to try.

We got the answers Garrett had been wanting, and still the guy brooded. It was never enough. I left Zaire's parents to their discussions, and they had a lot to discuss. But Garrett was all bark and no bite. I felt the pride in him when his gaze wandered toward Zaire. And who wouldn't be proud of the little butterball?

Reyes and I headed back to the apartment building and I promised him I'd stay in while he went to check on things at the grill. I went home and had planned on doing research on the suicide-note victims, but Cookie was on top of that. If she had yet to find a connection between them, I sure wouldn't. So, I did a different type of research. After meeting Zaire, I was so caught up in the whole baby thing, I decided to see how it all worked.

I mean, I knew the basics just like everybody else, but I figured I should learn more of what was involved. It was the biggest mistake I'd made in a long time, minus that whole orange fur-lined sweater catastrophe.

Cookie came in as I sat glued to my computer screen, horrified and slightly intrigued.

"How's it going?" she asked, starting a pot of coffee.

"Everyone and their dog is mad or has been mad at me at some point today," I said absently.

"Way to stir the hornet's nest."

I didn't answer. The video I was watching was just getting good.

"They're from different parts of the country," she said, washing a couple of mugs. "The suicide victims. Two are native New Mexicans and two aren't. But I found something rather interesting." She walked over and handed me a news article. "The identical case two months ago in Los Angeles? Another note. No body found."

I tried to nod but couldn't quite manage it. What the hell were they doing to that woman?

Cookie went back to the kitchen. "Her name was Phoebe Durant, and guess where she was from?"

"Uh—"

"Exactly. Right here in Albuquerque. And guess what I did. Go ahead."

"Um—"

"You guessed it. I went to talk to Phoebe's aunt before picking up Amber from school."

That got my attention. "You did what?"

"It was in the same area, so I thought, 'Hey.' She still lives here. Works at a nursing home. Oh, this really nice elderly man wants me to smuggle Viagra to his roomie and gin in to him. He said we could start a smuggling ring. He's going to cut me in for twenty-five percent. What do you think?"

"Sounds legit. You went on an interview?"

She flashed me a nuclear smile. "I knew you were busy almost getting killed by the crime boss and playing paternity lawyer, so I thought, 'Hey.'"

"You think that a lot. But look at you. Miss Private Investigator. Now that you have a concealed carry permit, we might have to get you a fedora and a trench coat. The whole nine yards."

She shrugged sheepishly. "It was nothing. Like literally. The woman knew nothing. She and her niece were fairly close, but she said they hadn't talked much since Phoebe's move to Californ-eye-ay. That's actually how she said it. And what the hell are you watching?"

But I'd returned to the woman on the screen and didn't dare take my eyes off it. "She's pregnant," I said.

"You think? These things are going to give you nightmares and—" She stopped and leaned closer. "What is she in?"

"Shhh." I waved absently. "It's almost here."

"Is that a wading pool? In her living room?"

"Cookie, wait. She's having a baby. Look."

"What is that man doing down there?"

Shaking my head, I said, "That woman does not seem to be enjoying the moment."

"There's no reason for his hand to be doing that."

"I think he's massaging her."

"Her what? Her vagina?"

"Oh, wait!" I said, squirming in my chair. "It's coming."

We tilted our heads in unison, trying to see the baby emerge. Then, again in unison, we both cried out in horror.

I covered my mouth and spoke from behind my hand. "Is that supposed to happen?"

"Okay, seriously," Cookie said, recovering quicker than I, "who's the new guy? And why does he have a spatula?"

"What are you two watching?" Uncle Bob asked from behind us, but our gazes were superglued to the screen.

"Is that even legal?" Cookie asked. "It just seems wrong."

"I think this was shot in Mexico."

"Okay. But still, is it moral?"

"What the hell is that guy doing?" Uncle Bob asked, leaning over my other shoulder, tilting his head until it matched ours. "Are you watching South American porn again?"

"Oh, crap," Cookie said, straightening. "You're here."

"I am," Ubie announced proudly.

"We have to get ready for dinner. I'll call and have Italian delivered."

"Works for me," he said, heading to my kitchen for a cup of devil's blood.

I twirled in my chair and stood. "What is this dinner everyone keeps talking about?"

"The dinner. You know."

"That is not helpful, Cookie."

She pursed her lips. "It was in last week's memo."

Ah, the Concorde. It met a fiery end on Central. My window had been open.

"Dr. von Holstein?" she continued.

"The cow doctor? He's coming here for dinner?"

"He's coming here to talk to you. Garrett was supposed to pick him up at the airport. We're supposed to have dinner. Please tell me Garrett didn't forget."

"He's a little busy with his ex."

"No, he's not," Garrett said, walking right in. Nobody knocked any-more. It was weird.

Cookie cast him a worried frown. "He isn't coming?"

Garrett hung up his phone. "He died of a heart attack two days ago. I just got off the phone with his secretary."

"Oh, no," I said, sitting back down. "I'm sorry, Garrett."

He shook his head. "I'm sorry, too. That explains why I didn't hear from him." He glanced around self-consciously. "I thought maybe you could, you know." He wiggled his fingers.

"I can wiggle my fingers, thanks for asking, but what does that have to do with the cow doctor?"

My phone dinged with a text. I grabbed it off my desk and checked it.

"You know what I mean," Garrett said.

"How'd it go with the ex?"

"She's not really my ex. I mean, we never really had a thing."

"Sure you did." It was Osh asking if he could come in.

I typed back,

Of course.

"You had a kid. That's a tad more important than a thing."

"I guess."

Cookie went up and hugged him. He hugged back as though she were a prickly pear cactus, clearly uncomfortable with the subject of fatherhood. "I don't care how it happened, it's still wonderful. Congrat-ulations."

He wiped his mouth when she stepped back. "Thanks."

"He's adorable, Cook. His name is Zaire and you nailed it with the voodoo stuff."

Garrett's gaze snapped back to hers. "How did you know?"

She chuckled and walked back into the kitchen. "Marika has a blog. I'm a little surprised you didn't find it."

"Wow. I never dug in that direction, I guess."

Uncle Bob shook his hand. "Congratulations. I'd offer you advice, but I've never been married."

"Neither has Garrett," I said, stating the truth. "He's a slut."

Cookie giggled. "I love it when you call men sluts."

"Right?" I said, giggling back. "It's much funnier than the alternative." It was odd how I despised that word when talking about women, but when talking about men, all bets were off. Maybe because of the centuries-old double standard where a woman who enjoyed sex was a slut, whereas a man who enjoyed sex was a stud. That one never sat well with me.

I slowly got the feeling something was out of place. I glanced around, then bent down to Belvedere's fishbowl. Only it wasn't Belvedere. He'd been kidnapped!

"Cookie," I said, straightening and turning to look at her. "This is not my goldfish."

"What?" she asked, guilt radiating out of her.

"Cookie!" I said, astonished. "Why would you abduct my goldfish?"

She let out a hapless sigh. "How on earth did you figure that out? It's a goldfish. They all look alike."

"Belvedere had a white patch on his side. This . . . this impostor, does not."

"Hey," Cook said, walking over to cover the bowl as though covering a child's ears. "She is very sensitive. Belvedere didn't make it, hon. This is Mrs. Thibodeaux."

"What? I barely had him a day."

"I know." She stepped forward and patted my shoulder. "It was his time."

I sank into a chair at the kitchen table. "I killed him. I knew it. I'm going to be a horrible mother. How can I keep a kid alive if I can't even keep a goldfish alive?"

"Charley, this has nothing to do with your parenting skills. Any number of things could have happened."

I sniffed and glanced over at Mrs. Thibodeaux. "Did he go peace-fully?"

"Yes." She patted again. "I found him floating upside down with a smile on his little face."

"Mrs. Thibodeaux is very pretty."

"Yes, she is."

"So, can you try?" Garrett asked, going back to the wiggling-fingers thing as someone finally knocked on my door.

With a sad sigh, I stood and opened the door to a very embarrassed and uncomfortable kid named Osh. When he didn't come inside imme-diately, I rose onto my toes and hugged his neck.

"You are welcome here anytime, Osh. I know you didn't summon them. Reyes knows it, too."

Osh let me hug him but didn't hug back unless I counted the slight patting of my rib cage. When I finished, he said, "Rey'aziel has a point. There are only a handful of entities on this plane who could have sum-moned the Twelve."

"Come in."

He stepped inside at last and I went to pour myself a cup of his cap-tor's blood. "Coffee?" I asked.

He shook his head, then offered a tense nod of acknowledgment to-ward Cook and Garrett. They had both been there that morning during World War III.

Cookie rushed up and hugged him, too, her arms barely reaching around his shoulders. He bent to let her. It was sweet.

"Are you okay, sweetheart?"

His gorgeous mouth slid into a smile. "I'm fine. And I'm a centuries-old demon. I've lived through a lot worse."

She stepped back. "You're a sweet boy nonetheless. Anyone who risks his life for our Charley is family in my book."

He was taken aback by her assessment of him. I got the feeling he didn't get many compliments like that. "Thank you, ma'am."

"Okay, who's up for Italian?" When everyone nodded in agreement, she went to her apartment to call in an order and check on the offspring who had to do her homework before she could join us.

Uncle Bob turned on the television and Osh walked up to me as I sat back at my computer. "You knocked my ass out this morning," he said, clearly impressed.

"Yeah, sorry about that. You sure came up swinging."

"Yeah. I'm sorry about that, too."

"Not at all. That was on Reyes, love. Who will be here in a few minutes."

"What is that woman doing?"

I'd paused the video. "Oh, you won't believe this crap."

I replayed it, to his utter mortification. "I've been alive for centuries, and I've never seen anything like that."

"Thank God that's unusual. I was worried."

Reyes showed up and—instead of apologizing to our guest, the one he'd tried to beat senseless that morning—went straight to his apartment for a shower. Osh was cool with that. He sat and watched a game with Ubie and Swopes as Cookie cleared a space in my kitchen for the food when it arrived. Gawd, she was handy. I needed like three of her.

Remembering she needed actual utensils, she ran back to her place to grab some. No idea why plastic forks wouldn't do. Much less work involved later.

"I have a joke for you," Amber said as she sashayed into the room, her long dark hair hanging in tangles down her back.

"Okay," I said, giving her my full attention.

She stood beside me, drinking soda from a can. "You know how you have a bun in the oven?"

I stifled a laugh. "Yes. Yes, I do."

"Okay, and you know how Reyes calls you Dutch?"

"Yes," I said, wondering where she was going with this.

"Well, you're like a Dutch oven. Get it?" She giggled.

"I get it," I said, giggling, too.

"You're still coming to the carnival, right?"

"Abso-freaking-lutely."

She deflated. "You don't know anything about it, do you?"

"Sure I do." I seemed to recall something about a carnival. Cookie may have mentioned it. Or it may have been in that 747 I'd crashed into the toilet. Memo or no memo, I was not fishing that out. "I just forgot when it is, exactly."

"Awesome. It's tomorrow night."

"Oh, that's right."

She giggled again. "You're such a bad liar."

Oh, my god. Clearly, I needed lessons.

"Let's go into my room," I said. "I need to change."

She shrugged and grinned as her phone dinged with a text.

"Quentin?" I asked, leading her that way.

After a quick glance at Osh, who nodded a very cool acknowledgment, she said, "Yeah. He got in trouble today in shop."

"Uh-oh. What'd he do?"

"He made a wooden heart for me, but his teacher said it didn't look like a heart. I have no idea what else it would look like, but he got detention for the rest of the week."

"Hmmm, I'll have to call Santa Fe in the morning, see what's going on."

"Okay."

"But things are good with him?" I asked. She seemed quite taken with Osh. Then again, so was I. What teenaged girl wouldn't be?

She sat on my bed, her expression morphing into dreamy. "Things are wonderful."

"I'm glad." I chose a white sweater, then put it back. White and Italian didn't always mix. Going for a soft black sweater, I took off the vest I was wearing and tossed it on a chair in the corner, then unbuttoned my blouse. "Don't look. You'll be scarred for life."

"Okay," she said with a giggle. "I have a question for you, though."

"Shoot."

"Did you ever, you know, experiment with a girl?"

"I did once in high school. She was my lab partner, and we had to dissect a frog."

"No, not that kind of experiment. The other kind."

I was worried she meant the other kind. "Oh, okay. I did experiment once in college. It was kind of the thing to do."

"Did you like it?"

"I certainly didn't hate it, but I did find out I'm not gay. Still, twenty bucks is twenty bucks."

"Yeah. Misty Rowley says if I want to give it a try, she's game. But I just think I like guys, you know?"

"She's not pressuring you, is she?" I asked in alarm.

"Oh, no. She just said if I wanted to try, it was okay with her."

"I'd go with my gut on this one, kiddo."

"Yeah. Her family is kind of weird anyway. She said her mother has a strap-on named Event Horizon."

I hid a burst of laughter behind a cough, then asked, "Do you know what a strap-on is?"

She gave me a look of incredulity. "Of course. I know what a bra is. You strap it on."

"Right." I patted her shoulder. "Well, some people name their bras. Personally, I find the practice bizarre."

She giggled. "You name everything."

"Not my bras. Who does that?" I asked, refraining both from explaining the error of her definition of a strap-on and the fact that I was currently wearing a bra named Penelope.

After lifting a delicate shoulder, she said, "I have another question for you. But this one is kind of hard."

"Anything. Unless it involves math. Four out of three people are bad at math."

She fidgeted for a moment before continuing. "No math. I was just wondering, is Reyes's . . . you know, *package,* is that an accurate representation of what a guy has?"

I stilled and slammed my lids shut in mortification. I'd almost forgotten Reyes had torn into my apartment with nary a stitch on the other day. She came in right after and got the full monty.

I couldn't help it. I referred back to one of my favorite movies: *The Jerk.* "Um, do you mean his special purpose?"

"No, I mean his cock."

I dived forward and slammed my hand over her mouth. "You're twelve! How do you even know that word? I didn't even know that word when I was twelve. Well, no—actually, I've known that word since the day I was born, but I didn't *use* it when I was twelve."

Amber pursed her mouth and said from behind my hand, "I'm thirteen. I've been thirteen for a week."

"Right, okay." I let her go. "Well, from here on out, it's called a special purpose, okay?"

"I've seen the movie. So is it?"

"Wow, um, I'd have to say not really. Reyes is a tad . . . well, larger than the average male."

"Oh." She deflated.

"But the anatomy is the same. I mean, they all have pretty much the same equipment."

"Oh." That seemed to make her happy.

I finally found my sweater and pulled it before sitting beside her. "Why, hon? What's up?"

She shifted her mouth to one side of her gorgeous face. "It's just I thought he was really nice. You know, to look at."

Stifling a grin, I said, "I agree completely."

Cookie walked in then, her brows raised in question. "What are you two talking about?"

"We're talking about special purposes," Amber said. "We're talking about how Reyes has a spectacular special purpose."

I closed my lids as Cookie walked up and put a hand on her shoulder.

"Honey," she said, "we all have a special purpose. Some are just bigger than others. You'll have your own special purpose someday."

It took every ounce of control Amber had not to burst out laughing. Her face reddened with the effort as she stood, not sure how long she could hold it. "Thanks, Mom. I look forward to my own special purpose someday."

I dropped my face into my hands as she walked out.

Cookie let out a long, exaggerated sigh. "*The Jerk?*"

"*The Jerk.*"

"Why do I fall for these things?"

"Because you're you," I said, giving her a sympathetic hug.

14

If I'm upset, hold me and tell me how beautiful I am.
If I growl, retreat to a safe distance and throw chocolate.
—BEST. ADVICE. EVER.

We enjoyed—*enjoyed* being relative—a quiet evening as Garrett told us stories about some of the conversations he's had with Dr. von Holstein. Those were great. Clearly the man wasn't nearly as stodgy as I'd imagined. The tension came from the two otherworldly beings in the room—minus Mr. Wong, since he didn't seem to care about much of anything. Osh was very determined to stay put, to make sure I stayed safe despite the glares Reyes kept giving him. It didn't help that Osh grinned every time Reyes glared. I was growing quite annoyed with the lot of them, if two could be considered a lot. It was kind of iffy, kind of like how two crows was only an attempted murder.

But we made it through dinner with nary a punch thrown or an eye blackened. It was another good evening. In other words, it made me nervous.

I walked into the bedroom after making Osh a bed on Sophie. Reyes was none too happy about our slumber party, but Osh was worried. He wanted to be here. To help in any way he could. And I had no problem letting him. Reyes would just have to deal.

When I stepped past the threshold of our room—our beds still butted up against each other, since he'd taken the wall separating our rooms out a couple of weeks ago—I was struck by the picture that met me. Reyes lay across both beds, propped up on several pillows, shirtless with only his dark lounge pants, his legs stretched out in front of him, his feet bare, a drink in one hand, and a book in the other. It was like one of those "at home" photos with models that looked like movie stars.

I almost came at the sight. It was the sexiest thing I'd ever seen. And I'd seen a lot of sexy lately. Would I ever get used to just having him? To just being able to look upon him and know he was mine? Know that I didn't have to share him unless I got really kinky as I got older and decided to get into threesomes. But I couldn't imagine ever wanting to share the man before me. I got jealous of his talking to a departed woman today. Granted, she was a gorgeous departed woman.

"Be still my Betty White," I said softly.

"What?" he asked without looking up, one corner of his mouth lifting playfully.

I walked forward and stopped at the edge of the bed. "You. Reading. That is probably the sexiest thing I've ever seen a man do."

His mouth widened and he finally looked up at me, closing the book in his hand and setting it aside. "Clearly you've never seen me pole dance."

A bubble of laughter burst out before I could stop it. "I think you and your pole should keep your dancing private. It sounds like a very intimate act."

"You're probably right." He let his gaze travel over me, and I wished I hadn't chosen to sleep in the shirt that said FOR ENTERTAINMENT PURPOSES ONLY.

I snapped out of my trance and said, "By the way, I'm very angry with you."

He raised a knee and draped an arm over it. "Are you?"

"Yes. Don't think I've forgotten that you've been spying on me."

"I wouldn't dream of it."

"Who is she?" I asked as I crawled onto the bed, kneeling at the foot of it, well out of his reach.

"What makes you think I have only one?"

I raised my brow, impressed. "The one I saw was beautiful."

"I think she drowned at a dinner party."

"That explains the evening gown."

"Her makeup is smeared."

"Yeah, but you like that kind of thing."

"Only on you." He grinned and reached for me anyway.

I slid off the bed and sidestepped past him to gather my dirty clothes and toss them in the laundry basket. "How many do you have?"

"What would you like me to tell you?"

I wondered why that was a difficult question to answer. "The truth would be nice."

"I have an army, then. Is that what you want to hear?"

I walked to my dresser and scooted onto it. "If that's the truth, then yeah. How many is in an army, exactly."

"I have several," he said, acquiescing. "Seven or so. You're getting stronger. She knew you'd detected her today at the coffee shop."

"I smelled her perfume. I've never done that with a departed."

"Your senses are heightening. Good."

"What exactly does your army of spies do? I don't like being watched."

"Then perhaps I shouldn't tell you."

I didn't know how to take that.

"I'm not risking you just because you don't want to be guarded, Dutch. It's like you said earlier. It's not just about you anymore."

He had a point.

"Let me see what you're capable of," he said.

"You know what I'm capable of. I seem to be the only one who doesn't. And from what I understand, if you tell me my real name, my celestial name, I will just know what to do."

"Yes, but it will also change everything. We can't use that card unless we absolutely have to."

"I don't understand. What's really going on?"

He glanced down. "I'm not sure that if you learn your celestial name, you won't become the grim reaper completely."

"Do you mean, you're afraid my physical body will pass? That I'll become the reaper and—"

"You'll forget about me. You'll have a job to do. Reapers aren't known for their social skills. They do their duty. Period. They become, how do I say it? Void of emotion."

I could tell it actually worried him, though I knew in my heart I would never, no matter what happened, no matter what I knew, forget him. It was as improbable a scenario as the world turning to dust. But I let it drop for now. "Fine. That can be our ace in the hole should we ever need it."

"Now, let's see what you're capable of." He crossed his arms over his wide chest. His hair curled around his ears, the thick dark mass shimmering in the low light. "Just play along for a minute."

"Okay, what do I do?"

He lowered his head and gazed at me from underneath his lashes. "Imagine I'm one of the Twelve," he said, his voice soft, smooth.

"One of the Twelve. Got it."

"Now drop me."

"Drop you."

"Like you did today."

"No," I said. "What I did this morning was not okay. You couldn't breathe."

"It was brilliant."

"It was reckless," I argued.

"Dutch," he said in warning.

"Fine." I lowered my lids and morphed into a lean mean fighting machine. I'd imagined myself as a coffee machine for so long, it was difficult, but I managed it. I opened my eyes and bore my gaze into his. "You are the disease and I'm the viral inhibitor that blocks attachment to the host cell and prevents the release of cloned viral particles, attacking from both ends."

He fought a smile, then asked, "Where'd you get that?"

"Theraflu commercial, mostly."

"Dutch," he said in warning again, "drop me or you'll wish you had."

I didn't doubt his words, though I had no idea what he would do to make me wish I had. After drawing in a lungful of air, I concentrated, ordered myself to *drop* him.

He kept his gaze locked on mine. "Dutch," he growled, giving me one more warning.

But I couldn't figure out what to do to drop him. I didn't want to hurt him. I didn't want to put him through what I'd put him through that morning.

I blinked, and in that instant, he was on me. He grabbed me by the throat and lifted me as though to body-slam me on the bed. Without thought, I slowed time to his speed, then slowed it more, until I had the advantage. Until I had the strength to break free from his hold, to twist my legs around, to grab him by the throat, and to use time itself to help me force him over my shoulder, to flip him and slam his body onto the ground.

As I allowed time to grab its footing again, the sound deafening as it ricocheted into place, I said one simple word to make sure I kept the advantage for a few seconds more.

"*Excruci.*"

Reyes's back arched as the pain hit him. He threw his head back in agony and growled between clenched teeth, his muscles tense as though seizing. I watched for a split second and wondered, as time settled around us, if I could cause pain, could I do the reverse? Could I cause pleasure?

"*Laetitia sine poena non habet,*" I said. "There is no pleasure without pain." I released a steady stream of air as he lay beneath me. After a moment, I said softly, "*Voluptas.*"

He threw back his head again with a loud gasp, only this time I felt the purest, most ethereal form of pleasure I'd ever felt radiate out of him. He grabbed my leg as I knelt beside him, his other hand going to the bed, blindly grasping at the comforter as wave after wave of unimaginable pleasure coursed through him. I should have stopped it, I should have released him, but I was riding the wave as exquisitely as he was. Just as it pulsed inside him, it pulsed inside me, pooling between my legs, hardening my nipples until I gasped at the tightness of my skin as it shrank around me.

I couldn't tear my gaze off him. He was so beautiful, writhing in a combination of pain and pleasure like I had never felt before. The force I'd created urged my legs apart and pushed into my abdomen, growing and spreading like molten lava, scorching me from the inside out. I guided it deeper, and in an act of pure lust, I reached into his bottoms and wrapped my hand around his rock-hard cock. Blood rushed beneath my fingers, the power coursing through me more delicious than anything I'd ever tasted.

"Dutch," he said, the agonizing ecstasy racing through his veins and swarming his nerve endings as painfully as it was mine, the sting as sweet as fruit off the vine.

But I wanted more. I ripped down his bottoms and swallowed every inch of him as he groaned and plunged his fingers into my hair. He tried to push me back, to slow my attack, but with one simple thought, I disabled him. Helpless, he threw his hands over his face as his climax neared.

"Dutch, please," he begged through gritted teeth, and I doubted he knew what he was begging for. An end to the pleasure or its indefinite continuation?

I tasted a droplet of salt on my tongue and knew he was close. Skimming my teeth along the underside of his cock, I silently ordered his release.

"Fuck," he said, crying out as he exploded inside my mouth. He bucked against my hold, driving himself deeper. At that exact moment, my own orgasm surged up in one giant wave. It lanced straight to my core and burst in white hot light as I dug my nails into his flesh.

The sweet sting pulsed inside me for several fleeting moments before my heart slowed and the afterglow of ecstasy warmed me through to my marrow.

I fell against him, more sated than I'd ever been. And more powerful.

"How was that?" I asked, genuinely wanting his assessment of my performance.

His gaze spoke volumes. Mostly shock. "I've never felt anything like that."

"Me neither," I said, snuggling against his rib cage.

"Dutch," he said, taking my chin in his hand and lifting my gaze to his again. "I'm serious. I never knew anything like that existed. I knew you would be powerful, but you completely disabled me with a thought. You took me out with the force of your mind. And you used time to your advantage. You used everything you had at your disposal to incapacitate your opponent. You're a warrior. You really are the Val-Eeth."

I leaned up onto an elbow. "What's a Val-Eeth?"

After running one hand down his face in astonishment, he said, "Do you remember when I told you that you were different, special, even among your own kind? Your own species?"

"Yes. You said I was royalty."

"No, you are so much more than that. You're the Val-Eeth. Through-out time, since before the creation of Earth, even before the creation of your sun, there have been only twelve Val-Eeth. One is born into your world every few million years. You're the thirteenth."

"I'm the thirteenth?" I asked. "Like the prophecy you read about the thirteenth warrior."

"I'm not sure. Prophecies are so open to interpretation, but—"

"I'm going to be my own undoing?" I asked. "Not Antonio Banderas?" That was disappointing, to say the least.

He took my chin into his hand again. "Do you ever take anything seriously?"

"Not especially."

He lay back, his brows furrowing in thought. "But why would they let you go to become the reaper? It's almost—" He fought for the word he was looking for. "It's almost beneath you. In fact, it's very much beneath you. You're destined to be their leader for millions of years. You're destined to be a god. I don't understand."

"Unless they knew about the prophecies. Maybe they knew our daughter would be an absolute badass. She would have to be to take on your dad."

"I'm dumbfounded at their sacrifice. To finally have another Val-Eeth born among them after who knows how many millions of years, and then to give her up to this dimension? This plane?"

"I'm glad they did, either way."

He shook his head. "No, they wouldn't have." He leveed a heated gaze on me. "They would never have sent you. Never. You must have volunteered. You must have insisted. You hadn't ascended to the throne yet, but pretty much anything you would have said would be law. It must've been you."

"Cool. So this is like when I volunteered for the Peace Corps. It's like a temporary venture to better myself and to aid other people in their time of need."

A dimple appeared beside his mouth. "Exactly." He said it, but not without adding a healthy dose of sarcasm.

"Okay, so getting back to what I can do, clearly I have power over you while you are flesh and blood, but what about something that is incorporeal, like a hellhound?"

"That, my dear, is the million-dollar question."

I beamed at him and snuggled closer, ignoring the corner of the dresser in my back, and giggled softly. He called me dear.

———

I felt a cool touch on my shoulder as I slept in Reyes's arms, but after the night we'd had, I wasn't terribly inclined to respond to the summons. Our *training session* had exhausted me. I'd have to practice more, learn to control myself and not ravish my affianced every time I had the upper hand. He was just so darned delicious. And Reyes Farrow vulnerable? Too tempting to resist, not that I had the best self-control as it was.

The touch returned, along with a soft, "Ms. Davidson? Are you awake?"

I couldn't quite place the accent as I forced one lid open. Just one. I let the other rest. Our room was pitch black, but that never stopped me from seeing the departed as though they were onstage with a spotlight.

A man stood before me, pudgy, well dressed, and looking like he'd just stepped out of the 1940s. He had round-rimmed glasses and a thin mustache that looked like an insect over his top lip.

"Ms. Davidson, I had to see you before I left. I had no idea any of it vas real. I— I vould have come sooner had I known." German. He had a thick German accent, and I realized who he was.

At that same moment, I also realized I had another visitor. Osh stood beside the man, his head down, his dark gaze glaring at the departed man beside my bed.

I sat up and rubbed my closed eye, coaxing it open to join the other. "Osh, what are you doing here?"

"Mark him and he'll be mine."

"Osh," I said through a yawn, "I'm not marking this man's soul for you just because you're hungry."

"What do you want?" he asked the man, taking him by the collar.

The man winced, his expression full of fear. "I just need to talk to Ms. Davidson. She is ze one, is she not? Ze daughter of light from ze prophecies?"

Osh glanced at me, then back to him. "She is. What's that to you?"

"I— I have been translating zem. Ze documents. I— I zink I died before I could come to you."

"I'm sorry, Dr. von Holstein," I said. "You died two days ago."

"No," he said, lowering himself onto the edge of the bed. "Zat's impossible. It vas only a moment ago."

I leaned forward and put an arm on his shoulder. "Time is different there."

"Apparently." He took off his glasses and cleaned them on his shirt.

"Can you tell me what you learned?"

He shook out of his stupor with a deep sigh. "Zere is so much I never imagined possible. If you are vat I zink you are, I can just show you, *ja*?"

"You can," I assured him.

He put his glasses back on and slipped through me. I leaned forward, bracing my arms on my knees as his essence slid over me and his memories filled my brain to capacity. I skimmed past his childhood in West Berlin, unaware of the turmoil and strife that surrounded him. His family sent him to America as an exchange student and he'd come back to attend university here. His love of both countries was a constant struggle for him. He longed for home but loved the United States so much, he stayed and taught here.

I scanned forward in time until he was contacted by a westerner named Garrett Swopes about an ancient text he'd come across. I had yet to find out how Garrett came across the documents containing the prophecies in the first place or how he'd stumbled upon Zeus, but I knew it had something to do with his trip to hell and back, thanks to Mr. Reyes Farrow.

Then there it was. The doctor's breakthrough. He'd finally found a pattern to the chaos. He had only copies to work from. Garrett must still have the originals stashed somewhere safe. But Dr. von Holstein found what he believed to be a grave error in his previous translation.

There were twelve. We already knew that. But there were more. The phrase went something like: Twelve sent and twelve summoned. That was what we believed would be Beep's army: the *good* twelve. She would handpick twelve defenders to help her fight the fallen as they rose from hell. But the army was not part of either of the twelve.

Twelve sent and twelve summoned.

It was hard for the doctor to make out exactly what it all meant. The texts were written in riddles, in much the same way Nostradamus had written his quatrains, but von Holstein had begun to believe that Beep's hand-chosen army was in addition to the good twelve. It would be the thirteenth warrior that would tip the odds in favor or against the daughter. And the war that could tear the world asunder or bring peace for a thousand years would be decided in a split second.

But I would never go against her, so surely I wasn't the thirteenth in this situation. Maybe Beep herself was the warrior, but Dr. V got the distinct impression from a variety of contextual clues that the thirteenth warrior was male. And the thirteenth warrior, who had been born in darkness, would tip the scales one way or the other.

There was a lot more—so much, it was hard to absorb it all—but when I lifted my lids, Osh was sitting in my chair in the corner, waiting patiently.

He stood when I focused on him. "Well?" he asked.

"You'd better tell him," Reyes said beside me. "He wouldn't leave until you came out of it."

"Out of it? How long was I in it?"

Osh looked at the clock on my nightstand. "Three hours."

"Three hours?" I twisted around to see for myself. "That's never happened before."

Reyes rubbed my back. "You had a lot to learn."

"I did, but I don't think it's anything that will help us with what is happening right now."

I called a very sleepy Garrett and explained to them what I'd learned from Dr. V. He was a nice guy in the end, and I hated that he'd died of a heart attack after finding what he considered his own personal Holy Grail. He wanted to publish eventually with the texts and make the prophet Cleosaurius as famous as Nostradamus. I doubted that would ever happen, but he did find correlations to the prophecies of Cleosaurius and things that had happened throughout history. Again, the same could be said for Nostradamus and a few other prophets, but that concept was rather cool.

I couldn't sleep the rest of the night. I was still absorbing everything I'd learned and everything Reyes had told me. But I decided to focus on the bottom line. How were Reyes and I going to fight the Twelve and save our daughter? Nothing else really mattered at that point.

Well, besides the fact that I still had three, possibly four murders to solve and the fact that I still had a missing body and the fact that I was getting terribly worried about my dad. As I sat at my computer in the wee hours of morn, listening to Artemis breathe as she slept at my feet, I did search after search on every database we had access to, both legally and illegally, looking for a connection among the suicide-note victims. It was all I could do at the moment until the sun came up.

Reyes walked up and rubbed my shoulders for a few.

I lifted my coffee cup. "Your father's blood?" I asked, offering him a sip of my decaf, but he just kissed my head and went back to bed. Osh lay on the sofa, but I got the feeling he couldn't sleep either. Finally, after the longest sunrise in the history of the world, I picked up my phone and called Denise—my stepmother, for all intents and purposes. I knew she wouldn't be up yet, but she'd once told me never to call her unless the sun was up. It was up!

"Hey, you!" I said as cheerfully as I could. I woke up Artemis, who groaned in protest and went to sleep with Reyes.

"Charley?" she asked, her voice sandy from sleep.

"The one and only. Have you heard from Dad?"

"No," she said, perking up. "Have you?"

"Not a word. I need to know where he was staying when he moved out."

"How would I know?"

"Denise, I will send an army of dead people to haunt you for all eternity."

And that was when our usual dance, also known as the Tyrannical Two-Step, went downhill. She berated me for five solid minutes, telling me Dad's leaving was all my fault. If only I'd done this or that or hung the moon or some shit, they would have made it. Instead I made my father's life a living hell.

Because she had *nothing* to do with that.

After we hit the five-minute mile marker, I interrupted her. "Are you off your soapbox yet, because I need to do laundry."

"Your father is missing, and all you can do is sass."

"Well, it is my specialty."

"Do you even have a conscience?"

Getting more annoyed by the second, I said, "I used to until it was picked clean by a vulture in polyester clothing."

After a very long standoff, she finally flinched. "He was staying at the La Quinta. The one closest to you, by the airport."

Having nothing more to say to her, I hung up. An hour later I found myself, along with a comely man with a newfound respect for my badassness—or possibly just my ass—at the La Quinta on Gibson.

"But I'm a private investigator," I said to the desk clerk, who clearly hated his job.

"And I'm an ordained minister," he said in a thick Indian accent. "Doesn't mean I can get into any hotel room I want to just because I have a little piece of paper."

"Little piece of paper?" I took out my license and waved it in his face. "This is laminated, I'll have you know."

Thankfully Cookie called, because I was about to go Val-Eeth on his ass. I filled my lungs, vowing to use my powers only for good, then said, "Charley's House of Edible Paint."

"His boat is still at the docks in South Texas," she said, her voice panicked. "It took forever for the harbor patrol officer to confirm. I'm calling Robert."

"Don't bother. I have to call him anyway to get a warrant to Dad's hotel room because someone—" I glared at the desk clerk. "—woke up on the wrong side of the Albuquerque, apparently."

An hour after that little dispute, Ubie showed up with a warrant. He'd also filed a missing persons report and put out a BOLO on Dad's vehicle. God love 'im. When he showed the warrant to the desk clerk, I smirked. The guy raised his chin and led us to Dad's room.

"Maybe you should laminate your little piece of paper, too," I said as he left us. I was such a child. But the moment I walked into Dad's room, all thoughts of childhood left me. I took a few steps farther in and did a 360, my jaw open, my gaze transfixed.

The air had been sucked from the room and I started to feel light-headed. Page after page, picture after picture, article after article lined the walls in an explosive collage of . . . me. It was all about me. It started on the south wall in my childhood. Hundreds of pictures, most I'd never seen, were taped up. There were articles, letters, schoolwork, interviews, all about me. He even had pictures I'd never seen from my time in Uganda in the Peace Corps.

I looked at Uncle Bob, questioned him with a gesture.

"I don't know, pumpkin. I mean, he was asking a lot of questions about you, but not in the way that you think."

"What does that even mean, Uncle Bob? Look at this place."

"He was asking if I'd ever seen anybody following you. Keeping tabs." A quick glance toward Reyes told me he thought Dad had been talking about him.

"He was asking about Reyes? Why? I mean, he met him. Reyes bought the bar from him."

"It's not me," Reyes said, studying the paraphernalia. "He asked me a few questions when we first met. His intentions had been honorable. He cares for you very much. But this is something else. Look at them."

He pointed to one picture in particular, and both Ubie and I stepped closer. "He's in this one, and it looks like—"

"A surveillance shot," Ubie finished for him.

"And this one."

We followed him to another area.

"See these? They aren't of you, but of a man. Do you recognize him?"

He was average height, average weight, but it was hard to make out anything else. "I've never seen him," I said as Ubie shook his head. "But that's—" I leaned closer. Squinted. "—that's my apartment building. He's right outside my apartment building." I pointed to another. "And he's on my fire escape in this one!" I shrieked. "He's looking in my window. The camera was on night vision when someone took this shot."

Reyes slipped a hand into mine when my anger slipped and the ground shook, just barely, beneath us. Uncle Bob stepped back and grabbed hold of a lamp. Not sure why.

"Was that an earthquake?" he asked, astonished.

"Must've been," Reyes said, lifting my chin until our eyes met. "We good?"

I filled my lungs. "We're good. Sorry."

"Anger is something I'm very familiar with."

After offering him a pensive smile, I turned to Uncle Bob. "So, what? Dad is following this guy? Do you think that's why he's not picking up?"

"That would be my guess. I wouldn't worry too much about it. He did tell me he was investigating something and that he would be un-reachable for a while."

"Uncle Bob, why didn't you tell me that?"

He lifted a sheepish shoulder. "He told me not to. Now I know why."

"But why is this guy following me?"

"And from the looks of it," Reyes added, "he's been doing it a long,

long time." A dimple appeared at one corner of his sensuous mouth. "Not that I can blame him."

I grinned. "Yeah, but you followed me for a reason."

"This guy looks like he has a reason."

"Or he thinks he does," Uncle Bob said. He was on the phone with the captain. "I'm not really sure what to do here, pumpkin. It's your dad's investigation. Maybe we should leave it for now, wait for him to clue us in to what he's up to."

"I agree. But for now, I want to know everything he does about this guy." I sat at the desk and tried calling once again, but Dad's phone was turned off this time. His battery may have died, and now we had no way of tracking his whereabouts.

"We can triangulate from your earlier calls, pumpkin. If nothing else, we'll figure out where he's been."

I nodded and started sifting through papers.

"Okay," Ubie said, hanging up, "just don't remove anything. I have to get downtown."

"Go," I said. "We're good. And thanks so much, Uncle Bob."

He walked forward and kissed my temple. "Anytime. And don't give that desk clerk too much crap. He was just doing his job."

"I know. But that's what makes it fun. Wait," I said, spotting a familiar picture. "I've seen this picture."

Ubie and Reyes took a look. It was of me in Uganda. We were helping a group of refugees to a safe camp we'd set up with fresh water. I was carrying a little girl, her head resting on my shoulder. The memory was one of my more powerful, and I knew why it was of interest to the Vatican. A lion had been attacking villagers, but word soon spread that the lion was afraid of me. That it wouldn't come near an encampment where I was. I had no idea how that rumor got started. There was zero truth to it, but we began getting new refugees every day.

What I hadn't known at the time, and what the photographer had captured beautifully, was that the lion stood crouched in the brush to the right of us. I couldn't see it in the smaller black-and-white Father Glenn had brought, but I could see it now in full color, its amber eyes almost glowing in the setting sun as it watched us.

The shot was spine-tingling and heart-stopping at once. The lion was close enough to reach out and sever my jugular before I even knew it was there. The Ugandans would have taken that as a sign of a miracle. No wonder they thought I was protected.

"Where did you see this?" Reyes asked.

"In the file the Vatican has on me."

Ubie ogled us both. "The Vatican has a file on you?"

"Didn't I mention that?"

"As in the actual Vatican in Italy?"

"No, Uncle Bob, the fake one in Poughkeepsie. Yes, the real one in Italy."

He scrubbed his face with his fingers. "What does that mean?"

"It means someone in Italy has a little too much time on their hands. Go, we got this."

He nodded absently, then closed the door behind him.

Reyes and I studied Dad's investigation for a couple of hours. One thing we didn't find that I was hoping for was a name. An address. Anything. Just weird documents, receipts, pages torn out of an accounting journal.

Finally, Reyes found a card from a storage company buried under a pile of fast food receipts. "Safety Storage, Unit 17-A."

"We need to check it out, don't you think?"

"Normally, considering the circumstances, I would say it could wait. But it's not like your father to decline calls and not check in with someone."

"Exactly. But, once again, we'll need a warrant. No way will they let us in there. Unless," I said, scheming.

Reyes pulled me onto his lap. "How about we grab some lunch and call your uncle. If he can't get a warrant, we'll try it your way. Whatever that way may be."

"Deal. Ubie's like my own personal warrant man. Some judge must really owe him. Sadly, he couldn't get a warrant to dig up that grave, but I have a plan."

We stood and started out the door. "Do you know how terrifying those words are coming out of your mouth?"

"I do. I really do." Before I could elaborate, a high-pitched shriek hit me from my left.

"Charley!"

I jumped at least a mile. Jessica ran up to me, her arms flailing. "My nephew. Hurry!" She grabbed my wrist and tried to pull me along with her.

"Jessica, stop," I said as Reyes crossed his arms and leaned against a post outside Dad's room. "Stop, seriously." I jerked out of her grip and rubbed my wrists. Her nails were lethal. "What's going on?"

"My nephew got hit by a car last night. I didn't know. I didn't know until now. Please, help him."

"Help him?" I asked, shaking my head. "Jessica, I can't save people. Unless he needs help with his homework, and he's still young enough that I'd understand it, I can't help him."

"Please, Charley," she said, pleading with tears streaming down her face. "He's in critical condition. They don't expect him to live. He's— he's everything my sister has left."

"I didn't know Willa even had kids."

"She only has the one son. They've been trying, but— Please, just try to help him."

I gave Reyes my best sheepish slash apologetic brows. "Do you mind?"

"It's your world, Dutch."

Since we had no idea how long we'd be, we grabbed tacos and sodas from Macho Taco on the way to the hospital. I was a little concerned with his compliance, his willingness to come on this mission. He seemed curious, and I realized he wondered if I could do anything to help the kid. He'd been testing me for days. This was just another test of my abilities.

Sadly, everyone was about to be very disappointed. Just like I could not save my father from cancer, I could not save this boy from his injuries. But Jessica was certain I could. After all the years of her snide remarks and derision, I wondered why I was helping her at all, but this wasn't for her. Willa was nice when she wanted to be. We'd gotten along for the most part, besides that one fight to the death I had to break up between the two of them.

"Jessica, if he's in ICU, they won't let me in. You have to be family."

"Then tell them you're family!" she screeched, panicking. "Tell them you're my cousin Kristi from Louisville."

"And if they want an ID?"

"You lie all the time. You can't make something up?"

The elevator doors opened, and Jessica pushed me to the end of a corridor, where a very intimidating door stood between us and the patients. Reyes followed along at a slower pace. I pushed the buzzer.

"Yes?" a woman said.

"I'm Kristi. I'm here to see—"

"Dustin!" she shouted.

"Dustin."

"He's in number three," she said as the giant metal doors opened. "You should hurry, hon."

Jessica's face fell. She ran forward and I lost sight of her. "Be right back," I said to Reyes as I stepped across the threshold.

"I saw a *Good Housekeeping* back there that's calling my name."

I nodded and headed for ICU room 3.

I walked around the nurses' station until I saw a glass room with a big *3* on it. I stopped short. It was full of people. At least a dozen people lined the room. That meant only one thing: Dustin didn't have long. They allowed only two people in a room at a time in ICU. This could not be good.

"Come on," Jessica said, urging me forward.

"Jessica, I can't go in there. Your family is in there."

"But you have to. You have to touch him or something, right?"

"Jessica, honey, this is not what I do. I don't heal people. I'm sorry. I shouldn't have come."

As I stood talking to her, I noticed a little boy sitting in a chair outside the room. He looked scared and lost, and I knew that had to be Dustin. Jessica had disappeared back into the room, so I walked up and sat beside him.

"Hi," I said.

He didn't look up.

"I'm Charley. You must be Dustin."

I wasn't too worried about what people thought. Everyone in the area was pretty busy. Nurses worked at their stations, and visitors visited with either a patient or each other. So I didn't feel the need to take out my phone. Plus they weren't allowed, so it would have done me little good.

"Your aunt Jessica is really worried about you," I said, looking over my shoulder inside the room. "Everyone is."

"Am I dead?" he asked.

I craned my neck and looked at his monitor. "It doesn't look like it. Your heart's still beating, so that's a good sign."

He finally looked up at me. "But I'm going to die, right?"

Damn it. I didn't know what to tell him. I'd never been in this situation, talking to someone just before they actually passed. "I'm not sure, hon. I hope not."

"I hope not, too. My mom is so sad."

"I'm so sorry this happened to you."

He lifted a small shoulder. "It's okay. It was my fault. I was riding my bike and fell off right into the street. Stan Foyer says I'm a klutz. I guess he's right."

"Stan Foyer's a doody-head."

Dustin looked up and me and laughed. "He is, huh?"

"You know it."

We high-fived before he grew serious again.

"Why are you so bright?" he asked.

"It's part of my job. I help people like you."

The blue in his irises glittered in delight. "Like an angel?"

"Well, kind of, but not really. I'm more at the other end of the spectrum."

"Can you help my mom?" he asked. "She's going to be really upset when I die."

My heart constricted painfully in my chest. I felt Reyes near. He must have come in incorporeally to keep watch. I glanced around until I found him. He nodded, urging me to go inside. To see what I could do, if anything. And for this brave kid, I would.

"I'm going to step inside real quick," I said, grabbing a nurse's stethoscope off a workstation nearby. I wasn't dressed for the part, but hopefully the stethoscope would serve as an all-access pass.

"Are you going to touch her? That's what you do, right? I don't want her to be sad. I'll be fine."

The backs of my eyes stung and I had to turn away. After a moment, I knelt in front of him. "I'm going to touch her. She'll be okay."

"So, I can go now?"

I looked at the monitor, growing worried. "Can you hang on just one minute more? Just to make sure this is going to work?"

"Okay."

I stood and slipped inside the room, going straight for the monitor. Dustin's loved ones stepped aside as I passed. They were sniffing, touching him, waiting for the inevitable. I fought past their grief, the weight of their sorrow like a boulder on my chest. My lungs stopped working. I tried to block their emotions, but they were too strong.

Struggling for air, I pretended to press a few buttons on the monitor, not daring to actually touch anything. Then I turned to the pale boy, so tiny and frail in the huge bed. His head had a bandage around it and his face was scratched and swollen, almost unrecognizable from the boy I talked to outside.

I reached down and touched his wrist as though taking his pulse. Surely someone in the room would realize how futile an act that would have been. They were all aware of the direness of the situation. I glanced up and saw Willa, Jessica's sister, sobbing into her mother's shoulder, her fingers entangled in the purple blouse her mother wore. I'd always liked Jessica's mother.

When I thought no one was paying any particular attention to me, I closed my lids and slid my fingers around Dustin's fragile wrist.

I didn't do this. Healing the sick was not my job, so I had no clue what I was doing, but I did know Latin, and that seemed to be working like a charm lately. *"Resarci,"* I whispered, asking the Big Man upstairs to forgive me if I was crossing any of his boundaries in attempting to do what I was attempting to do.

When I'd finished, however, I felt nothing. No power coursing through me. No lightning bolts shooting from my fingertips. No seas parting before me. Not that New Mexico had many seas, but . . .

I'd failed.

I let the wetness gathering between my lashes spill over them. What was the point in hiding anything now? I picked up the little guy's scraped arm and kissed the inside of his palm.

Unfortunately, that got me some attention. I put his hand back and tried to hurry out of the room, but it was packed with grieving family members. My escape proved harder than I thought it would be.

Before I got halfway to the door, the beeps on the heart monitor quickened and grew stronger. In another instant, Dustin moaned and moved his head from side to side. Even I stood in awe as he slowly opened his eyes. Just barely. The lights clearly bothered him because he squinted, then closed them again, but Willa cried out to him.

"Dustin!" she said, gently draping herself over his fragile body, petting his face with her fingertips, smoothing back a stray lock of brown hair. "Dustin, please," she said.

He fought to open his eyes again. A nurse rushed into the room to check his vitals. Another nurse was fast on her heels, weaving through the crowd to get to him.

Dustin tried to focus on his mother, but he couldn't quite keep his lids from drooping down before he managed it. He tried again, his irises rolling unsteadily until he found something else to focus on: me.

I gave him a quick grin as recognition registered on his swollen face. After a nod of affirmation, I tossed him a wink, then placed an index finger over my mouth as discreetly as I could. Dustin nodded with a wince, but couldn't seem to hold back a mischievous grin.

My lungs seized and tears flowed freely now. Had I done it? Did I actually save a child's life?

Before anyone could ask questions, I excused myself and wound through people to the exit. The nurses, as astonished as anyone, were kicking everyone but the mother and grandmother out anyway, so I blended in as the crowd, now hopeful, was ushered out of the tiny cubicle.

As I passed Dustin's chair, I rejoiced that he was no longer in it. I didn't know what happened, but I didn't care. I beamed as we were led to the huge metal doors, but I was brought up short by a soft, feminine voice.

"Charley?"

I stopped as everyone else kept going. Turning around, I smiled sadly at Willa. "Hi. Um, I was just visiting an old friend when I saw you in there. I'm so sorry I—"

"Stop," she said, her voice cracked, her cheeks flush. "It was you. Mom saw you pick up Dustin's hand. She saw what you did."

"What?" I asked, backing away from her. "I didn't do anything."

She caught my shoulders in her hands. "I know what you are. I was listening that night when you told Jessica." Her sadness returned with the thought of her departed sister. "She was just scared, Charley. She was just, I don't know, a stupid kid."

"Willa, I was kidding that night. You know how kids joke around about those things."

"Five minutes ago, I would have believed you." She put a hand on my face and looked at me with such awe, such regard. "Not anymore. I know what you did. How can I ever repay you?"

Jessica put a cool hand on my shoulder. "Tell her I love her. Please, Charley. I will never ask anything of you again. We were not on the best of terms when I passed. I just want her to know that I love her."

I crossed my arms and put my hands on Willa's. "She sent me here, you know. She's the one who saved Dustin. If not for her, I would never have known about him."

She covered her mouth with both her hands as a sob racked her slender body. She looked like a pixie with short brown hair and big brown eyes. She was always so stunning.

"Oh, my god," she said, her voice hitching.

"She wants you to know that despite your differences, she loved you beyond measure. She always has."

Willa collapsed into my arms, holding on to me as though her life depended on it. Her mother walked up behind her and put her hands on her shoulders as they shook. Willa leaned back.

"I will never forget this," she said, kissing my cheek and then picking up my hands and kissing them, too. "I will never forget this. Please tell her I love her, too."

"You just did."

Jessica was sobbing from behind me, her head on my shoulder. "And my mom. Please, Charley."

"And you, Mrs. Guinn. Jessica loves you very much."

She hiccupped with every breath she took and could only manage to nod her head. "He's asking for you," she said at last, squeezing Willa's shoulders.

Willa nodded, gave me one more quick hug, then rushed to her son's side. Jessica hurried after them.

I walked out dazed and confused. Reyes was right there.

"Did that really just happen?"

"You're Val-Eeth," he said, reminding me. "You're a god on your plane. I told you. You're capable of anything."

"Yes, there. But here? On this plane? In this world? It already has a God, in case you've forgotten. Do you think he'll be upset that I've done this? That I've invaded his turf?"

"I think that he's glad to have you. I just wouldn't make a habit of it."

As we left the hospital and headed for Misery, I picked up a rock in the tread of my left boot. I stopped and leaned against the building to pick up my foot. As Reyes surveyed our domain, I squeezed my lids together and practiced my Latin before removing my hand from the brick building.

"Race you," I said, running past him for a head start.

The exuberance of being in the lead, the sweet scent of victory, lasted approximately 0.7 seconds. It was the boots. And the fact that he had the prowess and strength of a freaking panther.

We finally made it back to the office. Reyes went to check on things at the bar while I hurried upstairs to check on my wayward assistant. I like to surprise-attack her sometimes. Keep her on her toes. I wasn't paying her to play spider solitaire. Unless I was playing spider solitaire. Then we were good.

I opened the door to my office slowly. Cookie was at her desk, so I tiptoed across my office floor.

"I hate you with the force of a thousand suns," she said. I hadn't even scared her yet.

"Why do you hate me today?"

She sat at her desk with an ice pack on her head. "It's hit. The caffeine withdrawal. I think I need a morphine drip."

"That's weird," I said, picking up her stapler. Hers was much cooler than mine. "My head is fine today."

She whirled toward me, then reeled in agony. "What?" she asked, fire blazing behind the depths of her killer blues.

"Yeah. I'm fine. I thought you said it was going to last two weeks."

"It should have. It's your supernatural crap." She waved an index finger at me. "Why did I do this? I don't even like you anymore."

"Sure you do," I said, adding a sprinkle of cheer to my voice. "I'm like crack. People don't want to like me, but once they get a taste, they always come back for more."

A nasally groan oozed out of her. "Why can't I quit you?"

"I just told you. I'm like crack. You never listen." When she groaned again, I laughed. "Cook, I told you not to give up caffeine just because I had to. It's hardly fair for you. We can get two coffeepots. Mr. Coffee has been saying he wants a friend anyway. And I think by *friend* he means he wants a profile at Match.com." I winked conspicuously at her.

"Or," she said, jumping to show me something she'd printed out. "We can get one of these newfangled single-cup brewers. Then you just buy the different kinds of coffee. They have flavors and everything."

I snatched the paper out of her hand. "What mad genius is this?"

"They've been around for years now."

"It's brilliant. I've never seen anything so brilliant."

"No," she said, erasing the air. "I can do this. It's just two weeks, right? What's two weeks in the grand scheme of things?" She leaned back and put the ice pack on her head.

"Well, a lot if you have work to do. Any updates?"

"No. And please step back. If my brain explodes, I don't want you to get any brain matter on your D and Gs." She loved my Dolce & Gabbanas. Sadly, I loved them more.

"Aw, that's so considerate."

"This is like the worst hangover I've ever had."

"Not so. The worst one involved your head in my toilet for seven hours while you moaned the chorus to 'Swing Low, Sweet Chariot.'"

"Oh, yeah. Freaking tequila."

"Right? So, I kind of just healed a kid."

She straightened again. "Charley, really?"

"Yeah. It was pretty amazing. To know that he is going to live. I've never felt such purpose."

"But you really healed someone? I mean, you can do that?"

"Apparently," I said with a shrug.

"Then what the hell are you waiting for? Lay your hands on me, baby." She leaned back in her chair and spread her arms wide.

"I don't think it works on just anyone."

"And I'm not just anyone. Come on, give it your best shot."

I giggled as I watched her wait. When she did her motherly glare thing, I finally leaned over and put an index finger on her head. *"Resarci,"* I said, and waited.

Cookie blinked and then shook her head to test it, at which point she clawed at her temples with both hands and groaned. "You're not even trying. Put your back into it." She reclined again.

"I just don't think it works this way. I think your illness has to be pretty dire."

She plopped her elbows on her desk and pointed to her head. "You think this isn't dire? You think my brain is somehow expendable?"

"I didn't say expendable."

Draping herself over her desk melodramatically, she put the ice pack on the back of her neck.

"What's on the agenda for the rest of the day?"

"We still have the suicide-note victims. But Robert said they may have found something."

"Really? He didn't tell me."

"Yeah, he said to put that case on the back burner for today while they work this lead."

"Hmm, okay. What next?"

"We have Amber's carnival in a couple of hours. Besides that, you don't have anything until tomorrow morning. You're meeting with the priest at the Amityville house."

"Sweet. A possessed house that knows my name. But this whole two hours of free time is weird. I never have free time."

She pulled herself up onto her elbows again. "No, I never have free time. You have all the free time in the world, which is why you make paper airplanes out of my memos."

"Good point. And that's another reason why you need to get back to work. Chop, chop. I'm not paying you barely enough to survive on for you to drool uncontrollably on your desk."

15

Lead me not into temptation.
Follow me instead! I know a shortcut!

—T-SHIRT

Two hours later, Cookie, Reyes, Osh, and I found ourselves roaming the halls of the Roadrunner Middle School during Carnival. It was their big annual fund-raiser for library books and educational field trips. A noble cause, but I could've done without the moans of agony from my sidekick. She was really taking the whole caffeine withdrawal hard. While I, on the other hand, had grown quite fond of the blood of Satan. A little creamer, a dash of sweetener, and voilà! Fake coffee. I could live with it for the next eight months or so until Beep decided to make her grand entrance.

"I'm not saying I'm going to resent Beep for the loss of my girlish figure," I said to Cook, who was only half listening through the fog of agony, "but seriously, have you seen my ass?"

"Charley!" Amber said, waving us over. She was wearing a long blue veil with gold trinkets dangling off it, and she had on heavy liner and a stark smattering of blush for effect.

Quentin stood beside her, a tall, beautiful, blond-haired blue-eyed devil who made Amber's heart go pitter-patter. I'd met him when a demon had decided to possess him to get to me, because Quentin could see things others couldn't. Namely, my light.

Fortunately, Artemis took care of the demon, and Quentin became a very good friend.

"Hey, you," I signed to him before pulling him into a big hug. "I didn't know you were coming."

"I invited him. I wanted him to meet Osh." She spoke and signed at the same time, ever aware of the rules of Deaf culture. And she was getting really good. I loved it.

"Oh, he's outside patrolling," I said, doing the same.

"Okay, Mom, do you want to be first?" she asked.

Quentin smiled shyly to Cook and accepted a hug from her. Then, in an act that rather surprised me, Quentin held out his hand to Reyes.

Reyes took it and offered an approving smile.

It was a big step. Quentin had been afraid of him for the longest time. He could see the departed almost as clearly as I could, but he could also see Reyes's darkness. I'd seen it only a couple of times, but had I not known him, the darkness would have scared me, too. So Quentin accepting Reyes as one of the good guys was a very big deal in my book.

"Or you can, Aunt Charley," Amber said.

"Fantastic," I said, having no idea what I'd just agreed to.

Cookie pointed to a sign on the floor painted in bright blues and yellows.

MADAM AMBER: A TELLER OF FORTUNES

"You're a madam?" I asked, taken aback. "Do you think that's appropriate at a middle school carnival?" They weren't kidding when they said kids grow up fast.

"Not that kind of madam," Cookie said.

"Or you, Uncle Reyes," she said, twisting on her toes shyly.

Reyes glanced at her in surprise.

"I don't have to call you that. I just thought since I'm losing Uncle Bob."

"You're losing Ubie?" I asked her. "Is he dying again? You know he just says that to gain sympathy."

"Well, no, you know, since he and Mom hooked up, the term *uncle* seems a little weird. So I thought since you're marrying Aunt Charley, maybe—"

Reyes took her hand into his and bowed over it, sweeping a light kiss on her knuckles. "I'm honored."

She beamed at him and threw her arms around his neck before planting a kiss on his cheek, leaving a heart-shaped imprint of ruby lipstick. Apparently, fortune-tellers and ladies of the night had a lot in common, including their choices of color palette.

"I totally have to go first," I said. I never had the patience to wait in line. "I have a lot of questions about my future. Be prepared."

Amber skipped in excitement and clapped her hands as she held open her tent, which looked alarming like Cookie's bedspread.

"Wish me luck," I said to Quentin.

"She's good," he promised.

I gave him a thumbs-up, winked at Reyes, then sat at the short table she'd set up. The curtain fell and Amber sat across from me, becoming Madam Amber, a teller of fortunes. She started laying out tarot cards, flipping one at a time to reveal my sordid future. Or sordid past. Either way. I took a closer look and picked up one of the cards.

"Amber, these are gorgeous."

"Thank you. I made them in art."

"You made these?" I asked, astonished. They were lovely, with flowing colors and soft angles. "Wait, they let you make tarot cards in art?"

"Yeah, our teacher is very New Agey."

"Ah. Well, I'm completely impressed."

She squirmed in delight, but I thought now might be a good time to broach a subject that needed to be broached. Perhaps with a nice cameo.

"Hon, are you okay with Uncle Bob dating your mom?"

"Are you kidding? I love Ubie. He's like a hero and one of those crazy uncles rolled into one."

"He is that."

"And he makes awesome spaghetti."

What a great kid. I hoped Beep would be as wonderful. As outgoing and accepting of her circumstances. No theater productions. No drama.

"Oh, my god, I totally lost a press-on." She held her hand up to the glowing crystal ball and snapped a shot of it to post on one of the gazillion social networks she belonged to.

I had to remind myself, I did the same thing once when I'd slipped in the bathroom on my Clorox ToiletWand and broken my toe.

"Okay, are you ready?"

"Dang straight. Hit me, O wise one."

She giggled, then slid a hand over the cards, letting it hover before touching one.

"Death," she said, and I wondered how I knew she'd go there. Tarot readers went straight to the Death card every time I'd had my fortune read. Which, including this one, was twice.

"A new beginning," she added. She touched the card with one hand, her lids drifting shut as she took my other hand into hers. Then she flattened our palms together until my hand was resting on hers. After a moment of concentration where I felt a ripple of electricity course between us, she began. "Twelve have been summoned and twelve have been sent."

At first her knowledge of the Twelve surprised me, but I remembered she heard a lot across the hall. She was a smart one. Still, she nailed the look. Her back was straight and her lids closed as the trance seemingly overtook her.

"Their eyes are unseen yet everywhere. They are blind yet they miss nothing. Twelve beasts lurk in the shadows. Twelve more lurk in the hearts of men. They wait. They watch for the uprising, when the daughter of the ghost god will stand alone on the rock and await the thirteenth's decision. With her. Against her. It does not matter, for she was made for this day. A day of death and a day of glory. With or without him, she will taste the victory of her enemy's blood on her tongue."

Holy.

Shit.

I sat stunned. That was a little too close to home. How much had she heard last night? I'd only just learned this stuff myself, and she couldn't have overheard me tell Cookie. She'd already been at school. But how did she know about the thirteenth warrior? How did she know he could tip the scales in the uprising of Satan and his army on this plane?

Without further ado, Amber snapped back to the present and held out her hand. "Three dollars, please."

I replaced my lagging jaw and dug into my bag for some ones. Either Amber was one of the best actresses I'd ever seen, or she just channeled Edgar Cayce.

"Hon, did you hear Reyes and me talking last night?"

"Pfft, no. I was out like a lamppost."

Kids and metaphors didn't always mix. I handed her a five and told her to keep the change.

"Sweet," she said, stuffing the money into a cup beside her. "Next!" she yelled, effectively kicking me out.

I stepped out and saw Ubie. Still stunned by Madam Amber, I asked, "What are you doing here? Is there something new on the case? Is it Dad? Did you find him?"

He raised his brows and waited for me to notice the fact that he was holding Cookie's hand.

"Oh. Oh! So, you're here in a nonprofessional capacity."

"Yes, pumpkin. I'm surprised you'd forget so easily after all the trouble you went to to get us together."

Cookie blushed a pretty pink.

"Next!" Amber shouted from her blanket tent. She was so impatient.

"I'll go next," Cookie said. "She practiced on me, so this should be short and sweet."

Quentin was busy checking out two kids trying to juggle samurai swords. Middle school boys and samurai swords. Those boys had very brave parents. Or really good health insurance.

I sidled up to Reyes and said, "Did you hear any of that?"

"I did. And can I just say, what the fuck?"

"Right there with ya. You know, part of the prophecies say that those who can serve and protect the daughter will be drawn to me. Maybe all of this, everything, me moving into that building, meeting Osh, meeting Quentin, knowing Pari, who can also see the departed, and now with Amber, maybe it's all part of some big plan. Some kind of security system for Beep."

"I'm beginning to wonder. And I'm really beginning to wonder who the thirteenth warrior is. If he could tip the scales and he could tip them out of our daughter's favor in her most desperate hour, maybe we should see to it that he doesn't live long enough to choose."

"I'm beginning to wonder. But how will we know who he is?"

"Next!" came Amber's insistent shout.

"Your turn. Maybe she'll shed more light onto this situation."

He nodded, then ducked, really low, to get into the tent. I stepped closer and listened in, but Amber went through the usual routine with him. No trances, just her giggles and fascination with my affianced, which was utterly charming.

He paid up, lest he face the wrath of Amber the Astonishing, and ducked back out again. Not an easy task for someone who was six-four.

After a round of games and some of the unhealthiest fare in the state, Reyes, Osh, and I left Cookie at the carnival. She'd promised to help tear down.

"Okay," I said, sidling up to her, "don't forget about the plan tonight."

"How could I forget about the plan?" she said, rolling her eyes. "It's ridiculous."

"No, it's not. If it works, it's not ridiculous. And it's going to work."

"Okay, but I don't even own a shovel."

"I have two. No worries."

"I'm going to regret this, aren't I?"

She asked it as though there were a chance I'd soothe her qualms. "Duh."

I did a little research when we got home, before going to bed. Osh took Sophie again, lounging against her armrest as I typed in everything from *the Twelve,* to *hellhounds,* to *the thirteenth warrior,* which yielded much Antonio, so that was fun. But I found nothing on my current-slash-future predicament.

Having synchronized our watches earlier, Cookie snuck into the apartment right on cue.

"Are you ready?" she asked, whispering.

"Ready as a drunk virgin on prom night."

I went to the bedroom. Reyes was fast asleep, his breathing deep and rhythmic. I hated to wake him. I didn't, however, hate to wake Osh. He'd supped on the souls of many a desperate man in his time, and he deserved to be deprived of a few hours of blissful slumber. Someone had to go with us. No way was I going out into the night without backup. There were beasts out there. Twelve of them. Once we got to the cemetery, we'd be safe. Consecrated ground and all. It was the in between here and there I worried about. But the only time we could dig up a grave with any hope of going undetected was at night.

So, I tiptoed over to him, put a hand on his mouth, and leaned close to his ear.

"Osh," I said, kneeing his hip. "Wake up."

"I wasn't asleep," he said from behind my hand.

I snatched it back. "Sorry."

"So, grave digging, huh?"

"How'd you know?" I asked, holding a shovel in my other hand.

"Okay, that was a good drive," I said, looking over at a traumatized Cookie as I pulled to a stop in the cemetery.

"You ran three red lights."

"Yeah, but it's two in the morning. No one was around. And I didn't want to be sitting ducks for any hellhounds that might happen along."

"And you drove through the university campus where there are no streets."

"Yet plenty of sidewalk."

Osh grabbed the shovels out of the back and followed us to Lacey's grave.

"Hey, guys," she said with a wave. "Who's the hunk?"

Osh grinned, and if the departed could blush, she would have.

"Um, sorry. I didn't know you could hear me."

"Not at all. Which one?"

"Oh. Over here."

Lacey led Osh to her gravesite.

Cookie and I lagged behind, partly so I could ask her something and partly because we were hoping Osh would do all the work.

"Have you noticed anything strange about your daughter?" I asked Cook, not certain how to bring up tonight's event.

"Something?" she asked. "As in only one thing?"

I chuckled and relayed what had happened at the carnival to an astonished Cookie.

"Yeah, I was right there, too." I stopped her and put a hand on her arm. "She's special, Cook. And I don't mean a little. I think we were destined to meet. I think she's going to somehow be a key player in my daughter's life."

Cookie sat on a headstone, and while normally that would be a tad profane, I understood her need to sit down. "I don't know what to say."

"I don't either. I was floored, Cook. She was amazing. And those cards? Where did she learn to do that?"

"I asked her that, too."

"And?"

"Prison, apparently."

"She's such a smart-ass."

"Tell me about it."

I summoned Angel and made him and Lacey be the lookouts. "No flirting either," I said in warning. "I need lookouts, not make-outs. Got it?"

"Sheesh, *pendeja,* chill your blue jeans. She's so bossy," Angel said to Lacey, hooking a thumb toward me.

And again with the almost blushing as they went off to be our lookouts.

Luckily, Lacey was right. The ground had recently been disturbed, so digging was way easier than I thought it would be, which still meant it was one of the hardest, most effortful things I'd ever done in my life. I'd dug a lot in Uganda, but apparently I was in much better shape then.

Osh sat against a headstone, scanning the area while Cookie and I dug. It was my own fault. I should have blackmailed him into actually helping, but I got the feeling he was enjoying the Cookie and Charley Show.

We were getting somewhat of a rhythm, though. Two hours later, Cookie was wheezing and involuntarily moaning every time she swung the shovel, like a tennis player every time she hit the ball, while I just sweated like a running back during Super Bowl. Every once in a while, I'd accidentally dump a shovelful of dirt on Cook's head. It seemed to upset her tremendously, and never one to take an insult lying down, she would accidently dump a shovelful of dirt on my head, too.

"Wouldn't it suck if we did all this work and Lacey's body was still in there?"

"Bite your tongue."

"I heard that!" Lacey said from afar. Dead people had really good hearing.

Osh strolled up to us, chewing on a blade of grass like we had all the time in the world. Reyes would figure out I wasn't back home soon enough; then I'd have hell to pay. Literally.

"So, you two have been at this for two hours and—"

"Dog!" Lacey screeched in the distance. She'd been doing that all night, scared to death one of the hellhounds would show up.

"—and you've managed to shave off only the top layer of dirt."

I gaped at him. "This is much more than the top layer. This is at least—" I held up a hand to get a visual calculation. "—four and a half inches."

"Out."

Cookie and I couldn't have scrambled out of the grave fast enough. Which, at four and a half inches deep, wasn't difficult.

Osh took both shovels, tested their weight and balance, chose one, and then went to work.

An hour later, Cookie, Lacey, and I sat in the graveyard, watching a slave demon who looked like a nineteen-year-old kid—a very well-built nineteen-year-old kid—dig up a grave shirtless, his wide shoulders shimmering in the moonlight.

"I'm going to hell," Cookie said, unable to rip her gaze off him.

"Well, if you go, there are probably others who look like that. It might not be such a bad place."

"I want to have his demon babies," Lacey said.

Angel scoffed behind us, the only one besides Osh actually doing his job.

Just then we heard a thunk, and Osh looked up over the grave. "Found it."

We hustled over as he scraped dirt off the coffin and opened it. Sure enough, no body.

"Told you," Lacey said. "You know, the more I think about it, the more it had to be Joshua, my ex. Maybe he hid my body somewhere else. He was so obsessed with it when I was alive. Can I haunt him?"

"You sure can. I advise it, actually. It's very therapeutic. But I'm not sure it's him."

"What do you mean?" she asked as Osh jumped out of the grave. Like literally. Freaking demons.

"You said there are two more graves with missing bodies?"

"Yes, I can show you."

We walked to the other two graves, and I took the names, dates, and lot numbers down.

"I have a feeling that once we find your body, we'll find the others, and these two have been here awhile. I'm thinking someone who works here is stealing them."

"But why wait until they're buried?" Cookie asked. "Wouldn't it be much easier to steal bodies while they're in the morgue?"

"If my assumption is right, which it usually is, this is someone who has access to the equipment here and knows the schedule. It's a lot harder to sneak a body out of a morgue than one might think. It's better to steal the bodies after they are in the ground where no one will notice they're missing, don't you think? Much less likely to get caught that way."

"True. Sick, but true."

We took another trip through Albuquerque in the dark, but this time we had to make a quick pit stop at a convenience store, one that I happened to know used fake cameras out front, and called the police. We told them someone was digging up a grave at the Sunset Cemetery. We told them to hurry. Then I called Ubie from my cell and explained what was about to happen, how there would be a grave robbery soon and that the detective on the case needed to look into the cemetery's employees, specifically groundskeepers, and to check out the culprit's property once he was found, as there were two more missing bodies.

The horizon was just beginning to brighten when we pulled up to the apartment building. We hurried in, and I fought Osh for the first shower. Literally and quietly, so as not to wake up the demon in the next room. I went for the hair. Grabbed handfuls. It was a dirty trick, but I was a dirty girl. Again, literally. I had dirt in places I didn't know existed.

Once victory was mine, I closed the bathroom door, flipped on the light, then pulled back the curtain to turn on the shower. Reyes stood there. Leaning against the tile. Arms crossed. Deadpan expression in place.

"Oh, hey," I said, smiling brightly. "I was just looking for you." When he didn't say anything, I continued. "You would not believe what happened while I was taking out the trash." I scoffed and pointed to my hair. "Yuck. That's all I have to say."

"Grave robbing is a federal offense."

I gasped. "What? I would never. We weren't robbing. We were just digging. Exercise is good for Beep. And did you follow me?"

"Your every move."

My jaw fell open. "I am so indignant right now. I was trying to let you rest."

"Mm-hm."

"And if you were there, why didn't you help us dig?"

"Because it was far too amusing watching you do it." He stepped out of the tub and kept walking until he'd backed me against the wall. "And you left without me. At night. When the hellhounds are free to roam the lands and eat little girls for breakfast."

"I took Osh." I couldn't imagine how bad I looked.

"You left. At night."

"Are we going to have this conversation again? I. Took. Osh."

"Why?" he asked, seeming genuinely confused. "Why would you take a risk like that for a dead body?"

I tried to push past him. He didn't let me. "It's what I do, Reyes. Someone stole that sweet girl's body."

"She took her own life."

"Reyes," I said, scolding. "She had a disability. She felt hopeless and lost. You cannot fault her for that."

"And what about me?" he asked, leaning closer, but not to seduce. Not to lure. To intimidate. He slipped a hand around my throat, gently and methodically, his signature move. "Do you know how I would feel if the Twelve got to you? *Hopeless and lost* doesn't even begin to describe it."

"There's a guy out there stealing the bodies of young girls out of their graves."

"And they are already dead. It couldn't have waited until after we settled the matter with the Twelve?"

"You get ahead of yourself. That should be *if* we settle the matter with the Twelve. What if I don't make it? I could do this now. I could solve this case now, so I did. Why put off until tomorrow . . . ," I said, letting my voice trail off.

"Then why would you not wake me? Why would you risk your life and the life of our child for something so inconsequential?"

"I couldn't risk you, too," I said quietly. "I'm compelled to help the departed, Reyes. It's like my calling. If they are in pain, in need, in straits, I feel compelled to the marrow of my bones to help them. It's just who I am."

He dropped his arm and stepped back. "I think I know why your people let you come. Why they let you leave your plane to come here for what amounts to menial labor."

This was going to be interesting. "Okay, I'll bite."

"You're a god, and yet you want to help. Gods don't help, Dutch. Gods have to know when to aid their people and when to step back and let them learn from their mistakes."

"So my stint on Earth is supposed to help me become a better god?"

"Yes. Because no being can live in a perfect world. Life is destined to fight to survive. To thrive. To prosper. To have more than the have-nots. All life destroys in order to live. You can't fix everything, but you would try."

"Are you saying I'd be a horrible god?"

"I'm saying you *are* a horrible god. You risk the wrong things for the wrong causes. You strive for perfection instead of taking pleasure in the imperfect."

He started to walk out, but I put my arm across the doorway to block him. He looked down at me, his deep mocha gaze shimmering angrily.

"You're wrong," I said, matter-of-fact. "You, Mr. Farrow, are far from perfect."

I dropped my arm and turned from him. Partly because I needed a shower really bad and partly because there was a grain—just a grain—of truth to what he'd said.

16

Never underestimate the power of termites.
—BUMPER STICKER

I showered and then made a cup of Satan's blood as Osh took his turn. I was exhausted, but the sun was in full swing, and I had things to do. Cookie came over and made herself a cup, too.

"Every inch of my body is sore," she said. "And my head is going to fall off at any moment."

"I'm really sore, too," I said, playing along.

"No, you're not. He busted you, didn't he?" she said, taking one look at me as I sulked behind my mug.

"Yes. He followed us out there."

"Seriously?" she asked, sitting on Osh's bed. "And he didn't help?"

"Right? But that's not all. He said I'm a horrible god."

She gasped. "He didn't."

"He did."

"Well, we all have to be horrible at something, sweetheart. Take me, for example. I'm horrible at selling vacuum cleaners."

I shrugged a shoulder. "You're just saying that to make me feel better."

"True. I rock at selling vacuum cleaners. And you have a house to dispossess. Chop, chop."

After I got dressed, I searched Reyes's apartment for him, but to no avail. I stepped back into my own pad to see Osh dressed and wearing his top hat like he was going places.

He stood. "Rey'aziel had to go check on things at the bar. He asked me to escort you today."

The sting was quick and brutal. I fought to suppress it. "Okay," I said, wondering if Osh was like Reyes and me. If he could feel emotion.

Either way, we ended up going to the Amityville house together. In absolute silence. Maybe he *could* feel emotion. We crossed the Rio Grande at eight thirty and found the house with relative ease about ten minutes later. Sadly, it looked nothing like the real Amityville house. And it certainly didn't look possessed.

Father Glenn stood out front, waiting for us.

"Where's the family?" I asked as I climbed out of Misery.

"Work. Kids are at school." He shook my hand and nodded to Osh, who stood close behind me.

"It looks so normal," I said, and the father chuckled.

"That's what I said. It seems very interested in meeting you."

"Wonderful. Shall we?" I asked Osh. I'd of course packed Zeus, but if there was a real demon inside, I could easily get rid of it with my light, or my *inner glow,* as I liked to call it. I'd done it before.

Osh nodded and followed me to the door.

"It's open," Father Glenn called out. "I want you to get a feel for the place before I join you."

" 'Kay. Thanks." I wasn't sure what else to say to that.

"It has a dark aura," Osh said quietly.

I slowed my step. "That's bad?"

He nodded. "Houses don't have auras."

"Oh. So, yeah, bad." Probably an angry demon.

He went inside with me, but just in case, as we crossed the threshold, I summoned an even angrier demon. "Rey'aziel," I whispered.

"I'm here," he said at my ear. Of course he would already be there, watching over me incorporeally. I felt his heat slide along my skin, the scorching sensation oddly comforting.

As we searched for the room Father Glenn told us about, the one with the most activity, I asked Osh, "How do you do that? How do you see auras? I've done it, but I can't do it every day. And I'm the grim reaper, for heaven's sake."

"It took a while for me to learn it, too. You were made to see the departed, to focus on them. Maybe that's why the auras of the living are unimportant to you."

"They're not unimportant."

"Just a thought."

"So, how did you learn?"

"First, you have to realize human sight is different from our own. We see a thousand times the number of colors that they do."

"Seriously? Okay."

"Then you have to adjust. To see things from more than one plane at a time."

"And how do you do that?"

"You catch fire."

I stopped and turned to him. "You what?"

He lifted a shoulder. "That's the only way to describe it. When I was first learning, it felt like I would catch fire. Then I could see every color the sun had to offer. And every nuance of every color. Every gradation in between until the shades between black and white were in the millions."

"Yes. That," I said, pointing to him. "I want to do that."

"Push inside yourself until it feels like you catch fire. And hurry, because it's here."

I whirled around, looking but not seeing. "I don't understand. I've seen demons a dozen times. Why can't I see it?"

"You've seen them when they've allowed you to. You need to see them with or without their permission. And, yeah, I'd hurry."

My adrenaline kicked in, my gaze darting from corner to corner in a narrow hall. The wood floorboards creaked with every movement. I did what Osh said and concentrated. Tried to catch fire. A spark of heat flared to life inside me and grew, spreading until it consumed every inch I had to offer, until it blurred and shifted my vision from what I saw as a human to what I saw as a supernatural entity. And slowly a figure took shape in the darkened corridor.

"I see it," I whispered.

He leaned closer. "You see the one that wants you to see it. You still aren't seeing the other two that don't."

That did it. I pushed in and pushed out at the same time, sending my light out to illuminate the world around me, and two more demons came into focus. Sadly, they were all three hanging from the ceiling, their slick black heads twisting in curiosity, their teeth glistening.

One fell from the ceiling like a spider and partly unfolded itself in front of me, its limbs full of sharp angles and odd positions. Osh quickly traded places with me, his head lowered, his fists at his sides as he prepared for an attack. I could feel excitement rush through his veins with the promise of battle.

The demon hissed and scurried back, and I could have sworn I heard the word *champion* on the air. It was in a language I knew but didn't recognize. Either way, they knew who he was. What he was.

I could also see Reyes, his cloak enveloping me like a protective layer undulating around me as he stood at my side. I felt the heat of his visage slide over my skin.

Along with my newfound sight, the colors like a kaleidoscope glittering before my eyes, came other sensory clues that I was no longer just on the earthly plane. The scent of the demons hit me hard, like someone burning an animal that had been dead for days, its fur acrid, the smell of death strong.

"You've been making an awful lot of commotion to get me over here," I said to them. "It will be a costly mistake on your part."

"Reaper," one of them said, its voice nothing more than a rasp, one that stabbed me like a dentist's drill hitting a nerve. And it came from behind us.

I turned while Osh stayed glued to the ones in front of us. The one behind us was still attached to the ceiling. Its face upside down came nose-to-nose with mine. Or it would have if it had had a nose. They looked so alienlike. So misshapen.

I could so very easily turn them to dust, but I was curious as to why they would practically invite me over for tea and scones. "Why are you here?" I asked in the same language they were speaking.

"You realize that by summoning me here, you signed your own death warrant." Demons were nothing to take lightly. I'd seen what they were capable of, but I also knew they were no match against the light that shone inside me.

"I do," it said, and I fought to place the language we were speaking. I knew it was ancient. Possibly the first language ever spoken in the universe. "Unless we sign yours first."

"Is that what you think will happen here?"

"Dutch," Reyes said into my ear, "stop playing with your dinner."

"I just want to know why they've come onto my plane so brazenly. So callously."

"We are *quedeau*," it said, and I had to translate the word in my mind.

"Hunters," I said, but it was more than that. "Bounty hunters."

"Close enough."

"If you're going to do something, now would be a good time," Osh said.

I glanced around. The hall had filled with the slick, insectlike beasts. I felt a ball of oppressive energy gathering near the end of the hall, where the demons were entering through a crack in the wall. They looked like a horde of spiders emerging from a nest. Before I knew it, there were dozens of them surrounding us.

"Why did you want me here?" I asked the one staring me down.

"We are strongest here."

"Look closer," Reyes whispered, and I saw that beyond the crack in the wall was a darkness, thick and a million miles deep, and it was literally hemorrhaging demons.

"A gate?" I asked him, taken aback.

"One of several gates to hell," Osh said. "But the trip even to get this far is perilous. They must have emptied hell of these lice to get this many across.

"There are more," the demon said, his head twisting as though curious about me. "The Twelve have been sent. You are not long for this world, Reaper."

"There are more gates?" I asked Osh.

"Yes. I came through one similar to this centuries ago, but I looked a lot better than these roaches."

As we spoke, the demon closest to me decided to take advantage of the distraction. He lurched toward me, claws extended, teeth bared, and in one blinding moment, I let loose the light that would burn them all alive. I focused my energy on the gate, tried to close it, but even my light couldn't accomplish such a feat.

Still, after I reined in my energy, they stopped coming through. Either they'd wised up and decided to stay on the other side, or I'd killed all those that had made it this far.

"We should go just in case one of the Twelve had a passport stamped at this particular checkpoint."

"How many are there?" I asked as we hurried out of the house. "How many gates?"

"It's not that simple."

"What do you mean?"

"They aren't what you think."

I stopped short and glanced up at something shiny in a corner where wall met ceiling. A small circle reflected light down at us, and if I was not mistaken, it belonged to a camera lens.

"Coming?" he asked.

I nodded and followed him out, wondering about the good father who'd summoned me here. Did he know this house sat on a hellmouth? Of course, the family could have placed cameras about the place themselves in an attempt to catch paranormal activity. It wasn't the camera itself that caught my attention, but the fact that it was so well hidden, almost undetectable. And it looked like a professional installation.

I pulled him to a stop in the foyer. "Is that what you looked like in hell?" I asked Osh. "One of those things?"

"Hell no," he said, offended. He adjusted his top hat. "I looked like me."

"Then what were they?"

"Demons."

"But you're a demon."

"Let's just say there are as many species of demons as there are animals on Earth. Those are the lesser demons. Kind of like worker bees."

"They were below you?" I asked. "Below the Daeva?" I didn't want to use the word Reyes used to describe them: *slaves.*

He shook his head and looked away as though embarrassed. "No one was below the Daeva."

I stepped even closer, my curiosity burning. "After they threw Reyes off that grain elevator and I kissed him—"

"You brought him back," he assured me.

And maybe I had. He'd fallen seven stories. He'd been crushed and lay dying at the bottom. All he'd asked for was a kiss, and when I kissed him, I'd felt an electricity run from me and into him. A warmth. But it was still hard for me to believe I had such a gift. I was the grim reaper. It was my job to escort the dead to heaven. Not to bring them back to life.

"Fine. Let's say I did, but for a few seconds afterwards, I saw something else. Something dark. Something very much like those demons. And then it was gone. Did I kill the demon inside him?"

He offered me a sad smile. "Sugar, he *is* the demon inside him. You cannot separate the two." This time, he stepped closer, his expression hardening. "Make no mistake, Charley, there is a part of him that is as dark and dangerous as Lucifer himself. That part lives in all demons."

I raised my brows in question. "Even in you?"

"Yes, even in me." He stepped back and dropped his gaze to the floor. "Especially in me."

"Thank you for being honest." I looked up. "And thank you for being here, Reyes," I whispered before we stepped out into the light. But he didn't respond, and for the second time that day, I felt a sting, quick and brutal.

"The good news is they're gone," I said to Father Glenn as we walked toward him.

"What? Just like that?" he asked, straightening. "You weren't in there five minutes."

"We're super-efficient. The bad news is, this family is living smack-dab on top of a gate to hell."

He stilled, then opened a journal to jot down a note. "How do you know?"

"I saw it."

His lids rounded into saucers. "Can you describe it?"

"I have another case to get to," I said. "But we can talk another time, yes?"

"Yes, of course. What do I owe you?" he asked as we walked to Misery. Despite my suspicions, he didn't seem deceptive at all. He had a burning curiosity, but who wouldn't when told of the location of a gate to hell? I thought about the file he'd given me, the one from the Vatican. "Paid in full, Father."

He shook my hand, then tipped an invisible hat as Osh tipped his real one and climbed into the driver's seat.

"I think I need to know more about your world," I said to Osh as we headed back to the office. He drove, which was probably a good thing, since I was shaking and a little light-headed from our ordeal. Being surrounded by dozens of demons in that form felt a lot like standing in the middle of a room crawling with flesh-eating spiderlike roaches. I shivered. "And the gates. What the hell are those about? And the whole marking-of-souls thing I'm supposed to be doing."

"Okay," he said, more compliant than I'd expected.

"And just how, exactly, do you feed off the souls of humans? Is it like a vitamin-deficiency thing?" I winced as Osh changed lanes to avoid ramming into the back of a Sunday driver. We had places to be, damn it. "And do all demons do that? Or are you like an incubus?"

He laughed. "If I were an incubus, sugar, I'd have had you in my bed weeks ago."

"Osh," I said, scolding him teasingly, "you really need to work on your self-confidence. Low self-esteem is such a tragedy in today's youth."

"Isn't it?" he said, his mouth tilting up at one corner. His eyes were such a fantastic shade of bronze, a color I'd never seen on anyone before, and I wondered if he was lying about the incubus thing. I had a feeling he didn't want for womanly affection.

Ubie called before we could dive deeper into the conversation. He had good news and bad news. He'd managed to get a warrant for the storage unit from the card we found in Dad's hotel room. That was the good news. The bad news was that a woman had called the police to her house off Academy. She hadn't heard from her son, so she went to his house that morning and found a suicide note but, of course, no son.

"I can meet you there," I said, my phone beeping with another call. We could still save him.

"Actually, pumpkin, I'm headed over to the station. I'll call you when I know more."

He was acting awfully weird. "You're acting awfully weird," I said to him, my mouth echoing my thoughts involuntarily.

"We have a lead. I'll get back to you." His tone was tightly controlled. He was in full detective mode, which was fine since he was a detective and all, but I was on the case with him. Why would he keep the lead from me?

"Okay. Keep me in the loop."

"Pumpkin," he said, then hesitated a moment before saying, "you know I love you, right?"

My chest tightened. That was beyond weird. "Of course, Uncle Bob. Tell me what's going on." Fear spiked within me like the percussion of a nuclear blast.

"I'll explain later."

I hung up so I could answer the other incoming call.

"I wanted to call you," the woman on the other end said. "I figured it out. I know who's writing the suicide notes and kidnapping people."

"Mrs. Chandler?" I asked, recognizing her slightly Texan accent. She was the widow of one of the "suicide" victims. "What do you mean?"

"I called the police this morning, and now they have someone in custody. I got him. I got that bastard."

"Mrs. Chandler, tell me what happened. How do you know who it is?"

"Okay, well, I don't watch a lot of TV. Hardly ever, really. But my son was home, and he had the TV on. It was that woman. That newswoman from Channel 7 who goes out and interviews people in Albuquerque? Ted always said she was dumb as a box of rocks."

"Okay." I couldn't argue that. "Sylvia Starr."

"Yes! But I didn't know he'd been released. It's him. He's the kidnapper."

"Who, Mrs. Chandler? I don't understand."

"That Reyes Farrow boy."

My vision blurred and darkened around the edges. Osh must have sensed my distress. He pulled over to the side of the road. Horns honked behind us, but they could have been a million miles away, for all the attention I gave them.

"The guy she did the story on. Said he was innocent and the state let him go after ten years in prison. That's how I knew. My husband was on the jury. I called and told them to look into it, and they said I was right. Said all the victims were on the jury."

Osh put Misery in park. Mrs. Chandler was practically screaming into the phone. He couldn't have missed a word she said.

"Mrs. Chandler," I said, swallowing back the acrid taste of bile in my throat, "I'm afraid that isn't possible."

"It's him, I tell you!" She was growing frantic. "I wanted to let you know I figured it out. I have to call Betty back. She's not picking up. I'm calling everyone."

Another false accusation against Reyes Farrow. If they investigated him or questioned him in any way, he would never trust cops again.

"How did you come to this conclusion?"

"I remembered where I saw that other victim. She was a juror. It didn't hit me till I saw that news story. He'd been accused of killing his father, and both my husband and that other one, that Anna girl, were on the jury that sent him to prison. But he's been released! Now he's coming back for revenge!"

"Your husband was on the jury that wrongfully convicted Reyes?"

"Yes! No! The evidence was overwhelming. I understand now it was a setup, that his father was still alive, but they didn't know that. Now Farrow is exacting his revenge. Ten years in prison changes a man. I have to try Betty again."

She hung up before I could say any more. I turned to Osh, his image blurry through the wetness gathered between my lashes. "This can't happen to him again, Osh."

He nodded in understanding. "He got a call this morning before he left," he said, putting Misery in drive and making a U-turn. "It . . . upset him. I think it was your uncle asking him to go down to the station to answer a few questions."

"No," I said, anger welling up inside me. Uncle Bob didn't even have the guts to tell me. "That's why he sent you with me."

"That's my guess."

"Where are you going?" I asked, looking around.

"To the station. Where else?"

We pulled up to the APD station where Uncle Bob worked fifteen minutes later—to a media frenzy. Cameramen and reporters lined the front of the glass building. A podium had been set up. Someone was about to make a statement.

I jumped out of Misery before Osh had turned off her engine and hurried up the steps, until an officer held me back.

Uncle Bob rushed out to let me through.

"You knew, didn't you?" I asked, growing more volatile by the second. We pushed through the front doors. "You knew this was about Reyes's trial."

"We just found out, pumpkin," he said, leading me back to his office. "Just?"

"Yesterday afternoon. One of the guys ran the names in a court-system database and got a hit."

"And when were you going to tell me?"

"It was my idea to wait."

I turned around. Captain Eckert was trailing behind us. "Well, then you're an asshole."

He frowned. "You can't call me an asshole."

"If the sphincter fits."

"And you wonder why we didn't tell you straightaway," he said, urging me into Ubie's office. "Can you get her some water?" he asked Ubie.

"I don't need water. I need to see my fiancé."

"We're holding him for the time being," he said.

I gaped at Uncle Bob. He, of all people, should know how very thin the ice was on which they walked. "You cannot be serious. You know he didn't do this, Uncle Bob."

"I know, Charley, but we can't just ignore the evidence."

"What about the one in California. She disappeared two months ago."

"Weeks after Reyes was released."

I scoffed and walked to Uncle Bob's window. It overlooked . . . another window. "You know what this will do to him," I said without turning around. But when I did turn around, I pinned all my anger on him. "You know how incredibly unfair this is."

"I do." He raked a hand through his hair, not about to argue with me on that point.

I turned away, unable to look at either of them. "What about Anna's phone records from work? What about the woman who called her out of the blue, wanting to meet?"

"We're still going over the records," the captain said. "We don't even know when she received the call. So far, nothing out of the ordinary has popped up."

"Anything unusual about this new case? Did the guy mention anything to anyone?"

When I turned back, Ubie had lowered his head. "He told his mother he wanted to talk to Reyes. He told her he found out he'd bought a bar and was going to go by there and talk to him. That was last week."

"So, what? He goes down there and Reyes convinces him to write a suicide note so he can abduct him? I've never heard Reyes use the word *glorious* once, by the way. You know, in case you're keeping track."

I swept past them. They clearly weren't going to let me see Reyes, and I needed to be on the phone with a lawyer instead of wasting my time here. Uncle Bob followed me out to a surge of questions from the reporter.

"Detective! Detective! Are you once again trying to accuse Reyes Farrow of a crime he didn't commit?"

I stopped and spotted Sylvia Starr in the crowd of reporters. Wonderful.

"Is this about the lawsuit?" she asked.

I rolled my eyes. Though I would not have condoned a lawsuit, Reyes had every right to pursue one, and I was beginning to think it might not be a bad idea. Maybe if the city lost a few million to him, they'd think twice about dragging him in here on a whim.

Ubie followed me all the way to Misery, where he grabbed my arm and turned me toward him. "I don't think he's guilty," he said under his breath. "But, pumpkin, you cannot expect me to ignore the evidence when it's staring me in the face."

"Of course not," I said, pulling free. "But the last time you knew he wasn't guilty, he spent ten years in prison for a crime he didn't commit."

I climbed back into Misery and slammed the door.

"If it makes you feel better," Ubie said through my window, "you were right about that corpse stolen out of the cemetery. We went right to the head groundskeeper's house and found the body of a young woman who'd died recently in the closet of the guest room."

"It really doesn't," I said as Osh backed away.

I called Cookie. "I need to know exactly who was on that jury."

By the time I got back to the office, Cookie not only had a list of jurors, but she'd pulled up recent DMV photos of almost all of them as well.

"I'm so sorry, honey," she said, pulling me into a hug the minute I walked in.

"Thanks, Cook. Anything?"

"I'm still working on the current photos, but I did find this."

She pulled up an article about the trial we'd never seen before. It was dated over a year after Reyes was convicted.

She pointed to a passage. "See here? One of the jurors said she was bullied by the other jurors, coerced into changing her vote to guilty, even though she believed him to be innocent. She goes on to say . . . here." She pointed to another passage. "She said they badgered her, and one juror called her a lovesick fool. She also received threatening letters during deliberation, and another one told her to just let them all go home. Said even his idiot kid could see Reyes was guilty. She changed her verdict and sealed the fate of Reyes Farrow despite her gut instincts." Cookie stood back to let me peruse. "She sounds more than a little miffed. Apparently, there was an investigation at her insistence, but I can't imagine anything ever came of it."

"And who was this again?"

Cookie looked through her list. "Sandra Rhammar. But you haven't seen the best part."

I turned to her, almost afraid to hope she'd found anything that would convince the cops Reyes was innocent. She slid a picture over of Sandra Rhammar from the trial. "Look familiar?"

I snapped it off the desk. "Oh, my god, Cookie. You are amazing."

"I am. I really am."

I jumped up and hugged her neck, realizing I'd forgotten about Osh. He stood over me, looking at what Cookie had found. "Isn't that chick on TV?"

I grinned. "Yes, she is."

"She changed her name," I said into the phone, trying to convince the captain to listen to me. "She was a juror." I'd tried Ubie about a hundred times—to no avail. I guess he was done with me for the day. Or he was giving a press conference. Either way.

"And who is this again?" the captain asked. The background noise was deafening, and he was having a hard time hearing me.

"It was Sandra Rhammar."

"Sandra Rhammar," he said to someone else. Hopefully that person was doing a background now.

"She changed her name to Sylvia Starr. She's right there in front of the station."

"Right. The newswoman."

"Yes. It's her. I really think it's her, Captain, but I don't have time to look into it. The last guy was still alive for a while, so I'm guessing maybe she was keeping him alive for some reason or maybe he was in a confined space and it took him a while to suffocate. Or I don't know. Why else would it take him so long to pass?"

"She may have hesitated," he said. "Or she could have poisoned him and it took a while for it to kick in."

"True. I'm going to her house."

"Davidson, don't do anything you'll regret when you're sitting in a courtroom."

"Look, just tell my uncle, okay? Tell him to meet me at 2525 Venice Avenue, Northeast. It's right off Wyoming."

"You can't go in without a warrant."

"I know," I said, completely offended. "I'm all about the warrants. But if this guy is alive, we need to get to him now."

"Where is your uncle, by the way?" he asked me. "I thought he left with you?"

"No," I said, driving slowly down Venice, looking for the house number.

"There," Osh said, pointing ahead.

"Why would he leave with me? Isn't he doing the news conference?"

"That's where I am. I'm about to give a statement now."

"Captain," I said pulling over, "don't say anything about Reyes."

"I wouldn't either way, Davidson. Especially without a formal arrest."

"It won't come to that. Thank you."

"Let me know what you find. And don't break in. I don't need your uncle on my ass any more than he is."

"He's on your ass?" I asked, surprised.

"He about flipped when I told him to bring Farrow in for questioning."

That alleviated some of the sting I'd felt earlier. "I'm glad. He knows Reyes. My affianced had nothing to do with this, Captain."

"Prove it," he said before hanging up.

If ever there were a challenge. "After the zombie apocalypse, I'm raiding these houses for sustenance," I said to Osh. The homes were gorgeous—huge territorials with Spanish-tiled roofs—and the views incredible.

We pulled into the drive, and knowing Sylvia was at the station, we walked around back.

"Oh, look," Osh said after scaling a cinder block wall and then opening the gate to let me in, "this door has a broken windowpane."

I nodded, studying the pristine glass. "It looks broken to me."

He hooked his elbow in his shirt and smashed in a single pane.

"You realize we're most likely going to set off an alarm."

"I'm counting on it," he said with a wink. He reached in and unlocked the door. Sure enough, an alarm blared to life.

"Neighborhood like this, that'll get them here in no time," he said.

"Okay, when the cops get here, let me do the talking."

"Why? I'm the one who saw a burglar in a ski mask and a semiautomatic go inside this house."

"See, that's what I'm talking about. He clearly had an Uzi. Just try to keep your sentences short and to the point." We'd just let the cops search the place for us.

"But just in case they ask, why are we in this neighborhood in the first place?"

"I told you." People never listened to me. "We're scoping houses in preparation for the zombie apocalypse."

"Right. Preppers. Okay."

We hurried back to Misery and waited for the cops. It was amazing how quickly they got to these posh neighborhoods.

Twenty minutes later, the four patrol officers came out of Sylvia Starr's house empty-handed. "We didn't see anything," Taft said to me. He was Strawberry Shortcake's older brother, and we'd almost been friends since I told him she was still here on this plane. Our relationship was a little on the cool side, but he was okay, for the most part. He knew better than to believe I had nothing to do with that broken pane, but he didn't let on to the other cops. Though they probably knew, too. I was rather infamous around these parts.

"Really?" I asked, disjointed. "There was nobody tied up and drugged in there?"

"No."

"Damn it."

"I gotta admit, Davidson, you're fucking weird."

"Yeah?" I said as he turned with a grin and walked away. "Well, right back atcha, buddy. Your sister said you used to paint your toenails tea rose pink."

He laughed but kept walking.

"Damn it," I said again, trying Ubie for the umpteenth time. He was picking up my dad's bad habits. Just as I was about to call Cook, my phone rang. It was the captain.

"We got a hit on the phone call," he said to me. "You were right. It was Sylvia Starr."

Exhilaration laced up my spine. "Is that enough to let Reyes go?" Technically, they could hold him for twenty-four hours unless I got a lawyer involved, which was what I should have done immediately. I just got so excited once we'd figured out Sandra/Sylvia was involved, I kind of spaced that part.

"I've already released him. We had a patrolman take him out the back way."

"Thanks, Captain."

"Don't thank me. It was your uncle who kept insisting we had the wrong guy."

"Can I talk to him?"

"He's AWOL."

"Still?" I asked, growing concerned until my utter stupidity hit me like a ton of masonry. "If Sylvia is behind this and it has to do with the fact that the jury bullied her and put an innocent man in prison, a man with whom she fell in love, what do you think she would do to the arresting officer?" I asked him.

"Son of a bitch," he said. "She wasn't at the news conference."

"She was when I was there."

"And so was your uncle." He hung up before I could comment further, but I knew he would put every available resource on it.

Before I could put Misery into drive and peel out, Cookie called. I hesitated, unsure of what to tell her.

"Cook," I said when I answered.

"Anything?" she asked.

"At Sylvia's house? No. The cops searched the entire place."

"Well, her parents have passed away, but I did find some property that belonged to them in Tijeras."

"That's just thirty minutes from here."

"Yep. They owned a cabin."

"And what a perfect place to take someone you'd just forced to write a suicide note and abducted."

"That's where I'd take someone I'd forced to write a suicide note, then abducted." When I hesitated even longer, she said, "I'll text you the address. It'll take you a little over half an hour to get there from your current location."

"Cook," I said, biting my lip, "have you heard from Uncle Bob?"

"Not in a few. Why? What did you say to him?"

"I wasn't very nice, but that's not the problem. He was the lead officer in Reyes's case."

"I know, hon. I don't underst—" My meaning sank in. I waited for her to absorb the reality of the situation. "Where is he?" she asked, growing wary.

"We can't find him. He's not answering his cell and he hasn't been at the station in over an hour. Sylvia was there, and she's gone, too."

"Charley," she said, her voice a whisper.

"She forces them to write suicide notes," I rushed to assure her. "And even after that, she doesn't kill them right away. There's still time, Cook. We'll find him."

"Oh, my god, Charley."

"Reyes is headed your way. Explain what's going on, and tell him to get his fine ass in that muscle car of his and meet us out there. And call the captain. Tell him what you found."

"Okay. Okay, I'll do that now. Charley, please," she said, pleading with me.

"We got this, Cook. We're the best team ever. You solved this one. You. Let me do the rest."

17

I already know I'm going to hell.
At this point, it's really go big or go home.

—T-SHIRT

The sun set just as we pulled onto a long drive that, according to the GPS, was the road to Sylvia's parents' cabin. Tijeras had trees galore, but this area was out of the way and pretty barren. If she was out there, she'd likely see us coming.

I turned off Misery's lights just in case and drove slowly. There was still enough of a pink afterglow on the horizon to lead the way. We crept over a small hill and were engulfed in trees once again. I had no choice but to turn on the headlights, but hopefully the trees would cover our approach.

After about a mile, we came to another clearing. A cabin sat in the middle, its windows illuminated.

"Stop here," Osh said, jumping out of Misery before I'd managed a full stop.

He closed the door quietly and sprinted through the trees as I killed the lights again and tried to call the captain. No signal. Just in case, I sent a text to Cookie explaining that someone was at the cabin and telling her to call the captain to let him know. I hit send, then jumped out and followed Osh into the surrounding woods. He was going for the back of the house. Less likely to be seen that way, as the front was lined with massive plate-glass windows.

Scattered about the grounds were several departed. They were strategically placed to watch every opening, every nook and cranny. Reyes's spies? I definitely saw the woman in white, the woman Reyes had been talking to who'd drowned in her flowing evening gown. That was definitely the way I wanted to go: in style.

She turned around, spotted me, and disappeared. "Hello," she said, reappearing by my side, causing me to jump.

I looked up from my crouching position. "Hey. Did Reyes send you?"

"He did. We haven't spotted any yet."

"Any?"

"The Twelve. As far as I can tell, they aren't aware of your presence. Here all alone. At night. Completely vulnerable." She scolded me with a gathering of her delicate brows. If I were anyone else, being scolded by a dead woman in an evening gown with makeup smeared down her face would have freaked me out. Thankfully, I was me.

I scolded her right back. "My uncle might be in there. Can you see anyone in the house?"

"I'm not worried about in the house. Reyes sent me to guard you, not your uncle."

I straightened to my full height. She still had two inches on me. In my own defense, she was in heels. "Can't you just do a quick look-see? Pop in and out and just tell me if she's in there and who she's with?"

She didn't answer me. She was looking toward the drive, where another set of headlights was approaching. If they belonged to Sylvia Starr and she saw my Jeep, she could do anything to Uncle Bob, assuming she did actually have him. How that tiny lady could kidnap anyone was beyond me. We knew she'd drugged at least one of the victims, Mrs. Chandler's husband. She could have used Rohypnol, but how would she have done that with Ubie? It wasn't as though they were having drinks into which she could slip the date rape drug in the parking lot at the station.

And Ubie was a big guy. She would've had to use a lot to make him compliant. I just couldn't figure out how she was doing it all. I might soon find out, however. The vehicle approached slowly, its lights making it impossible to tell what kind of car it was.

I ducked down again just as the lights flashed twice, then went out. Recognizing the wicked black muscle car, I hurried through the woods as Reyes killed the engine. I rushed into his arms before he'd found his balance, but he caught me to him and held me tight.

"You're here," I said, my fear for Uncle Bob easing knowing Reyes was there.

Then again, Uncle Bob had just taken him in for questioning for a crime he didn't commit—for a second time. He might not be very inclined to help.

The passenger door opened and Cookie came flying out. "Is he here? Did you find him?" she asked, her gaze darting about wildly before she made it to me and embraced me with the enthusiasm of an offensive tackle.

"I don't know yet, but what are you doing here?"

She gaped at me. "Are you insane?"

"She threatened to jump on the hood if I didn't let her ride on the inside," Reyes said. "She was very determined to come."

"I can see that." I nodded in approval, loving her all the more for her dedication. "But you have to get right back in that car, missy."

"What? No. I'm going with you."

"Cook, we don't know what's going on in there yet."

"She has him," Osh said, jogging back to us. "They're in a basement below the house."

Cookie's hands flew to her mouth with a loud gasp.

I was right there with her. Fear consumed me in one spinal-tapping rush, and Reyes tightened his hold. "Is he—?" I started to ask the fifty-thousand-dollar question, but it got stuck in my throat.

"Is he alive?" Cookie asked for me, her voice soft with hope.

"For the time being. It was hard to see, but I think he's been shot."

That was all I needed to hear. We were out of time.

I took off, heading at a breakneck speed across the dark and uneven ground, having every intention of tearing through the front door and beating that bitch to a pulp.

Reyes was on me before I made it halfway. He tackled me in the clearing and we tumbled head over heels to a stop. Osh was right behind him, ready and waiting for anything crazy I might do.

I fought him, using the vast arsenal at my disposal to slow time and drop him to his knees. I needed him, so I didn't want him hurt, but I wasn't about to argue. I had to get to Ubie.

As he fought for a hold on my wrist, I twisted and turned the move against him. But he was a warrior. A general in hell and a champion on earth. And rather deadly at both. In hand-to-hand combat, I didn't stand a chance. We fought for dominance. He was also trying not to hurt me; otherwise, I probably would've been whole wheat toast much sooner. But his reluctance to cause me physical harm was his weakness. I took complete advantage.

I was on top once again and just about to utter a word that would disable him momentarily, when Osh tackled me to the ground. We hit the rocky terrain hard and skidded across the landscape, his body taking most of the abrasions. But my lungs seized with the impact. My diaphragm contracted, making it almost impossible to take in air. The impact disoriented me, and I lost my grip on time long enough for it to crash back with a vengeance. Which disoriented me even more.

That was when I felt an ice-cold grip on my forearm. The departed socialite had wrapped her fingers around it and pulled at me, as though I were on a track with a train barreling down upon us and she was trying to drag me clear. Her eyes rounded as she looked at me. Her mouth opened to scream.

Then I heard it. A growl, guttural and deep and inches from my neck.

I turned just in time to see Reyes dive toward the silvery black outline of a beast. It was so close, I felt its blistering hot breath fan across my cheek like dragon fire, causing an eruption of goose bumps over my skin.

The clock slowed of its own volition that time, and I watched in horror as a second hellhound bound out of nowhere and hit Reyes midflight; his body—like a swimmer's darting through the water—buckled under the force. They soared over Osh and me, and plummeted to the ground in a whirlwind of dust and limbs. All I saw as they fought was the slick glint of its razor-sharp teeth. They sank into Reyes's rib cage, burrowing deep into the flesh and bone there. Reyes showed no sign he'd even felt the bite. He ripped the beast off him and in one quick movement broke its neck. It crumbled with a whimper as another took its place. Reyes easily bested it as well, grabbing its jaw and jerking its head back until, again, the neck snapped. But something happened to the first one. After a moment, sparks of a silvery light glittered around it and it slowly regained its footing, shaking its head as though Reyes had only rung its bell.

It lunged and sank its teeth into Reyes's shoulder as he fought a third one. The second one he'd taken out was already coming to, and I realized what a futile battle we fought. They really were indestructible.

One sank its teeth into his left thigh, and he went down onto one knee, but before I could get to him to help, I felt just how sharp those teeth were. The one closest to me turned its attention to Osh and attacked, knocking him to the ground as they tumbled and rolled. Another took its place instantly. Its teeth sank into my calf, and it pulled me into the darkness of the forest beyond. The socialite lost her grip, but she turned as another hound barreled down upon me. She stepped between us, her shoulders set in determination. It grappled her to the ground, its growls thundering against the silence of the night.

That's when the magnitude of the situation hit me. The entire dozen hellhounds had made an appearance, and the departed, Reyes's spies, whoever they were, fought beside us with a ferocity I'd never expected.

I kicked at the hellhound dragging me into the brush, but my efforts served only to make my wound worse. Crying out in pain and fear for Reyes, I arched my back to get a better view of him. I could now see the beast's outline better because it was covered in Reyes's blood. Both of them were drenched in crimson. I heard a grunt in the darkness, but could no longer see Osh. Like a raging inferno, fear engulfed me.

I kicked at the beast again and it released me that time only to crawl over me, its mammoth body like a small house as it placed a paw on my chest. It spanned half my torso, the weight crushing me to the point of breaking.

Unlike the departed, the Twelve were even more invisible in the darkness, almost completely transparent, but the silvery black dust of their coats shimmered in the moonlight, allowing me to make out a shoulder here. An ear there. I looked to either side. My throat lay between two massive claws I could barely see past. The beast bent its head until we were nose-to-nose. His mouth quivered as he prepared to sever my head, but another growl mingled with his. I tore my gaze off the amber eyes of the hellhound and looked up. Another canine had materialized and was now in a deadly face-off against my captor.

Artemis pushed her head over mine until she was between us; then she rose up, forcing the hellhound back. Even if only inches, even if she bought me only seconds, I rejoiced at the borrowed time. Artemis quivered with anger, exposing her teeth in a vicious show of authority. She didn't give their inconceivable difference in size a second thought. It reminded me of a scene outside my apartment once, where a Chihuahua had been attacking, mostly verbally, a huge pit bull. The adorable pittie didn't know what to think about the miniscule assailant and seemed more worried about its ankles than anything else as the Chihuahua danced around it, snarling and nipping. But Artemis held her own. She slowly eased forward, David forcing Goliath back.

Artemis had distracted the beast long enough for me to get to my boot. I gasped for air as my fingers sought and found the hilt of the blade there. In one quick move, I pulled Zeus out of my boot and slashed at the hound. I felt resistance when the blade met flesh, when Zeus sliced into the hound's side, but the beast whipped around and caught my forearm in its mouth with lightning-quick speed. Teeth sank to the bone. Pain rocketed through me.

With the beast's attention averted, Artemis went for the jugular. She lunged forward and sank her teeth into its neck, but did they bleed? Could she really do it any harm? The weight of its paw on my chest was causing the edges of my vision to blacken; then a sharp, scalding pain splintered my body in two. The beast had cracked one of my ribs. I cried out as another gave way, my eyes rolling back as nausea roiled up like an ocean wave to drown me. I felt my lung fill with blood as fragments of bone punctured it. Breathing grew even harder as the beast fought Artemis, using me as its canvas.

I glanced across the landscape. Reyes fought as though unfazed by the beasts' teeth and claws, by the massive amount of blood loss, by the fact that we were facing almost certain death. His expression void of emotion, his instincts on automatic, he finally untangled himself from the melee and sprinted toward me. Before he made it, however, another creature dived for him. He slid underneath it and caught two handfuls of its fur, then slammed it into the ground. It yelped as another of its kind tackled Reyes to the ground. They rolled farther away from me. That seemed to be their goal, in fact. To keep Reyes as far from me as possible, all the while ripping him to shreds.

Fighting through the pain, I welded my teeth together, lowered my lids, and gathered my energy, forced it to my core until the molecules compressed to the density of marble, until the pressure built like steam with no escape route. In one violent eruption, light burst from me, exploding into the atmosphere like the blast from a nuclear bomb.

The beast that stood over me winced and jerked away with a startled whine. It faltered and fell to its knees, but regained its footing just as quickly. Then it shook its snout and snorted as though it had sniffed something it didn't like. Glancing about, I realized that was the extent of the damage.

It didn't work. It had stunned the hounds momentarily, but they were back in full form in no time. Their disorientation lasted just long enough for Reyes to make it to his feet before one pounced again.

I lay there hopeless.

It didn't work.

It didn't work.

It didn't work.

The beast sank its teeth as another dived for his jugular. Tiring, Reyes blocked its lethal jaws and hooked a leg around to break its neck. Instead, they both somersaulted, the beast ending up on top again, blood dripped from its snout as it watched him. Another one eased forward, and they exchanged silent glances. As though plotting. As though planning their attack. The second one crept around and crouched, ready to pounce.

Reyes glanced at me then. His face streaked with blood almost exactly like the first time I'd seen him, when I was in high school and Gemma and I were out in the middle of the night, trying to catch shots for a school project. He had the same look then that he had now: Acceptance of his fate. Approval of his impending death.

He whispered to me in Dutch, his voice soft and unhurried as it traveled over the terrain and into my ear. *"Houdt haar veilig,"* he said: "Keep her safe." Beep. He was talking about Beep.

Then he relaxed against them, let his arms and his head fall back, giving them clean access to his jugular. When a black mist raised out of him, I realized he was going to keep them occupied with his physical body so he could fight them with his incorporeal one. But they would kill him before he could do any damage. The other departed were gone. The beasts were too strong. Too fast.

Fear bucked inside me—when a seed took root. A thought that started as an infinitesimal kernel burst inside me. I realized the problem: Where I came from, I was pure energy. An elemental made of spirit and light. That light, which was supposed to be as bright as a thousand suns, was being filtered through the human body I possessed. It should, at the very least, have sent their asses running for the hills, but it had done nothing more than made them sneeze. Their hide, thick and scaly, seemed impenetrable.

I had to set it free. I had to stop them from ripping Reyes apart. He materialized in a great mass of darkness, rolling around me like a sea of ink. He did it on purpose. So I wouldn't see what was about to happen to him. So I would not have that vision in my head for the rest of my life. I heard the sing of his blade, a growl, a sharp whine. But even his blade wouldn't kill them; I was certain of it.

I had to set it free.

As the beast on top of me tossed Artemis away like a rag doll, all I could think was *I had to set it free.* I took Zeus, the mystical knife that had somehow found its way into the hands of Garrett Swopes. The one that could kill any demon on this plane. The one that vibrated with power and strength, as though it were alive. As though it possessed a will of its own.

I didn't want to die. If I died, Beep died. If I lived, a darkness would settle upon the earth, and all on it would eventually perish. Those were the terms Rocket had given me. While the choice was clear—not that it was much of a choice—I couldn't help but question the legitimacy of Rocket's vision.

Up to that point, I'd kept thinking all things in the supernatural realm, just as in the earthly one, could be manipulated. Satan could have fed Rocket false information about my demise. Rocket's prediction that if I didn't die, millions, possibly billions, of others would perish could have been concocted. A complete fabrication.

But maybe that was the plan all along. Maybe this had been in the cards since the beginning of time, and when my daughter took the bastard down—because she would eventually take the bastard down one way or another—it would not be from a life lived on earth, but one lived in another realm. Another dimension where her soul, her essence would grow into adulthood.

My final thought was of Reyes. Of his shimmering eyes and his lopsided grin. I was going to die anyway. I'd known it for weeks now. At least I could save Reyes. Before the hound could finish what it had started, I let my lids drift shut and promised my daughter I'd see her in heaven.

I heard Reyes call my name. Once. Twice. The deep timbre thundering across the sky. And then again in desperation. Softer this time. Pleading. He must have seen the dagger at the ready.

With his face on my mind and our daughter in my heart, I plunged Zeus into my chest. The searing pain was like nothing I'd ever felt. It hurt when it penetrated my flesh, but when it sliced through my sternum and pierced my heart, the agony was so quick and so sharp, my mind reeled from it, and I thought for a moment, just a moment, I saw heaven open up above me. I saw angels looking down. Not the cherubs of children's tales, but warriors, tall and stoic and fierce. One of them, a dark-haired creature with wings that expanded across the horizon, raised a single, quizzical brow.

When my last breath as a human left my lungs, I felt a warmth spread through me. In the next instant, an incandescent light burst from my heart, as though by piercing it, I had penetrated the barrier between my earthly vessel and my spiritual energy. In one silent atomic flash, everything changed. I sent out the part of me that had been released, the essence of who I was, to each hellhound. Their razorsharp teeth glittered as I brushed a tendril of light along their scales. A fire spread throughout them, igniting each molecule until the beasts glowed like molten lava.

The hound closest to me yelped and twisted in agony, tossing his head back as though to bite the offending blaze. The silvery black dust of its coat disintegrated into a powder that drifted away on the wind. At the last minute, it charged forward, but by the time it reached me, there was nothing left but floating particles of blackish orange embers. Slowly, even those drifted away.

It happened again and again. Each lick of light caused a chain reaction that literally disintegrated the hellhounds where they stood until there were none left.

I scrambled onto my knees and looked down at Zeus. Then at my chest. Then at Reyes and Osh and Cookie, who were sprinting toward me. I patted my face, wondering if I were dead. I didn't feel dead. In fact, I felt very much alive.

Reyes slid to a stop on his knees in front of me, his face a mask of astonishment.

Unable to wrap my head around the unrealized state of my demise, I examined my shirt. A crimson stain had spread over my heart, but my chest remained completely unmarred.

"How did you do that?" he asked me as Osh arrived in much the same manner.

Having not the faintest idea, I shook my head.

I examined Zeus and felt none of the power I'd previously felt from it. It had been drained of its energy, now able to do nothing more to a supernatural being than give it a paper cut. I stuffed him back into my boot nonetheless, realizing the true power of the dagger now resided inside me. And inside our daughter. It had fused us together, not only on a physical level, but on a spiritual one as well. And that bond had created a supernatural weapon of mass destruction. It was not something I could have done before. I could do it only through the power that Beep gave me. What strength I had, woven with Reyes's DNA, combined to create a true child of the gods.

Reyes sat there stunned. Osh as well, and I was right there with them. Cookie, who would not have been able to see the hellhounds at all, seemed to be in a state of shock.

Only then did I realize it was raining. A downpour, in fact.

I held out a hand, palm up, and looked toward the heavens, wondering if the quizzical angel was sending me a message.

"I think I died for a minute," I said to Reyes. Water poured in rivulets down his handsome face. The heat from his body radiated out and warmed me as icy droplets drenched me to the core. He reached out with one arm to embrace me, but I leaned away from him. Shocked once again.

"You're ripped to shreds," I said, one hand covering my mouth, almost unable to look.

He shook his head. "It's not so bad this time. We're learning."

"Beep?" Osh asked, his impatience shining through when he grabbed my shoulders and turned me toward him.

I nodded in affirmation.

Relief flooded him visibly. He lunged forward and placed his palm on my abdomen, an act that Reyes didn't entirely appreciate. I had to slam my eyes shut at the sight of them. At the blood that saturated their soaked shirts and jeans.

Cookie stood shaking, her face the picture of shock.

After an eternal moment, Osh nodded. "She's okay. She's—" He lowered his head in thought. "—she's even stronger than before."

"She's the future of the world," I said, as though I'd planned such an outcome the whole time. "That's a lot to place on a girl's shoulders. She'll need all the strength she can get."

"Oh, sweetheart," Cookie said, kneeling beside me and pulling me into her arms. "You— You were going to take your own life."

"I'm sorry, Cook. I thought it was the only way." Then I looked at Reyes, who was none too happy about that fact, if his rigid jaw was any indication. "Are they gone?" I asked him.

"For now," Osh said, answering for him. "But you have to understand," he added, "just like me, just like Rey'aziel, they were created for this kind of thing. I don't think it killed them. And I think it's safe to say beyond a shadow of a doubt, they definitely all made it onto this plane."

"Reyes?" I asked, hoping for a different answer.

He nodded reluctantly in agreement, scanning the horizon. "Osh'ekiel is right. They won't be back tonight, but they will be back. These aren't fallen. They will not die so easily."

"There was nothing easy about that," I said, anger over that fact spiking within me. But Reyes was certainly evidence of what Osh had said. I could hardly look at either of them without almost passing out. I never knew a body could take that much trauma and survive. I never knew bone actually looked white beneath torn flesh. They had been shredded and yet they stood, in all their glory, ready to fight again.

Then the reason we were all there hit me. "Uncle Bob," I said with a gasp of recollection. I stumbled to my feet and took off toward the cabin again, in the back of my mind very aware that I should be dead. Instead I felt no pain. No soreness. Even my fractured ribs had healed. "Cookie, stay back!" I shouted, but before I got far, Reyes tackled me and lifted me off the ground. He then gestured for Osh to go first as I fought his hold. I'd just fought a dozen hellhounds. Certainly I could take on one crazy human. But she did have Uncle Bob. He was not indestructible.

"If this woman is here," Osh said, jogging in front of us, "she has to know we're here, too. No way did she miss the battle royal going down in her front yard."

"Reyes," I said, squirming until he set me down and let me walk on my own, like a big girl, "I'm going in there."

"Not before I do."

We got to the side of the cabin and hunkered down as Osh crept to the front window for a quick peek. "There's a light on, but I don't see anyone."

Reyes gestured for me to stay—as if—and tread swiftly across the porch to the front door. Naturally, I followed. When he tested the door to find it unlocked, I put a hand on his. Both of us crouched on our toes as he turned toward me.

"Let me go first," I whispered.

"No," he whispered back.

I stabbed him with my best glare, my gaze traveling slowly, purposefully, to his mouth. Even set as it was in the grim line, it was fuller than a man's had a right to be. Sensual. "I could make you," I said, my voice soft with what was part threat and part promise.

He leaned forward until our mouths were almost touching and said, "You could make me do a lot of things." After a tense moment where he studied my lips, he dipped his head as though to kiss me, before adding, "But on this, you'll trust me."

Then he slowed time before I had a chance to and ducked inside the cabin. From my point of view, it literally looked like he'd vanished into thin air. I cursed and hurried in after him, but by the time I stumbled over my first piece of furniture, he was in front of me.

"He's downstairs. There's a basement."

I glanced around and found a staircase leading down. Osh stepped to it and looked into the cavernous opening.

"She's with him," Reyes added. "And I think she drugged him."

"How is he?" I whispered, angry Reyes did the time trick thing when I'd least expected it. That was cheating.

Before answering, he took a firm hold of my wrist, as though to anchor me to him. "He's definitely been shot."

I took off without another thought, dodging Osh as he reached out for me. But I'd shifted time to my advantage, taking them both off guard, and flew down the stairs.

When I emerged from the darkened staircase into a half-finished, dimly lit room, I saw Uncle Bob lying on his back, his tie loose and hanging to one side, his white button-down stained a dark crimson. Blood pooled beneath him, spreading slowly as though there wasn't much of it left. I didn't take the time to look for Sylvia. I rushed headlong toward him.

"Uncle Bob," I whispered, sliding next to him to examine his bindings. Sylvia had bound his wrists behind his back, but Reyes was right: He'd also been shot. And he was unconscious. "Uncle Bob," I said again, my gaze blurring with wetness. His short brown hair and the left side of his face had dried blood like she'd hit him with something. Surely not to subdue him. Unless she hit him very, very hard, knocking him out would not have been easy.

I cradled his head in my lap and patted his cheek, leaning over and whispering into his ear. "Please, Uncle Bob. Please be okay."

The fact that he was warm registered in the back of my mind, sending a glimmer of hope spiraling up my spine. I felt for a pulse on his neck. Strong as a mule, and just as stubborn. I kissed his forehead.

As I was about to check the wound that seemed to be centered along the right side of his rib cage, I felt a sharp sting at my neck. Reflexively, I slowed time and flung my arm back, dislodging the needle. I could only hope that whatever she'd injected me with wasn't lethal. Time bounced back before it had a chance to stop completely. But everything else slowed.

I spun around to look at my attacker, and even she slowed. Or, well, blurred.

Sylvia Starr stumbled back when I knocked her arm away. She immediately went for the syringe again as I grabbed Uncle Bob under the shoulders and tried to drag him to the stairs. But the world toppled to the left. I adjusted, trying to topple with it, to keep myself upright. It just kept toppling, the floor beneath me tilting until it stood completely vertical. It rested against my shoulder and cheek, and I couldn't help but wonder how gravity had maneuvered itself that way. We would all fall off the Earth if this kept up. Then where would we be?

I felt a sharp tug on my hair and then cold metal resting against my temple.

"You don't understand," she said, talking as though we'd been having a conversation the whole time. "He put you there."

"Where?" I asked.

"You went to prison because of him."

"I've never been to prison," I argued. "Not as an inmate, anyway. There was this one time—"

"Don't do this, Ms. Rhammar." It was Uncle Bob. Maybe my poking and prodding had awakened him.

"My name is Sylvia Starr," she said, hissing at him. Then her voice changed to a pleading whine. "If he hadn't arrested you in the first place, you would never have spent ten years in that hellhole."

"And what do you know of hell?"

It was Reyes. He'd come for me! "Hold on!" I said, my tongue thick in my mouth as I pointed to the floor at my ear. "We're going to fall off. Grab on to something!" How we were not sliding down the floor, I'd never know.

"They convicted you of a crime you didn't commit," Sylvia said.

I looked up at Reyes, baffled. "I've never been convicted of a crime. Well, not one I didn't commit."

"I told them." She pressed the metal into my temple. A long lock of her dark hair fell into my eyes. It was very painful. I tried to swipe at it as she continued. "I told them you were innocent, and they ignored me. Treated me like I was an idiot."

"You *are* an idiot."

"They convicted you. You went to prison for killing a man who was still alive!"

I started to argue with her and explain once again that I'd never been convicted of any crime aside from that little breaking and entering gig, which was wiped from my record when I turned eighteen—but then I realized she wasn't talking to me.

Reyes stood there, his clothes saturated in crimson, a bored expression on his face, as though he were completely unimpressed with her. I, on the other hand, was completely impressed with her ability to remain perpendicular without falling over.

"I knew all along you were innocent. But they treated me like shit."

The emotion I felt radiate off him was not what he was presenting to Sylvia. He crossed his arms over his chest, his expression passive, but an anger welled within him, deep and turbulent and violent.

Uncle Bob spoke then. "Ms. Starr," he said, his voice hoarse and cracked, "Charley was not on that jury. If you hurt her—"

"What?" she asked, jamming the cold metal against my skull even harder. Poor Fred. "What will happen to me?"

Uncle Bob! I'd forgotten he was shot. I'd been drugged. Ubie was shot!

I couldn't decide which one of us needed my most immediate attention. I fought the effects of whatever she'd injected me with, struggled to right the world and see it for what it was: a big blue ball that had not toppled over, and we were not going to slide off it. Knowing that theoretically and knowing that instinctually were two different beasts. I was having a hard time marrying the two with the more logical side of Barbara, my brain, when Sylvia jerked my head back and scraped the metal along my temple until it brought forth blood.

Uncle Bob lurched, but with his hands bound could to little more than that. "Put it down," he said, his voice even.

"Shut up!" she shouted at him before turning back to Reyes. "I had to get retribution for you."

"You sought retribution for you."

"No, I could tell you were innocent. I knew, Reyes. I knew you were innocent, and they bullied me and mocked me. They made me feel stupid until I changed my vote. They threw you away like you were a piece of trash. Like you were somehow less, when anyone with eyes could see you were so very much more. They don't deserve the glorious life that's been given them."

"All the evidence pointed directly at me. Detective Davidson was only doing his job."

I heard a derisive jeer directed toward Ubie. It was so time to bring it. And I planned on bringing it. I would've already brought it if I could've remembered how. Or what it was I was supposed to bring. A cheese ball, perhaps?

"You're wrong."

"I'm rarely wrong," he replied, and I couldn't argue that point. "The jurors were doing what they were instructed to do, to weigh the evidence and make a decision based on what was presented to them. You chose not to see what they saw."

"They saw a juvenile delinquent. A hooligan. A monster."

"Then they saw everything that I am."

Another thought hit me. Actually lots of thoughts. I was having trouble focusing, but this one had me curious. "Did you know it was her?" I asked Reyes. "Did you know she had been on your jury when she approached you for an interview?"

He frowned at me. "Yes."

"You saw the pictures of the other jury members. You knew she was killing them?"

"I was hardly paying attention to your uncle's case. I had other things on my mind."

"How could you not pay attention to something of this magnitude?"

"Two words: Hell. Hounds."

I scoffed and tried to turn away from him, but couldn't quite manage it with Conan's death grip on my wet hair.

Sylvia plowed forward, convinced she'd done the right thing. "They all deserve to die for what they did to you. I sat there day after day, watching as the evidence was presented, knowing you were innocent. I just wanted to make everything okay."

Unmoved by her speech, his impatience grew exponentially. "I have been bitten, pounced on, and generally mauled by angry hellhounds, and now you dare pull a gun on my fiancée?"

"A gun?" I squeaked, catching on.

"I had to seek retribution for what they did to us."

He paused, his anger pulsating over me before asking, "Us?"

"I could have taken care of you if you'd been exonerated. We could have been happy. I would have given you anything you ever wanted."

He stepped closer, regarded Sylvia from behind a stormy expression.

"I felt your infatuation throughout the trial just as clearly as I felt their conviction of my guilt. At the time, I thought you *all* imbeciles. I've since changed my mind."

I became cognizant of one simple fact: He could have slowed time and ended this confrontation immediately. He was doing all of it, getting not only a confession out of Sylvia, but also her motivation, for Uncle Bob's benefit. Ubie could serve as a witness to her ramblings, but he was still bleeding to death.

I could fight a dozen hounds from hell, I could bring down the son of Satan with a word, but put me in the ring with a psychotic chick, and I go down in the first.

"Rey'aziel," I said, switching to Aramaic, "we need to get my uncle help immediately."

Reyes nodded. In the next instant, he was in front of us, eyeing Sylvia as a predator eyes its prey right before it attacks.

"Don't hurt her," Ubie said, pinning him with a warning stare. He wanted her alive, but hardly for noble reasons. He wanted to see her face when the jury pronounced her guilty. His desire for revenge was strong, pulsating inside him, but it hadn't reared up until she pointed a gun at my head.

Try as he might to fend them off, a tidal wave of feelings rushed forth inside Reyes as though a dam had broken. He'd spent ten years in a maximum security prison, and he'd always acted blasé, as though it hadn't fazed him. But it had. He looked at me, the fury inside him explosive. He pulled her forward and said something in her ear. I buried my face to stop the reeling, to calm the raging seas, and to focus. I listened with every part of me as a soft whisper spilled from his mouth and filtered into her ear.

"How dare you assume so much when you know so little," he said. Then, in one lightning-quick movement, too swift for my mind to register, he grabbed her head and twisted, causing a sharp crack to splinter the tense air. He pushed her to the side and dropped her lifeless body in front of Uncle Bob. She crumpled before him, and a big part of me wanted to scream.

This was not happening. He didn't just kill someone in front of a police detective. He would go to prison all over again. At the very least, it would be a nightmare. There would be a trial, a media frenzy, but Reyes didn't care. His fury scorched along my skin as he leaned down to Uncle Bob.

I rushed forward—at least I tried to—afraid of what he might do. But he only spoke to him, his tone almost as soft, almost as dangerous as it was when he'd whispered to Sylvia. "You owe me that."

Still unable to perform my award-winning routine on the balance beam, I stumbled into Reyes, clawing at his arms, worried he might decide to kill the only witness in the room who could put him back in prison for taking a woman's life. But I had nothing to worry about. Reyes lifted me into his arms just as Osh rushed into the room.

He barely spared a glance for Sylvia before saying, "He's still alive. The other one she took. But not for much longer."

The latest suicide-note victim was still alive? "Where is he?" I asked him.

"Safe enough for now. He's in the small outbuilding behind the cabin. But she must've given him something. He's foaming at the mouth."

"She poisoned him," I said. Deciding to try to heal Uncle Bob, I squirmed out of Reyes's arms and reached down to him. I had no idea if I could do it or not, but that didn't matter.

Ubie put a hand on mine. He seemed to know my intentions. "No, pumpkin," he said, regarding Reyes as though uncertain whether he should arrest him or give him a medal. Not that he could do much of either with his arms tied behind his back. He cringed as he tried to stand. "This has to look very, very good."

I helped him to his feet as he examined the unstable staircase before giving us a once-over. "I'll ask later where all the blood came from. For now, we need to get rid of any evidence that you were ever here." He nodded toward the back of the basement. "She was going to set it on fire.

The whole thing. She knew she was out of time and was going to kill me, then run off into the sunset with you, Farrow."

Reyes blanched inwardly at that.

"So the way I see it," Uncle Bob continued, "as she held that lantern up there—" He raised his chin, indicating a lantern at the top of the stairs. "—she doused the place in gasoline and tripped on her way up the stairs, breaking her neck in the fall."

"Uncle Bob," I said, worried. It was a good plan, but if it didn't work, he could go to prison as well. "You don't have to do this."

"I do," he said sternly. "She was also dowsing me to make sure I died down here."

"No," I said, changing my mind. This was a bad plan. "You aren't going to put gasoline on yourself."

"You're right. I can't with my hands tied behind my back. You'll have to do it."

"Absolutely not," I said, almost falling over again. "No way in hell."

"Pumpkin, you have to do this." He looked so vulnerable. So pale and fragile. I'd never seen him be anything other than the ox I'd grown up with.

"Pick it up and pour some on me, then douse the place. I'll break the lantern and hightail it out of here."

"No. What if you aren't fast enough? You've lost so much blood."

"Farrow," he said, handing the reins over to him. "Do it now and get out before I bleed out."

He nodded. Osh took me as Reyes grabbed the gas can and proceeded to douse my uncle in gasoline. Its scent made me gag, and tears rushed down my face. It wasn't very long ago that I'd had a similar experience. The memory caused an upwelling of emotion. Such tragedy happening to me was one thing. The same thing happening to those I loved was quite another.

"That's enough," I said, clawing at Reyes's shoulder. My hand slipped in the slick blood there, and my nausea jumped into warp drive.

Reyes lifted me into his arms again and rushed up the stairs two at a time as Osh took over, sprinkling the foul-smelling liquid over the contents of the room—careful not to spill any on Sylvia, lest it look suspicious—and up the stairs. He helped Uncle Bob up them as he ascended.

Uncle Bob offered me one last smile, then nodded as he pushed the lantern to the floor. The gas caught fire immediately and spread like a beautiful dancer across the floor.

"I'm right behind you," Ubie said. "But I need to inhale a little smoke first."

"Reyes, make him come," I said, pleading with him.

"Pumpkin, it has to look very, very good." He gave Reyes another warning scowl, and this time Reyes obeyed.

He whisked me out to a frantic Cookie. Without another word, he indicated for her to follow us and carried me to our cars. Osh followed us out and climbed into Misery to drive her back for me as we piled into Reyes's 'Cuda.

Cookie had gotten ahold of the captain, so the cops were already on the way by the time we pulled onto the highway. We stared straight ahead as they passed us with lights flashing and sirens blaring. The glow of a fire lit the sky in the rearview, thick gray clouds billowing into the air, and my uncle had been drowned in gasoline. The fumes alone could catch a wayward spark and burst him into flames. If he made it outside, he'd be okay. The downpour would keep the heat at bay and it would also keep the flames from spreading into the brush. Purposely setting a fire was never a good idea in New Mexico. The rain had been a godsend.

We rushed home to change out of our bloody clothes so we could meet the ambulance at the hospital. I had to leave Reyes and Osh to see to their own duct tape. Even though the Twelve had disappeared, we had no way of knowing if they would stay that way. Reyes called Garrett to escort us to the hospital.

A group of officers lined the front of the building. One of their own had been injured. They were there to pay their respects as the ambulance pulled up. We pulled in right behind it, and Cookie was out of Misery, running after the ambulance before I could stop her. I pulled around to park, staying close to the emergency entrance, trying to decide if it was too soon to call her an ambulance chaser.

"Robert!" Cookie screamed, dodging a cop and sliding under the arm of an EMT. The girl could move when she wanted to. "Robert," she said, and I jogged up to the melee. Despite a polite officer trying to gently urge her back, Cookie had a death grip on the gurney as they unloaded Ubie from the ambulance.

"She was throwing gasoline everywhere, going to torch the place," he was telling the captain, who'd apparently ridden in the ambulance back. "She doused me, then took the stairs, sprinkling fuel as she went up. I couldn't see what happened. I guess she just slipped. She fell down the stairs. Next thing I know, the place is burning and she's unconscious at the bottom of the stairs with a broken neck."

Another ambulance pulled up with the other suicide-note victim. He was alive, and they were pumping his stomach.

"Robert," Cookie said, and when his gaze landed on her, I thought the heavens had opened up for the second time that day.

Captain Eckert let her walk beside the gurney as they rushed him inside to prep for surgery. Fortunately, the bullet hadn't hit anything vital. I teased him that it must've hit his brain, then. Or his penis. He laughed, clearly relieved to be alive.

As Cookie, Garrett, and I sat in the waiting room, Reyes and Osh strolled in like they owned the place. They both wore hoodies, and Osh had donned his top hat, which looked painfully sweet when coupled with a 49ers sweatshirt. But they had to cover the duct tape somehow.

Reyes sat beside me, his heat blistering as Osh went straight for the vending machines. He walked back to us with waters for Cook and me, even though we both craved coffee like there was no tomorrow.

"How did you do that?" Reyes asked as I took a sip. He'd pushed the sleeves of the hoodie up. His forearms corded. His hands strong yet almost elegant as he gazed at them.

I turned to him with my brows raised in question.

He looked at me from beneath his lashes. "I had my hand around your wrist in the cabin. You . . . slipped through my fingers."

"I had to get to Uncle Bob," I said, mesmerized by his probing gaze.

"You did the same with the handcuff in front of the asylum," Garrett said. "It was like you passed through it."

"Really?" I asked, thinking back and taking another sip. "I just slipped my hand out."

He shook his head. "You couldn't have."

"Hmm," I said. I poked my wrist with my index finger to make sure it was all there, not overly worried about it either way.

Reyes took my hand in his then. He brushed his fingers over the inside of my palm, up my wrist, as though examining it, as though testing it, as a magician does when he taps his top hat before making a rabbit disappear.

"Then the knife," Reyes said, his voice now soft, accusatory. "You tried to take your own life."

"So did you, if you'll remember," I volleyed.

Frustration flared within him, but he bit it back, kept it to himself.

"You have to heal," I said, worried about both him and Osh. He was scorching, and I was beginning to realize he grew hotter when he was injured and needed to heal. "You need to rest."

"We need to get to safe ground first," he said. "Hold on." He unfolded from his chair and strode to the socialite standing in a dark corner, which normally would have made me a little testy, but she was dead. What could they do?

Captain Eckert walked up to us then, his face somber.

I froze as I tried to get a read, then jumped out of my seat in alarm. "Uncle Bob—!"

"He's fine," he said, urging me to sit back down. I didn't. After a moment, he said, "The other victim didn't make it."

"I know," I said, nodding to the seat on the other side of me, where one Mr. Trujillo sat petting a weary Rottweiler named Artemis. Before Reyes and Osh arrived, we'd been making plans on what to tell his wife. How to get her a message before he crossed. Like so many departed, he was more worried about his family and their well-being than about the fact that he'd just passed. He schooled me on where to find the life insurance policy and the extra keys to the Harley-Davidson he'd bought during a midlife crisis, stating explicitly that his wife could not, under any circumstances, sell it to his cousin Manny, because Manny was an asshat. His words.

The captain nodded; then his gaze darted to Reyes, a curious look on his face, before he went back to talk to a few of his officers standing nearby. He knew more than what he was telling me, and I wondered what all Uncle Bob had said to him in the ambulance. What could he have said, though, with the EMT right there?

Reyes seemed completely unconcerned. He stood in the corner, talking to the socialite. Apparently, the departed who'd helped us battle the Twelve were okay. He walked back to us, his expression grave.

"They're still here on this plane."

Osh nodded. "I know. I still feel them."

I didn't feel anything but anger at that point. What the hell would it take to kill them? And how hard was it to get one's hands on a small nuclear device? Just in case.

"We need to leave tonight," Osh said.

"What?" I glanced from him to Reyes. "What do you mean? Leave where?"

Reyes drew in a deep ration of air, as Cookie looked on in concern. "We need to get to sacred ground. They're from hell. They shouldn't be able to cross it."

"Reyes, I can't leave. My uncle is in the hospital. My father is missing. And someone has been taking pictures of me for what looks like years."

Reyes gave me a look that should have had me shivering in my boots. It failed. I was not about to leave my uncle.

"We got lucky," he said, his expression firm. "Next time, it might not be so easy."

"And once again: I stabbed myself through the heart with a dagger."

He flinched at the memory.

"There was nothing easy about that. But I found my light. I can keep doing whatever it was I did. I can keep them at bay."

He stepped closer and lowered his voice even further. "It took a syringe and one small lunatic to bring you down."

That time I flinched at the memory.

"One dose of a sleeping agent, and you couldn't even stand, much less fight off a pack of hellhounds. It's too risky. Osh has a plan."

"Oh, now we're letting the *Daeva* decide?" I asked, mocking him. "Suddenly we trust him?" I'd trusted him all along. Reyes was another story.

"We have no choice," Reyes said, and I felt the defeat he'd been hiding, an oppressing sense of failure, engulf him.

Guilt washed over me. "Reyes, I didn't mean—"

"Stop," he said, lowering his head and gazing with his sparkling brown eyes from underneath his impossibly thick lashes. He hated my empathy. I hated that he hated my empathy. There was certainly nothing I could do about either.

I stepped even closer. Placed my palm on his shadowed jaw. "Never."

He buried a hand in my hair and pulled me so close, our mouths almost touched. "I failed in every way possible," he said, his voice hoarse, husky. "There's no way to make that right, Dutch. But I can try to keep you safe from here on out. I can try to keep our daughter safe."

"You didn't fail."

One corner of his mouth lifted sadly. "You're such a bad liar."

"I'm an excellent liar," I said, placing my mouth on his before he could argue any more.

He opened to me immediately, drank me in as though begging for forgiveness. Instead, he left me struggling to satisfy my body's need for oxygen and wanting to find a dark corner of our own.

He broke off the kiss, then said, "You're also a sucker."

Feeling a cold strip of metal at my wrist, I gasped and looked down. He'd handcuffed me to him. With handcuffs! Real ones! I lifted our cuffed wrists, appalled. "Oh, this doesn't look odd in a room full of cops."

He lifted a shoulder. "I don't trust you as far as I can throw you. Sue me."

I gasped again, glancing at Osh, who had a shit-eating grin on his face.

"It was my idea," he said, quite proud of himself.

"This is so wrong. I am not leaving Uncle Bob."

"He's out of surgery," the captain said, walking up to us. "And coming out of the anesthesia as we speak." He spared a quick glance at the cuffs, then motioned for us to follow.

I stood aghast. What if I was in real trouble? What if I was being kidnapped by a man with handcuffs? One glance was all my imprisonment warranted?

I set my shoulders and followed him. "I'm not leaving my uncle," I said to Reyes as we walked toward the ICU.

"How much you want to bet?" he asked, making it sound like he was trying to seduce me. Of course, Reyes could read the phone book and make it sound like he was trying to seduce me. Or a grocery list. Or an instruction manual. I had a most wicked thought of him reading the instruction manual of something that used a coupling, like an engine, perhaps. I loved that word: *coupling*. I wondered what it would sound like sliding off Reyes's tongue, the deep timbre of his voice slipping like warm water over my skin.

Coming to my senses before I melted on the spot, I glared at him.

"And what holy ground?" I asked, taking Cookie's arm as she fell into step beside me. "Where are we going?"

Osh and Garrett were following us even though they wouldn't go in to see Ubie. Clearly they wanted in on the conversation.

"A convent," Osh said. "Doesn't get much more sacred than that."

"That's fine and dandy, but what about you two?" I asked Osh softly. Cookie and I were walking arm in arm. Reyes and I were walking cuff-in-cuff. "You guys are, you know, from hell as well. Can you go onto sacred ground?"

"We were born human," Osh said. "We can pretty much go any-where you can."

"Oh." I didn't know, but it made sense. Reyes had been to the cemetery, and that was consecrated ground.

"But the hellhounds can't?" I asked suspiciously. How much did they really know? "You're certain?"

Reyes shook his head. "No, we're not, actually. But it's worth a try."

I took a deep breath. "Well, we can't go just yet."

"Dutch," Reyes said in warning.

"No, I mean it." I lowered my voice again even though I was certain the captain could hear everything. The halls echoed worse than an amphitheater. "We are not going to *do it* on sacred ground without the bonds of holy matrimony to make us legit, and no offense, but I ain't going eight months without a piece of that ass."

Reyes pulled us to a stop, wrapping his long fingers around my wrist so the cuff didn't chafe. The entire entourage stopped as well as he grinned down at me. "Are you asking me to marry you, Dutch?"

I pressed my mouth closed in admonition. "No, you already did that. I'm asking you to marry me *now*. We can't disrespect the Big Guy like that. It's just wrong. And Beep needs her baby daddy's name."

He seemed stunned speechless. Cookie certainly was, but only for a few seconds. Her face brightened and she pulled me into a hug. "Oh, sweetheart. We can make this work. We'll find a justice of the peace or a priest or something tonight. I know a homeless man who was an ordained minister and had a small church in the valley before he went crazy and started going to all the local Catholic churches to drink the holy water, fearing contamination by Beelzebub." She glanced at Reyes, embarrassed. "Sorry, that's what he calls your father."

An impish dimple appeared. "I've called him worse."

She sighed, her expression slightly lovesick. "We already have the license. It'll be so romantic."

"Cook, I'm not sure we can manage this all tonight," I said, loving her enthusiasm.

"You'd better," Reyes said. "We leave at dawn. Saints or sinners, we are going to holy ground."

I sighed aloud. "Fine. We can manage it tonight." I looked at her. "How hard can it be?"

18

The hospital staff actually let us all go into the ICU: the captain, Reyes, Cookie, a couple of detectives, and me. Gemma came rushing in as well, her face as pale as Ubie's sheets. We hugged, the cuffs making it awkward, before we continued inside.

When we walked in, the Iron Fist was there, the judge who hated me. Or at least she used to hate me. I doubted her feelings had changed very much, but she seemed to tolerate me rather well. It was nice. And had been at the hospital visiting her grandmother when she heard the news about Ubie. It was kind of her to stick around to see him.

Ubie was groggy, which made him all the funnier. They gave him free rein on a morphine drip, which could not be good. He gave me a sleepy wink and told Cookie she looked like angel hair pasta. Not sure what that was about, but she literally melted. Clearly I was out of the loop. Either that or Ubie meant an angel but was thinking of food and in his dazed state blended the two. It happened. I once stayed up for two weeks straight and blended coffee and sex. I asked a server to bring me a coffeegasm. He said they didn't serve them but if I'd wait until he got off work, he'd do his darnedest to fill my order. He was cute.

I leaned forward and hugged Ubie's big head, afraid I'd hurt him if I hugged anything else.

He managed a drunken smile and said, "It's all taken care of, punky." He hadn't called me punky since I was a kid. It brought back fond memories. And a few disturbing ones, but nobody was perfect. How I loved this man with all my heart.

"I'm so mad at you," I said into his ear, partly to hide the annoying onset of wetness gathering between my lashes. How could he risk his life like that all to set up a scene to make sure Reyes didn't get arrested for murder? Or, at the least, manslaughter. Maybe he felt he owed Reyes. He was indeed the arresting officer over a decade ago.

"I know, sweetheart." He tried to pat my arm and patted Will Robinson instead. Normally that would be awkward, but considering the circumstances . . .

I laced the fingers of my cuffed hand into his. The deal was done. He'd been thoroughly and undeniably shot. Everyone saw that. He'd almost died. He'd heard the confession of Sylvia Starr before she *fell down the stairs* and broke her neck. He'd almost become a charcoal briquette for Halloween, not nearly so effective a costume as his Spidey outfit, in my humble opinion. Uncle Bob in tights was a sight to behold. Sure I'd needed therapy afterwards, but who doesn't need a little counseling now and then? And he'd tried to save Mr. Trujillo, Sylvia's final victim. If there was anything I could do, now was the time.

I kissed his cheek, whispered one teensy word in Latin, then stood back and let the others take turns wishing him a speedy recovery. His cheeks flushed instantly, his pallor returning to health as he gave me a sideways, suspicious glance. I didn't think I healed him completely. Just enough to ease the pain and mend his innards. Just enough to make what I was about to ask him tolerable.

We spoke a few minutes more before we were all ordered out. "I have one quick favor to ask," I said before we got run out completely.

"Anything, pumpkin," he said, his gaze glassy with a morphine haze.

Now was certainly not the best time, but I explained our situation to a room full of smiles, and thirty minutes later we were standing beside Uncle Bob's bed in ICU again, this time with a more matrimonial purpose.

Cook fetched Amber while Reyes and I ran to the apartment for the license and a couple of other trinkets. I'd insisted on being de-cuffed so I could clean up my face, brush the grass out of my hair, and throw on a white cocktail dress with silver slingbacks. Reyes donned a black dinner jacket and a gray tie. He'd shaved and tried to slick back his hair, but the dark locks fell over his forehead anyway. When he strolled into my apartment, he left me speechless—me!—and we almost didn't make it back to the hospital.

But Cookie and Amber insisted as Gemma fussed over my hair, pinning pieces here and there back with baby's breath–covered bobby pins and trying to hide the onset of tears.

"All my plans," she said, devastated that I'd ruined her big wedding plans.

Score!

Nurses and a couple of doctors had gathered outside, most likely because of the bizarreness of the situation more than for the romance, as Judge "Iron Fist" Quimby married us. Uncle Bob gave me away from his hospital bed, insisting that under no circumstances could Reyes give me back, while Cookie and Gemma stood beside me.

Reyes had to ask Garrett and Osh to stand with him, which was so ironic, it was unreal. He'd started out disliking both, and now they served as groomsmen to witness our journey into wedded bliss. I tried Dad one last time before the ceremony began, to no avail. I didn't bother calling Denise. I could surprise her with an announcement of my nuptials next time we met, though hopefully that would be in hell.

Despite the harried situation, despite the cramped room and sterile atmosphere, butterflies attacked the lining of my stomach, and my heart doubled in size as I looked at Reyes.

I was marrying him.

Him.

The man of my dreams was about to be mine, forever and ever, amen.

The words spoken by the judge slipped in and out of my consciousness, my mind racing a thousand miles a minute. I was about to be a married woman with a baby on the way. And I'd never been happier. Domestic bliss had never been part of my plan, but apparently someone had other ideas. If, that was, we survived the Twelve.

"May I have the rings?" Judge Quimby asked, and Garrett presented rings we'd each secretly given him.

Mine for Reyes was a simple band with both gold and silver woven together. In my mind it represented the two of us and how our lives had been woven together since birth. I went first, speaking the traditional vows that for the first time in my life really meant something. They were no longer just words, but a true testament to the commitment I was making to the man I loved.

He stood straight and proud, but when I went to slip the ring on his finger, I felt the smallest tremble, as though he was just as stunned as I. And hopefully just as honored.

Then it was his turn. He took the ring he'd been saving and slipped it partway on my finger, holding it there while he repeated his vows. I was so busy staring at him, waiting for those two words that would make him mine, that I didn't notice the ring until he said, "I do," and finished sliding it onto my finger. Then I gasped. I looked up at him, then back down at the gorgeous work of art that rested on my hand.

"Reyes," I whispered, "it's gorgeous."

Two perfectly matched dimples appeared at the corners of his mouth. "It matches your eyes."

The amber gem that sat in a flurry of gold waves looked like fire, and indeed, the gem was the color of my irises. "What is it?" I asked him.

"It's called an orange diamond."

I looked up. "Where did you get it?"

He leaned forward and whispered into my ear. "From hell."

I stilled, completely taken aback.

"It's from where I was born, deep in the hottest part of what you call Hades. Not many people know this, but we have the best diamonds there. Lots of heat. Lots of pressure. Perfect conditions."

The judge spoke about commitment and not allowing men to put us under—under what, I had no idea—while we spoke softly. "Why would you do that? Why would you risk a trip back there, Reyes?"

"I got in and out with no one the wiser. And the look on your face was worth it."

I wiped all expression from my face, then examined the ring again. I didn't know what to say. Before I could say anything, Reyes pulled me into his arms and kissed me, his lips scalding against mine. A thrill ran from the tips of my toes to the top of my head. We were no longer affianced. We were the real deal, baby, in a state of wedded bliss. I was so putting this on Friendbook.

Amber sighed aloud and the room erupted in laughter and applause. But only for a minute before the charge nurse shushed us with a stellar death glare. Then she smiled brightly and I wondered if she was normally on medication.

"We bought a cake," she said, bringing in an ice cream cake that was clearly meant for a child's birthday party. It was beyond perfect.

We stood around eating frozen cake and drinking ginger ale from cone-shaped cups as Uncle Bob told stories from my childhood, doing his darnedest to embarrass me. We didn't have much time before we had to get home and pack. Apparently, Osh had a place set up, an abandoned convent in the Jemez Mountains that had been built on Native American sacred ground: double whammy.

I gazed lovingly at my ring again. "A diamond from hell. Who would have guessed?"

"I helped pick out the setting," Gemma said, clearly missing what I'd said, as she spoke from a few feet away.

"Me, too!" The corners of Amber's smile almost reached her ears.

"The gold is very special, too." I looked back at Reyes.

"And where is it from? The gates of heaven?"

He grinned. "Yes, but I'm not allowed in. I had to have it sent over by courier."

I didn't know whether to believe him or not. About any of it. But I didn't care. I was married.

No.

I looked up at him. *We* were married. And knocked up. Did life get any better?

I grabbed the gift bag—aka a Walmart shopping bag—I'd brought from home and handed it to him.

"What's this?" he asked, squinting in suspicion at me.

"It's your wedding present." I grew excited as he opened the bag and took out the T-shirt I'd bought him.

He read it aloud: " 'I don't need Google. My wife knows everything.' "

I giggled like a mental patient as Reyes bent to plant a kiss just below my ear.

"I can't believe you're my wife."

"And I can't believe I don't get to call you my affianced anymore. I really like that word."

He laughed softly, then scanned the room. But the longer we stood there, the more distant he became. He put the T-shirt back in the bag, pretending to be happy, and my heart lurched in alarm. Was he regretting marrying me already? It'd been only ten minutes. If so, we were in a lot of trouble.

I took him aside as Ubie told the story of how I got the scar along my hairline—which was totally his fault for leaving a chain saw next to a stuffed raccoon in the first place. What child wouldn't want a piece of that?

"Okay, what gives? This is supposed to be the happiest day of our lives. You're not letting the fact that you are being held together by duct tape get you down, are you?"

He tried to smile, but it didn't quite solidify. "I have to tell you your name now."

"What?" I asked.

"I promised you. I just—" He shook his head. "I just don't know what will happen once you know it."

"That's right," I said remembering. "You promised to tell me my celestial name on our wedding day."

"I did."

"Don't do it," Osh said, coming up beside us. He was glaring at Reyes. "We aren't sure what will happen once she knows it. We don't know what will happen to Beep."

Reyes glared back. "I promised, *Daeva*. I keep my word."

But his promise was causing him distress. As much as I wanted to know my celestial name, it could wait. There were much more important things at the moment. I took his hands into mine. "Tell me later," I said. "We have the rest of our lives, Rey'aziel. It can wait."

Relief flooded him so completely, I almost laughed out loud. Sometimes he was like a kid. A tall, sexy, lethally dangerous kid who struck fear in the hearts of supernatural entities everywhere, but a kid nonetheless.

That seemed to satisfy Osh. He went to talk to the judge as she ate ice cream cake. I grew worried for her soul. The kid was a silver-tongued devil, and everyone—everyone—wanted something bad enough to risk his or her soul. But he'd promised to be a good boy and sup only on the souls of bad guys. He'd darned sure better keep that promise or he was going back to hell sooner than he'd planned.

The captain came in and reported that they had found a gold mine of evidence against Sylvia Starr at her house. A diary from the trial, pictures, notes she'd written to Reyes while he was in prison, along with a shrine. Reyes inspired shrines a lot. It was weird. And the evidence was enough to corroborate Uncle Bob's story. As far as the captain was concerned, the case was closed, and I couldn't help but breathe a sigh of relief.

A short while later, we said our good-byes. I kissed Uncle Bob all over his face until he blushed a brilliant red before we headed back to our respective homes. Osh was going to meet us at our place once he was packed. We had an hour. I was never the best packer. I inevitably forgot underwear or toothpaste or both. Thankfully, Reyes promised to help as soon as he was finished.

He went to his apartment and I went to mine even though we had no wall between our bedrooms. I'd hurried into my bathroom to scoop my toiletries into my overnight bag, wondering if I would need my Clorox Magic ToiletWand, when Jessica popped in.

She stood back, biting her lower lip as she waited for me to acknowledge her. After a solid two minutes of silence, she caved. "I just wanted you to know, I always felt guilty about everything that happened between us in high school."

"Yeah, I could tell," I said, testing a particular shade of lipstick on my wrist. Was it wrong to wear bright red lipstick in a convent? I just didn't know how to dress for this.

"You have no idea how shallow and self-centered I can be."

"Yes, I do. Trust me." Maybe I should stick to pinks.

"But none of that matters anymore. I'm so glad I died," she said, and I stopped. Turned toward her.

"What do you mean?"

"If I hadn't died, I would never have even thought to go to you for help when my nephew was hit. I'm so grateful for what you did, Charley."

"I didn't do anything, Jessica. You don't owe me anything."

The fact that she was okay with giving up her life if it meant saving her nephew spoke volumes to me, almost enough to drown out the nasally whine in her voice as she turned to me and said, "I owe you everything,

Charley. I will never forget this. To pay you back, I'm going to stay with Rocket, Strawberry, and Blue. I'm going to do the right thing and leave because I'm—" She lowered her head, then whispered, "I'm in love with your fiancé."

"Reyes?" I asked, stunned.

"Yes. I'm sorry."

Growing possessive, I said, "As of tonight, he's my husband."

Her head snapped up. "Already?" she asked, her face ashen and forlorn.

"Just like that."

"Then I'll leave."

I fought my innate desire to do a fist pump. "That's probably best."

"Because, really, I'm completely, unconditionally, and irrevocably in love with him."

"Okay, *Bella*. You need to find your own man, now. *Capisce?*"

"I did find my own man, remember? Freddy James? And someone took him from me."

Crap. The guy I'd lost my virginity to, and all to get back at a shallow, self-centered—she'd nailed the descriptors—freshman whom I'd called best friend for years before she did a 180 on me. Still . . .

"And I'm glad I did," I said, trying to sound sincere and not hurtful.

She crossed her arms over her chest. "And you suck because of it."

"No, Jessica, what I'm trying to say is that . . . Freddy wasn't very nice. In the long run. I'm glad you were spared his issues."

"Oh." She blinked in surprise. "Well, then, I'm sorry you had to find out the hard way."

"Yeah, me, too."

"So, he's really married?" she asked, her voice turning whiny again. "Like forever?"

"Go," I ordered, pointing toward the door.

She disappeared. Hopefully for a very long time.

Before I made it back to my bedroom, a harried Rocket popped in. Apparently, my visiting hours had changed. I'd have to post a sign.

"Rocket Man!" I said, surprised as I waited for him to adjust. He didn't get out of the asylum much, and the last time I'd left him, I was being attacked by an angry hellhound.

He blinked, orienting to his new surroundings before giving me his attention. His pudgy face and bald head glowed in the low light of my living room.

When he finally focused on me, he crossed his arms over his chest. "No breaking rules, Miss Charlotte."

Here we go. "I know, hon." I put a hand on his shoulder. He would never have come here if he weren't distressed. "What rule did I break?"

"All of them!" He threw his arms in the air, completely disappointed in me.

Damn my disdain of rules.

"I had to erase, Miss Charlotte. Three names." He held up three pudgy fingers. "Three. One, two, three. Three."

I frowned in confusion. "You had to erase? You mean you had to take names off your wall?" Hope engulfed me. "Was one of them mine?"

"No. You already died."

I did die. *I did die!* Wow. I knew I saw an angel. A real one with a quizzical brow. Odd, that.

Reyes appeared beside me, framed by the door to my bedroom as Rocket scolded me. I looked at him, and Betty White overflowed with joy. I'd died, so I could cross that off my to-do list. Next up: honeymoon.

"Not you," Rocket continued. "The others."

"Okay, well, now that that's cleared up." I patted his shoulder to encourage him to leave.

"The ones in the hospital. Heaven is so mad."

I stopped as a sickly kind of dread crept up my spine. "What do you mean, 'heaven is mad'?"

"It was their time. You can't just do that. You can't just save people for no reason. I had to erase!" he shouted, reiterating his original point, the one that seemed to be at the fore of his misgivings.

My curiosity of how he would erase names he scored into a plaster wall notwithstanding, I steered the conversation back to heaven. "Rocket, heaven. What's up in heaven?"

"Chaos!" He flailed his arms again. "They are very upset that I had to *eeeeeee-rase!*"

He was apparently not into erasing. "I'm sorry, Rocket," I said, giving Reyes a worried glance.

He lowered his head, and his mood hit me. It was somber once again.

"And just so you know, great. I have to go erase another one. No more touching hospitals. That's cheating. Michael says so."

"Michael?"

"The archangel."

"The archangel?" I asked, knowing who Michael was but a little surprised he'd been brought into the conversation.

"He's only the biggest archangel ever."

He'd been hanging around Strawberry way too long. Her attitude was rubbing off. "No, I know who Michael is, but—"

"Miss Charlotte, I have to go erase."

Before I could stop him, he vanished, and I stood gaping at Reyes. "Did I really piss off an archangel?" When he didn't answer, I strolled past him into my room. "That can't be good. That cannot, in any way, shape, or form, be good."

I grabbed an armful of clothes out of my closet and turned, first spotting Reyes, his head inclined, his gaze averted, then spotting my dad.

"Dad!" I yelled, tripping over an evening gown I doubted I would need in an abandoned convent, but one could never be too prepared.

"Hi, sweetheart," he said. He was in front of my window, silhouetted by the streetlight outside, his hands in his pockets.

Ecstatic, I dropped the clothes on my bed before a ripple of disbelief hit me. I straightened and paused, curling my fingers into the pile of clothes in front of me.

"You should get that," he said, and only then did I realize the phone in my pocket was ringing.

Consumed with disbelief, I dug it out and slid the bar over.

"Ms. Davidson?" It was Captain Eckert, his voice low and formal.

"Yes," I whispered.

"We checked out that address your uncle gave us. The one with the storage unit you found in your father's hotel room."

"Yes," I said again, dread rising from the floor and drowning me.

He cleared his throat and said, "We found a body."

My vision blurred as he spoke, as I looked at my dad, at the two gunshot wounds in his chest.

"We have reason to believe it's your father." After a long moment in which he allowed me to absorb what he'd just said, he asked, "Did you find anything more about what he was doing? Whom he was investigating?"

Though I didn't feel it, the phone slipped from my fingers. Reyes caught it and told the captain I'd call him back before ending the call.

"Dad," I whispered, unable to take my gaze off the gunshot wounds, the blood that had saturated his light blue shirt.

I started toward him, but he took a step back, ducked his head as though ashamed, so I stopped.

"I don't understand."

"I'm sorry, pumpkin. I never knew."

"What?" My vision was so blurred, my heart so suddenly empty, I could barely focus on him. I could barely keep my knees from buckling.

"I never knew how truly special you were. I mean, I knew you had a gift, but I never knew the depths of who you were. Of what you were. You're amazing."

"Dad, what happened?"

"You're a god."

"Dad, please. Who did this?"

He nodded as though coming to his senses. "There are people out there, honey, people who know what you are. I tried to stop them. I was trying to find out exactly who they are when they caught on."

"Where did all of those pictures come from?" I asked him, referring to the pictures of me in his hotel room. "Is that who . . . Did the people who took those pictures do this?"

"No. But they know who did. They've been following you. Studying you. Recording every event in your life since the day you were born." He bit out the last words as though disgusted with them. With himself for not realizing it. "They know more about you than I ever did. But you can't trust them. They aren't here for you. They're here only to observe and report back."

I knew it. "The Vatican. They report to the Vatican."

He seemed surprised that I knew. "But there are others. They're called the Twelve."

"Yes," I said, nodding. "We know about them."

"They were sent," he said, beginning to fade.

"Dad, where are you going?" I asked, rushing forward.

"I have to go. I'll let you know when I learn more."

I made it to him, but he put his cold hands on my shoulders to try to force me to pay attention.

"Charley, listen. They were sent. The Twelve. They were sent by something very, very bad."

"I know," I said, his essence fading from my sight.

"No," he said, shaking his head. "They weren't—" He glanced behind him, and just as he disappeared, he said, "They were *sent*."

I stood staring into an empty space as the last word drifted toward me. The coolness on my shoulders faded slower than my father had. I closed my eyes, unable to bear the void in front of me. The void in my heart.

"Dutch," Reyes said.

I turned and rushed into his arms, overwhelmed by the sobs bursting from my body. How would I tell Gemma that our father had died? That he died because of me? Because of what I was? The loss crushed me as nothing had before. I clung to Reyes and let the pain slip inside me, let it rattle my bones and score my flesh.

After an eternity of anguish, I peeled off his shoulder and went to the bathroom to get cleaned up. Then I came back out, my shoulders set in determination. "I can't leave," I said, prepared for an argument. I now sounded like I had a cold from all the crying, and I wondered how long I'd sobbed into Reyes's wet T-shirt. "I have to find out who killed my father, and I can't do that from a safe house in the mountains."

Reyes lowered his head. "You have to trust your uncle to find that out."

"My uncle doesn't know what he's facing. I do."

He stepped closer, growing ever wary. "We're leaving."

I stepped closer, too, reached up, and wrapped a hand around his throat. "I can drop you right now and leave you quivering in my wake."

He nodded and spoke softly, as though speaking to a wounded animal. "You can do a lot more than that to me, Dutch."

Satisfaction welled in my chest.

"But before you do, think of our daughter."

That one threw me. Reluctantly, I lowered my hand and retreated a step, not wanting to think about anything but the fact that my father had been shot and left to bleed out in a fucking storage unit.

"We have to get her to safety," he continued. "You know that as well as I." He lifted my chin. "The moment it's safe, we'll figure out who did this."

"And when will that be, Reyes? When will it be safe? We have no idea how to stop them, much less kill them."

"We'll figure those things out," he said. "But we can't do that here. We're too vulnerable, too available, but we will figure this out."

In a fit of fury, I jerked my chin out of his grasp, grabbed my overnight bag, and stuffed a few random articles of clothing inside it.

"You keep telling yourself that," I said before scooping up Mrs. Thibodeaux's fishbowl and storming out the door. I would go with him.

I would become a prisoner at some abandoned convent for the sake of our daughter, but the moment she was safe on earth, the moment I knew they couldn't get to her, there would be hell to pay for those who had done this. Not to mention the fact that Reyes's father would soon discover the folly of trying to position himself between an angry mother and her cub.

The earth rumbled with every step I took, with each idea that formed and solidified in my mind. If I had to, I would raise hell from the depths of the unseen myself and rip that bastard to shreds.

He wanted a war? He'd get one.

Excerpt: Reyes's POV

I watched as Dutch stormed out of her apartment, fishbowl sloshing water over the sides, overstuffed bag dropping articles of clothing in her wake. The light that radiated from her core burned hot with anger, turning it to a gold as dark and shimmering as her eyes. That, combined with the pain of her father's death, washed over my skin like an electric wind. She was so incredibly powerful and growing more powerful every day. Soon she'd be an uncontrollable force. An unstoppable creature. She would be the god that she was born to be, and she would no longer need me. No longer have use for me.

I waited to hear her footsteps on the stairs before I summoned the mutt. Angel, she called him. Her investigator. He appeared beside me and I tilted my head in question.

After stuffing his hands in his pockets, he nodded. "You were right. He's spying for someone."

"For whom?" I asked, not in the mood for games.

"Look, *pendejo,* I'm doing this for her. I work for Charley. Not you. She deserves to know."

The punk had always been afraid of me, but he was getting bolder. I'd have to rip that bandanna off his head and wrap it around his throat soon. But now was not the time.

Instead of acting on my instincts, I glared at him.

It worked. The mutt bit down and said, "I don't know who it was. Some guy in a black Rolls. A rich fuck with more money than sense, if he's doing what you say he's doing."

I nodded. That would be my father's emissary. And the spy the kid had been following on my orders was one of Dutch's newest hard cases. He'd been watching her for a while. And I'd been watching him.

I wondered how to tell her that a deadhead, one she considered a friend, was spying on her for my father. With everything else going on, she would not take it well.

His name was Duff, and Dutch, like so many before her, had been taken in by his baby-faced charm and childlike stutter. But I knew him for what he really was. He'd been in prison for a reason, after all.

"Keep an eye on him. Let me know if there are any changes."

"What if Charley needs me?" he asked.

"Then be there for her, but get back to the deadhead the minute you're finished."

With a nod, the mutt started to leave, but then stopped. "Will this guy hurt her?"

"Duff?" I asked him.

"No, the rich fuck."

"Only if we give him the chance."

The kid bowed his head. "I can take him out."

"And deny me the pleasure?" I took a purposeful step closer. "I would not suggest that course of action."

He took a wary step back. "Fine. He's all yours. But I get the ghost."

"Duff will be all yours when we're finished with him."

"Hell yes," he said. Pleased with that, he disappeared.

I followed Dutch out the door, wincing at the soreness I still felt from the fight with the Twelve. That one had me stumped. They seemed impossible to kill, but there had to be a way. I had to find a way. For Dutch and the kid. Our kid. I just needed a few more pieces to the puzzle. Once I figured out who'd summoned them, the hellhounds, I could take that guy out. They'd be more vulnerable then. Easier to crush.

I had yet to figure out the part that the Daeva Osh'ekiel played in all this, but I'd use him for now. If he so much as blinked wrong, I'd sever his spine. It was the least I could do.

I stepped into the ink-like night. Dutch sat in her Jeep, the engine idling, her expression hard. I walked around to the driver's side and opened the door. Her emotions hit me like a freight train, and I felt her fight tooth and nail to hold back the grief that threatened to consume her.

"I have to call Gemma," she said.

"You can call on the way. I'll drive."

After a moment, she turned to get out. A tear pushed past her lashes and slid down her cheek. She brushed it away angrily, the incredible energy radiating out of her rumbling the ground beneath us.

I didn't dare stop her as she pushed past me to walk around and get in the passenger's side. The emotions roiling inside her were like at that stage of a nuclear bomb when the first atom has been split and the rest are on the verge of exploding. She had unlimited power and no means to control it. Not yet. She could destroy so many in such a small span of time and not even know what she'd done until the deed was complete. It would devastate her beyond anything she'd ever felt before, so I stepped aside, not wishing to be responsible for the damage she could inflict, for the immeasurable loss of life. And I didn't want to be eviscerated myself. Not just yet. I wanted to see our daughter. I wanted to see, if only for a moment, the being destined to destroy my father once and for all.

Then I could die knowing he would suffer for his crimes against humanity and I would spend eternity with the only creature in the universe who could bring me to my knees with a mere whisper.